Dearly Beloved

Dearly Beloved

INSPIRED BY TRUE EVENTS

WILT RHYS

MARGINAL IMPACT PUBLISHING

CONTENT WARNING

Your mental health is important. Take care of yourself, check your triggers here:

Dearly Beloved

PROLOGUE

I. Hate. You.

Almond-shaped, medium brown doe eyes that were too big for the small, milk chocolate oval face they inhabited, shot a feral glare.

Respect had nothing to do with why she didn't speak the words to the emaciated woman standing before her. It was fear and loathing. This could be her scary future if she played her cards wrong. The fact she knew this at five years old said a lot about her life. Five felt like forty.

THIS is your brain on drugs. Way better than that egg skillet commercial. Somebody should hit her with a skillet, the little girl thought, glower glued to her "mother." The woman couldn't even stand still. She fidgeted. Picked at the tattered, black leather upholstery of the couch she stood behind. Shifted her weight from one foot to the other.

"Mama, we got one of them notices again," her twelve-year-old half-sister Kathy said from the archway separating the kitchen and living room.

"I paid rent yesterday, baby. Mama's broke," the woman rasped, now fingering a hole in the sleeve of the flashy sky-blue dress she wore. Not even noon, but she looked ready for a pageant. Or the club.

With cat-like onyx eyes, Kathy took after her father instead of their so-called mother. They might not be full sisters, but their clothes—two sizes too small, and so threadbare they were nearly transparent—and fed-up glares, were identical. "Mama, that was two months ago. They gon' make us leave," Kathy reminded. Frustration deepened skin a couple of shades darker than her own.

Yep, she loathed this *woman*. The self-centered, she-devil didn't deserve respect. She'd wasted enough tears on her and her lost childhood. She wouldn't waste words. Their mother had left two months prior, with the promise of grocery shopping only to return this morning. She left her daughters without food, electricity, or running water. Thank God, for nosy neighbors. They paid for the electricity and water, no questions asked, out of pity.

The babysitting services her older sister provided neighbors in exchange for food would only last so long. Otherwise, they would starve. Kathy also kept her out of sight so not-so-understanding neighbors wouldn't realize she hadn't been to school in months and call the authorities.

Kathy depended on adages like out-of-sight, *out-of-mind* to keep questions to a minimum. Selfless to a fault, she cared for her little sister better than any mother. They were a team. Kathy's mature appearance aided in keeping suspicions low. Her body had matured light years ahead of her twelve years. She possessed a gentle, almost fragile soul. An iron will and fierce loyalty assured she did the necessary without complaint. Even though their mother let them down in so many ways, misguided belief ensured she never betrayed their mother's secrets. Kathy had a near child-like naivety. For her, the same couldn't be said.

While only five, she'd been born an adult. Possessed an arcane knowledge of people and the world. Being a child wasn't a luxury she could afford. Her older sister loved their mother and gave her the benefit of the doubt. She didn't.

The junky reached down, picked something off the floor. "Mama's gon' go make this money right quick. Sell this"—holding up a dark blue carrying case—"blow dryer. I'll be back."

She and Kathy traded sidelong, skeptical looks. "Mama, they're gonna evict us," Kathy pleaded.

"I know, baby. That's why I need to see bout this money now. I'ma be back," their mother crooned, pulling the front door open. She disappeared before either child could protest.

Ten minutes later, Kathy sat on the couch reading one of the two books they owned. Fortunately, books weren't an accepted form of currency for crack, or they'd have no source of entertainment.

The five-year-old made her way toward the front door.

"Uh… excuse me," Kathy said, turning to watch her sister, "where you goin'?"

All-too-knowing, brown eyes collided with questioning onyx ones. "The porch." A small brown hand yanked the door open before Kathy asked anything else.

She knew the answer, but something inside her needed undeniable proof. Maybe a tiny part of her wanted to believe it wasn't true. Perhaps she wasn't as jaded as she thought. Whatever it was, she had to know.

Relentless Arizona sun smacked her. Her skin flushed as she stepped onto the porch. To her immediate left, the storage closet. With unnecessary caution, she approached the closed door. She sucked in a deep breath through her mouth, then opened the door. Froze. There was the blue bag their mother went to "sell" on the cement floor.

CHAPTER ONE

"How's the bulge?" Christopher Clark sauntered into his roommate and best friend's bedroom.

Green eyes full of murderous intent shot toward where he stood in the doorway. "Are you fuckin' serious? I'm not checking out your dick print, bro."

Chris examined his childhood friend, Andrew "Drew" Sutton, through narrow eyes. Creased gray slacks, black long-sleeved dress shirt, black silk tie, and black dress shoes—what the...? He wasn't into guys or anything, but his six-foot-three, brown-haired, green-eyed friend never looked this good. "Where the hell are you going?"

Sliding his mirrored closet door closed, Drew turned toward him. "It's called a date. You know, one of those things a man takes a woman on. Man picks said woman up, takes her somewhere nice, they eat, get to know each other, then man pays and escorts woman back home. They don't have sex on the table or in the car."

Frowning, Chris rolled his eyes. He knew what dates were. Just didn't believe in them. Pot. Kettle. Who was Drew to criticize...?

They'd been friends their whole twenty-seven years on Earth. They'd been born within days of each other, and their parents were best friends. He *knew* Drew. And knew when he was being lied to. Until a couple of months ago, the asshole had the same philosophy on women as he did: if there's grass in the field... play ball! Now, some mystery woman had Romeo's punk-ass sprung. Just the thought of being whooped over some chick gave Chris the shakes. Unless...

Not going there. He didn't want or need a subscription to her issues. He liked his bachelor status. There were too many women in the world. God did not bless him with his rock-hard body, six-five height, blond hair, blue eyes, and nine-and-a-half-inch dick to give it to one woman for the rest of his life. Especially not a woman who made being sodomized by Satan with a spiked club sound fun.

Chris stood next to Drew and checked himself out in the mirror. Fixing his hair and straightening his clothes, he didn't miss the incredulous side-eye coming from Andrew—nor did he care.

"Oh, I'm sorry, *Your Highness*, was I in your way in *my* room, standing in front of *my* mirror? Asshole."

"You know, you're gonna go gray from all the whining you do. Unclench. Let the stick fall out."

"Stress—*jackass*—stress makes you go gray. If you, being annoying, turned me gray... I would've been completely gray in second grade. Anyway, this is my room. I'm allowed to not want you in it. And there's a mirror in your room. Several, to be exact." His best friend pointed out.

"We were in the same kindergarten class. You were there when we learned to share. Plus, the mirror in my room is portrait size," he informed Drew. "I need a good look at the package since some people—who shall remain nameless—are no help."

Damn, I'm fine!

Chris continued fixing his wavy hair. He wagged his eyebrows at his reflection. Cupped himself. "I *know* what women want."

Revulsion curled Andrew's upper lip. He glared at the image his friend presented in the mirror.

Dick.

The guy was a grade "A" jackass. He loved him like a brother, but like a brother, Chris pissed him off to no end. So far past conceited—dude couldn't see conceited if it head-butted him. The fact Chris hadn't forgone women altogether in favor of asexuality shocked him. The narcissist attached mirrors to his bedroom ceiling, not because he was a visual man. No, he did it to evaluate himself during sex. Make sure he didn't sweat too much or make any unattractive expressions.

Had Chris been anybody else, Drew would've beaten his ass and disowned the self-proclaimed "cookie crook" long ago. God, if his little sister ever met a guy like Chris, he'd kill him. Given his profession, he knew how and where to hide the body. Buuut, Chris had good qualities... deep, deep, deep down.

Somewhere trapped inside him was a fiercely loyal, chubby, acne-riddled kid. He'd give the shirt off his back to anyone in need. Of course, there were other reasons for their continued friendship. Chris's invaluable, no-bullshit honesty—no matter how blunt—was one. Chris was Chris; take him or leave him. No guesswork required. He was a straight shooter. Told it like it was, and Andrew appreciated that.

Andrew's ire cooled a bit. Yes, if he were being honest and risking sounding a little gay, he'd admit his friend was attractive. He looked better than most male models, even dressed in simple blue jeans and a black T-shirt with his multi-hued blond hair artfully mussed. Not only did he get mistaken for a young Matthew McConaughey, but the guy possessed the deep, slight, southern drawl to boot. No cap. It was how he spoke, which shocked the shit out of Andrew since they were both born and raised here in Arizona.

Finished with his covert appraisal of Chris, something on his king-sized bed caught his attention. Shit! He forgot. The usually unobservant Chris noticed, too.

Fuck!

"Movin' out?" Chris asked, gaze fixed on the large, black duffel bag atop Andrew's royal blue comforter.

Damn, damn, dammit! He'd hoped to get away without Chris knowing. Typically, Andrew told Chris everything. Borderline, TMI-style, everything. However, he didn't prefer to share this one of two things. The first, he kept from Chris and everyone. It wasn't only his secret, and he wasn't ready to go public. The second—*this*—he kept from Chris for his sanity.

"If I say yes, will you pretend you didn't see that?"

"What the fuck, man?" Chris snapped. "Why all the secrecy? We're supposed to be boys. Now I'm public enemy number one—you keep shit from me? I'm the bad guy—fuck you, too, dude."

Damn! Leave it to Chris to go all little girl sensitive. "If I tell you, promise not to ask to come."

"Go wherever you want. I'm a grown man, not a lost puppy. I don't need to follow you around. I've got people to see and women to screw. And, in the immortal words of Reverend Lil' Wayne,

I'm the pussy monster. Ladies need me around here. I can't take a day off." Chris boasted, planting himself on the corner of his mahogany desk. Arms crossed, he watched Andrew.

Andrew released a loud, long-suffering breath. If only it were that simple. But for reasons unknown to him, he knew the second he told his best friend, he'd want to come with him. Chris liked to live dangerously. After a deep sigh, he conceded. "You know my parents' anniversary is in a couple of days, right?"

Chris arched a thick, golden brow. Nodded.

"They're going to Hawaii on some sort of second honeymoon type deal the day after tomorrow. I'm house-sitting until they get back."

Chris sat, eyes narrowed. Pensive. "Why would you need to house sit? Isn't—when do we leave?" he asked, interrupting himself as realization struck. He hopped to his feet.

Andrew raked a hand through his brown locks. Sighed. "Chris, that's why I didn't say anything. What happened to you being a grown man? Thought you had pussy to attend to?"

An indecipherable expression flashed in Chris's deep blue eyes but disappeared before Andrew could decipher its meaning. "I am a grown man and as such... I choose to go with you. Ain't shit to do here."

"You have work to do," Andrew pointed out, knowing he'd already lost this battle. Chris would reschedule all his training sessions at the gym, where he worked as a personal trainer and nutritionist. Funny, he'd never pegged Chris as a masochist.

"What? You don't think I'm up for a little sparring match?" Chris smirked, lifting his fists and mimicking a couple of boxing jabs. "Afraid I won't be able to take a few punches from little Sugar Ray Leonard?"

Drew rolled his eyes. No, he in no way, shape, or form wanted to spend his much-needed, eight-week-long vacation playing referee. "I always thought you liked your dick?" As soon as the words left his lips, he and Chris winced in unison at the memory they invoked.

"Poor... poor... Rand," Chris said in a mocking, sympathetic tone, shaking his head. "At least the one nutt still works."

Poor one-testicle Rand. He'd never seen it coming. When they were around fifteen, he, Chris, and their other two best friends, Alex and Rand, had been hanging out in the kitchen of his childhood home when his twelve-year-old sister came in. Rand said something to the effect of... she'd filled out. Andrew would've gladly readjusted his friend's nose for the comment, but the little ninja got to Rand first. One well-placed kick turned him into Mr. Uni-ball. Blood everywhere.

With that, his thoughts took an unpleasant turn. He'd hurt her, too. To refocus on the here and now, he shook his head. "You can't come. My parents didn't invite you."

Chris snorted. "Please! Since when do I need an invitation? I'm always welcome. Your casa *es* my casa."

"What about Samantha? She'll be pissed if you up and disappear for two months. Don't you guys have some other restaurant, amusement park, mall, church, or somewhere to defile?"

"First—motherfucker—I don't answer to her. She can throw a tantrum all she wants, but she knows the score. Second, there are these newfangled devices called cell phones I can use to tell her I'm gone if I choose. She'll wait. Who's better than me?" Chris grinned.

"I don't know. I mean, you're so humble. How could she ever tire of waiting for a catch like you—douchebag?" Andrew sat on his bed.

"You really don't want me to go, huh?" Chris asked, crossing his arms over his heavily, muscled chest.

"No. I don't. You know how it'll turn out. I don't want to play mediator, UFC referee, bodyguard, or judge," Andrew answered, hoping to appeal to some latent sense of decency within his friend.

Chris almost ran his fingers through his perfectly coiffed hair but stopped mid-action. His hand fell to his side. God forbid his hair should ever be out of place. He exhaled a clement breath. Shrugged. "Fine. If it matters that much, I won't go." And with that, his usual self-centered friend strutted out of his room.

Ho-ly, shit! Christopher Patrick Clark was doing something unselfish. Where was a camera when he needed one?

CHAPTER THREE

"And how does that make you feel?" asked a smooth, soothing professional tone.

"I couldn't give a shit less," Renée Sutton answered. "It was nineteen years ago. I'm over it. I'm not the first kid it's happened to, and I won't be the last. It was a dream. I only told you because you give out the meds." Yeah, that voice was supposed to calm her, or whatever, but it pissed Renée off to no end.

Hazel eyes narrowed, condemned. Mrs. Anne Mendoza, M. D., seemed to have a hard time keeping her emotions in check, sitting behind her large oak desk. She struggled to pinch her too many times tucked face while twisting in her big, black, I'm-somebody-important leather chair. The degrees hanging on the wall gave her the authority to prescribe medicine and the right to think she knew everything.

Looks like someone's giving away their power, Renée thought. It took conscious effort to keep her mental sarcasm off her face.

She'd been told that same thing during one, or forty, of her sessions with Dr. Mendoza over the last three years. According to Dr. Mendoza, no one can make another feel anything without their permission. To let someone provoke you to anger gives away your power. Damn, therapist psychobabble! Renée didn't buy it, which was why she worked extra hard to poke the bear.

Renée was here for two reasons. Neither had anything to do with thinking this white blond haired, middle-aged lady in her gray pants suit knew anything. At least, not anything about her. This fulfilled one of her well-meaning parents' stipulations for her "moving" back home. The second reason: the excellent psychiatrist prescribed the only Western medicine Renée would take.

Usually, she stayed pretty healthy. She rarely drank. Didn't smoke. Didn't eat meat. Exercised her mind and body. She used natural remedies for any aches, pains, or illnesses. But, there was one condition nothing but good old-fashioned Xanax would cure: panic attacks. Her traitorous nervous system... Hangnails and being held at gunpoint elicited the same physical response.

"Renée? Renée, did you hear me?" Dr. Mendoza asked, breaking into her reverie.

"No. What'd you say?"

"How are you and your parents getting along? Your living situation?"

"Great, it's the best experience of my life. I love it. I recommend every twenty-four-year-old be forced under the threat of an involuntary psychiatric hold to move back home," she said, then tossed in a grin for good measure.

What did she mean—how were they getting along? They got along like too many queens in a castle. Barely.

"You know, sometimes sarcasm is used to hide deeper pain," the good doctor informed in the condescending tone that drove her crazy. "It's a way of deflecting."

"And sometimes sarcasm keeps annoying people from asking too many questions," Renée rebutted condescendingly.

"Renée, I'm here to help. Have you given any more thought to our discussion from a few weeks ago?"

God, give it up, lady! Less talk, more prescription writing. "Jeez, memories, dreams, they're all the same. Everybody dreams. Once I dreamed, I married a big, nine-foot-tall slug. Should I find a slug to keep that dream at bay? See if we have any chemistry? Or, wait, you know... I had a dream about being alive inside my coffin at my funeral. Should I go down to the local funeral home and lay in a pine box?" She shuddered. "No. Thank. You."

Dr. Mendoza ran a shaky hand through her chin-length hair. "Ms. Sutton, you could try the patience of a saint."

Gotcha, bitch! "I do what I can," she said in a breathy, dreamy voice.

"You can't keep running from your past—your feelings—forever. Waiting to examine things until later. The past will catch up with you. Confront those things that haunt your nightmares. For instance, you could try talking to me about them. Your parents pay for these sessions. The least you could do is use me. These degrees here,"—she pointed to the wall behind her—"aren't just for covering the holes I punch in the wall after our sessions, you know?"

Renée flashed a brief smile. Okay, that was funny. She didn't mean to be such an ass. But she didn't want to talk about it. For years, she'd been having nightmares about her past. But they weren't dreams. They were memories of the most harrowing experiences of her childhood and life. Memories she'd love to forget. But her subconscious didn't get the memo. And after "The Event" three years ago, the memory nightmares increased, which meant so did her anxiety attacks.

Dr. Mendoza believed the increased dreams and panic attacks were because of Post-Traumatic Stress Syndrome, PTSD. Renée agreed. After "The Event," she couldn't take another trauma or stressful situation in her life. The next big thing would more than likely kill her. Her fragile mental health couldn't endure another hit.

"This isn't my first rodeo. I've talked about this stuff with therapists before. It doesn't go away, no matter how many times I repeat the stories. Nobody understands what it was like for me, and I'm honestly over it. But, hey, good lookin' out." To further illustrate her point that the topic was closed for discussion, she gave Dr. Mendoza the wink and the gun.

"So, how are our relationships?" the doctor asked, changing the subject to one she thought safer. "Your friends? Your brother? Are we dating yet?"

The doctor didn't understand the universal sign for stop-talking-and-get-to-the-prescription-writing.

Hmm... she'd have to work on her sign-giving. "Er, I don't know about you, but I'd rather clear out my right and left eye with a rusty nail than date anybody. On a happier note, friends are good. The brother's doing well, I guess. We don't speak much."

With a smile and nod, the doctor reached into her desk drawer—a white prescription pad.

Thank God!

"Have you given any more thought to how you identify?" Dr. Mendoza asked, fancy pen tip to paper.

What the hell was she doing? Besides her resolve to never date or marry and her hate of mouth noises, everybody knew—very well—Renée had zero patience. And this bitch was toying with her. Yeah, patience wasn't a virtue she possessed. We all have our battles.

"My identity isn't wrapped up in skin color. Some people get left. Kids get left. There's no deeper meaning," she snapped, harsher than intended. The very idea she might not be as comfortable with herself as she believed didn't sit well with her. It had weighed on her mind since her psychiatrist brought it up a month ago. But she'd be damned if she admitted it. "I identify with me."

Thankfully, her response seemed to suffice because the pen glided across the paper. Sweet freedom was within her grasp. An hour had never seemed so long.

Arizona sun pummeled asphalt. Blurry, shimmering heat haze distorted a rundown beige and brown townhouse. Two white, four-door sedans were parked outside of it. Doors of the idling vehicles hung open. A black, spear-top iron perimeter fence bordered an Astroturf-covered front porch.

The home's front door flew open. Distraught screams and cries rent the air.

"No! Please..." screamed five-year-old Renée. A young, light brown-haired, professionally dressed Caucasian man struggled under her slight weight. "I don't want to go!" she yelled. "Kathy!" Tears streamed down a tiny, round chocolate face. Brown eyes were wild.

Kathy followed close behind, sedate. Her mouth turned down, a frown of resignation. A petite, red-haired woman with worried green eyes—dressed in a professional A-lined, gray skirt and sleeveless, cowl neck, black blouse—escorted her from the house.

"It's okay, it's not forever. We'll see each other again," came Kathy's hollow assurance. The woman led her to one car. The man led Renée to the other. "Renée, it's okay. Shh... I love you."

The attempt at comfort fell upon deaf ears. Renée knew better. She kicked, struggled harder against the man's hold. He forced her into the back seat. A jagged piece of metal from the doorframe sliced through her right wrist. Cut to the bone. Blood ran from her wrist to her elbow. She didn't feel it. Deeper, excruciating pain lanced her heart. Overshadowed the physical pain as she watched the other car pull away. The only person in the world who loved her sat rigid in the back seat, facing forward. Kathy never looked back.

Renée jolted awake. It was dark. Sweat ran from her forehead, down her hairline, off her chin. Her body shook. Tears flowed, unchecked, down her cheeks. Her heart compressed yet thundered in her chest. Breath ragged, she reached toward the nightstand beside her bed. Hand bumping into the lamp atop it. She tapped the metal shade. Muted light trickled out. She turned her alarm clock toward her—three-thirty-three in the morning.

Great!

Hands shaking, she opened her top drawer. Pulled out a prescription bottle, opened it, shook out two pills, and swallowed them dry. To give the Xanax time to do its thing, Renée focused on breathing. In through the nose. Out through the mouth. Waiting for her body to relax, she scanned her room. She attempted to re-familiarize herself with her surroundings.

Hoping to make her feel comfortable after her adoption fourteen years ago, her parents allowed her to paint the walls her favorite color: maroon. Her other favorite colors, black and royal blue, which were the colors of her bedsheets, always brought her peace. Right now, she needed all the peace she could get. She gazed across the room at her oak dresser with an attached mirror. In the mirror's frame, she'd tucked pictures of her friends. On the dresser were more framed photos.

As her medication calmed her system, flashes of her memory-dream replayed in her mind. She didn't allow her conscious mind to dwell in the past, but the chances of falling back asleep now were slim to none. So, she let her mind wander down the cracked memory lane. The day her sister had called Child Protective Services and reported that their mother abandoned them was as clear as if it happened yesterday.

She remembered most of her life experiences and events as if they'd happened yesterday. They'd diagnosed her at twelve years old with Hyperthymesia. People with the syndrome have superior autobiographical memory. Her memory was her most significant ally, and worst enemy. It reminded her of all the things she wanted, never wanted, and never wanted to happen again. It kept her grounded, maybe too grounded, which left the guard walls around her heart high with barbed wire and choked full of electricity. No one got in, or out, easily.

Of course, she knew her thinking wasn't healthy, and it limited her, but that didn't make it any less a part of her, nor did she know how, or even if, she wanted to fix it. Most people weren't worthy of her heart, anyway. Her guard wall allowed her to stay aloof. Able to detach from anyone. Barring two events in nineteen years, she never let her guard down. Let no one in that she couldn't kick out in a nanosecond. Those two exceptions only fortified her resolve, especially the last slip-up.

It pained her on a soul-deep level to have to maintain such a view of people. More than anything, she wanted to let someone in. Be close to someone. Have someone see her. Know her. But every time she tried, she learned the accurate measure of mankind the hard way. Humans' penchant for committing brutal, cruel, cold, and heartless acts against each other confounded her. She couldn't be that way. Yes, she treated people like they were disposable, but that covered her genuine care. It killed her inside.

Although she knew now that her five-year-old self's thought process wasn't fair... it didn't change the fact that Renée included Kathy in the long list of people who'd abandoned her. Who'd let her down. Now, of course, she realized Kathy hadn't known they'd be tossed knee-deep into the craptastic foster care system and separated. But some wounds run to the very fiber of a person's being. Age and wisdom scabbed them over, but they never truly heal.

Three weeks after their "mother" said she'd be right back, neighbors got wise to their situation. One neighbor Kathy babysat for threatened to call the police. Scared, Kathy did the only thing she could think of: She called the police herself.

Less than twenty-four hours later, two social workers came to investigate. One look at their barely furnished town-house—barely furnished because their tweaker mom sold any-thing of value for drugs—empty refrigerator and cupboards. They seized emergency custody. They took her and her sister that same day, each with a tiny garbage bag of dirty clothes. Renée never saw Kathy again.

Kathy could have found her later in life; they were seven years apart. She'd reached adulthood far before Renée. Yet she never came back. Never looked for her.

Renée rubbed the crescent moon-shaped scar on her right wrist and yawned. She laid down. Her final conscious thought: *Does she ever think about me?*

"Isn't it a little early to set up camp in front of the TV, young lady?" a rumbling voice asked.

Turning from her position, curled up at the end of the stone-colored plush sectional, Renée dropped the television re-mote. She squinted. When filtered through off-white curtains, the sun bathed the contemporary-style living room in a harsh orange glow, making it hard to discern her father's image in the arched entryway.

Randall Sutton. Possibly the most handsome fifty-six-year-old man alive—at least in her opinion. At six-three, he was a big man, but not fat. He was in fantastic shape for his age. Cropped brown hair peppered with gray complimented sky-blue eyes. Lugging four large, black suitcases—one under each arm and one in each hand—he'd forgone his usual cowboy attire. In its place, he wore a tacky, multi-colored, floral print, button-down shirt with khaki shorts, and Timberland boots.

Not every outfit can be a winner, I guess.

"Don't you have work to get ready for? Or a mall excursion to plan?" Randall asked.

Renée gave a wide, ditzy smile and twirled a lock of long, mahogany hair around her finger. "Like, OMG, Dad. Like, the mall's not even open this early. Duh!" she said, affecting her best Valley Girl accent, which wasn't far from her usual speech pattern.

"Hilarious, Renée," he replied, eyes narrowed. "Is this your plan for the entire time your mother and I are gone? Watching soap operas?"

"Dad!" she exclaimed, offended. "Do you see how fast I'm flipping through the channels? I couldn't be watching anything if I tried. I'm surfing. And soap operas aren't really a thing anymore."

God, the way her dad made it sound, one would think she asked to live here. She wasn't some freeloader mooching off her parents. She managed a luxury apartment community close to their Paradise Valley home. On-call all the time, this was the first day of a much-needed vacation. Shit!

Randall put down the luggage. Sat in his favorite, ugly brown La-Z-Boy recliner. It contrasted starkly against the other furniture: the curved stone sectional where she sat, the plush stone couch, her mother's stone recliner, the glass-top oak coffee table with matching end tables, and a burnish-brown oak entertainment center. His La-Z-boy was also a source of contention between her parents.

A familiar, disapproving clucking echoed through the hall, grew louder by the second, and annoyed the shit out of Renée. Six seconds later, buxom, five foot five, Susan Sutton came into sight. Her outfit was almost identical to her husband's, except she wore flat white sandals and a black carry-on bag. Censure dimmed emerald eyes. Pink gloss-coated lips pressed into a firm line in a wrinkle-free, heart-shaped face. Her honey blond hair, up in a ponytail, made her look younger than her fifty-two years.

Eyes cut at her daughter and a hand propped on her hip, she shook her head. "Always sarcasm from you and your brother. A simple 'No, I'm not watching TV,' would suffice." She turned to her husband. "Honey, remember I told you Née has the next few weeks off?"

Randall arched a curious brow in Renée's direction.

Susan returned her attention to Renée. "You doing anything today, or just hanging around the house?"

Renée released a deep sigh. It's not like they'd be here. What did they care? This over-interest in her life shtick pissed her off. Too much. Her interrupted night's sleep was catching up with her. She glanced at each of her parents; warmth and love warred with annoyance. "Gosh, sorry, you act like you don't want me here. What? Afraid I'll throw a wild party? I will gladly move out if it helps alleviate your fears."

Susan entered the room and sat at the opposite end of the sectional. "Stop, Renée," she chided. "We were just curious—no ulterior motive or hidden agenda. And we said we didn't want you to move out before you were ready. You're not ready," she clarified.

Renée understood her mother's comment for what it was, a command. Oh, so now they were splitting hairs. Two could play that—

Ding. Dong!

Saved by the bell. Thank God! She would've given the *I have to potty* excuse to escape this escalating conversation in another minute. She hopped up on bare feet to answer the door. Renée pulled the door open and froze.

A smile lit Renée's face. "Hey, you!" she exclaimed. "Nice of you to grace us with your presence." No sooner than the words left her lips, she jumped up and threw her arms around Andrew's neck.

He looked good. Debonair in his gray T-shirt and jeans. She'd almost forgotten what he looked like in casual clothes. Since moving out, whenever he came by, it was after some meeting with a client, so he wore business attire. A successful private investigator, Andrew could not only find half a needle in a haystack but also determine who put it there, why they put it there, when they put it there, and get pictures of it happening in seconds.

He was one of only three men she tolerated. The serious workaholic never dated, which was sad because he was gorgeous with above-average height, green eyes, and chiseled features.

Bone-crushing strength returned her gentle embrace. He lifted her off her feet. She'd missed him but would bite her tongue off before voicing such a weakness. Renée glanced over Andrew's shoulder. Something—yeah, some-*thing*—caught her eye. Her smile morphed into a fierce scowl. She backed out of her brother's arms, grabbed the door, and pulled it close to her body. Wrapping her left arm around it, she blocked entry into the house.

Just when she thought the day couldn't get any worse. Now, all that was missing was an AK-47 and a rooftop.

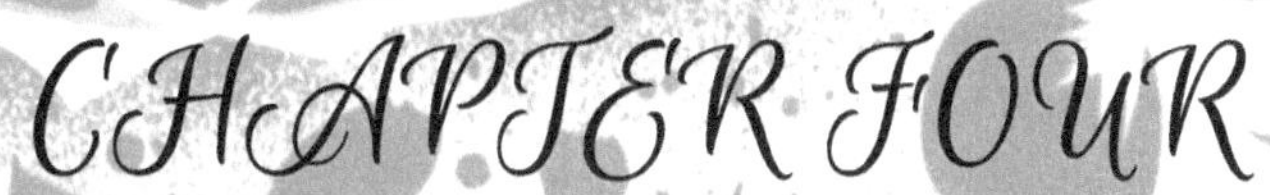

CHAPTER FOUR

"Andrew," Renée said, glaring daggers over her brother's shoulder, "aren't you breaking some leash law for your dog?"

"Missed you, too, Renée," Chris greeted in his sinfully deep bass.

Tingles shot down her spine. A rush of liquid fire pooled between her thighs.

Damn him!

In black cargo shorts, flip-flops, black muscle shirt with a white short-sleeved shirt left unbuttoned over it, he looked hotter than sin. Thank God, dark black tinted Oakley's hid Windex blue eyes that could turn her into jelly. He looked... disgusting! No, she wouldn't think of anything, but how gross he looked with tanned, muscular calves, arms, and rock-hard pecs. The man bled charm and game. If looks could kill... he'd be a nuclear weapon. And that irked her to no end. Of course, stupid, shallow, self-centered, dumbass jerks got all the looks—*asshole!*

She didn't voice her ire, but she'd been working on her non-verbal communication skills since her session with Dr. Mendoza. She hoped her glacial stare conveyed the message.

It didn't, or the bastard was slow on the uptake. He broke into a straight, pearly white-toothed, panty-dropping smile. But not her panties, no sirree Bob—nuh-uh—she wouldn't have it. Nor would she acknowledge the pulsing ache and wetness between her thighs. No, not wetness; it was... dew. Yeah, dew. Her shorts were tight, and it was a hot day. Her panties were firmly in place.

As the thought crossed her mind, his smile grew wider. It was as if he could read her thoughts—*jackass!*

Yeah, read that!

If eyes were indeed windows to the soul, his spoke volumes. She didn't have to see him to know they were empty. Full of deception and shallow, like him.

Chris always stood sure of himself: tall and straight with his broad shoulders, large muscular arms crossed over a wide, lickable chest. No! Not lickable, disgusting. His large muscular arms crossed over a wide lick—disgusting chest. *Shit!*

Standing must make her light-headed. It had to be because Hell would freeze over, thaw, and then freeze over again before she licked his chest. Half the Arizona female population had licked that chest. She'd be damned if she got added to his roster.

Chris's smile widened, unbothered by her rage. He always acted so unflappable, but she'd be damned if she didn't rattle him constantly. Nobody could be that sure of themselves; it wasn't natural. He needed to be knocked down a few pegs.

"Been saving that one for a while?" Chris drawled, deepening his voice. Renée tried to hide her desire, but he saw the flames clear as day in those hypnotic, bourbon-colored eyes, and he knew exactly the effect his voice had on her. He also noticed how her tongue snaked out to glide across her bottom, then top, lip. The way her eyes perused his body. "I'm happy you think about me so much."

To his utter amazement, Renée's face lit up. She gifted him with a sexy yet adorable, dimpled smile that nearly knocked him to his knees in front of his best friend, God, and everyone outside. "Oh, Christopher," she said with a sigh. He tried not to cringe at the use of his government name. "I think about you all the time."

His heart stuttered.

"Late at night, when I'm sitting alone in my room, I think about you," Renée admitted. "And all the ways I could kill you without going to jail." She released an exaggerated breath.

It was his turn to glare. Though it seemed longer, their entire exchange lasted a brief minute, and he'd done well masking his desire with practiced aloofness. He couldn't hold his annoyance now. For years he'd known, should his genuine feelings for Renée become public knowledge, it would ruin his friendship with Drew. End it altogether.

Although they seemed to have drifted apart, Drew and Renée were super close. Given that there were only three years between them and most of their respective friends, they both had strict rules about dating each other's friends. Chris was one hundred percent certain those rules were more brutal on Drew's side with his friends dating his beloved, pain-in-the-ass sister. To date, no one had ever tried to do the unspoken and forbidden: date Renée. And he didn't plan on doing it either—kinda.

He'd tried to talk himself out of coming with Drew—he did! He wanted to be the good, selfless friend Drew needed, but in the end, he was Chris. And Chris wasn't known for his patience, but he'd given the ever-mercurial Renée five years to run from their mounting attraction, what they could have, and he could wait no more. He'd stayed with his grandparents in Flagstaff for over a year, so she didn't tempt him to cross the line before he thought she could handle the type of relationship he expected with her. Age was no longer a factor. Neither of them was seeing anyone. See, he didn't want to date her. He wanted her.

Completely.

Mind, body, and spirit.

Forever.

Something inside her called to him on a primal, life-altering, heart-capturing level. Chris was tired of living without her, tired of denying, not only himself but her, too, what belonged to the other. He was hers, and she was his. Now he needed to convince her of that.

"Seriously, Christopher," Renée said, breaking into his planning, "why do you come here? I don't think we have enough mirrors to feed your insatiable need for your own company."

Chris gritted his teeth. He hated being called Christopher, and she knew it. He allowed only his elders to get away with it.

Biting back his irritation, he responded, "Not an issue. I brought a couple portable ones and a compact. I'll be fine. But, thanks for your concern. And, please, call me Chris."

"I reserve nicknames for my friends, *Christopher*." She smirked.

"Chris," he corrected, narrowing his gaze.

"Chris-to-pher," she responded, enunciating each syllable.

She enjoyed getting on his nerves. If she wanted to play, he'd play. Though she wasn't ready for the game he wanted to play. He played dirty. For keeps. Chris trapped her with a hard, penetrating stare.

With the lesser part of his attention, he caught Drew's groans, but he wasn't about to back down. He had a feeling no man ever challenged Renée. "Chris."

"Christoph—"

"Renée Marie Sutton, stop!" a booming voice ordered from somewhere behind the door.

Since Renée still blocked their entrance, he couldn't see where the voice came from, but he recognized Mr. Sutton.

"Let them in already. I reckon it's mighty hard to house-sit from outside the house—no matter how appealing that idea is to you, young lady," Mr. Sutton continued.

With a last glare, Renée let her breath out in a huff, stepped back, and opened the door wide enough for him and Drew to enter.

"Explain to me again why you need Andrew to house-sit?" Renée asked through clenched teeth, shutting and locking the front door. She followed them the short distance to the living room, where Mr. and Mrs. Sutton sat. "Aren't I a better choice? I mean, I live here. He doesn't," she complained, sitting opposite her mother on the stone-colored sectional.

"C'mon, sis," Drew said, sitting on the arm of the sectional beside Renée. "You know as well as I do you can't be trusted home alone, no matter how old you are."

Chris settled in for the show on the comfortable couch near Mrs. Sutton. This was about to get good. Renée bitched and whined with the best of them. Don't get him wrong, he adored his little firecracker. Especially loved the way her five-two, petite, Coke-bottle frame poured into her tiny navy-blue shorts and white, lace-trimmed, V-neck camisole that showed a healthy portion of her full, milk chocolate breasts. But the girl carried a King Kong-sized chip on her shoulder.

She took everything the wrong way. In her mind, everything was a ploy to do her wrong. An angle to get over on her somehow. However, he supposed the situation would frustrate or insult him if he were her, too.

He didn't understand why her parents needed Drew to watch the house when she was here either. Nothing made sense about how the Suttons, including Andrew, were suddenly overprotective of Renée in the last few years. They walked on eggshells around her most times and tolerated her little temper tantrums like she was a toddler. They'd always been protective of her, but they'd never been as indulgent as they'd become in the last three years. He'd have to break her out of her bratty behavior.

Renée grimaced at her brother. "What will I do by myself? I'm twenty-four. I'm all growed up now," she said, mocking a child's voice.

This was one side of Renée Chris rarely saw. He loved her playful sarcasm. There were more, gentler, layers to her. He knew it. Couldn't wait to pull back that hard shell to find them all.

Randall Sutton stood, stretched, and then patted Renée on the head. "We're more worried about what you'll do to the house, sweetheart, not yourself. And... we might be concerned about our little girl's safety," he teased, going over to the mouth of the hall where several black suitcases sat.

"I've never been a little girl, *Dad*," Renée snapped. "And anyway, I'm more mature than Drew on my worst day."

Andrew snatched up a maroon throw pillow and bopped his sister in the head with it. "You say that now, but when you see a scorpion or hear a noise in the middle of the night, you'll be screaming, 'Drew, help! Drew, did you hear that? Drew, kill it!'" he said, impersonating her voice, then he finished in his regular baritone, "Like a little girl."

Renée turned a glare on her brother so fierce it should've eviscerated him on the spot. Then a quick, playful smile spread her lips.

God, he wanted to be the one she had fun with. He'd never admit it, but he was jealous of his friend. She'd never looked at him that way before. Not playfully, anyway.

Dismissing his surge of irrational jealousy, he tossed his arm around the back of the couch and patted Susan Sutton on the arm. "Hey, Mrs. Sutton, excited about your big trip? Gonna give the resort something to talk about?" He winked.

Andrew and Renée made gagging sounds in unison.

"Hay is for horses, Christopher," Susan reprimanded, getting to her feet. "And I'd appreciate you not using filthy talk around my poor, innocent babies," she crooned. A hint of humor laced the last part.

Innocent his ass! He couldn't say for sure, but he'd be willing to bet with her fiery temper and tight little body. Renée might not be too experienced, but she wasn't innocent. As for Andrew?

Puh-lease!

Drew's world was full of pussy. Girls found out he was a P.I., which they equated with danger. Drew needed a catcher's mitt for all the pussy thrown his way. The guy got more ass than a toilet seat. Shit! He almost got more ass than him. At least, he did until a few months ago.

Susan picked up a black carry-on resting at her feet. "We better get going."

"Need a ride to the airport?" Drew asked.

"Thanks, sweetie, but no. We're stopping at one of your father's friend's houses. He and his wife are borrowing the truck. He'll drop us." She rushed over to Drew and Renée, gave them each a quick squeeze. After a slight hesitation, she turned and gave him a brief one-armed hug. Susan's strong perfume drowned him, filled his nostrils.

Randall grabbed the suitcases, one under each arm and one in each hand.

"Need help, Dad?" Drew offered, standing.

"Yeah, let us help with that," Chris chimed in, not wanting to seem like a total ass.

Randall scowled at both younger men. "I'm not that old yet, boys. I can carry my own bags. Besides, wouldn't want Christopher to break a nail." He chuckled, turned, and walked toward the front entrance.

"Hilarious!" Chris hollered after Randall Sutton, who might as well be an uncle, considering he'd known him all his life and ribbed him like one.

"I thought so. You kids be good," he called, heading down the short hall.

"One day, that man's going to hurt himself, thinking he's gotta compete with you boys," Susan groused, following her husband. "Goodbye, my sweethearts. Be careful. Don't destroy the house. No parties! We have our cell phones for emergencies, and please, look after each other like I would look after you. Understood?" She yelled from down the hall, opening the front door.

In unison, Andrew, Renée, and Chris shouted, "Understood!"

"Damn, twenty-seven years old, and she treats me like I'm fifteen," Drew complained.

"Andrew David Sutton!" Susan yelled, "I heard that! You're not too old to put across my knee."

"Sorry, Mom!" Drew shouted and then asked under his breath, "Exactly what age does hearing go?"

CHAPTER FIVE

"Hey, Née, isn't your brother staying with you?"

Soft-spoken Christina Lee, one of two of Renée's best friends, asked two weeks after her unwelcome house guests arrived. A sizable green umbrella shaded the three friends from the brutal afternoon sun while sitting at a table outside Starbucks.

Chris had tried to corner her a million different times, a million different ways, every day since he got there. Places to hide were scarce. Pretending to be in the bathroom or sleeping took a toll, especially when it meant going to bed at seven to avoid him. One time, he attempted to follow her into the bathroom, but Drew walked by, and he made some lame excuse and left. She didn't know what his game was, but she wasn't playing.

"Oh, yeah... Isn't he supposed to be babysitting you or something?" her other best friend, Ashley Moore, asked in her I'm-al-ways-up-for-stirring-some-shit-up voice.

Renée regarded her friends through narrowed eyes. The two women couldn't be more different.

Twenty-three-year-old, five-foot-four Ashley, had an average frame—not too big, not too small, but just right—and a light smattering of freckles on the bridge of her nose. Her eyes were a beautiful hazel, strawberry blond hair hung in waves to the middle of her back, and she wore her trademark jeans and T-shirt ensemble. Guys referred to Ashley as adorable until she opened her mouth and spit fire. No one ever saw that coming. Ashley believed in living life out loud—literally. The mouthpiece of the group, she spoke her mind all the time and screw the person who didn't want her opinion. They got it no matter how they felt about it.

Christina was the total opposite. A pretty Asian and petite like her—maybe an inch taller—black-as-night hair hung stick straight to the top of her shoulders, but today, she wore it in a ponytail. Soft brown eyes complemented her gentle nature. Christina screamed girlie girl. On rare occasions, she wore jeans. Still, her usual go-to was what she rocked today: modest pumps, a cute frilly shirt, and a flowing skirt.

Two years ago, Renée and Ashley had encountered a distraught Christina sitting in the food court of Paradise Valley Mall. Ashley, being Ashley, helped herself to a seat at Christina's table and a nose into her business. They bonded over shitty boyfriends, annoying parents, Jacob Elordi's abs, and Oreo blizzards. They'd been inseparable ever since.

All their personalities were distinct. Renée was the mama bear of the group, or The Godmother, as some called her. She didn't let many into her circle, but once she cared about you and you were in—you were in. The only way out was death. Renée protected those she cared for with ferocity, the likes of which the world would never suspect someone of her size capable. She could also go girlie like Christina or casual like Ashley and be comfortable.

She loved her friends and would do anything for them, but she'd cut them off if they screwed her over.

Renée threw a glare at each friend. "I'm not being babysat at all—ass," she snapped at Ashley after a sip of her caramel macchiato. "He's staying there because my parents don't want me to be alone—which I don't understand. But, yes, he's there. Along with his annoying friend, meaning I won't be there as much as possible," she said, dousing each word in all the aggravation she felt.

Christina wiggled her eyebrows at Ashley, then Renée, from behind brown-tinted Gucci sunglasses. "You mean to tell me you have your brother *and* one of his many hot friends staying with you?" she asked, propping her elbow on the table to support her chin. "Life is *so* unfair."

"Annoying friend?" Ashley asked, brows furrowed behind oversized pink Dolce & Gabbana sunglasses. "Which annoying friend?"

Renée lifted her cheap brown Target sunglasses and rubbed the bridge of her nose before replacing them. With her uncanny ability to lose sunglasses, no way in Hell would she waste money on expensive ones. She could buy twelve of the cheap ones for forty dollars. "It's not a good thing, Chrissy. For one, it's my brother, so, ew, what do I care? And second, I could never be attracted to his friend. Plus, he can't attract anyone. He's too busy admiring himself. He makes me sick."

Ashley pushed her grande caramel Frappuccino away as if it disgusted her. "Ugh... Chris," she said, groaning. "Say no more. I hate those types of guys."

"Me, too." She sighed in agreement.

Chris was the type of guy a girl had to watch her make-up around—not that he wore make-up. She likened being with Chris to how Prince's wife must have felt. The guy was an extraordinary musician, a legend. But that poor lady probably had to hide her shoes every night just to keep him from stealing them. So vain!

She hated girlie men, or "metrosexuals," as they were now called. Being metrosexual wasn't a bad thing. It just wasn't her thing. Yes, she used to have a crush on Axel Rose, but that was different. He oozed raw sex appeal; '80s hairband rockers were manly. Kind of like Chri—shit! What the Hell was she thinking? Scratch that thought.

"Oh, really? You hate those types of guys, too?" Christina asked, pulling Renée out of her stupid ruminations. "Let's recap, shall we,"—she ticked off each point on her fingers—"white guys aren't your type. Black guys aren't your type. Asian guys aren't your type. No Germans, Russians, Serbians, Croatians, Italians, British, Scottish, Australians, Irish, Native Americans, and no Mexicans. Oh, and let's not forget, no tall, short, hot, or ugly guys." She arched a brow. "That rules out all guys. So, what exactly is your type of guy? Do you even have one? Or... are you playing for the home team now?"

Ashley laughed, then choked on her drink.

"See? That's what you get. No, Chrissy. I'm strictly dickly, thanks," she snidely responded. "There's a type, but I can't be in a relationship right now. My focus is elsewhere. I need to find myself."

Ashley slammed her hand against the table. Their drinks wobbled. "Find yourself? Née, don't start this shit again," she scolded. "How long have I known you? Since what, before the Suttons—fourth grade? Before all this shit." Waving her hand, she encompassed the general area. "If you don't know who you are—I do. You don't need some people you don't know, who just so happen to share some DNA with you, to tell you who you are. And, no offense, but it's not like they've been knocking down your door to get to know you. Remember, they left you."

She didn't want to have this conversation in front of Starbucks. Unlike Ashley, she knew a thing or two about privacy.

Christina looked as uncomfortable as Renée felt. Stupid her for confiding in her friends about her talk with the good doctor, Anne Mendoza. The whole, "Who do you identify with?" question had gotten to her more than she cared to admit. So much so, she'd shared her concern with Christina and the Queen of Little Tact.

With an overabundance of memory dreams and the ever-exciting panic attacks, she'd been tossing around the idea of finding her birth family. She'd told them that, too.

Of course, she'd heard bits and pieces about her birth family from different caseworkers over the years. All they'd ever told her was that they were unfit and had some emotional issues. The state had to think that to justify taking kids into the system. But she didn't know how much truth there was to that assessment.

"How long has your puppet master—oh, excuse me, therapist—been suggesting you go find your loser family?" Ashley asked, bringing her back to the topic at hand.

"She hasn't been suggesting I find them. At least, she says that's not what she means. But how else does a person confront their past? Just talking about the past doesn't help."

"Maybe she's on to something," Christina mused. "Have you ever looked for any of them? Found anybody?"

Laughing without humor, Ashley rolled her eyes. "Or maybe, just maybe, that quack is full of shit."

Damn, Ashley had a way with words. However, her thoughts weren't far from Renée's own. Most counselors, therapists, and psychiatrists were full of shit. At least, she thought so. They based their entire modus operandi on knowledge from books. Not experience. People were complicated. Unique. Not meant to be forced into nice, neat, labeled boxes. What worked for one might not work for another. However, this nagging feeling in the pit of her stomach made her want to know. What if finding them filled in the gaps of her identity? Helped her move on in life? She was tired of surviving life. She wanted to live.

"Ash," she said with a sigh. She finished her drink before going on. "I know you don't think it matters, but it does. This crap with my past needs to stop. It impedes everything. This waiting for life to start? I don't want to end up some eighty-year-old woman with a million cats, still having panic attacks and bitchin' about what might have been. I gotta do something."

"So, is that a yes? You have found somebody from your family or a no you haven't?" Christina inquired, picking a piece of ice out of her tea and popping it into her mouth. She was always chewing ice, constantly hot, just like this conversation.

That girl was far too observant. Renée had told no one that she'd searched online for family members she had names, or parts of names, for.

"Yes and no." She hesitated, confirming her friend's assumption. "I found some names, but no addresses or anything of any actual use."

Crazy enough, for the wealth of information the Internet possessed, it couldn't deliver something as simple as an address without charging an arm and a leg for it. And none of her birth family had any social media. To be fair, her parents didn't either; they could barely email with an attachment.

"You know," Christina said around the ice in her mouth, "there is one person you could ask for help. He wouldn't be offended. He might even understand if you explain everything."

"How would this offend him?" Renée argued. "What I'm doing can't offend anyone. I'm not trying to take anything from my adoptive family or be disloyal. I'm trying to improve myself like they want me to."

"If you believed that, you would've told your parents. And you might've mentioned it to your brother, The King of Research. He could've gotten names, numbers, addresses, and social security numbers in five minutes," Christina pointed out.

"He's not my keeper," Renée spat, speaking more harshly than intended. It wasn't Christina's fault she and Andrew weren't as close as they once were. It also wasn't her fault she felt guilty. Searching for her birth family made her feel like she was betraying her adoptive family.

The next time she spoke, her words came calmer. "It's none of his business. I don't have to tell him everything."

"Renée," Ashley chimed in, "since when is Andrew someone you keep out of the loop? You guys used to be close—uncomfortably so. Best friends. Gag reflex-triggering, close. Tell him what's up and move on. Stop punishing him for something he had no control over."

Yep, no heartfelt conversation was complete without Ashley chucking her fifty cents at you. She wanted bygones to be bygones with Andrew. After all, it was her fault their relationship changed. Intellectually, she knew that, but when it came right down to it, she couldn't get past it.

"You guys ready to go?" Christina asked, fanning herself with her hand. "I'm hot. Hanging out at Starbucks shouldn't be a major life choice. We've been here for three hours."

Later that night, after another of her all-too-common, startling flashback dreams, Renée padded on bare feet to the kitchen. She searched the cabinets for her favorite comfort food: Cinnamon Toast Crunch. Her mom always stashed a box behind the fat-free oatmeal cookies, oat bran, and other crap Renée wouldn't eat with someone else's mouth. So, she didn't see her dreaded nemesis move through the kitchen and over to the pantry in stealthy silence. But she felt it. Her body tensed.

She got a bowl down, poured her cereal and milk, put them both away, grabbed a spoon, and sat at the oak table before being forced to look at him.

Damn! She glared at—and checked out—his broad, corded, naked tan back while he dug through the pantry. He looked like a freakin' Calvin Klein model in low-slung, plaid pajama pants.

She squirmed in her chair, focused extra hard on eating her cereal and not drooling over his tight gluts. The boy could crack walnuts with that ass. She'd never been an ass woman, but his was worthy of praise...or a smack.

Crap! *What am I thinking?* This was Chris. Chris, the town bicycle—every girl over eighteen got a ride. He made Narcissus seem modest.

He turned around. Noticed her sitting there. Renée rolled her eyes to mask the desire, need, and longing in them. Although, what she wanted was to go over and brush back the wet strands of blond hair falling over his eyes.

Chris's cocky grin took her breath away. "Hey there, short stack," he said, unwrapping one of two power bars he held. "You always eat cereal at one in the morning?"

"What's it matter to you? Do you always walk around someone else's house like you're expecting a camera crew to pop up?" she retorted. Renée shoved a spoonful of cereal into her mouth before she said anything else stupid.

Chris arched a brow at her compliment. And aggressive chewing. *Progress already, excellent.* "So, what you're saying is... you like the way I look?" he asked, taking a seat across from her at the table.

In all honesty, he shouldn't eat this late either. It went against his meal plan. But when he'd heard Renée's bedroom door open, he'd needed some excuse to be in the kitchen with her. He didn't think she'd appreciate him coming in and just staring. For two weeks, she'd avoided him like the plague, and he'd had as much of that shit as he could take. She would talk to him tonight.

When he came into the kitchen, he'd nearly forgotten himself, ran over to her, bent her over the counter, and thrust into her with gusto. She looked scrumptious in a pair of black boxers—which he refused to believe belonged to another man—and a sports bra. Her hair was in a sloppy ponytail that he'd love to pull while he hit it from behind.

Good thing she'd been busy getting her cereal because, at that moment, his dick could've drilled through granite. He'd needed those few minutes in the pantry to regain composure. If she had looked at him with those honey-brown bedroom eyes of hers, it would've been all over.

An awful sound from Renée pulled him from his pleasant thoughts but did nothing to lower the tent his reverie raised in his pants. Thank goodness he sat down.

Renée inclined her head toward his snack. "Are we watching our weight? Having fat camp flashbacks, Chub-chub," she asked, using the nickname he'd love to leave in the past where it belonged.

He knew she needled him to distract herself from his effect on her. Chris wouldn't let her get to him. He saw the spark of desire she couldn't hide when he approached. She wanted him. He wanted her, too. Patience was needed here because when he claimed her, it would be irrevocable—no turning back for either of them. No more letting her treat him like crap. No more hiding their feelings.

"I don't need to watch my weight," he said in answer to her question, though he knew she didn't expect a reply. "You're watching it for me."

At that, warm brown eyes bored into his. Chris allowed everything he felt for her: hunger, lust, and need to seep through his intense stare. She saw it. Might never admit it, but she did. He knew it. He kept her trapped in his gaze for several moments before she broke away and took an extreme interest in her cereal.

"I wouldn't watch anything, or care to watch anything, about you," she said, maintaining her fascination with her cereal. "Your arrogance disgusts me. I can't stand you or this conversation for another second," she growled, looking him in the eye.

Glare trained on him, Renée pushed back from the table, got up, and then shoved the heavy oak chair back under the table. The chair slammed into the table, tipped on its hind legs, and crashed to the floor. On top of Renée's foot.

"Ow! Shit! Ow!" She hopped around, hit the table, and almost knocked over her cereal bowl full of milk.

Trying hard not to laugh, Chris rushed around the table and picked up the chair. "Smooth move, Ex-Lax." He chuckled, bending to look at her toe.

Renée glowered at him. Jerked her foot away. "Shut up! You think I meant to do that?"

He reached to pull her foot toward him.

"Keep your hands off me. I don't need your help!" Renée shouted, backing away so fast she nearly fell. She grabbed the table to steady herself.

Amusement upturned the corners of Chris's mouth. He tried smothering his smile, but Renée's attempts to avoid his touch were too cute. Like him, she probably knew one touch would change their relationship. Something he counted on.

He reached for her again.

She shrugged away. Teetered.

"Oh, yeah, sure, you don't need help. Do you have some sort of ability to walk on one foot I don't know about?" He laughed. "You can barely stand."

It was too late before either of them guessed the other's intentions. Renée reached to steady herself on the chair. At that exact moment, Chris went to pull it out for her. Their hands touched. Something he could only describe as an electrical shock hit him. Tingles shot up his arm. He didn't have to ask. The startled expression on Renée's face and sharp intake of breath confirmed she felt it.

He'd felt nothing like it before. It was like his every desire, need, and vulnerability burst from his body and into hers. Had she not already owned him, she did now. That one touch sealed them for all eternity. As corny as it might sound, the electricity between them seemed to fuse their souls, making them one. She would forever be a part of him, and he'd forever be a part of her.

Their eyes locked. Every emotion coursing through him shone in her brown eyes. Matched his intensity. Except for the flash of fear.

Chris tried to pull her into his arms and protect her from whatever frightened her. He made a silent promise to her. Let it flare in his eyes. As long as he drew breath, no harm would come to her again. He would care for her. Protect her with his life. It might be too soon, but he didn't care. He was kissing her—tonight. Right now.

Quick on the heels of that thought, she evanesced. Vanished, as if she'd never been.

CHAPTER SIX

Pitch black. She couldn't even see a hand in front of her face.

But she heard footsteps. They were coming toward her. Her heart pounded so loud in her ears, it drowned out all other sounds, which scared her more because now she couldn't tell where the footsteps were or how fast they were coming.

Seconds that seemed like hours ticked by, and now, not only couldn't she hear or see, but she couldn't move. And...

Someone was close, very close. She felt it. Hot breath came from above. Right above her. And oddly enough, someone was behind her too. A shorter person, her height. Innocuous.

"I told you I would be back in fifteen minutes!" the deep male voice roared as loud as thunder.

Her heart stopped. Then it took off at beat-neck speed. Her stomach dropped. She knew that voice, recognized this moment.

Knowing what was to come, she squeezed her eyes shut. Her throat went dry. Tears stung her eyes. Her palms sweat.

"That was six hours ago! Where the Hell have you been?" her voice shouted from behind her.

"I told you not to talk to me that way. You're not my mother. I have a mother, and she wasn't a short, black, ugly bitch last time I checked! Watch your mouth when you talk to me. I'm the man in this relationship," the man hollered.

Renée made a loud sound at the back of her throat. "Making fun of women? Some man you turned out to be," her past self retorted.

A loud bang reverberated through the emptiness. Only an observer in this black obis. Yet the blow felt like it'd been dealt to her again.

Finally, a dim spotlight lit the angry pale face of a tall, blond-haired, brown-eyed man.

Fear was a living, breathing entity. Her breath hitched. Not one word escaped her lips, or the lips of her past self, who lay crumpled against the floor in a whisper.

Not a word. One name. "Corey."

Renée and Ashley walked through the Hall of Fame, her parents' loving name for the long hall, separating family bedrooms and bathrooms from the rest of the house. Pictures of Renée's and Andrew's age progression through the years and members of their extended family as they grew over the years lined each wall. For whatever reason, whenever Ashley or Christina visited, they loved to scope out and make fun of the pictures. Since Susan Sutton religiously updated the walls, there was always something new.

The lady was a ninja photographer. Renée didn't even remember half the candid pictures being taken, but there they were. Documented proof of her awkwardness, which is why she called the hall: The Dreaded Hall of Blackmail.

While her friend giggled at a picture of Andrew picking his nose in his sleep—two years ago—Renée stopped. Stared at one of her dad from last Christmas. He wore a red T-shirt with green lettering that read: *Sit on Santa's lap. Let's talk about the first thing that pops up.* An arrow pointed to his lap. Yeah, her brother and father thought the shirt hilarious. She and her mother... not so much.

Thoughts wandering to the previous night, she stared through the photo. As much as she hated to admit it, her memory-dream, or rather nightmare, still had her on edge. Last night was the first time she'd ever had two nightmares: one before she ate her cereal and one after. Her nerves were all over the map. She'd taken her Xanax twice already, and it was only two in the afternoon.

That wasn't the only thing weighing on her mind, though. The moment in the kitchen with Chris hadn't escaped her notice. Had she stayed there, he would've kissed her. She knew it like she knew her name. Why he'd want to do that made no sense, but his intentions had been clear as day. Worst of all, for a split second, she *wanted* him to kiss her. She'd wanted his firm lips against her softer ones. Have his muscular arms embrace her—protect her. Something indefinable passed between them in their pseudo moment, and it scared her shitless. Hurt toe or no hurt toe, she'd run out of there so fast she left a vapor trail in her wake.

If it was such a non-moment, then why did it affect you so much?

She didn't know the answer and didn't want to examine it too closely, either. Something told her she wouldn't like what she discovered.

Renée looked askance at her best friend, clad in a violet satin, spaghetti strap tank top with lighter purple trim. Worn, skimpy blue jean shorts with strategic holes placed in the back and flip-flops. Her hair braided in low pigtails. For the first time in quite some time, Ashley dressed girlie. Renée might as well be wearing a moo-moo instead of red sweetheart boxers with hearts all over them and a scoop-neck black tank top.

Silly her, she'd invited her beloved, obnoxious friend over to help dull the weird feelings and terrible memories of a time she'd rather forget. However, she suspected that the whole Chris incident triggered the nightmare too. The last thing she needed was another nightmare trigger. She had plenty of those.

"So, Chris is still staying here, huh?" Ashley asked in a ho-hum voice, knowing full well he was. When she didn't answer but stared at the side of her friend's head, Ashley turned, wagged her eyebrows, and grinned.

She didn't appreciate the insinuation behind Ashley's grin.

I knew I shouldn't have told her about last night—shit! "What?" she asked, pretending she didn't know what that stupid grin meant.

"Don't play dumb with me, bitch, you know what."

Renée narrowed her eyes at Ashley.

Ashley's grin turned into a full-fledged "Hey, Kool-Aid" smile.

"Shut up," she snapped. This was why she didn't tell Ashley about this stuff. Since Christina was at work, and she needed to talk, she'd buckled and called her. When would she ever learn? She knew what the strawberry blonde was getting at. "I was thirteen," she reminded her.

"Mm-hm..." Ashley nodded. "You could still be carrying a torch for him."

"Uh... No. There's a lot of stuff I liked then that I don't like now. Come to think of it. There's a person I liked a second ago. That I won't like too much longer if she doesn't stop talking about the thing she vowed never to speak of again in mixed company."

Ashley flinched, wrinkling her nose. "Mixed company? We're the only two people out here," she pointed out. "Who is there to hear me mention the enormous crush you had on Chris that made you cut his picture out of Drew's yearbook? And who could hear me say that when Drew asked what happened, you told him he did it in his sleep?"

Mouth pinched tight, Renée gave Ashley a wide-eyed, murderous glare.

"What?" Ashley asked. "Have I said too much? You worried Chris'll come out here, and what... spank you?"

Renée was about to tell Ashley where she could stick her bullshit opinion when she heard a voice she hadn't heard in eons, come from behind Drew's closed bedroom door. She stepped closer to listen.

"What are you—?" Ashley whispered, joining her.

"Shh..." she mouthed, putting a finger to her lips.

CHAPTER SEVEN

"Dude, when did you get back?" Drew asked, bouncing his miniature orange basketball, preparing to shoot it into the mini basketball hoop mounted on the back of his bedroom door.

His parents had months to do anything they wanted with his room. Most would've turned it into a den or a sewing room, but not his parents. They left it just as he had. The walls were still indigo. His cherry wood, executive-style desk remained in the corner, making his childhood room seem smaller. They hadn't so much as touched a paper clip since he'd moved out.

The only exceptions were his king-size bed sheets. When he'd left his *Ace Ventura,* sheets covered the bed. Now, a thick, black, goose-down feather comforter was in their place and matching black with white sheets. It stunned him that his mom would go through the trouble of changing the sheets—it wasn't like he was an actual guest. Of course, that wasn't the only surprise he'd gotten in the last two weeks of being back in his parents' home.

The second shock showed up unannounced, about an hour ago. A twenty-six-year-old, six-foot-tall, dark brown-haired, rich brown-eyed, light caramel-skinned, Latino man with a lean body that was muscled more than he remembered. It'd been a little over three years since he'd seen the man. It felt like some weird lucid dream when he saw him standing on his front porch.

Shooting the ball—and missing the basket he wasn't even a foot away from—he looked at his friend expectantly. Alejandro "Alex or Lex" Gutierrez lay kicked back on his bed dressed in gray and blue Ballin shorts, gray muscle shirt, and a backward black hat. Hands behind his head, he leaned against the wall and crossed his legs at the ankles. White sneakers hung over the edge like he owned the place. Or better yet, like he'd never left.

"Today," he answered, yawning. "The parents and I agreed it was time. Three years is long enough—don't you think?" He shrugged. "So, I jumped in the car, and six hours later... heeeeere's Alex!"

"Man, I think your sister's gonna try to kill me in my sleep." Chris, sitting at the desk, chimed in off-topic.

The off-topic part wasn't shocking. Self-centered Chris rarely paid much attention to conversations or anything not about him. While Alex had been updating them on his life in California, Chris had been where he loved to be, a world of his own. Here and there, he contributed an "oh, really," and "uh-huh," or a "no way," or nod to the conversation, but nothing else.

"Did you see how she looked at me earlier this morning? Shit, the last couple weeks I've been here...?" Chris continued.

Alex laughed and caught the ball. "Why wait 'till you're asleep?" he muttered.

Chris glared at Alex. Flipped him the bird. He picked something up off his desk and extended it to him.

Drew felt the blood rush out of his face as he saw what his friend held. Shit!

"What's up with the bling? You got a side hustle as part of Drake's entourage?" Chris smiled before doing a little dance—a rhythmically challenged head bob and shimmy, shake, bounce combo—and singing, "Twenty-one can you do somethin' for me?"

Alex leaned forward to look at the object.

Drew snatched the decent-sized diamond stud—obviously a woman's—earring and pocketed it. "I don't think it's you," he said, in answer to his friend's earlier question and ignoring his *faux pas*. His little secret was getting harder and harder to keep, especially with slip-ups of this magnitude. "She treats all guys like that," he finished, speaking of his sister.

Chris and Alex exchanged curious looks but said nothing about his change of topic, which was weird for his friends. They all got immense joy out of giving each other shit.

Alex chucked the ball at Chris without shooting it. Chris caught the ball and took the shot. He made it without so much as a glance at the hoop.

"Whatever." Chris sighed, exasperated and agitated, which was odd. "I don't even kind of envy the guy who ends up with her," he said, tossing the ball back to Drew.

He took the shot, missed, caught the rebound, and pegged a laughing Alex in the head.

Alex rubbed his head, feigning injury. "Maybe she just doesn't like you," he suggested to Chris. "Ever think of that?"

With a fake-out pretending to throw the ball at him, Alex changed up at the last second and threw the ball at Chris, hitting him square in the junk—hard.

He had to give his friend props; he didn't wince, cough, or cry. Chris didn't show that it hurt at all, but he and Alex didn't miss the fire in Chris's eyes as they narrowed.

Okay, so maybe they were acting juvenile. They were all well into their twenties, but it was like being stupid boys again when they got together. Boys who defined their relationship by how shitty they treated each other. They knew, without a doubt, that any of them would give their life for the other and have the other's back in a minute if necessary. All they were missing was Rand to complete their quartet of merry idiots—as Renée and his mother called them. It was their play on Robinhood and his merry men.

"I was watching this thing on TV the other day," Chris said after taking a minute to regroup, "about praying mantises... that's what Renée is."

Now, he and Alex exchanged eye-tightening, brow-furrowing quizzical looks.

"What the hell are you talking about?!" he exclaimed, voice rising an octave.

"Praying mantises," Chris repeated as if that should explain it. "They trap their mates," he elaborated off their blank stares, speaking in a tone that suggested they were the stupid ones, "with their beauty, then after they mate, they bite their heads off."

No words could suffice in this situation. Alex and Drew stared at their friend, deadpan and mouths agape.

Alex recovered from his stupor first. "That's what you think about when you see Renée?" he asked. "Do me a favor? Let me be there when you tell her that." He chuckled.

He didn't know how his sister fit into this conversation, but he needed to clarify one thing. "Never talk about my sister's mating habits again," he snapped. "My sister doesn't mate!" His bedroom door slammed open, knocked off balance, Andrew tripped into the wall. "Ow! What the hell, Née?"

Of course, she didn't hear his complaint. Not over the eardrum-piercing squeal she let rip as she barged in. Ashley strolled in much slower, but just as unwelcome, behind her.

CHAPTER EIGHT

"Alex! Oh. My. Gosh. I missed you," Renée squealed then, much to Chris's dismay, launched herself onto the bed, on top of Lex, and into his waiting arms.

What the fuck?

She'd never treated him like that. She often acted as if he weren't even in the room, like now. When he'd tried to help her last night, she'd treated him like he had the Ebola virus or some other infectious disease. He'd just got done hearing how she hated all men, but there was one man she liked. And by the way, her petite, barely dressed body draped over his alleged best friend with her breasts—sans bra—smashed against his chest? She more than liked him and Lex more than liked her. His arms wrapped around her said it all.

That should be me. Friend or no friend, I'll rip his motherfuckin' heart out if he's touched her, Chris thought, mouth clenched so tight he thought his teeth might shatter.

After what seemed like an eternity, watching his woman embrace another man—his best friend no less—her best friend voiced the words he couldn't without also committing homicide. "Should we leave you two alone?"

With a light-heartedness he'd never heard come from her before, Renée giggled—fuckin' giggled. She rolled off Lex but stayed lying on the bed as close as possible to him and held his hand.

"When did you get back?" she asked the traitor, gazing at him as if he were some sort of celebrity.

He guessed Lex could be considered good-looking if you liked that whole tall, dark, and handsome, mysterious bullshit. To him, he reminded him too much of that guy who played Fez on *That '70s Show*. Last Chris knew, the ever-unpleasant Ashley was the object of Lex's infatuation.

If he was furious with this PDA, Drew must be ready to draw blood. Chris turned and was struck speechless. The bastard stood there smiling—smiling!—accepting this open display of... Shit, he didn't even know. Guess the hands-off oath their friends forcibly took regarding Renée didn't apply to Lex. The double standard had him ready to spit fire. He gripped the chair he sat in to keep himself from beating his childhood friend to death.

"Today," Lex answered Renée. "How are you?" he asked, bringing their intertwined hands up and kissing the back of hers.

"Still alive," she smiled at him with a frustrating, dreamy grin.

In a gut-tightening, sickening exchange, Lex kissed his other index finger, tapped Renée on the nose with said finger, then turned a flirtatious eye and smile toward Ashley, who stood in the doorway. "What's up, Ash?" His voice dropped to a seductive level.

What the hell? What'd Rico Suave think he could do—have every woman? Three unexplained years in California seemed to have inflated his ego.

Ashley's eyebrows rose, the corners of her mouth turned up in their familiar, uncomfortable, yet disgusted way they did when Lex flirted with her.

At that moment, he found a secret ally in Ashley. At least he could count on her for the correct response, unlike his woman, who he wanted to grab off the bed, throw over his shoulder caveman-style, smack on the ass and carry out of the room.

Ashley averted her gaze and shrugged in response to Lex.

"How long are you in town?" Renée asked, bringing everyone's attention back to her.

"Indefinitely," Lex answered, not taking his eyes off Ashley.

"We need to celebrate. Let's go out tonight," Drew suggested.

"I'm so down," his sister agreed with more enthusiasm than Chris had ever seen her display in the twelve years he'd known her. "Let's go to Big D's."

"I'm not in the karaoke bar mood," he grumbled, pissed and aggravated by this new cockblock to getting Renée to accept him.

Ghosts of all her hang-ups and her preconceived notions about him were one thing to fight. Fighting his visible, and if he were being honest, better-man-than-he'd-been-in-the-recent-past friend was quite another.

Since he'd spent the year with his grandparents and only came back to town a day before Lex left for California, it'd been more like four years since he'd seen his friend. But time couldn't damage their bond or the vow they'd made to never let women come between them. However, Renée wasn't just any woman. She was his woman, his soulmate. He couldn't let her go; wouldn't let go of her. He'd fight for her and ruin his friendship, whether or not he wanted to.

His friends were his brothers, and he couldn't imagine his life without them. They were all impressive—him being most impressive. Together, their personalities melded to form the perfect man. He couldn't dream of having better men in his corner, one day standing up for him at his wedding—to Renée.

"Fine. Whatever. You don't have to be in the mood," Renée said, breaking into his thoughts. "Nobody asked *you* to come."

Damn, praying mantis Renée replaced happy-go-lucky Renée just like that. Ready to bite his head off without the courtesy of a fuck first. What would change her perception of him? Make her stop treating him like old gum or like the tenderhearted chubby kid nobody wanted around and the girls ran from.

He raised a brow at Drew. "Told you."

Drew looked confused, then comprehension spread across his face. "Shut up!"

"Come on, Née," Ashley said. "We should tell Christina. She's never met Alejandro."

"Alex," Lex corrected. "Alex or Lex, there's no Alejandro here."

"She's never met Alejandro," Ashley repeated, as if Lex hadn't spoken.

"Alex," he reiterated in a strained voice.

Renée released his hand and got up.

Much to Chris's dismay, other than her one shot at him, she hadn't otherwise acknowledged his presence. She exited without a glance in his direction. They'd had a moment last night. By the way, she acted now; it would surprise a person to know they knew each other. Oh, if she thought she would trade him for Lex, she had another thing coming. It was full-court press time, starting tonight.

"See ya tonight, Alejandro!" Ashley called over her shoulder.

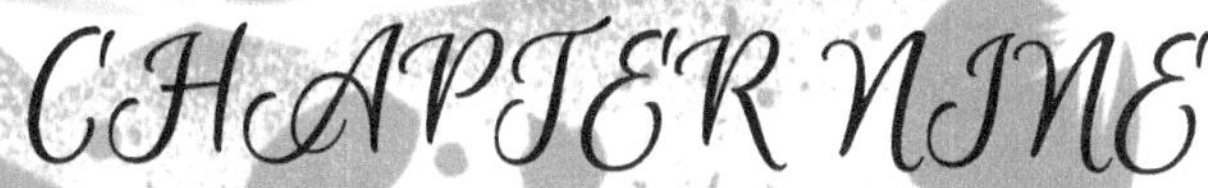

"I'm surprised I was invited to this here shindig."

Chris rolled his eyes at the snide comment made in a fake twang by the fourth member of their crew. At their usual table in the tiny dive bar, he, Lex, and Drew sipped beers and scrutinized Randolph "Rand" Wallace, kicking back in his chair. If he was the pretty boy jerk of the group, then that made Drew the serious-responsible one, Lex the ultra-relaxed one, and Rand the preppy muscle.

A six-foot-three, light-skinned, green-eyed black man with a black skull-trimmed, fade and a neat goatee. People often mistook Rand for a pushover. Polo shirts, creased khaki pants, and loafers didn't help his cause. But, hidden under his cool façade was a well-muscled hothead.

Ladies loved his looks, charm, courteous nature, and money. The guy was filthy rich. Nobody knew what his parents did, and no one asked. But everyone speculated that even as nice as Mr. and Mrs. Wallace were, they had mafia ties. Men only tested Rand once before they realized who they were dealing with. They didn't want that smoke. Step to someone the man cared for, and he'd throw the first punch before they completed their sentence. Rand was the guy you brought when you'd tried everything to deal with a situation, any situation, and got no results. He got results by any means necessary. Confrontation didn't scare Rand. Good thing, since he was in law school to become a criminal defense lawyer.

Chris scanned the bar. No sign of Renée and her posse. It was packed for a Thursday. They'd had to rely on Rand's powers of persuasion to get an extra table to push near theirs so the girls would have somewhere to sit. Given how rowdy and drunk the crowd already was, it'd be an exciting night once the DJ got the karaoke set up.

He'd never been here on the same night as Renée. Chances of her doing karaoke were slim. Ashley, he was positive, would. He'd only met Christina a few times. Each time, she stared at the floor as if she were falling in love. She hadn't said over two words and answered only when spoken to, so her singing was a stretch.

"You're one of the boys, right?" Drew asked Rand.

Two pairs of thick thighs, long-legs, and denim-encased asses attached to two brunettes passed their table. Held them in thrall.

Once they were out of sight, Rand took a swig of beer. "I couldn't tell. What's up with the blow-off, brah? You too good to return phone calls? Your phone don't make outgoing calls? You're in town, two, almost three weeks, and I'm just now seeing you."

"Been busy, man. Got shit going on. Been making big-time adult decisions, you know?"

That got everyone's attention. Three pairs of suspicious eyes flung toward Drew.

"Adult decisions?" Chris wondered aloud.

"You know," Lex retorted, kicking his chair, almost making him fall, "those things you avoid."

Lex didn't know how close he was to being maimed. He hadn't forgotten about him touching all over his woman, nor would he.

"Screw you," he said, fixing his chair and kicking Lex hard in the calf.

"Shit! The fuck, Clark?!"

Drew cleared his throat, recapturing their attention. "Umm... like I was saying. I've been making *adult* decisions—*making* moves."

"What's that you say, Lassie? Timmy fell in well," Rand said, hand to his ear. "Uh... today, Drew. Shit!"

Drew never beat around the bush, which was what he was doing.

"What does that mean? *Adult decisions,*" Lex joined in. "You get a prostate exam or something?"

Everyone but Drew laughed.

"Not that adult, dumbass! I said *adult decisions*, not middle-aged decisions."

"Well, shit!" Chris shouted. Enough was enough already. "You gonna tell us, or is this a Tampax moment? 'Cause I'm fresh out," he quipped, patting his pockets, pretending to search. "We can stop and get some, then go get a latte and talk this shit out like the woman you're acting like—*oomph!*"

This time he got knocked off his seat—by a fist to the chest from Drew. He stood and picked up his chair, glaring daggers at his friend to his right. Normally, he would do something like pour his drink on him, but trying to be a better person, he took the high road. He knocked Drew's beer into his lap.

Drew caught it before it spilled. "You're lucky it's almost empty, stupid! You guys done interrupting me or—"

"Wait," Rand interrupted. "Umm... you need some Monistat? Vagisil?" At Drew's blank stare and flared nostrils, he raised his hands in surrender. "All right, I'm done. Continue."

"Okay, this is about to get little-girl-on-the-swing set, real. You can't repeat what I'm about to say," Drew cautioned.

"Damn, it wasn't already? Is this, like, a secret secret?" Rand asked, mimicking a prepubescent voice. "Should we pinky swear? Cross our hearts and hope to die?"

Drew slammed his beer bottle on the table. "Fuck, y'all! You know what would be great? If I could finish a damn sentence."

"Stop leaving yourself open then," Rand advised, tipping back in his chair.

Drew scowled. "I've—"

"Shoot. Go ahead, shoot."

"Will you shut—"

"We're listening. Shoot."

After staring stone-faced at Rand for several seconds, Drew spoke in such a quiet voice they had to lean forward to hear him over the din of the bar. "I've been kickin' it with one of Renée's friends."

Oh, this was good! And opened the door for what he wanted to do—in a way. Maybe getting Drew's approval to be with his sister wouldn't be as hard as he thought. He smirked. "Which one?"

"Don't even think about saying Ashley, Sutton," Lex interjected before Drew answered. "I saw how close you two were standing earlier in your room. There will be all the smoke if you say something that even sounds like Ashley."

Rand studied Drew while taking a sip of his drink. "That little chubby one?" he asked, lip curled. "What's her name...? Umm... Elise?"

"Elise?" Drew recoiled as if someone had slapped him. "God, no! I wouldn't fuck her with your dick. It's..." He trailed off, gazing over Lex's shoulder. "Shit! Shut up! Nobody says anything else. Here they come."

"No matter who it is, Renée's going to have a cow, two ducks, and a chicken when she finds out. Castration will be the least of your problems." He heard Rand say with the lesser part of his focus.

The sight before him riveted his attention. Each of the three women wore black, ankle-length, long-sleeved, tight sweater coats and black high heels that were at least four or five inches tall. Light gleamed off their matching silver hoop earrings. Their matching stopped at the earrings.

Ashley's wavy, strawberry blond hair scrunched to define the curls. A spike brow ring went through her left eyebrow, and a tiny sapphire stud replaced her standard silver labret piercing. The top two buttons of her sweater coat were undone.

Christina wore her straight black hair in pin curls that framed her face. Around her neck, a simple platinum choker. Two buttons at the top of her sweater coat were open, along with the buttons starting from her knee down. They walked with a confident, sexy gait. Renée held him spellbound.

Renée looked magnificent. Far too appealing for her own good. He scooted his chair closer to the table to hide his erection. Swallowing several times, he tried not to drool. Her long mahogany hair was curled in a Farrah Fawcett feathered style. A black, lace, Victorian choker hugged her elegant neck. A delicate ruby teardrop hung from the center. At the top of her sweater coat, one button was undone, emphasizing her sex appeal. The open bottom buttons revealed chocolate thighs and smooth calves.

Chris couldn't peel his eyes away from her. They'd gone dry from staring without blinking for so long. He followed her progress through the crowded bar to their table.

Is it hotter in here?

He was sweating. In his peripheral, he noticed Drew and Lex having similar issues. Even Rand seemed impressed by the three beauties headed their way. Lex's response to Ashley didn't surprise him. Drew's gaping mouth and wide-eyed expression did, though. He had no clue who triggered it.

Drew appreciated a beautiful woman as much as the next guy, but never Renée's friends. At least, no one in her immediate circle.

Had he not lost some brain functionality from his blood traveling south to his groin already, he would've investigated the situation further.

"Hey, boys," Ashley drawled in a sultry southern belle accent, approaching the table, "any room for us?"

"Alex," Renée said. She sauntered up behind Ashley, pulling Christina with her.

Lex remained fixated on Ashley.

"Alex?" Renée tried again, louder.

Nothing.

Chris would've laughed if he weren't suffering the same ailment gawking at Renée. He tried but couldn't take his eyes off her. Her chocolate thighs looked good enough to lick, and her heels made her legs miles long. Those legs belonged wrapped around his waist while he pumped in and out of her body. His heart raced, and his mouth went dry just thinking about it. She could keep the heels on while he claimed her.

"Alex!" Renée shouted, breaking him out of his lustful thoughts. Lex still hadn't recovered. "Hello?" She snapped in front of Lex's face. "Earth to Alex."

Lex blinked. "Sorry, sweetie, what?"

Chris ground his teeth and rolled his eyes at the endearment.

"I wanted to introduce you." Renée gestured to a blushing Christina. "Christina Lee, this is Alejandro Gutierrez, also known as Alex or Lex. He will kill you if you call him Alejandro. That's a privilege reserved for only Ashley—I'll explain later—but I'm sure you figured it out." She nodded toward Lex. "Alex Gutierrez, this is Christina Lee. If you hurt her or make her feel weird, I will gut you," she threatened, saccharin sweet.

He, along with everybody else, knew she wasn't joking. That was one, among many, things he loved about her. Her protective nature turned him on. It reminded him of an angry koala bear or something else non-threatening. Another thing he loved was her inner strength; it shone through her eyes. Like a beacon, it called to him. She was also innocent and vulnerable. Of course, she'd never cop to it. Still, it was there in the depths of her eyes, along with gut-wrenching sadness and loneliness that he craved to erase from her life.

"Nice to meet you, Alex. You can call me Chrissy," Christina said, offering Lex her hand.

Lex took the proffered hand, turned its palm down, and kissed her knuckles. "Ditto, doll. The nice to meet you part. You don't have to call me Chrissy. It could get awkward."

To Chris's astonishment, Christina laughed. Hard.

Damn, Rico Suave can't keep his hands off anybody.

Drew pulled out each of the girl's chairs. The women sat, Ashley beside Rand, Renée next to Drew, and Christina brushed past Drew—breast to arm—to take the seat next to Lex, leaving him at the head of the tables with Drew on one side and Lex on the other.

Chris shook his head. The night was not going according to plan. He couldn't woo Renée from across the table, which meant he couldn't run his hand up her thigh to see if it was as slick as it looked. Maybe it was a stupid thought, but he found himself fascinated with the idea that she could taste like chocolate. Even if she didn't, he'd bury his head between those chocolate thighs and lick—

"Don't you guys understand where you live? Why are you dressed like that?" Rand asked the girls, interrupting Chris's thoughts since he was on the verge of disgracing himself in his pants.

"Oh, you big mad or little mad?" Renée asked. "Worry about yourself," she snapped.

Rand cut his eyes at her but said no more. The guy had no more nuts to spare and, although aggressive, he wasn't stupid. He'd learned his lesson with Renée.

"So, uh... hey, Mr. Money Bags," Ashley said to Rand. "Saw the new ride outside. Nice..."

With a cocky grin, Rand leaned back in his chair and put his hands behind his head. "Like that, do you? Paid for in full... cash."

"What kind of car is it?" Christina asked, eyeing the table.

"That's the newest Tesla, baby—you better recognize."

Through long, thick lashes, Christina gave a clueless, I-know-nothing-about-cars smile.

"Drew," Renée whined, elbowing her brother and batting her lashes, "I'm thirsty."

Chris wanted to be the one to get her what she needed, but not only would Renée not have received it well, it would've sent up a red flag he didn't want to raise yet. However, he couldn't wait for the day when she would rely on him. Need him.

Drew glanced at his sister out of the corner of his eye. "Hi, Thirsty. Nice to meet you," he said, extending his hand. "I'm Drew."

Renée smacked the hand away. "Drew... *pleeease?*"

"Ugh... what do you want?" Drew asked.

She smiled wide, exposing the deep dimples Chris would give his right arm to kiss.

Bloody Mary.

"Umm... a Bloody Mary," she answered.

He knew it! Chris knew everything about Renée. Likes, dislikes, and pet peeves. When he first realized he was in love with her, he made it his mission to learn as much as possible about her to ensure he was in love and not infatuated—as Lex was with Ashley.

Whatever anybody might think, pursuing his best friend's sister wasn't a decision he took lightly. After all, if he got together with her and broke her heart, it would end his friendship forever. Hell, getting together with her at all could do that. Now knowing what he needed to, he was sure of not only his unconditional love for her but of their future. And he was her... future.

Ashley turned, beamed at Rand. "You paying for our drinks, Mr. Big?" she asked, nodding at Christina.

Rand scoffed and rolled his eyes. "No. Why would I do that?"

Ashley narrowed her eyes, flipped her hair. "You're an ass. When your car gets keyed, remember you said that."

"Fine. What do you two want?" Rand demanded, jaw tight.

"Don't worry about it, man." Drew stood. "I got 'em."

"I want a Latin Lover," Ashley answered.

Lex winked, clucked his tongue, and smiled at her.

Ashley stared, confused.

Chris saw the wheels turning in her head as she tried to figure out why Lex was grinning like an idiot. Realization sparked in her hazel eyes as she digested the double meaning of her words.

"Oh, I get it." She rolled her eyes. "Ha-ha. Cute. I meant the drink, smart guy."

Lex shrugged. "Just checking. Let me know when you want a real Latin lover."

Ashley pretended to gag and averted eyes.

"Corona with lime, right, Chrissy?" Drew asked Christina with a wink.

Christina beamed like Santa brought just what she asked for; she gazed into Drew's eyes.

Chris felt like he was intruding on a private moment. He wasn't the only one to notice the weird exchange, either. Suspicion darkened Renée's eyes as she watched her brother and best friend.

After several rounds of drinks, everyone felt nice. Chris watched the short, shaggy brown-haired DJ wearing baggy pants and a Celtics throwback jersey, as he set up two monitors and placed three microphones on a nearby table at the front of the bar/makeshift stage.

"Hey, where'd the girls go?" Rand asked. He scanned the bar.

He, Drew, and Lex did the same.

The girls had disappeared a few minutes before with the promise of being right back but had yet to return.

"I think Ashley needed some moral support in the bathroom," Drew said, looking toward the rear of the packed bar toward the restrooms.

"What's that about?" Lex asked, then finished the last of his beer. "Imagine if every time I went to the bathroom, I asked one of you to go with me."

"I should be so lucky," Rand joked.

"All right, ladies, gentlemen, now is the portion of the night we dedicate to the ancient art of... Kar-a-oke," the DJ announced, cutting through the music and noise of the crowd. He broke the word into syllables using an offensive, stereotypical Asian accent. "Sign-in sheet is on the table to my left. —don't be shy. —But, first, we have a special treat. Welcome Ashley, Christina, and Renée, to the stage, please."

Each of the guys perked up. They swapped curious looks. Their attention yanked to the front of the bar, where the girls moved in fluid unison toward the stage. A familiar slow sort of jazzy intro played. He, Lex, Drew, and Rand did a double-take.

No. Fucking. Way!

Gone were the sweater coats they'd worn earlier. In their place: skin-tight little black dresses identical except for their length. It also didn't escape his notice that they'd applied cherry-red lipstick.

Ashley's dress went to her knees. A slit up the right side stopped mid-thigh. Christina's dress landed a couple of inches above her knee with a mid-thigh slit. Renée's...

Well, Chris attributed the strength it took to not get up, throw her down right there, and drive into her to the fact that he couldn't breathe. His lungs ceased functionality. She took his breath away. Never in his life had he seen anything sexier, more alluring, more captivating, than Renée's black dress. Slits on each side of her legs rose too close to the top of her thighs; it wrapped her slender curves like a glove and revealed ample cleavage. He couldn't remember a time he'd been harder than he was at this very moment.

In all fairness, the other girls looked good, too, but once he saw Renée—fuck!—they might as well have been sumo wrestlers.

Once on stage, deafening whistles rang out from the crowd along with catcalls as the girls' hips swayed provocatively, sensually to the beat. Their backs were to the audience. The hypnotic, back-and-forth motion of Renée's hips mesmerized him. She might not have a Kardashian ass, but the small one she had was plump, firm, and made him drool. God, if she moved like that on stage, what would she be like in bed?

On top of him.

Underneath him.

Chris shuddered in anticipation. Somehow, his pulse went straight to his cock. The intro to the song was long, familiar. Drums, bass, trumpets—he couldn't put his finger on which piece it was. Though as soon as he found out, he planned to buy it for their future use. She better not think this was a one-time performance. Now that he knew she could move this way, he'd demand an encore—behind closed doors.

Stark possessiveness and jealousy, the likes of which he'd never experienced, coursed through him. Other men were lusting after his woman. He couldn't be angry at her; she was having fun, which she rarely did. He wouldn't ruin it by making a scene. Punching every man who dared ogle his lady was a hard impulse to fight. Especially when each woman turned. He heard the startled intake of breath the men in the crowd took at their beauty.

Ashley sang—well—the lyrics to an old-school En Vogue song, "Given Him Something He Can Feel." Renée and Christina sang backup. If he remembered correctly, which he indeed did, they were copying the moves from the video.

The men in the audience salivated, and so were Drew and Lex he discovered, taking his eyes off his Nubian princess to check his friends' reactions. The real question was, who was Drew looking at?

CHAPTER TEN

B ack at their table, Renée sent Chris a devious smile. He glared. She loved it.

Serves you right, she thought, relaying the message through her gaze.

Slave days were over. She wouldn't stand for being treated like property. Minor possessiveness from a boyfriend was one thing. Blatant, aggressive possessiveness over something stupid was ridiculous.

And he's not your boyfriend, she reminded herself.

Yeah, that, too.

She'd already agreed to more than she wanted to for reasons that defied logic. At his not-so-subtle insistence, she put her sweater coat back on after his sixty-fifth reference to her showing her hoo-ha to the entire bar—his words, not hers.

Grabbing her wrist and shaking his head when she went to sing the Black-Eyed Peas' "My Humps" with Alex, was out of line. She owed Alex her life; she'd never treat him as less than the hero he was. While she was on the plywood stage, Chris had never taken his glacial stare off her. His anger was comical. As if he had a right. He might have looked delicious in—yeah, after a few drinks, she could admit it—his tight gray T-shirt that traced each defined muscle of his sculpted chest. Dark blue jeans encased legs of steel. She pretended not to see or look at—often—the healthy bulge in the front of those jeans. Being sexy as sin gave him no right to dictate to her.

Plus, he was one to talk about inappropriate karaoke songs.

Besides sitting through a drunken, middle-aged man singing an off-key "Friends in Low Places" and a plastic, busty blonde's okay version of Pink's "Trouble"—which she was sure should be the woman's anthem—she'd suffered through Alex, Drew, Chris, and Rand knotting the front of their shirts, rolling their sleeves, and singing a very flamboyant rendition of The Village People's "Macho Man." At one point, they even stuck their butts out and wiggled them while rubbing their butt cheeks in circular motions. Everyone in the bar laughed until they cried at the spectacle they made of themselves. Thank God, she and Andrew shared no family resemblance. No one would connect him to her. At least she'd thought so until he brought his sweaty ass over and kissed her cheek after their number.

Now everyone sat at the table talking and exchanging cutting remarks like they often did when they got together. Although no longer angry, Chris's deep blue eyes remained plastered to her with some unreadable emotion shining through.

It conjured visions of angry sex, which she knew nothing about but thought wouldn't be half bad. She wanted it—with him. Wanted it with an unfamiliar, relentless need. She could almost feel his powerful arms around her. Feel him slam her against the nearest wall, feel his large, rough hands push aside her thong. Yank open his pants and pound into her with enough force to take her breath away. The thought consumed her, set her body ablaze. Trapped in her mind as she was, she didn't realize she stared at the object of her fantasy with unrestrained desire until want-glazed eyes met hers.

Chris gifted her with his signature lopsided grin.

That grin made her ache in ways she hadn't since before her three years of celibacy. She crossed and uncrossed her legs to ease the discomfort. Unfortunately, what she wanted to relieve it sat diagonally from her with her brother between them, giving her a knowing smile.

Damn, now she knew what Roberta Flack meant in that song "Killing Me Softly." It felt as if Chris read her thoughts. All the passion she saw echoed in his eyes made her uncomfortable having such private emotions in mixed company. Instead of using a song, he killed her softly with his eyes. With his colossal frame taking up too much space.

He was too much.

Engrossed in her thoughts as she was, Renée didn't notice when the karaoke performances stopped. Ashley's voice came from beside her. She jumped.

"I have a surprise for you," Ashley said in her ear in a sing-song tone.

Renée turned narrow eyes on her friend. What had she done? The mischievous grin on Ashley's face said whatever it was, sucked.

"What did you—"

Before she voiced her full concern, the DJ interrupted.

"Our next performer is Renée Sutton doing"—he glanced down at the sign-up sheet clipped to the clipboard he held—"Christina Aguilera's 'Voice Within.'"

Oh, no, she didn't.

Renée shot her smiling friends a look that should've stopped their hearts on the spot.

Ashley grabbed her hand, pulling her from her seat. Christina helped push her toward the stage. She shuffled over to the DJ as if she were going to the gas chamber.

Singing with her friends was one thing; singing on her own was something she did in the shower. Music was a secret passion of hers, a way of expressing oneself that allowed everything a person felt to be laid out for the world to see. To her, music came from the soul. She preferred to sing songs with significant meaning—something her friends knew, but not her brother's friends or everyone in the bar. She reserved this song for when she felt alone or when dealing with more than she could bear.

Renée snatched the mic from the DJ.

She took a deep breath as the piano intro came over the speakers. Her heartbeat thundered. It felt like it would break through her sternum.

Ready or not, here goes nothing.

Chris's mouth wouldn't close. He thought he'd learned everything about Renée. She was compassionate, loyal, funny, sensitive underneath her abrasive armor. Jaded, yet an innocent dreamer, a beautiful, unique blend of strength and vulnerability. A survivor. Never in a million years would he have ever guessed she was an absolute angel sent to Earth to ensnare and steal his heart. He thought she already owned him. Still, he felt the last pieces he'd kept safe in case she rejected him, slip away as she opened her luscious lips and showed him Heaven.

Not the false Heaven he thought he felt between the legs of some nameless, faceless, random woman. Not the Heaven he believed his body, the body he worked so hard to change, to be. No, this was Heaven in its purest form. It shamed him for his previous playboy ways, made him want to be a better man, and filled him with inexorable pride in the woman he knew was his. Her voice was a soothing celestial balm made to comfort and provide peace to... everyone; it seemed by the varying expressions of awe and contentment on the faces of the audience.

Enthralled by this beautiful, brown-skinned angel, he could only stare. Everything and everyone faded away, which was why he didn't notice when the mood in the bar shifted from one of perfect peace to a living nightmare—for Renée.

Halfway through the song, Renée felt good. She hadn't passed out, her voice didn't crack, and she hadn't messed up. For the first time, she felt at peace, like she belonged somewhere. Happiness she'd denied herself for so long descended upon her. She felt whole, worthy…

Then she saw him.

Time hadn't been kind to the burly black man. Middle age transformed a head full of tight-cropped ebony curls into a receding hairline with a patch of hair in the center of two small cul-de-sacs on each side. Black slacks and a white button-down fought to contain a beer belly that used to be flat abdominals.

His presence overpowered just as the commingled scents of booze, unique perfumes, colognes, and sweat from too many bodies compacted into such a small establishment. Though the man had changed in so many ways, everything about him still screamed, "Fear me!" Her nervous system obeyed. Her gut tightened, muscles spasmed. Chills made her shake.

Renée's breath hitched. She broke apart like a beautiful clay sculpture fresh from the kiln, or blown glass smashed with a sledgehammer. Fragmented. He wrenched her from her heaven and flung her into her past hell.

Naked and scared, six-year-old Renée ran for her life around the sparsely decorated room. She almost tripped as she rounded the king-sized bed. Sweaty palms slipped on black satin sheets. She tumbled to the floor. She landed hard on her knees, ignored the stinging pain, and got to her feet. Asthma prevented her from running, but she did. Run. She had to get away.

Gasping, she crouched behind the bed. Her lungs hurt. Her legs shook. Frantic eyes peered around the end of the mattress, searching for a place to hide.

The long dresser across from the bed wouldn't work. It was too close to the wall. If she squeezed behind the tall, black dresser on the other side of the room, he couldn't reach her. She'd catch her breath. Maybe she'd be able to explain and he wouldn't hurt her as badly this time, she thought, then noticed something strange.

It was almost quiet, save for her wheezing.

From her vantage point, she couldn't see his jeans-clad legs or his bare feet. Had he left? No, she knew better than that. He wouldn't leave. He enjoyed torturing her.

Self-preservation demanded Renée figure out his location. She didn't put it past him to throw something at her. Find something long enough to hit her with.

She peeked over the top of the bed. There he was.

Crazed onyx eyes zeroed in on her. Sweat glistened on his bare brown chest, dripped off the ends of his curly hair. His nostrils flared with each exaggerated breath. Wrapped around his right fist was a long leather strap. She recognized it. It used to be a belt. Now it served as a torture device. The thick tail hung limp, ready to strike her already ravaged skin. He was going to kill her.

She shook, scared. Why wouldn't he listen? She hadn't done it. Her cousin, his daughter, got into the lunch meat in the refrigerator. Not her. But telling him that made him madder. As if he resented her taking away his reason to beat her. Then that anger provoked him more. He enjoyed hurting her. She knew because he was happiest after beating her.

Belt unraveling, he cocked back and prepared to strike.

Her heart battered her ribcage. Expecting the blow, her skin flinched. It would sting more if he got her from this distance. She moved. Swift as a snake stepped on by a hiker, she darted out from behind the bed as the leather strap sliced through the air.

He lunged for her. She dove to the right. Yes, she could've stopped, but something inside her refused to lie down and take another beating without a fight. Desperate to save herself, she ducked, dodged.

Weaved. Tears streaked down her face, but she didn't scream. Screaming made him fearful the neighbors would intervene. Then he beat her worse. Neighbors never came, though. No one ever came.

He cut to the left. Long legs provided him an unfair advantage. He caught her.

Rough hands yanked one of her braids. Sharp pain radiated all over her scalp. She resisted the urge to check to see if it had ripped the braid from her head. Her petite body sailed through the air, then landed on the bed. Her uncle's much heavier, more enormous body came down on top of her. Knocked what little air she had left from her lungs. He straddled her. With the hand wrapped around the belt, he angled his arm to the ready position. She knew what was coming. She tried to imagine her happy place. A place where she was a grown-up, comfortable, safe with a good, kind husband like the prince from her favorite movie, Cinderella.

This time, the pain doubled. His thighs squeezed her tiny frame. An audible crack—her ribs—ripped her out of her happy place and tore a shriek from her mouth.

"HELLP!"

Drew noticed something was wrong almost immediately. Renée's hand that held the mic lowered from her mouth, but not before it caught the hitch of her breath. The sound reverberated throughout the bar seconds before the mic rolled off Renée's fingers and fell to the floor. Eyes opened comically wide; she stood frozen. Her body visibly shook. Beads of sweat peppered her forehead. Something or someone held her gaze transfixed on the rear of the bar near the pool tables.

He couldn't think about who or what caused her metamorphosis now; he needed to get to his baby sister. Failing her again was not an option. Drew stood. A gray wall blocked his path. No, not a wall, but Chris's back.

What the fuck!

Chris rushed to Renée and scooped her into his arms. With her cradled close, he took off at a fast clip out the front door of the bar.

Drew shook his head to clear his befuddled mind. What the fuck just happened?

Now wasn't the time to figure out what the hell was up with his friend. His priority was his sister. He was following Chris before he realized his feet were moving.

On his way out, he called over his shoulder to their friends, "Chrissy, grab Née's purse! Rand, skip your shit and pay our tab. Alex, find out who that old motherfucker is next to the pool tables."

No one so much as sighed at his barked orders. The severity of the situation must have sunk in because they were right behind him when he stepped outside.

Renée was more out of it than he thought. Outside the bar, on the curb between Rand's black Tesla and a gold Chrysler Sebring, Chris sat on the ground. He cradled Renée in his lap. Her head tucked under his chin, he rocked her back and forth. Chris's features were a contorted mask of concern and anger. Though the area around the bar was well lit, Drew couldn't see Renée's face the way Chris held her. He bet she had tears in her eyes or pouring down her face.

Drew hadn't ever witnessed one of his sister's panic attacks firsthand. It was scary as shit to watch her abrupt transformation from the strong woman he knew to a paralyzed mess. His heart broke for her. Once again, he'd failed to detect danger to her. In his heart of hearts, he knew he couldn't have foreseen this happening, but his anal-retentive, responsible side, didn't care. The weight of his previous failure stomped on his conscience. As a child, he'd begged for a little sister. Now that he had one, he seemed to let her down at every available opportunity.

Anger rode him hard. He approached Chris and bent down. "Give me my sister," he demanded, hands extended.

Chris scowled, aggression deepening the shade of his blue eyes. Good. In his current mood, Drew wished he would fight. He might not want to hurt his friend, but he wanted to hurt somebody. At the moment, Chris would do. They were boys; he could explain later. His face wasn't made of glass. It'd heal.

"Let me up, please, Chris," Renée croaked.

He hesitated, studied Renée for a minute, then stood. He sat her in the spot he'd vacated and stepped back against the wall without a word, which again wasn't normal behavior for Chris.

Ashley and Christina, who'd redressed in their sweater coats too, rushed to her flanks. Ashley dug through Renée's purse, retrieved a prescription bottle, opened it, and then shook out two pills. She offered them to Renée. Without a sideways glance, Renée accepted them in a shaky hand, tossed them into her mouth, and swallowed them dry.

Lex and Rand leaned against the Chrysler, of course. Rand would never risk his precious new car, no matter how serious things were.

Okay, so maybe he was being an ass, thinking messed up stuff about his friends. He felt helpless. Vulnerability and he didn't work well together. Renée had been through far too much in her life, and she'd looked happy singing on stage. She used to sing in her room when they were younger. He'd sit in his room and listen for hours. It was the only time she seemed carefree.

Damn that man for taking that from her.

Drew paced between where his sister sat, head lying on Ashley's shoulder, and where his friend leaned against the wall.

Christina rubbed Renée's back. "Feeling better, sweetie? Did your medicine help?"

He listened to the answer.

However, no answer was forthcoming. Renée's emotionless, vacant expression said it all when she gazed dead-eyed at her friend and gave a slight nod.

That did it.

BAM!

He punched the wall beside Chris hard.

Chris didn't flinch.

Extreme pain should've followed the hit. His knuckles were shredded. Swollen. Split. A fair amount of blood trickled down the wall, but cold fury had him beyond physical pain. Vengeance would be the only remedy for his rage.

He turned, wiped the remaining blood on his jeans, and snarled at Alex, "Who the fuck is that guy?"

"The bartender said he comes in every now and again. Said his credit card says Davis Johnston, but you can't tell anyone where you got the info. She'll get in trouble," Lex responded.

Drew snapped. "I don't give a fuck if she gets in trouble. Did you see what he did to my sister? You don't know who he is, do you?" he asked.

Lex and Rand exchanged curious glances, then shook their heads.

Too bad for them, he didn't intend to explain. It wasn't his secret to tell. He knew what the bastard had done, and that was all that mattered. Fury blurred his vision. "I'm going back in," he said, heading toward the door.

Rand moved like the wind to block his way. "Dude, getting arrested won't help anybody."

Drew glanced at his zombified sister on the ground. "If you're not with me, you're against me," he said in a guttural tone, unrecognizable to even his ears. "Get the fuck out of my way," he growled, slamming his shoulder into Rand's, knocking him out of the way.

"You know I'm with you, Drew," Rand said in a smooth, reasonable tone. "I'm just saying think about what you're doing. This isn't some basketball court. There are witnesses here who could turn you in. You go down for this...? You're lookin' at hard time in big boy jail. We're not teenagers anymore."

He hadn't noticed Chris push off the wall, but when he turned to survey the situation, he stared into the pretty boy's face. "You gonna try to stop me, too?"

Expression a mask of calm, Chris shrugged. Shook his head.

Seconds later, he burst into the door of the bar. Chris and Rand pulled up the rear.

The stench of alcohol, musk, and sexual tension hung thick in the air. People laughed and talked as if a beautiful young woman hadn't just had a nervous breakdown right in front of their eyes. Must be nice! With the lesser part of his attention, he was aware of an old man on the makeshift stage singing The Charlie Daniels Band's "The Devil Went Down to Georgia."

Fitting. He felt like the devil now, or God, depending on how one looked at it. After all, he would decide a man's fate.

Halfway through the bar, they stopped. He scanned the room, spotted his prey.

Davis Johnston stood holding a pool stick at the back of the bar, a smile on his face as if he didn't have a care in the world.

That would soon change.

Not bothering to check if Chris and Rand were still behind him, Drew stalked toward the man. Power and deadly intent radiated from each step he took.

Drew ignored grumbled complaints from the other people playing pool as he stepped toe-to-toe with the large black man. If they knew what was good for them, they'd move.

A few inches taller than Drew, Davis Johnston scowled down at him. The man dared to fold his arms over his chest.

That might have intimidated people at one time, but now all it did was draw attention to the older man's beer gut.

"May I help you?" Davis asked.

Oh, damn right, he could help him. Help him by doing the world a favor and dying.

Chris and Rand closed in, one on each side of Drew, trapping the man between them and the pool table. If he wanted to get away, he'd have to go through them.

"You hear me talking to you, young boy?" the older man asked, unfazed by the predicament he must not realize he was in.

Drew clenched and unclenched his teeth. "You Davis Johnston?"

"Who wants to—"

That was all he needed to hear. Drew dropped him with a right to the jaw. The crack of bone-breaking carried through the entire bar. Davis's head snapped back. His knees hit the ground hard. Chris pulled the man's head and torso up, allowing Drew several more punches. Blood spewed from the man's lip, right eye, nose, and ear. A sadistic smile slid across Chris's face as Drew delivered more punches to the nearly unconscious man. He was enjoying this as much as Drew.

Wrapped up in the justice he dealt, Drew didn't see the crowd form around the small back room as much as he sensed being watched. A tap on the shoulder caused him to whip around. Raised fists prepared to fight anyone who tried to protect the bloodied waste of space kneeling before him. Seconds from fist connecting with cheek, he realized it was Rand.

Rand pointed to the owner of the bar, and two security guards heading their way. It was slow going with the crowd packed so tight.

"C'mon! We gotta go, now!" Rand shouted over the music.

Nodding, he turned back to the battered and already swollen-faced Davis Johnston. It looked like ground beef. Chris lifted him so Drew didn't need to bend.

He leaned forward, whispered in the man's ear, "Next time you feel the urge to break some little kid's ribs... remember me, asshole." He wiped his hand on the man's white shirt. "Next time I see you, I'll end you. And I don't mean that figuratively, like I'll make sure you go to jail. No... I'll stop your heart."

Chris released him. Davis face-planted in front of them. Chris kicked him in the ribs. If the deep scream the man emitted was any indicator, Drew would say Chris replicated the injury Davis inflicted on Renée years ago.

Before the owner and security reached them, Drew, Chris, and Rand beat feet out the back door.

Rand hocked a loogie on Davis, then yelled, "That guy likes little kids! Let him bleed out!"

Outside, Ashley's white Honda Civic idled in the middle of the parking lot. Christina, Ashley, and Renée waited inside. Lex sat behind the wheel of Rand's Tesla, idling behind Ashley's car. Chris, Rand, and Andrew hopped in the Tesla. Both cars peeled out of Big D's parking lot.

CHAPTER ELEVEN

"**W**hy did I come here? Why did I come here?"

"Because it was the right thing to do. Don't over-analyze it. This is tremendous progress."

Renée lifted her head off the floor. Her flat gaze looked in the direction the voice came from. "I was talking to myself." She lay back down.

"Don't you think it's rude to talk to yourself when someone else is in the room?" Wheels squealed as the good doctor, Anne Mendoza, scooted out from her desk. She stood. White blond hair brushed her jawbone as she peered over at where Renée lay on the ground. "Speaking of rude things, it's also rude to lie on the ground while talking to someone."

Hard eyes stared at the older woman. God, why was she here? After seeing her uncle last night, she couldn't stop the panic attacks. Ashley and Christina had helped her into her pajamas and bed. She was *Walking Dead*-style out of it. Nightmares of memories from her past had assailed her throughout the night. It was the worst possible segment of *This is Your Life*. She'd gotten a solid five hours of fitful sleep before deciding she needed to do something, which led to where she was now: lying on the floor in Dr. Mendoza's office. She didn't particularly want to talk but didn't know what else to do.

"I'm exhausted, but afraid to go to sleep. It's lie down here or fall down somewhere else. Anyway, you were saying something about a breakthrough...?"

"Yes. I know seeing your uncle was difficult, but it was the breakthrough we've been waiting for."

"*We?*" Renée scoffed. "Why do you always say that? *We* this, *us* that. Are *we* dealing with some co-dependency issues?" she asked with a smirk. "Is this the imperial *we* we're talking about? Because *I* wasn't waiting for a breakthrough. I was fine. Now I'm not, which is why I'm here. Make me better."

"Renée, you know as well as I, if not better, that there are no easy fixes. If there were, I'd be out of business. Last night was unpleasant, and it might not feel like it. Still, your being here illustrates that you're ready to confront your past—deal with those self-worth and abandonment issues. Change your self-talk. Those negative tapes that play over and over. That your self-talk reinforces."

Renée sighed and flung her right arm over her eyes. Damn, more of this bullshit. She muttered to herself then louder said, "I'm over the whole Mom leaving me thing. It was horrible. How could she? Blah... blah... blah. It's done."

"Yes, I know. But your mother isn't the only one who left you. You've mentioned before that you wonder why no one on either of your parents' sides of the family ever tried to find you. What about your father? You never mention him. I think now's the time to explore your feelings about him. And all men really."

She raised, rested on her elbows to ensure Dr. Mendoza saw her eye roll. Then put her head down. "Hey, most people get one deadbeat parent." Renée shrugged with a nonchalance she didn't feel. "I was lucky enough to get two and a deadbeat family. I've learned to embrace it."

Dr. Mendoza stood, gazed down at her. Stretching her neck, she made sure her stern, disapproving frown was in Renée's line of vision. "I wouldn't be worthy of my degrees if I allowed you to think I believed that."

"Believe what you want," she mumbled.

The good doctor was right about one thing. It didn't mean she was ready to open doors better left closed from her past. However, she wanted to get through this. Her reaction to seeing her uncle was not only irrational but eye-opening. She didn't want to forever respond to people and situations the way she had last night. There had to be a way to accept, acknowledge, and move through her past. At some point, she wanted to find someone to love her crazy ass, have babies. Maybe confronting the past was a necessary evil.

"How many panic attacks and nightmares do you have a month?" the doctor asked, retaking her seat.

Renée thought about it for a moment. Shit, they were so frequent, she'd lost count. "They aren't dreams or nightmares if they happened," she snapped, not angry but to avoid admitting the truth.

"If they happen while you're asleep, they are... even if they're real. Stop avoiding the topic."

Renée jerked into a sitting position. "What do you want? Me to say that after all this time it still pisses me off no one looked for me? No one cared what I went through. No one protected me. That I felt unprotected and helpless last night. How much I wish I knew what was so damn unlovable about me? I wish I knew why when there is a choice between me or anything else in the world, people always choose anything else. Let's face it... there's always something better than Renée?" She could've ended there, should've ended there, but couldn't. Exhaustion was causing verbal diarrhea. Made her thoughts erratic.

"Or, no, wait. Maybe you want me to get into how I'm my parents' lifelong get out of Hell free ticket. Taking in a damaged little black girl must be worth major karma points. I'm forever indebted to them. Andrew's not. He can just be. But they can say and do anything to me, and I can't get mad because I owe them. Is that what you want to hear?"

Dr. Mendoza leaned back in her seat. Hazel eyes peered at Renée. Nodding, she propped her elbows on her chair's armrests. She steepled her fingers. "That's exactly what I want, Renée," she answered. "Raw emotion. You're allowed to get mad. Get mad about last night. About your childhood. Get mad and address it. You have every right to be angry. You never express your authentic emotions. But what you said there? That was real. You deserve to be happy, healthy, and whole."

Tears slid unbidden down her cheeks. She had meant to say none of that, but—whoop, there they were. Her genuine feelings. She couldn't run from them anymore. Without another word, she stood, wiped her tears with her hand, gave the doctor a tight-lipped smile, and left. It wasn't rude. The open, honest gaze they exchanged was nonverbal communication enough.

"Are you gonna do it?"

Seated at her desk in her bedroom, Renée held her cell to her ear. Spun in her swivel chair.

"I don't know," she said, answering Christina's question.

After spending the rest of the morning alone, contemplating life, she'd walked out of Dr. Mendoza's office confident, empowered. Those emotions had waned considerably since then. On the good news side of things, she'd taken a two-hour nap without one nightmare. Having explained it all to the more sympathetic of her two best friends, she tried to regain some of her earlier courage.

"I don't even know how to look for these people. Like I said before, I couldn't find anything," she went on.

"You could always try my suggestion. I may not run my life for shit, but I give expert advice," Christina reminded her.

"Yeah!" a voice yelled in the background. "Ask Magnum P.I. He'll help you!"

Great! She groaned. "I thought you said you were in the car?"

"I am," Christina defended. "You didn't ask if I was alone. Ash and I are going to get her car from the shop; then she's gonna pay to get my oil changed."

Renée laughed. No matter how old she got, her mind drifted into the gutter now and again. Though it seemed to happen more and more with "what's his face" around.

"Yeah, there's this hot guy who works there. I wanna see if he'll show Chrissy how to work a dipstick!" Ashley yelled.

"Shut up," Christina said, away from the phone. "Don't make me turn this car around. I told you. I don't want or need that kind of oil change. Unlike you, not all of us need a tune-up every thirty miles." Then back into the phone, "So, you gonna ask him?"

Renée gave the phone an arched glare, as if her friends would somehow see it. "I don't know. I might. I have to come up with a plan of attack."

"Not to change the topic, but... did you see Chris checkin' you out last night?" Ashley shouted.

Yeah, not going there. Bad enough, she'd let him hold her and whisper sweet words of comfort. She'd noticed a difference in Chris. She didn't like it.

"And on that note... I have to go. Kick Ashley for me. Peace." She pressed *end* before anyone mentioned anything else she didn't want to talk about.

Late that night, Renée stretched and yawned as she trudged into the kitchen for her nightly bowl of cereal. She hadn't had a nightmare tonight. Quite the opposite. Tonight's dream was of the adult variety about the one person she shouldn't be dreaming about. Of course, right as things were about to get good, her internal alarm woke her up. Memory-dream or not, her body still wanted cereal.

She poured herself some Cinnamon Toast Crunch. Ate it in record time. This wasn't a night for her to run into the mirror monster.

As she rinsed her bowl in the sink, a chill went down her spine. Wait, wasn't true. The sensation was warmer than anything, but she shivered. After five minutes of washing, she turned off the water. Her special see-through glass bowl specifically for cereal, which she'd maim anyone for using, had never been so clean. She placed the bowl face down on a towel on the counter.

Time to face the music.

Renée turned. Her eyes met broad, tanned pectoral muscles. Resisting the urge to reach out and caress someone, she crossed her arms. Taking a stroll up the chiseled torso, she gazed into a set of beautiful, dark blue eyes. Her heart did a stupid flutter that she tried to ignore.

"May I help you?" she asked, injecting as much venom as possible into her voice.

Chris smiled.

Okay, the venom didn't work. It was hard to be venomous, with her emotions frayed and his defined bronze chest in her face.

Combine that with the dream… Yep, fate was conspiring against her.

"Bowl clean?" he asked, crowding her. She pressed back against the edge of the counter.

She'd known the precise moment he entered the kitchen and invaded her personal space. He'd stood behind her for the whole five minutes. She'd washed the bowl without a word. Now, she suspected he'd done it on purpose.

That was a lie—she knew he did it on purpose.

"It is. Thanks for asking. You know they make chairs for a reason."

"I know. I'm standing here. Is that a problem?" his voice dropped to a seductive level.

Liquid pooled at the juncture between her thighs. His voice should be outlawed. Speaking of illegal things, the intense, penetrating look he gave her also needed to be abolished.

"Yes," she said. "I don't like people in my space, and you stink." A childish lie. He smelled clean, mountain fresh, masculine, and of Chris. She needed to get away from him before he realized his effect on her, stat.

Without warning, he struck. Moved too fast for her to protest. Hand under each arm, he lifted her. Sat her on the small ledge of the counter in front of the sink.

She gasped and kicked at him. He dodged her kicks. Pushing her legs apart, he positioned his colossal body between them. Chris leaned in, braced a hand on each side of her hips. Blue eyes twinkling with humor gazed into hers.

Angry, she should be angry. She wasn't—uh-uh. Instead, arousal was as prevalent as her pulse beating at her.

Must. Fight. Temptation. Must be strong. "What are you doing?" she asked, surprised her voice was steady given her quivering insides.

He grinned.

Damn him!

"My neck was hurting from looking down at you," he explained as if it were the most rational excuse in the world. All the while, he stood close enough for her to know he'd brushed his teeth with Aquafresh.

She had to get away from him. "Chris, I—"

"Shh..." he interrupted, bathing her face in minty fresh breath. "How are you feeling?"

That was the last thing she expected him to say. Stunned silent, she blinked several times. The sincerity with which he asked made her want to believe he cared.

"How are you feeling, baby?" He smiled, repeating his question.

"Don't call me baby." That snapped her out of her lusty haze—a little. "I'm not your baby."

Chris wagged his eyebrows. Got so close she'd swear he'd kiss her. "You will be. And don't blow off my concern like it doesn't matter."

There was such conviction behind his words she almost believed him. But this was Chris. Self-centered, narcissistic, Christopher Clark. Her guard had to always be up with him. In no way did being another notch on his belt or tally on his bedpost appeal to her, but for some unknown reason, she wished she was special to him. She needed that right now. Needed to feel comforted—by him. He'd done it the other night, and it felt right. God, she sounded like one of those cheesy romance novel heroines, but there it was.

"Why are you saying stupid stuff to me?"

"It isn't stupid," he countered. "You were out of it, but don't you remember anything I told you last night?"

"No," she lied. Last night, he'd been a different man. Had cradled her as if she were a piece of fine China.

Typically, Chris wouldn't sully his clothes by doing something as vile as sitting on the ground. Once he'd gotten her outside, he sat down on the curb without hesitation. The entire time, he'd rocked and whispered soothing words to her. He'd apologized for not seeing the problem. Told her how beautiful her voice was. How gorgeous he'd always thought she was, and he'd promised he wouldn't let anyone hurt her again. It all seemed more like a dream. She'd needed his strength, and he'd given it tenfold.

Tilting his head, he regarded her through narrow eyes. He arched a brow, shook his head. "I don't believe you. You remember. Do you want me to repeat it?"

Not on her life; that'd lead to sex. She shook her head.

He smirked. "Thought so, liar."

God, why did he have to be so frickin' sexy? If he were ugly, this would be much easier. She could kick him in the nuts, jump off the counter and leave. But, no, he was sex personified. So, instead of doing what she should, she wondered if he was erect or not. The way he looked at her set her body temperature to an inferno. No matter how she moved her head or what she said, he hadn't taken his eyes off her face.

If she didn't know what he was about, didn't know that she and romance mixed as well as a gas tank and sugar—she'd want him. Not want his body, which she did. She'd want everything. The protection he offered. His heart. Soul. Little tomorrow babies with him. She'd like it all and give all of herself to him. But she'd learned long ago that she had a particular penchant for the unobtainable.

The more she wanted something, the worse it was for her. Mom referred to it as her "picker" being broken. At first, she'd taken offense to the judgment call. After several examples proving said phenomenon and now, sitting here on the counter with six feet four inches of over two hundred pounds of tanned, virile, muscled man between her legs, she agreed.

She would've loved to ponder her "picker" more, but Chris chose that moment to nuzzle her cheek with his. Her thoughts scattered. Good Lord, she could orgasm from the feel of his breath against her ear alone. It had been so long since she had intimate contact with another human being. Renée bit back a moan.

Chris hummed next to her ear. "Do you know what that smell is?" he asked, rubbing his nose up and down the side of her face. He exhaled slowly.

Chills skittered down her back. He bit her earlobe.

Words eluded her. She shook her head no.

Oh, no! Her spot. Her eyes rolled back in her head. Against her better judgment, she leaned into him, returning his nuzzle.

"Don't lie to me," he rasped in that deep timbre wrapped in an uncanny southern drawl. "You know as well as I do what that smell is," he spoke in her ear, lifted his head. Stopping his ministrations, he watched her out of the corner of his eye.

She returned his gaze with half-mast confusion. Her head swam. She couldn't think straight. He was speaking in riddles. On the one hand, maybe it was good he stopped messing with her. After all, that was her spot. A direct connection to the vijay spot. Speak in, bite, nibble, lick or do anything to her right ear, and it guaranteed you a place in her pants.

After an intense, passion-glazed stare down, he rubbed his nose against hers. Then nuzzled her cheek with his. He whispered in her ear, "That's pussy... your sweet, fragrant... pussy."

She wanted to speak. Protest. Rage at his vulgar words but couldn't. Like a guppy fish, she opened and closed her mouth several times. He must have foreseen her reaction because he snuck a hand between their bodies. Ran two brawny fingers over the damp evidence soaking the middle of her red, lace-ruf-fled, tanga shorts.

Well, denial's out.

"You know when I smell it?" he asked, continuing the assault on her senses. His fingers stroked her cloth-covered core. He blew in her ear.

Speech wasn't an option. Renée shook her muddled head. Did she want an answer to this question? If he got any dirtier, her head would pop off.

"Every time you're near me." He moved the fabric covering her apex.

Cool air hit sodden, sensitive flesh. She shivered. Lightly, he ran his fingers up and down the seam of her nether lips. Her stomach clenched in anticipation.

"It's your body's way of calling mine."

This wasn't right.

He felt right.

She should stop this.

Her body wanted him.

An innate desire for love—his love—and acceptance warred with her self-preservation instincts. Whatever this was would only hurt her. People lied. Men lied. Everyone pretended to be something or somebody they weren't to get what they wanted. Was Chris doing that now? Part of her said yes, but another part murmured no. She couldn't let another man do this to her, play a role. She might seem strong, but that was the gag. Inside, she was weak, a tad needy, and she couldn't have meaningless sex.

Wrapping an arm around her waist, he forced her forward on the counter. Ground his erection against her. "That's what happens when you're near me." Either Chris read her mind, or he sensed her need for reassurance. "Every time. Anytime. I am now a woody-hiding master." He chuckled.

For the love of all that was holy, Chris was hung like a stallion and the master of disguise. Somehow, in a move that a lot of guys seemed to have down, he'd shifted himself. The elastic waistband of his pants held his erection tight against his stomach. Although, she'd bet most guys weren't as thick and long as him. Even though he'd hidden it, pressed it snug against her, she felt its steely length. Her mouth went dry. She gazed down. The bulbous tip of his manhood protruded from the top of his flannel pajama bottoms. Stopped at his belly button.

She tried to swallow but came up dry; she bit her lip… Houdini slipped a thick finger past her tanga shorts and inside her at that exact moment.

Renée gasped. "What are you doing?" she breathed.

Pumping the digit in and out of her with a skill that should be taught in colleges everywhere, he said, "Need me, Renée. Rely on me."

She needed him—to not stop what he was doing. And she relied on him to not leave her without release. Her head lulled on her shoulders.

His labored breath assaulted her ear. Pleaded for something, something she couldn't do. Chris wasn't referring to just this moment. This was a request for more, which frightened her and sparked her curiosity. Could he be serious, or were these ramblings of a man desperate to get laid?

When guys just wanted a pump, she'd heard it all. One guy said he loved her even though he kept calling her Irene. Another guy told her she was the most beautiful woman he'd ever seen while she had the flu. Then one guy used her favorite line, "Just let me put the tip in."

Yeah, right!

Was Chris doing the same thing?

Ah… He added another finger. Shamelessly, she ground her hips against him and moaned.

Renée couldn't think anymore.

CHAPTER TWELVE

"That's it," Chris encouraged Renée. Grinding her hips, she forced his fingers deeper inside her tight channel. "You like that, baby?" he purred in her ear.

"Mm-hmm," she moaned, bucking against his hand.

His head reeled. Renée was everything he'd expected. Tight. So wet. She held his fingers in a death grip. The only thing better than this would be being inside her or coming in at a close second, tasting her. Her scent was out of this world. Didn't take a rocket scientist to discover her spot. He'd stumbled upon it when he first entered the kitchen and stood behind her.

Wanting to get a rise out of her, he'd stooped down and exhaled in her ear. She'd tried to hide it, but he'd seen her shiver. After that, he'd only planned to torment her a bit, but in her ruffled-butt red shorts and black tank top... He'd lost his damned mind when she turned and confronted him with all that round brown cleavage. How much was one man supposed to take?

He'd comforted her the previous night and wouldn't trade that for the world. He wished to God it had been him who'd fucked that guy up. Not that Drew wasn't well within his rights as her older brother to do it. He just felt that as her man he hadn't done enough to handle the guy who'd hurt her.

Usually, after a fight, his adrenaline pumped hard, and he'd work it out on some random chick or Samantha. Still, he couldn't do that now that he'd decided to claim Renée. For twenty-four hours, it had tied his insides in knots from needing some sort of release. Going to the gym hadn't helped. Lifting weights that morning did nothing. Running a few hours ago hadn't worked. But this, two fingers knuckle deep inside Renée's tight passage, knowing he provided her with a measure of pleasure, oddly helped.

"Why do you keep pretending you don't want me?" He nibbled her earlobe, delighted when her walls quaked around his fingers. "That you don't need, and think, and dream, and fantasize about me? Don't you know I'd do anything for you, baby?"

Maybe he was pushing, but he had to make her see what they could have. If forcing it on her with passion was the only way, so be it.

"Shut up," she moaned, tossing her head back when he thrust into her hard. "Anyone... would be... turned on... by what you're doing," she panted.

With his free hand, he lifted her head. Forced her to look into his eyes. Brown eyes darkened with longing. An unspoken command kept her eyes on him, trapped her caramel gaze with his. He continued his assault on her heated pussy, curled his fingers inside her. Let all he felt seep through his stare. To his surprise, moisture gathered in her eyes. He'd planned to make this about her, but she was too sweet for words. He leaned in, kissed the tip of her nose.

Keys jingled.

Panic flared to life in Renée's eyes. She squirmed and tried to move, but couldn't, with his body blocking hers. Reluctantly, he pulled his sopping wet fingers out of her and adjusted her shorts. Chris stepped back. Renée hopped off the counter and bolted for the exit. If she thought she'd escape without a word, she was sadly mistaken.

"Renée," he called, not loud, but he got her attention.

She stopped. Breathing ragged, she turned in the doorway.

In a split-second decision, he brought two glistening fingers to his mouth. Gaze locked with hers. He parted his lips and, in a savoring draw, sucked off her sweet juices. Light brown eyes followed the action with rapt interest. They darkened with lust. Swallowing, his eyelids drifted closed. He savored her sweetness. Knowing how turned on she was, he raised the fingers to his nose. Took a big whiff.

Fucking fantastic!

"Mm... strawberry," he moaned in the voice he knew drove her wild.

Her eyes widened.

The front door opened.

She glanced over her shoulder. Turning back, she whispered, "Asshole." Then ran off.

Waiting until he heard her bedroom door click closed, he dashed to the pantry. Pulled out some butter-flavored Pam and sprayed it in the air. As jingling keys drew closer, he threw the Pam back in the pantry and hurried down the hall to the guestroom.

As he closed the bedroom door, he prayed it worked. The last thing he wanted to do was explain to his best friend why his kitchen smelled—although delicious—like pussy.

The next afternoon, Andrew worked at his desk. His client's son's fiancée was hiding something. They had hired him to find out what that something was. He'd trailed the girl for six weeks to discover she was squeaky clean.

He'd be pissed if his parents ever pulled that shit. They got crazy, but not that crazy. He couldn't imagine the son would be too happy when he learned about what his parents had done. Andrew had half a mind to call the poor SOB and tell him, but that would break the confidentiality agreement he'd signed with his clients. He'd already bent enough rules in his personal life, which he hated doing. The last thing he would do was compromise his integrity further. All a man had was his word and his balls. His father instilled the lesson in him, and he firmly believed in it and wouldn't jeopardize either.

Plus, the guy would find out soon enough. The nut job parents planned to confront him about their suspicions with a giant notebook full of questions they wanted answers to. They'd shown him the questions, and the sad thing was the answers weren't any of their business. Most dealt with the girl's tragic past and the abuse she'd suffered. She reminded him of Renée. Every protective bone in him wanted to call the girl and warn her away from the loony family. If the parents were that crazy... Who knew what kind of lunacy the son hid?

A knock at the door pulled him from his thoughts. True to form, the knob turned, and the door opened before he responded.

"Knock, knock, big brother. Enjoying your mini vacation playing babysitter?" his sister asked, inviting herself in.

He sighed. Renée never seemed to grasp the concept of knocking on his door, then waiting for a positive response before entering. Several times, she'd almost walked in on him, rubbing one out and having sex when they were younger. Silly him didn't think he still had to lock his door—now he knew.

Andrew turned his chair to face her. "I guess." No use reminding her to knock. She'd nod, apologize, and continue to do what she did. Secretly, he thought it sweet that she felt so comfortable.

"What are you doing?" She sat on his bed. Fidgeted with the ruby birthstone ring she always wore on her right hand.

Uh-oh!

"Catching up on work. Crossing I's and dotting T's—know what I mean?"

Renée chuckled, eyes darting back and forth around the room. Her fidgeting increased.

Andrew examined his sister with open suspicion. Renée might be many things, but jittery and evasive weren't part of the package. She wasn't as bad as Ashley, but she said what needed to be said.

"Where's Captain Self-absorbed? Off looking in a mirror or something?" she asked, not meeting his gaze.

Okay, he was worried now. That put down was weak, not anything like her.

"Or something. Why, you looking for him?"

Maybe Chris had something to do with her behavior. He'd acted strange all morning before leaving to play ball with Alex and Rand. Andrew would kill his friend if he'd offended Renée. She wasn't over what happened a couple of nights ago. Neither were his knuckles. They were pretty banged up, but in good enough condition to beat Chris's ass if necessary.

"Absolutely not," Renée snapped, "the only reason I'd look for him would be if I were taking up serial killing."

"How could someone so tiny be so... ruthless?" he asked, hand to his heart.

Renée looked at him then—barely—and glared.

"So, did you come to provide comic relief, or did you need something?" The suspense was killing him; he hated this hesitation. There had been a time she wouldn't have ever hesitated to tell him anything.

She looked down, studied her hands as if the meaning of life was written on them, then chuckled.

He watched. Whatever was on her mind was monumental for her to do some nervous giggle. She hated girls who acted that way and openly mocked them.

"It's nothing. Never mind," she said with a sigh.

"Doesn't sound like nothing. You know you can tell me anything, right? This is a safe space," he joked, waving his hand to encompass the room.

The joke fell on deaf ears. Renée gazed at him stoned-faced, brandy eyes beseeching.

"Can you have an open mind and promise not to get mad or hate me?" she asked after a long moment of silence.

Andrew hurried away from his desk, wheeled over to the bed where she sat, and stopped in front of her. He took her hands in his to still her fidgeting. "I could never hate you. What did you do?"

She jerked her hands free. He yanked them back. Held them tighter.

"I didn't *do* anything, so to speak." She breathed deep and let the breath out. "Okay, so, you know I've been going to counseling, right?"

Andrew nodded, not seeing a connection.

"Well, because of the other night and other stuff, my psychiatrist suggested I confront some of my past issues."

He let out the breath he hadn't realized he'd been holding. Here he thought it was something terrible, like she was suicidal or pregnant. "How are you gonna do that?"

"I plan to embrace situations that remind me of my past and figure out better coping strategies," Renée answered, using her idea of an arrogant therapist's voice.

While adorable, it sounded like Doctor Ruth.

He shrugged. "Good luck with that. I guess."

Renée hung her head, sighed, then looked back up, expression grim.

Damn it; he would go prematurely gray if she didn't stop dicking around. He waited for her to find the courage to say whatever had her acting so scared.

"That's not all."

He figured.

"But I need your help with this next part."

"What do you want?" he asked.

"I need you to help me find some people from my birth family." He must have given a queer look because she rushed to add, "Not my parents or anything. Well, not my birth mother, anyway. I have some names, but that's it."

This time, he dropped her hands. "How does finding them help you?"

"It might not. I don't know. But it could. I'm tired of being a freak, Drew."

Damn! He'd do anything to help her, anything but this. Why did she have to ask for the one thing he didn't want to do? Not only would this kill their parents, but it could metaphorically kill her. Look what one time seeing an uncle she hadn't seen in sixteen years had done to her. He couldn't cope if these other people caused the same response or worse.

If he were being honest, a small selfish part of him didn't like those other people out there who had a claim to her. She was his little sister. What if she had some other brother and felt more connected to him, or felt more connected to her whole family? It might be a childish reason but, he couldn't help it.

"It might not seem like it, but one day I want to have a normal life," she continued. "One where people stick around and maybe even love me."

His eyebrows furrowed. "Now, you don't think people love you? What about Mom and Dad? What about me? Your friends love you."

Renée appeared uncomfortable with his questions. She fidgeted with her ring again. "Nobody loves me," her voice was meek. "People put up with me. When the people supposed to love you unconditionally turn their backs on you, it scars a person to their soul. I have to find out what about me screams *unworthy*. Maybe people care, maybe they don't. If I go back to the beginning, maybe I can start to believe for myself that I matter. Either way, I need to find my identity—who I am."

Andrew rolled his eyes. Man, this therapist his parents found had done quite the number on her. How could she believe this shit? "Identity doesn't come from blood, Renée, or skin color. It comes from soul connections you make with people." He couldn't think of the words to express what he wanted to say. Frustrated, he raked his hand through his hair. "This will kill Mom and Dad, Née. I can't help you hurt them."

Renée recoiled as if someone had struck her. "I'm not asking you to," she whispered. "I'd never intentionally hurt them. I love them. I love you."

Shit! Were those tears in her eyes? If she started crying, he'd feel like an even bigger piece of shit than he already did. He didn't mean to insult or guilt her. This was just... huge. He supposed he should have expected her to one day want to know about her birth family. He and his parents had even discussed it. In one of their family counseling sessions, years ago, they'd been told some adopted kids never reached out to their birth families. They figured Renée was one of those kids. Maybe the race thing mattered?

What was the right thing to do? Go behind his parents' back, or help his sister?

Renée seemed to have an internal debate of her own. A plethora of emotions crossed her face. She stared at him, studied him for a long minute, then got to her feet in one fluid motion.

She found something in his eyes. Her expression morphed into one of resolution. "Forget it. I shouldn't have asked. Sorry. I can do this alone."

What the hell? Talk about making it hard to say no. She wasn't pouting. This wasn't a ploy to get him to bend to her will. This was how Renée did things. When she realized she was wrong, she owned up. If she believed she'd hurt someone, she apologized. She would do it alone. It was one of many notable, lovable traits she possessed.

He owed her an apology. She needed him, and after years of not asking him for anything, she trusted him. And he was acting like a jealous ass.

He stood, pulled her into his arms. "I didn't say no. You're my little sister, and I can't—no, I won't—leave you high and dry."

She gifted him with one of her heartbreaking smiles. "Thank you, Drew. I owe you."

He hugged her tightly. God, he hoped this was the right thing to do. Either way, he'd be there for the fallout.

Two days later, Drew had the information Renée needed. Hopefully, she wouldn't be disappointed when she found out a couple of people on her list of names had passed away. He patted the black and white composition book on his lap that held the recorded information. She couldn't have known any of these people that well. The last time she'd seen them, she might have been three, four years old.

It was easy to get the information—for him. He understood how it would've been difficult for Renée. It had taken a day to compile all the telephone numbers and addresses. Then another day going back and forth with himself about whether he wanted to let her do this. Late last night, after talking to his lady, he'd decided it wasn't his place to stop her. His job was to support her, no matter what. Plus, this would be over in a day or two, tops. Once she called these people, they could put this all behind them.

Taking a deep, calming breath, he glanced across the kitchen table at Chris. The man wasn't acting like himself. Out of nowhere, he was asking people if they needed help with shit. Chris had gone and helped his parents clean out his old room, and didn't do his hair one day. Andrew considered alien abduction until a few minutes ago.

They'd been getting their breakfast, and Chris got cereal. Knowing he waited for the same cereal, Chris put it away like Drew wasn't standing beside him, saying, "I need that."

Now, he sat here at the breakfast table dressed in only jeans. The guy had no home training. Good thing Renée was asleep. She'd throw up or curse him out, whichever came first.

I guess a leopard can't change its spots.

"So, who had you drooling at the bar?" Chris grinned.

"I don't know what you're talking about. I was making sure those sloshed douchebags kept their hands off my sister and her friends," he lied.

Since when did Chris pay attention to what other people did? He planned to tell his friend his dirty little secret—he might need to use him for cover—but not now. Renée might overhear. They were in the kitchen with too many sharp objects. He didn't want to die today. For the first time, he was in love, a fact he hadn't shared with his woman yet.

"Know what I saw, though," Drew said, flipping the tables. "You looking at Ashley, man. Better hope Lex didn't see you."

"What!" Chris bellowed, eyes spitting blue fire.

Andrew laughed hard. Glancing at the entryway, his laughter died.

Disheveled and tired-looking, Renée stumbled in, wearing a maroon camisole and black sweatpants cut into shorts. Hands raised high; she stretched. Scratched her head before letting her arms drop to her side. "Could you guys be any louder?" she griped. "I don't think they heard you in Mexico."

He chuckled at her disgruntled scowl—until he looked at Chris. To his bewilderment, his best friend, since birth, stared at his sister like... like Chris gawked at women. Like he could eat her alive. To make matters worse, his eyes were locked on her breasts.

"Are you *ever* happy, or is this bad mood thing just part of your natural charm?" Chris joked, still focused on her cleavage.

Renée beamed at Chris. "I'm always happy—until I see you."

Yeah, as usual, she might have been insulting Chris, but something about this exchange made him very uncomfortable... and homicidal.

Renée went to the cupboard, lifted onto tiptoes to retrieve a cereal bowl and a box of cereal. Her ass cheeks peeked out.

Andrew turned to Chris. The fuckin' prick licked his lips like the coyote when he thought he'd finally caught the roadrunner.

Oh, hellllll, no!

"Renée!" Andrew snapped.

She started, lowered to flat feet, and turned toward him. Confusion etched across her face.

"Haven't you ever heard of clothes?" he shouted.

"Yes. Why?"

Was she serious?

"'Cuz you need to put some on. Or at least wear a robe or something—shit!"

Her mouth turned down into a moue. "Geez. What crawled up your butt and died?" she quipped.

He had a mind to go over there and drag her by the arm back to her bedroom. "Nothing," he shot back, "but I see what's crawling up yours. Go put some fucking pants on—now!"

"Fine, shit! I'll be back." She stormed out of the kitchen, shooting him curious glances over her shoulder until he couldn't see her anymore.

As soon as her door closed, Drew reared back his leg under the table, and as hard as he could, kicked Chris—square in the balls. "What the hell is your problem?"

Chris fell out of his chair, cupping himself. He groaned in pain. "I don't think I can father children," he answered between clenched teeth. "What's yours?"

"You! You were checking out my sister!"

Getting back into his seat slowly, Chris shook his head but couldn't elaborate further.

Renée stomped in wearing the same top, but with black sweatpants. She returned to the counter, where her bowl and cereal sat. She turned to Andrew with a raised brow. "Better, Versace? Or would you prefer I wear a turtleneck also?" she asked.

"Much better, Ms. Pint-size Naomi Campbell. You may proceed with your breakfast." He grinned, satisfied with not only her clothes but Chris's gaze, which stayed on the table and off his sister.

Renée glowered at him, then finished preparing her food. She sat at the table.

Andrew removed the composition book from his lap and slid it across the table to her. "This is yours. It's that stuff you asked for," he informed her cryptically, so he revealed nothing she didn't want Chris to know.

She picked the book up, flipped through the first couple of pages. Jumping up without finishing her breakfast, she dumped the contents of her bowl into the sink. She ran the garbage disposal, grabbed the notebook off the table, and exited the kitchen.

God, he hoped he'd done the right thing.

CHAPTER THIRTEEN

Renée went cross-eyed. She felt like she was looking at one of those weird paintings or pictures that you're supposed to put your nose on and stare at until a picture forms. She'd swear the black and white designs on the composition notebook were melting together.

Her butt was numb from sitting at her desk for so long. It had been hours since she'd moved. She'd barely taken a bite of cereal this morning, and that was... she glanced at the miniature Sylvester the Cat clock at the far corner of her desk. Eight hours! At ten this morning, she ate a single bite of cereal, and now it was six-twenty. So, how could a taste of cereal sustain a person? She didn't know, but it did.

Then why's your stomach in knots?

Good question. It wasn't hunger pains—of that, she was sure. These were know-what-I-have-to-do-and-it-scares-me-crapless pains. Tension bunched her muscles. And she thought the other day was hard. That was a long walk off a short pier compared to tonight. She felt light-headed, and her head throbbed, throbbed, and knocked.

Knocked?

Not knocked. The knocking was at her door.

Please… don't be Chris.

Now wasn't the time for his particular brand of bullshit. She didn't know his deal, but he was playing some game. If she were being honest, his *game* had a lot to do with the emotional turmoil she found herself in as of late. His mere presence affected her. Something about him was different, possessive, more… intense. His intensity stirred feelings. Old feelings, stuff she couldn't deal with, stuff that crumbled her resistance. To amend the words of the great Jay-Z, she had ninety-nine problems but a dick wasn't one, nor would she let it become one.

Please, please, don't be Chris.

"Come in!"

The door eased open. Andrew's brown-haired head peered around the door. "Hey, Little Bit, what's going on?" He smiled with apprehension. "You've been in here all day."

Taking a deep breath, Renée waved her brother in. Beating around the bush wasn't her strong suit, and his smile showed he suspected something. Might as well rip off the Band-Aid.

Andrew sat on the edge of her bed.

She turned in her chair. "I'm leaving." The words came out softer, less confident than she hoped—since she *didn't* feel confident. "I'm gonna go find my birth family."

Faster than she knew was possible, Andrew shot to his feet and leaned nose-to-nose with her. He squeezed the arms of the chair so hard the entire chair shook with his anger. Sweat dotted his brow. His jaw locked and set. Emerald eyes shot fire. "What the fuck do you mean?" Disbelief raised his voice. "You're leaving? You can't leave—that'd kill Mom, Dad… me. You said you wouldn't hurt them," he accused.

Tears pricked her eyes—that hurt. "I know," her voice cracked, "and I'm not going to. I'll be back before Mom and Dad are. They'll never know I was gone."

"Née." He lowered his tone to the one he used when trying to reason with clients. "You don't know these people. They could be serial killers. What are you going to do? Show up on their doorstep, hold them at gunpoint, and force them to spill their guts?"

Averting her eyes, she blew out a long breath. "I haven't worked that out. And it doesn't matter. I already bought the bus ticket online. I leave tomorrow."

"*What?*" he shouted—right in her face. Spittle landed on her lowered eyelids and cheeks. "No! You can't leave. I'm not letting you go. I got that stuff so you could make *phone calls.* They could be dangerous, or crazy, or both."

Raising her eyelids, she stared into her brother's eyes. She lifted her chin in defiance. Did she love Andrew? Yes, so much it hurt. But she was still wary of brothers, and people telling her what to do got on her nerves. "I'm not asking your permission. All I'm asking... is that you cover for me when Mom and Dad call. Nothing more."

Andrew pinned her with a glacial stare. "I won't let you do this. I'm your brother. I'm supposed to keep you safe, protect you." He took a deep breath. Guilt and regret softened his features. "I already failed once."

There it was...

Andrew always brought that sonofabitch up, and why wouldn't he when she made him feel that way—not on purpose, nevertheless, she was the reason he felt that way.

How could a person be pissed off and guilty at the same time? She didn't know, but her system worked it out. She didn't want him feeling inadequate. "The Event" wasn't his fault. Her lack of faith in the concept of *big brothers* shouldered a large majority of the blame for what happened. Yeah, she'd had a big brother before, a two-bit sonofabitch older brother who—

No!

She stopped those thoughts dead in their tracks; she refused to go there. The topic, the situation at hand, mattered more.

A lack of faith in the concept of older siblings made this her fault. She'd been close to Andrew once, very close, closer than she'd been to Kathy. She'd opened her heart to him in a big way, and like with Kathy, she let one situation no one could've foreseen—except her—shake her faith in him. And as much as she wanted to open herself to him again, she couldn't. There was a block in her mind. The past haunted her, which was more reason to follow through with her plans. Renée wanted to restore her relationship with Andrew.

The sorrow in his tone broke her heart. "No, you didn't fail. That was my fault, not yours." She covered one of his hands, gripping the arm of her chair, rubbed it. "I'm sorry, Drew. I have to do this."

Andrew let go of her chair, hefted himself to his full height. Stepping back, he raked his fingers through his hair, breathed in deep, and exhaled. He rolled his shoulders. His face, once pinched in anger, smoothed into a hard mask of resolve. "Fine. I'm coming with you."

Eyes bulging, she stared up at her brother. "No. You can't... I'm-I-I mean..." she stammered. It'd be weird enough with her going. She couldn't take him in some supervisory bodyguard role. Futile it might be, but she needed him to see reason. "Who's gonna cover with Mom and Dad? You can't come. And you can't take care of me forever, Drew."

"Yes, I can," he responded. "I'm your big brother. Besides harassing you, giving you a hard time, and chasing away would-be suitors, my number one job is to protect you. So, yes, I can... and

I'm going. Matter of fact, we're all going. Your friends, my friends; we'll road trip it."

"No!" she protested.

If she didn't want him to go, what would make him think she wanted a whole posse? Didn't he understand anything about self-discovery? It wasn't the type of work that needed witnesses. Showing up at these people's doors half-cocked might not be the best plan. Showing up with the cast of *Euphoria* behind her wouldn't help endear them to her.

Andrew sauntered to the door with all the swagger and confidence of John Wayne. "Yes. Now, get packed. I've got calls to make, and I need to get the Denali cleaned—"

"What? Why? I paid for a bus ticket. If you don't want to take the bus with me, then don't come."

"Oh, no, I'm going—we're all going. I'll get you back for the bus ticket. It couldn't have been that much. Call your friends, or I'll do it for you." He smiled a big toothy grin, opened the door, and walked out with mock enthusiasm. "Road trip, baby!" She heard Drew shout as he walked down the hall, then he sang, badly, "The more we get together, together, together, the more we get together, the happier we'll be. When your friends are my friends, and my friends are your friends, the more we—"

The slamming of his bedroom door cut off the rest of his little ditty.

Renée heaved herself up from her chair. She dropped to her knees, crawled to her bed, and pulled her duffel bag out from underneath it. "Well, this just got a lot more complicated. Fun times... fun times," she muttered.

The house came straight out of a movie. It had to. Places this big didn't exist in real life, at least not in her real life. When they pulled up to the single-story, north Scottsdale, southwest-style mansion—which she learned was two large houses pushed together to make one—with a tennis court, NBA-size basketball court, Olympic-size pool, and enormous rock garden with a walking path, her mouth fell open. A long circular drive led to the house, protected by a tall stucco wall with ornate, black, iron gates outside the front door.

Nine-year-old Renée watched a twenty-something, light, brown-skinned man with a thick mustache hug and kiss his mother. Why was she here? Yes, she liked her middle-aged, mocha-skinned, short, curly black-haired speech therapist. However, that didn't explain why she stood in the woman's foyer with two Hefty bags full of her belongings.

Eight hours ago, she'd lived in a shelter for abused and neglected girls close to her elementary school. An hour before school let out, her state-appointed caseworker showed up and chauffeured her to the shelter. They'd allotted her ten minutes to pack her meager belongings. Then her social worker drove her back to school, deposited her and her things in the speech therapist's office, and announced the widowed Mrs. Bobby Greensburg would be her foster mother. Just like that, it was done.

She didn't know this woman but was expected to live with her. Mrs. Greensburg informed her that her three grown children still lived at home on the drive here. This young guy dressed in a white polo shirt and fitted khaki pants must be her youngest.

Renée was confounded. Her life had turned from hell to heaven in a matter of hours. She needed time to breathe, time to absorb what was going on. She wasn't used to family life or how families behaved. However, she wanted to learn. It would feel so good to be a part of a family, have siblings, a mother. She'd seen tons of television shows where young girls had protective older brothers and secretly envied them.

Ever since she could remember, she'd been protecting herself. Checking over her shoulder for someone to do her wrong. Hurt her somehow. It would be nice to have someone whose job it was to watch out for her. Here, she'd have two big brothers since Mrs. Greensburg had two sons. As far as she knew, there was no such thing as a nice guy. A good man. Brothers were supposed to be that and more.

This would be great.

After kissing his mother, the man extended his hand to her. He smiled. "I'm Aaron." They shook hands. "Nice to meet you, Renée. I guess I'm your brother."

"I guess so." She shrugged, uncomfortable with the conversation. "Nice to meet you."

The entire situation made her uncomfortable. Even standing in the foyer, she felt inferior. Inadequate. They dressed to impress. The house's furniture belonged in a castle. Garbage sacks rested at her feet. She wore a shirt and pants two sizes too small. Hunger pangs gnawed at her insides, and her hair was in a ponytail with a million fly-a-ways pointing in every direction. She didn't belong here.

"I've never had a younger sibling before," Aaron commented, breaking into her thoughts. "I've always been the tortured youngest." He laughed. "I won't torment you too badly, though; I've always wanted a little sister." He winked and patted her shoulder. "You and I'll be close."

Putting her arm around Renée's shoulder, Bobby steered her away from Aaron and down a long, tiled hall. "Let me show you your side of the house."

Ornate doors lined each wall. There were about nine rooms in this one hall. Renée was awed. She assumed one door would lead to her room, but Bobby didn't stop at any of them.

It took several minutes to get to the forked end of the hall. To the left was a large kitchen. Peeking inside, she saw two ovens. A large island with a baker's rack hung over it, an industrial-size refrigerator, and stainless steel sub-zero freezer side-by-side—an entirely stainless steel wine storage unit with a glass panel front built into one wall. At the back of the kitchen was a cherry wood table with eight matching chairs set around it. In front of each chair were white and gold China plates with gold cloth napkins folded like origami crowns.

Bobby turned right. Renée quickened her steps to catch up. At the end of a short hall were tall, intricately carved, mahogany double doors. Grabbing the knob of each entry, Bobby opened them. Renée froze at the sight before her.

Cathedral-style ceilings. Built into the walls were shelves filled to the brim with books. An in-home library. Her fantasy brought to life. This must be how Belle felt in Beauty *and the* Beast. *Hardback, paperback, poetry, old classics, romance, paranormal, bestsellers, every genre a person could ever want to read. She stared, slack-jawed, at the magnificence surrounding her. Set on opposite sides of the room, two white wicker couches with fluffy maroon cushions. This was her idea of heaven.*

Caught in the splendor, it startled her when Bobby touched her shoulder.

"Come," she said in her magisterial, British accent. Hand placed in the middle of Renée's back, she nudged her toward double doors across the library. "Your side of the house is through here." She opened one door. "These doors don't lock, but this is your part of the house. Make yourself at home. No one will bother you."

They stepped through the doorway into another house. A modest four-bedroom home with a decorated living room, a small kitchen, three spare bedrooms, and a two-way fireplace. Again, Renée was taken aback.

"This is your domain. Your kitchen. Your living room, and down the hall there,"—she turned and pointed— "are two extra bedrooms. There's three, but my daughter January uses one when she's home from school. And the door near the fireplace, that's your surprise."

Bobby led the way across the room, opened the door.

Renée gazed inside. It wasn't an enormous room. Ugly pea-green sheets adorned a twin-size bed pushed against the far wall. A tall, antique oak dresser sat to the left of it. Next to the bed sat a night-stand with a lamp, phone, and alarm clock atop it. The room wasn't luxurious by any means, yet it was... perfect. She'd had nothing that was indeed hers until now.

"I thought you would like this room best," Bobby said. When she didn't react, she continued, "You can see the fireplace from your room and the living room."

"No, I like it," Renée assured her. "It's beautiful. I've never had my own room. It's the first time I've had my own... house. Thank you."

As sudden as a jack-n-the-box, Renée jolted up in bed. Tears streamed down her face, and her heartbeat erratically. Reaching over to her nightstand, she snatched her prescription bottle out of the top drawer. With shaky hands, she opened the bottle, shook out two pills, and swallowed them dry.

CHAPTER FOURTEEN

Damn, what is it with her and two o'clock in the morning?

Once again, Chris observed Renée shut her bedroom door in, an obvious attempt not to make noise, then tiptoe barefoot down the hall, heading toward the kitchen. Either the girl had insomnia or that weird sleep-eating disorder he heard about on one of those TLC Network shows like *My Strange Addiction* or *Freaky Eaters*. Or she was one of *those* girls, a woman who had a problem eating in front of people.

She'd never struck him as the type. Yeah, she was thin, but it didn't look eating disorder-induced. Renée might have a bucket full of issues, but that wasn't one. Whatever the reason, he'd know soon enough.

Opening the guestroom door wider, he peered down the hall. Left. Right. Coast was clear. Chris pulled off the muscle shirt he'd worn to bed with his plaid pajama bottoms, flung it on the bed, and slipped into the hall. Destination: the kitchen.

Operation Get Renée was on like *Donkey Kong*. Few women could resist him without a shirt, and he knew it was her weakness as well. He'd watched her try to stop herself from checking him out several times, but her eyes had a mind of their own. They slid up and down his body like a lover's caress. In the immortal words of one Steven Q. Urkel, he was wearing her down, baby.

In the kitchen archway, Chris crossed his arms over his broad chest. Leaning against the frame, he crossed his legs at the ankles. He watched his prey. Detouring from her typical late-night cereal, she made toast. Naughty girl—she had on the same outfit from earlier. The low-cut, maroon, V-neck camisole and black sweatpants turned into cutoff shorts. Smooth chocolate thighs begged for his touch. His tongue. The way she stood; one brown cheek was close to slipping out of the bottom.

Fuck!

He adjusted himself in his suddenly tight pajama pants. Sweat broke out over his brows. Without having a clue, the girl tortured him. Because of her short torso, her legs were long, although she wasn't tall. She had athletic legs. Nothing would please him more than to lick both her long legs from ankle to... well, it didn't take a rocket scientist to figure out where.

Before he realized it, his fantasy carried him from the entryway. He now stood behind Renée, a hairsbreadth away from his chest pressing against her back. A delicate mixture of almond mango shampoo and cocoa butter body lotion filled his nostrils. He leaned closer to pull her fragrance into his lungs, skin. His soul.

"Oh, my gosh!"

He jerked back to avoid being slammed in the face by Renée's head as she spun around.

Glaring at him, she clutched her chest. "You scared the crap out of me. What were you doing?"

Her low-cut camisole exposed perky, creamy brown breasts as they rose and fell. Beautiful. He craved nothing more than to hook his finger in the flimsy material and rip it down the middle. His eyes leisurely traveled down her body. Then up to her annoyed face.

Eyes narrowed, lips pursed, she pinned him with an icy glare. She didn't enjoy being startled.

He tried to hold back a grin, failed. "Wow! The forbidden pajamas again," he teased. "You're lucky it's me and not Drew. This would not be considered a minor infraction."

Ignoring him, Renée turned around.

Chris didn't move a muscle. She could try to shut him out all she wanted, *try* being the operative word. Her bratty mood wouldn't deter him.

"Why are you here?"

"Gosh, sorry to ruin your night," he said, feigning offense.

Pressing the toast down, she turned hard eyes on him. "You don't have the power to ruin my night." She smiled without humor. "I can ignore you."

Yeah, right!

The words were there, the evil eye was there, but her resolve was lacking. Especially since he noticed the heated once over, she thought she'd masked with a slow, annoyed, perusal up and down his body. He was harder than a diamond and didn't hide it. When her gaze found his erection, he felt it like she'd taken him in hand. Her gaze lingered. She licked her lips. God, help him—he wanted to bend down and suck that pink tongue into his mouth. The urge was so strong he had to lock his knees to keep from doing just that.

"I don't think you can." He smirked.

Her appraisal ceased.

Chris would've laughed at her forlorn expression if he didn't doubt she'd slap the shit out of him. Anyway, he had more important things to ask while he had her off guard. "Why do you think I'm so stuck on myself?"

She flinched as if startled by his question. Brown eyes narrowed. "Have you seen yourself?" Renée asked, gazing into his eyes.

Ah! So, she noticed him. Of course, he'd known that before, but it was nice to have verbal confirmation. "If I walked around like a slob, would I attract you?"

"Why does my being attracted to you matter? You have—what? —fifty, sixty groupies worshipping at the altar of the almighty Christopher Clark? Do you need more?" Renée smirked, quirked a brow.

Everyone thought they knew him so well. Had him figured out. To say their assumptions were pissing him off would be an understatement of grand proportion, hers more than anyone. Whatever; he'd table the topic for another time. Right now, he wanted to play with her. He moved closer. "So, you *are* attracted to me?" He grinned.

Renée, averting her gaze, stepped away. "Ugh..."

He hated when she pulled that dismissing him crap. Hooking an arm around her tiny waist, Chris yanked her close. She gasped. Finger under her chin, he tilted her head. Renée struggled, pushed at his chest—weakly. She wanted this, and he'd give it to her. Chris leaned in. Her lips parted, and her gaze latched onto his mouth. He wanted this, too. Hadn't realized how much until this moment. Her delicate breath warmed his chin.

He lifted her arm, draped it over his shoulder. Chris almost cried when she flung the other arm up there without prompting and laced her fingers behind his neck. His lips brushed hers.

Keys jingled. Toast popped up.

They jumped apart. Twisting, she retrieved her toast. She placed it on a plate then hauled ass out of the kitchen.

Sun glittered today. Not a cloud marred the perfection of the Arizona sky. Birds chirped. Leaves of a large eucalyptus tree swayed in a light breeze. What a beautiful morning for acid to destroy Andrew's stomach lining.

Lugging several duffel bags and a couple of suitcases, he walked down the sidewalk toward his black Denali parked at an angle in the driveway. He pressed a button on his key fob. The power liftgate lifted, exposing the rear cargo area.

He had a bad feeling about this trip. It was one thing when he'd thought his sister would make phone calls in some misguided attempt to fix her past. It was quite another to drive his baby, his precious SUV, across the country to find people Renée didn't know from Adam. These people hadn't given a shit about her while she suffered many abuses from her uncle and then in the foster care system. No one ever checked on her or tried to gain custody. What type of so-called *family* did that?

When first adopted, she was this frail little girl with big, sad eyes that had seen too much. While he didn't pretend to understand all that she'd suffered, he knew her wounds ran deep. It had taken a long time for her to let them in. But she was worth the wait and the hardship her often mercurial emotions caused others sometimes. His sister had a spark about her, a light in her eyes. She was a fantastic person lucky few ever got to know. How was it that someone so talented and beautiful couldn't see how loved they were? It pissed him the fuck off that this *family* she wanted to search for caused her deep-seated feelings of inadequacy and a low sense of self-worth. Yet, she risked hurting their parents to meet these people. And he used the term *people* loosely when referring to them. They weren't worth the air they breathed in his book. The ones from the list she'd given him who'd passed away were lucky.

Andrew was of a mind to kill the ones who remained so that they'd never interfere in his sister's life again. Maybe then she could get through these panic attacks and live a halfway normal life. She deserved that and so much more, which was why he was going with her. Her independent nature, while admirable, was sometimes a curse. She refused to rely on or trust anyone. So, until she learned it was okay to need people, he'd decide when she needed someone. She'd need him and their friends for this trip. And he would be there for her.

Plus, if he were being honest, there were definite benefits to this trip, he thought, glancing up the drive. The women were arguing about seating arrangements. Ashley, dressed in denim shorts and a gray-and white-striped, poncho-style, crewneck tee, glared. Christina, in a white flared shirt dress with a drawstring waist, slid on her sunglasses. Renée, wearing black cotton shorts and a red off-the-shoulder, cashmere sweater, shook her head no.

Just then, Lex and Chris exited the garage with a couple more bags.

In typical douchebag form, Chris tossed a gym bag at him. Andrew dropped the travel case he'd been prepared to pack in the Denali to catch the bag.

"Fuckin' dick!"

Chris straightened his black muscle shirt. Adjusted himself through his white Ballin' shorts. "We're driving to Indiana?"

"That's the plan. It should only take a few days."

Lex pushed past him, reorganized the luggage. He shoved the travel case in between a few bags. Dude was the king of *Tetris*. The way he organized the luggage proved it. He looked at Andrew. "You sure Renée wants us *all* to go? Isn't this kinda personal?"

Andrew snatched up a few more bags, took a suitcase from Chris, and worked the bags into the cargo area as best he could.

"Of course, it is, and no, she doesn't. But there's no way in hell I'm letting her do this alone."

"Are we all gonna fit in here?" Lex asked, leaning against the side of the SUV, careful not to get his white muscle tee dirty—as if Andrew would ever let his baby get dirty.

"Yeah," Andrew assured him, "two in front, two in the middle, and two in back."

Lex scoffed. "Cozy."

"I don't know if my big—"

Chattering from Ashley, Christina, and Renée coming down the walk from the front of the house interrupted Chris and drew their attention to the girls.

"I don't care if I have to cut off a leg. I'll fit in these damn seats," Chris finished as they watched the girls.

Each girl carried two additional carry-ons. Great. What didn't they understand about *pack light*? Shit! They wouldn't be gone more than a week and a half, yet the girls packed like they were moving there. He placed the last bag in the truck, shut the lift-gate.

Passing him, Ashley bumped his shoulder as if she were a linebacker protecting the quarterback. Damn, the girl was small, but not only did she have a big mouth, but she also packed a big—

"Excuse her," Christina said, brushing past him.

Andrew smiled. He wasn't a peach; he wouldn't bruise, he thought, watching Ashley and Christina climb in the truck. "No shoes on the leather, ladies," he reminded them.

Renée bumped him like Ashley had, but with less force. She tossed a smile over her shoulder. "Shake it easy, Andrew. This was your idea, remember? It costs to be the boss. You could always back out. Let me take the bus as I planned."

"Not happening. Get in the car. And I thought I told you one small bag—just you—in the car," he reminded her, glaring at her shoulder bag and the carry-on thing she held.

Hand on the door handle, foot on the retractable assist step, she shot him a snide, tight-lipped grin. She jiggled the shoulder bag. "Munchies... bro." Renée wagged her eyebrows, then climbed in.

"Indiana, here we come!" Ashley shouted from inside the cab.

Shaking their heads, Andrew, Chris, and Lex traded exasperated looks. His terrible feeling intensified.

CHAPTER FIFTEEN

G*allup, New Mexico*

Renée stared out the truck's window. She adjusted her oversized sweatshirt. Well, not her sweater, Alex's sweater. Who would've thought New Mexico nights were cooler than Arizona's? She'd heard somewhere that New Mexico was hot like Arizona, but it was cold, and she hadn't packed a coat, cardigan, or sweater. She'd taken the hoodie under Chris's frosty glare.

She sighed. There wasn't a star in the sky. If not for the gas station's lights that they were parked behind, there'd be no light at all. Between Drew insisting they go on this merry little road trip and Chris being...

God, what was he being? She didn't know and didn't care to find out. Chris confused the shit out of her. Renée had no interest in being one of his conquests, but when he got close, held her... She forgot all the reasons she despised him, and her teenage self, the one who used to have a crush, went weak-kneed.

Beside her, Ashley yawned. Renée swiveled in her seat. She and Ashley sat in the middle chair. Chris and Andrew slept in the front seat while Lex and Chrissy were knocked out in the third seat.

Ashley stretched. "Hey, what're you doing awake?"

"Couldn't sleep."

"What, Alejandro's stench keeping you up?" Ashley grinned. "Why would you wear that? You don't like him, do you?"

Renée put a finger to her pursed lips. "Shh... Could you shut the hell up?"

"Did we just meet?" she asked, modulating her tone.

"No, Ash, I don't like Alex. Not that way. It's a sweatshirt, not an engagement ring. I couldn't sleep. I'm nervous," Renée confessed.

Ashley readjusted in her seat, pulling her blanket close. The leather squeaked. She squeezed Renée's knee. "Don't be nervous. We'll go there; you'll talk to these people. The worst they can say is fuck off. The best, they give you some answers, you feel enlightened and shit, we leave, and you're better."

Very poetic, and not that easy. Them saying fuck off was why her intestines twisted. She hadn't seen these people in forever, wasn't even sure they'd remember her. Plus, there was animosity on her part. How did she talk to people who didn't give a shit about her? In her room, facing her past seemed like the right idea. Here at a rest stop, headed to do what was the most significant thing she'd ever do... Again, she was that scared, confused little girl who just wanted someone to tell her she mattered. Wanted someone to choose her. Being told to fuck off would kill her.

But she couldn't explain that to Ashley—Christina maybe—but not Ashley. Sensitivity just wasn't Ashley's strong suit. She was more brute force. The taser you brought if a deal went south. Renée took a deep breath.

"Née. Really? What's the worst that could happen?"

She took another deep breath before answering. "You're right," she lied. "Why are you awake?"

"I felt you watching me," Ashley joked. "A little too *Twilight* for me."

Renée chuckled. That was why she loved Ashley. Mushy words weren't her thing, but she had a sixth sense about this stuff. She knew when her mood needed lightening and then did it.

"Did we all have to come?" Ashley asked once they sobered.

Renée burrowed into her seat, thrust her hands into the front pocket of the hoodie. "Hey, I wasn't gonna be stuck with just Andrew. And he kinda forced the issue."

Shaking her head, Ashley whispered, "You guys used to be so close. Now you don't want to be alone with him. I don't get it, Née. Build a fuckin' bridge already."

If only it were that easy. This, Ashley never would understand. "Let's just say I have long-standing brother issues and leave it at that."

"Whatever," Ashley sighed. She pulled her blanket over her shoulders, curled in her seat, and faced the other direction. "All I know is that we better have some fun on this trip," she grumbled.

Sure, they'd have fun ripping off her emotional scabs.

"Renée, Jason, and Giovanni are going to live here for a few months. Would that be all right with you?" Bobby asked, setting her fork prongs down on her dinner plate. She interlaced her fingers.

How weird.

People asking for an opinion on anything was hard to get used to. Being in the foster care system, Renée got moved without notice, and life changed all the time. Her feelings were never considered. So, even though it had happened several times in the last two months since she'd moved in with Bobby, it still shocked her. Sitting at the dinner table with Bobby, Aaron, and Aaron's two friends, being involved in such a decision, made her feel important. Like they were an actual family.

Renée never had it so good. Bobby had taken her on her first shopping spree. She'd never had clothes someone else hadn't worn first. Mrs. Greensburg bought her a whole new wardrobe, got her hair done in a real salon, let her talk on the phone to her friends, and invited them over. None could come over, but just having the ability to invite a friend over to a place she wasn't ashamed of was nice. She also allowed her a couple of glasses of wine each night, which was so cool. Then there was Aaron.

Having a big brother was incredible. The TV shows had it right. Aaron spent tons of time with her. He showed her cool video games, taught her how to play said video games. Helped her learn to play tennis, played basketball with her, and introduced her to his friends. One of his best friends was Jason Cote, sitting at the dinner table to her right. He was so cute.

Jason was the epitome of a beach bum. At seventeen years old—two and half years younger than Aaron—Jason was the cutest boy Renée had ever seen. He resembled a blond Joey Lawrence with shaggy hair, long thick sideburns, and sky-blue eyes. He left his shirts unbuttoned and off sometimes. When they were playing basketball, he smiled at her and touched her arm the other day. Once, he flexed and let her feel his muscles. She got goosebumps. His brother, Giovanni DeSantis, was nothing like him.

Giovanni and Jason were both seventeen and stepbrothers. He was the polar opposite of Jason. Tall, slim, he had short chestnut hair and dark brown eyes. His awkward and painfully shy personality differed completely from Jason's confidant, happy-go-lucky. Giovanni rarely spoke to her or anyone. They were excellent, but it would be weird living with them.

Of course, this wasn't her house. She was thankful to be treated so well and for the opportunity to live in such a lovely house. No one ever hit her or made her feel invisible here. They doted on her. Bobby even made breakfast for her every morning like a real mom. One of the best perks of living here was that Bobby let her stay home from school whenever the wine made her feel funny. With all that, who was she to dictate to them who could and couldn't live there?

"Yes. They can stay; that's fine with me," Renée agreed.

Everyone smiled at her.

Bobby poured some wine into Renée's glass. "They're going to be staying in the spare bedrooms on my side of the house." She scooted the glass toward Renée. "You'll barely know they're here."

Aaron tapped the table in front of her, grabbing her attention. "We're"—he pointed to himself and his friends—"playing video games in my room tonight. You wanna hang out with us?"

Oh, my God!

Renée schooled her features into a smooth, expressionless mask. Inside, she did backflips. The robot. She couldn't wait to call her best friends, Becky and Sam. They would flip when they heard about her hanging out with high school boys for the night. In a room. Alone.

"Sure… sure I want to," Renée answered, trying hard not to smile.

Renée gazed around the room. She'd been here before, not at night, though. It amazed her how much the room didn't fit the house or the man who occupied it. Aaron was only twenty, but she'd thought he'd have more than he did. Sitting cross-legged on the floor behind Aaron, Jason, and Giovanni—who gathered around an enormous television on the floor playing video games—she scrutinized the room.

A king-sized bed with boring, faded, navy-blue sheets dominated most of the room. A massive armoire sat in the corner. Stacks of video games, a game system, a VCR, and a sixty-inch television sat on the floor just outside a door that led to his en suite bathroom. Compared to the rest of the house, his room was a dump.

Aaron glanced over his shoulder and smiled. "Having fun, little sister?"

"Yeah..." An accidental yawn slipped out. She covered her mouth and smiled. "Sure. I'm tired, though. I think I'm gonna go to bed, okay?"

It was three in the morning. Watching boys play video games wasn't all it was cracked up to be. Sleep was creeping in.

Aaron nodded.

Renée got up to leave.

"Goodnight," Aaron called out to her before she exited the room. She turned around.

Aaron grinned like the cat that ate the canary. "Every day, I enjoy having a little sister more and more."

Giovanni and Jason waved.

Attributing the odd, sort of flipping sensation filling her stomach to the combination of macaroni and cheese and wine from dinner earlier, she turned and left the room.

Renée couldn't sleep. She left Aaron's room because she was tired. But once she was in bed, her body didn't shut down as she expected. Listening to buttons clicking and electronic video game sounds for hours on end made it impossible for her to handle the quiet now thrust upon her. If counting sheep helped, she'd do it, but prior experience told her all that did was make her think about sheep and sheep facts.

Minutes stretched into an hour, and sleep still hadn't claimed her. The thought of getting up crossed her mind at the exact moment the door that connected her side of the house to the library creaked. Whispering voices wafted in through the opening in the two-sided fireplace.

"Hey, close that door," Aaron whispered.

A second later, a door slammed closed.

"Shh…" Aaron shushed someone. "I said close it, not slam it."

"What if she isn't asleep?" she heard Jason ask in a whisper.

"Look through the fireplace," Aaron ordered. "Is her back turned toward you or the wall?"

Renée didn't understand where the instinct came from, but something told her to flip toward the wall. She'd never been afraid of Aaron or his friends, but right now, that weird feeling churned in her stomach. She flipped toward the wall.

"What does it matter?" The question came from Giovanni's already quiet voice.

She wanted the answer to that question, too.

"A lot," Aaron stressed. "If her back is facing the wall, she isn't fully asleep. If her back is facing you, she's dead to the world."

"How do you know that?" Giovanni asked.

"I've been watching her since she got here," Aaron bragged. "She does the same thing every night. I had my mom get her this little peach tank top and shorts set to sleep in. She wears it all the time."

Statue-still on the outside, on the inside, Renée was an iceberg, chilled to the core, frozen solid. A shiver rolled down her spine. She had on the peach pajamas.

Why would he watch her?

"I wish she was awake. This would be so much better if she were awake." Lowering his voice more than it already was, Jason added, "And if you two weren't here."

The last part didn't sound as if he meant it to be heard by the others, and by the way they went on, they didn't seem to hear it. She did.

"Told you she was tiny, huh?" Aaron gloated.

Fear-induced tremors rocked her inside, but on the outside, she remained immobile. There was no way out of this. They had her. Most kids would scream. Two black eyes, a sprained ankle, and a set of broken ribs ago, she learned screaming didn't help.

Why did the bad people always find her? No matter where she was or how good she tried to be, bad things found her. Tears burned behind her tightly shut eyelids. She would not cry, ever.

"She is so cute... The way she sat there watching us play the game." She'd never heard Giovanni speak so much. A small part of her was shocked. "Did you see the look on her face when you put that strip poker game in?"

"I know. She acted jealous when that computerized woman took her clothes off. She didn't like that our attention wasn't on her," Aaron stated.

"I don't know about that," Jason drawled. "She was looking at me. I know she thinks I'm cute."

"She likes us both," Aaron said. "I heard her on the phone with her little friend."

They all gave a low, dirty old man chuckle. Renée's skin crawled. She heard a clapping sound she assumed was them high-fiving. Then came words she'd never forget.

"Let's make her dreams come true," Giovanni said.

The smack of bare feet shuffling and moving toward her bedroom seemed louder than average. Renée's heart pounded. Whether or not she felt she deserved it, this would happen.

As her bedroom door opened, she worked to slow her breathing. Three imposing shadows appeared on the wall in front of her. She shut her eyes again, not as tight as before, so they'd believe her asleep.

In her mind, she repeated the mantra; there's nothing to fear but fear itself.

Her bedroom door closed, but she wasn't alone.

CHAPTER SIXTEEN

R enée gasped, hyperventilated. Scanning her surroundings, she clutched her chest. Still nighttime. Still in the Denali. Light from the gas station lit the truck's interior. She worked to steady her breathing. Wiped the sweat from her forehead. Hands shaking, she grabbed her prescription bottle out of her purse. She downed two tablets, then returned the bottle to her bag. It was too confined in here. Breathing was impossible.

She got out of the truck; shut the door as lightly as possible behind herself.

Damn! It had gotten colder. Digging her hands into the hoodie's front pocket, she paced a small distance from the truck. The parking lot was deserted, except for one car near the store's entrance. No stars presented themselves while she dozed, so it was still dark out. She might need space, but she wasn't stupid. They were in the middle of nowhere. She wouldn't wander far.

Finding a precast concrete parking bumper among a copse of trees, Renée sat. Face buried in her hands, she wept silently. Big, fat tears soaked through the sleeves. Moistened her hands.

When would this shit stop? No matter how old she got, thoughts of brothers always elicited nightmares of Aaron, and what he did, his betrayal, which was why she couldn't just forgive Drew. There was nothing fair about how she treated Drew for his one misstep after a million right ones. But she'd once given her trust to a "brother," and he'd violated her.

God, she wanted to be better. Be over this stupid shit so she could hold on to one good and pure thing in her life. She tried to be good, pure. And Aaron and his friends had stolen that from her. She was damaged. Eternally fucking damaged.

"Hey, you shouldn't be out here alone," advised a deep accented voice.

Maybe he'd go away if she didn't respond. No way would she risk saying anything and revealing her husky, tear-laden voice or looking up and showing him her watery eyes.

"Amazing. Have I finally found a way to shut you up?" Chris laughed. "No snarky comeback for me—shocking." He kicked her booted foot.

Renée remained silent. Let him figure out how unwanted his presence was—

Whoa!

She was weightless.

Renée flung her arms around Chris's neck as he lifted her. He sat on the cement block, cradling her in his lap. For reasons unbeknownst to her, him being so not Chris, undid her. She sobbed into his cloth-covered chest. Sniffed his musky cologne and uniquely Chris scent.

"Shh... Renée," he crooned, attempting to soothe her. He stroked her ponytail. Patted her back. "What's wrong? It's okay. What's wrong? Talk to me, please."

Like she would ever tell him, the king of self-absorption. She wouldn't ever tell anyone. What Aaron, Giovanni, and Jason had taken from her was her shame. Her dirty secret.

"I-I..." she stammered between sobs, "can't. I-I-I don't want to talk about it. I'm... sor-ry... lemme go."

Although she asked to be released, she clutched his sweater. Tears continued to flow. She wiped her nose on her sleeve. How embarrassing. Once again, she'd fallen apart in front of the one person she couldn't stand—sort of. Shit! The lines were blurring. Renée rested her head on his shoulder. Damn, he felt good. Calmed her in ways no one else ever had or could.

"Shh... Renée." Chris kissed her forehead. Rubbed his nose on the top of her hair. "You're breaking my heart, baby. It's okay. You can tell me. What's wrong?"

"No"—sniffle—"Get... off... me. Let me go," she demanded, stronger.

"Let me help you?" Chris asked.

Renée felt his eyes on her but refused to meet his gaze. She looked a hot mess. Not that she cared what Chris thought, she just didn't like anyone seeing her broken.

"I let you cry all over my sweater," Chris teased, rocking her. "The least you can do is let me help you."

She burst into laughter through her tears. Leave it to Chris to say something arrogant amid her emotional breakdown. It made her laugh, though, but she was the only one.

Chris was quiet. Maybe he was serious about her ruining his shirt.

Renée glanced into eyes that had gone stormy. Something unreadable sparked in their depths. His eyes searched hers. She was helpless to look away. His nostrils flared as he breathed. Of its own accord, her head raised in an invitation she wasn't sure she meant to extend. He moved in. Crushed firm lips to hers.

Renée sighed. Melted. Gave in. Her fingers tiptoed up to his nape, tunneled through his hair. Butterfly wings fluttered in her stomach. With every brush of his firm yet smooth lips against hers, desire ripped through her like a lit match. Her lips parted on what she'd like to think would have been a protest. His tongue slid into her mouth, waylaying any objection. The duel that ensued between their questing tongues was as fiery as one of their arguments. Chris tasted fresh, minty. She was lost...

A car door closed.

Renée broke away. Chris's arms tightened around her as if he never wanted to let go. She turned her head. He grabbed her chin, tried to force her face back toward his.

"Don't," Renée said, shaking off his hold. "What are you doing?"

"That wasn't anybody we know," he assured, again trying to turn her toward him.

The moment died, as it should have. What the hell had gotten into her? Grief was a tricky business.

Chris heaved a loud sigh. His hold loosened. "Sorry. I was just trying to...help."

Renée jumped to her feet. She sat on the asphalt in front of him, knees raised and pulled the humongous sweatshirt over her upraised knees and legs. "It's cool, Fabio. We'll chalk that up to temporary insanity," she said, chuckling and wiping under her eyes with her thumbs.

"Why does it have to be insanity?" he asked, harsher than she expected. His features pinched.

Brows furrowed, she blinked, confused, several times. Renée shook her head. "What else could it be?"

Chris's eyes narrowed. He glared daggers. "Nothing. I guess."

They watched each other in silence.

What did she say? This was Christopher Clark. She'd be lying if she said she hadn't noticed something brewing between them since he'd been at the house, but it was Chris. Head in the sand, never seeing the world outside himself, Chris. Women passed through his world like water through cupped hands. He might hold on to them for a minute, but they slipped through the cracks. How serious could he be? He rejoiced in the uncomplicated.

Renée was anything but uncomplicated. A fling between them would lead nowhere good and jeopardize his friendship with Andrew. If she were honest, she didn't know why he'd wasted precious womanizing time coming on this trip.

"Why did you come with us instead of going home?" she asked, breaking their silent standoff.

He shrugged. "Why not? I've never been outside of Arizona. I had vacation time from the gym. Drew invited me, so why not?" Chris ran his fingers through his multi-hued blond hair.

She rolled her eyes, proving her suspicion. Everyone knew why they were traveling to Indiana. They grasped the seriousness on some level. Not Chris. It was a vacay for him. A way to escape boredom. Fuck what it meant to her.

"So, what's this thing you have with Lex?"

"What?" Flinching in shock, she chuckled. "There's no *thing* with Lex!"

Chris wrung his hands, gazed at the ground before looking at her. The harsh set of his jaw showed his seriousness. "Yes, there is. Your face lights up when you talk about him. Even right now, when I just mentioned him, you smiled, grinned, like you won the fuckin' lottery. You hang all over him. I've never seen you like that with anyone. You guys got something going?"

"*What?*" Renée fought hard not to gag, but didn't quite keep the disgust off her face. "Are you serious?" She smirked. "He's like a brother to me. I've known him forever."

"How's he any different than I am? I've been around just as long."

"I never said he was."

Chris studied her. Manscaped brows nearly touched. "But we kissed? Does that mean something happened with you and Lex, too, then?"

Okay. Understanding bloomed... Chris was jealous. Gazing almost endearingly at him, she gentled her tone. "Chris, I don't think of you as a brother."

He smiled wide, an indention appearing in one cheek. Straight, white, even teeth were a stark contrast to his tanned skin.

"You're too pretty," she finished. "I think of you more like a sister."

His smile morphed into a grimace.

Renée laughed.

"If that's true, then you just had one hell of an incestuous, lesbian moment with your sister. Your fruity Mentos taste is still on my tongue."

"Funny," she remarked.

Chris stood, closing the distance between them. Feeling disadvantaged, Renée untucked her sweatshirt from around her legs and stood. She dusted off her butt. They stared into one another's eyes. She felt as if Chris saw into her soul. Read her secret thoughts.

"I don't want you to think of me as a sister," he said, voice lower, resonant, "and I don't want you to think of me as a brother or a friend." He slipped an arm around her waist. Yanked her body flush against his. "I just want you to think of me... 'cuz I think about you. A lot."

If the bulge pressed into her stomach indicated anything, Renée knew his mind well. She took one giant step back, out of his reach. He let her go, which disappointed her. She'd been cold before but felt on fire now. Chris and his mild southern drawl did unacceptable things to her. Made her want to believe the empty words of a player. *Yuck!*

She stared at nowhere in particular above his head, avoiding eye contact. "Chris, I know right now you think you want me, but I don't think you know what you want. I'm not one of your groupies or conquests. I'm your best friend's sister. Other than that, you don't know me. And even if you did, whatever you want... you wouldn't want it from me."

Crossing his arms across his muscular chest, Chris arched a brow. "And what, exactly, do you think I'd find out that'd turn me off?"

God, where to begin? She wasn't one of his usual bobble-headed conquests. For one, she had a brain in her head. Corny lines, hundred-watt smiles, and tequila didn't make her clothes fall off. Anyway, she didn't care what he thought. He didn't need to know anything about her. That was the point.

"Let's just say you don't know me, and you never will."

He tossed her a lopsided grin. "So... your favorite color isn't maroon? You don't love pizza and plain vanilla ice cream with gummi bears toppings?"

Renée's mouth opened and closed, but no words escaped. How did he—

"Nothing to say?" He wagged his brows in challenge. "You hate the consistency of Jell-O and pudding in your mouth. You love historical period movies but won't read period novels. Edgar Allan Poe and William Shakespeare are your favorite playwrights and poets. Your favorite animated movie is *Cinderella*, and for some reason, you love *The Sound of Music*. You collect music boxes that play songs from *The Sound of Music*. You—"

"Stop, Chris, I under—"

He held up a hand, halting her interruption.

"Your right eyelid twitches when you're uncomfortable. You love late-night walks, burlesque dance in your bedroom, and classical music when stressed. Just in case you need to make a quick getaway, you sleep facing whatever side the door is on." He stared into her eyes. "You sleep in your bra because you think it'll prevent sagging in your later years."

Renée gasped, crossing her arms over her bosom.

"You had your first kiss in sixth grade during a heated game of truth or dare. You have no depth perception... Renée, I don't want you because you're the shiny new toy in the window that caught my eye. I want you because you relate more to country music than R&B or hip-hop but lie and tell people rap's your favorite. You love the X-games. I know you have a scar running from your wrist to your elbow where someone ran a hot iron down your arm as a child. And that's only one among many forms of abuse you suffered growing up."

Too stunned to give a false denial, Renée barely noticed she'd started rubbing the discolored wound he spoke of through her sleeve. Seeing Chris's gaze drop to her arm, she jerked her arms behind her back, laced her fingers.

"You are all I've been able to think of for months—shit! Years," Chris continued, fist-pounding his palm, emphasizing his impassioned speech.

Renée had never seen him so... fired up. This was the longest he'd spoken about anything that wasn't ninety percent about him. It was confusing.

"You are the only woman in my mind and heart. The only one I've wanted in my arms"—he held his arms out, emphasizing his point— "for a good long while. There has been no one else since I decided I would have you. I've learned everything there is to know about you. I'm a Renéeologist or Renée-ite. Yet, you still see me as self-centered—an egomaniac. Somebody beneath you. You can say anything to me since I don't have feelings, right?"

Chris's revelation left Renée immobilized. She just stared. He approached her, tilted her chin up, and placed a chaste yet oh-so-tender kiss on her lips, taking her breath away. Smiling, he stepped around her. She turned to watch him return to the Denali.

Turning, he winked. "I'm one hundred percent sure of what I want. My eyes are open. It's you who doesn't know what you want.

That's cool, though… I'm here to show you what you want. Get back in the truck."

Flabbergasted, Renée only blinked.

CHAPTER SEVENTEEN

"I'm starving!"

Andrew turned toward the back seat at Lex's guttural declaration. He shoved his arms through his hoodie and pulled it over his head. Oklahoma mornings were frosty as shit! Sun shining through the Denali's tinted windows provided minimal warmth. As usual, the girls hadn't packed appropriately. There were four bags between them, and not one thought to pack practical clothing for inclement weather.

Leaning over the middle seat, Lex snatched an encyclopedia-sized black leather-bound book with gold-trimmed pages from Renée's hands.

"Dammit! Alex!" his sister complained, kneeling on her seat to retrieve her property.

"Née, feet off the leather," he barked. Sleeping in the truck made him irritable. He couldn't help needling his sister.

Misplaced anger, giving siblings inappropriate outlets for centuries.

"Knees, Drew." She wiggled her feet at him, which dangled off the seat. "Shake it easy, bruh, your *baby* is fine."

"*The Complete Works of William Shakespeare*," Lex read the book's title, turned it, showcasing it for everyone to see the cover. "Does somebody have a crush they'd like to share with the group?"

Renée pegged Lex with a glare so evil that he cupped himself in fear. Balls were the girl's favorite target when pissed. Eyes wide, Lex recoiled.

"Shut up! I got this," she said, grabbing the book, "for my birthday. Since I'm on an impromptu group vacation, I figured what better way to pretend like none of you are here than reading." She gifted Lex with a smile sweet enough to cause a diabetic coma.

"Sounds like excuses to me," Lex smirked.

Everyone watched their exchange with great intrigue. Well, everyone except Chris, who sat in the passenger seat beside him. He'd become engrossed in inspecting his nails. No shock there. If it didn't involve him, Chris didn't care.

One never knew when Renée would explode or what method of self-expression she'd choose. Even with the bitter undertone of this trip, Renée was Renée. Ornery, mercurial Renée. She marched to the beat of her own drum, said what she wanted, did what she wanted, and was hilarious. A powder keg ready to ignite at a moment's notice.

These were the great things about her. Reasons people found her magnetic, reasons they loved her, which she either refused to or couldn't recognize. When she harnessed those attributes, focused on someone or something she cared for, the woman was a force to be reckoned with. Someone a person wanted in their corner. She might be blunt or brash, but it was done in love.

Andrew would never hit a woman, but he'd love to shake common sense into his little sister. Convince her to abandon this mission for her biological family. Sometimes water was thicker than blood.

"Oh, yeah!" Renée snarled. "Well, sounds like you're full of shit, Alejandro. I'm telling the truth."

"I thought you only read Shakespeare when you were feeling,"—he wagged his eyebrows—"romantic."

Christina's brow arched.

Then his sister's gigantic head and ponytail obstructed his view. Damn!

It did not thrill Andrew when they'd first decided on this seating arrangement. Lex was a brother to him, but he'd gained some of that Latin sex appeal that ladies were into nowadays during his time away. His friend had become woman catnip. Drove him crazy, and he was stuck sleeping in the uncomfortable front seat—no way in Hell he'd let anyone else drive his baby—with Chris.

Somehow, Chris violated his space over the center console. Legs and arms kicked and slapped him all night. Dude didn't get sharing or the fact that he wasn't the only person in the universe.

"Shut up!" Renée shouted in the small confines of his vehicle.

Ashley covered her ears and scrunched her face from her place beside Renée.

Andrew had enough of this argument. His sister was like a dog with a bone. She'd never let this go. He did the only thing left for him to do in this scenario. He sniffed the air.

"Oh, Renée!" he exclaimed, waving a hand in front of his face. "Your breath smells like hot garbage. Your dragon breath is heating the car." Andrew smiled at the wide-eyed mortification on his sister's face. Her brows jumped to meet her hairline.

Renée put a hand to her mouth, breathed out, and sniffed. Brown eyes narrowed. Reaching between the front and middle seats, she slipped her feet into her boots and grabbed her carry-on. "Screw you, Drew!" She opened the door and got out of the truck.

"Where are you going?" he called out.

"None of your business, asshole!" she shouted, stomping off toward a cement structure he knew to be the rest area restrooms.

Christina's stare bored a hole in his forehead. Her mouth tightened.

Shit! Not who he wanted to piss off. He shrugged apologetically.

She hopped over the middle seat, putting her chunky, wedge, flip-flops on his leather seat. His jaw clenched. If he wasn't mistaken, she ground her foot as if putting out a cigarette before following Renée.

Fuck!

The open door sent an arctic draft swirling through the vehicle's interior.

"Hey, I wanna go too," Ashley whined. She snatched Lex's blue and black flannel he'd just thrown over his shoulders and was about to put his arms into. She hurried to Renée's side, got out, and put the flannel on. "Thanks, Alejandro," she said. With an arrogant smirk, she slammed the door harder than necessary.

Fifteen minutes passed without a sight of the girls. He and Chris used the center console as a table to play Blackjack. Lex lay barefoot with his legs across the back seat and his head propped against the window. His eyes were closed.

"What's up with Renée reading Shakespeare?" Lex blurted, surprising them. They'd assumed he was asleep. "We need to kick some dude's ass or what?"

Finished arranging his cards, Andrew arched a brow at Lex. "You know as well as I do that's not possible. She'd rather eat hair."

True to form, Chris inspected his hand, oblivious to his and Lex's back and forth. He put down a five of clubs.

Andrew prepared to play a card of his own.

"Why"—pausing, Chris reorganized his cards—"wouldn't it be possible?"

He wasn't as oblivious as Andrew thought. Weirder still, what did he care? Chris didn't ask questions unless the answer served him somehow. Whatever. Trying to decipher Chris's motives did no one any good.

"Oh... you don't know what happened, do you?" Andrew put down an eight of clubs.

Chris's mouth curled into a frown reminiscent of a petulant child. "Don't know what?"

"That's right, huh?" Lex chimed in, astonished.

"What happened?" Chris demanded, slamming his cards face down.

Andrew growled at him. Boy, better not fuck up his ride.

"Where the hell was I?" Chris asked.

Lex sat forward, leaning on the seat. "In Flagstaff helping your grandparents, I think. Or you could've been making out with your reflection—it was one or the other, can't remember which."

Chris tossed a glower at Lex, then at him. "I thought I was family? Something huge happens, and nobody tells me? That's bullshit!"

Andrew put his cards down and turned as much as possible in his seat, so Chris and Lex were in his line of vision. "Fine, but hear this," he warned, glaring at Chris, "you breathe a word of this... and I don't know you. Our friendship is done. No using this to piss off Renée. Understood?" He quirked a brow.

Solemn blue eyes stared back at him. Chris nodded in understanding. Andrew didn't require assurance from Lex. This was more his story than... anyone else's. Neither of them preferred to talk about what happened. It's funny how the most significant thing in all their lives, the reason Lex left, the cause of Renée's panic attacks, and his guilt, was the one thing no one mentioned. But Chris had a point; he was family, and everyone knew except him.

Andrew took a deep breath through his nose, released it through his mouth. "You remember Renée's boyfriend from way back? Her senior year in high school, I think?"

"Tori? Your parents hated that dude."

On an exasperated sigh, Andrew corrected Chris. "Corey. Yeah, nobody could stand him. He was already out of school. I don't even think he graduated; he was just too old to go. He had a stranglehold on Née, though. She was stupid for him. They had that whole tortured childhood, first love bullshit connection going. So, anyway, he talks her into moving out, like, a second after her twenty-first birthday, and fuck what our parents think... she goes."

Lex grunted as if reliving the disgust and disappointment they'd all felt at Renée's unwavering devotion to the loser. To this day, it still baffled him how ride or die she'd been for this guy who'd done nothing to deserve it. She reminded him of one of those mindless bimbos, or cult members. The worst part was his sister was nobody's fool. Renée wasn't another pretty face. There was a brain in that beautiful head of hers, yet she'd refused to use it.

Shaking his head, he continued, "Our parents thought a little tough love—letting her see how rough it was on her own—would bring Renée to her senses. We decided as a family to give her the silent treatment, freeze her out so she'd come running home. We all know how well that shit worked. Renée was stubborn—"

"Was?" Lex interjected.

Rolling his eyes, Andrew rephrased, "Renée is stubborn. So that didn't work. She stayed gone for almost six months, didn't reach out or try to contact us once. If you want the rest of the story, you gotta ask Lex."

He and Chris turned, stared at Lex. Brown eyes glared back at them, daring them to challenge his silence.

"Dude, you gonna finish or what?" Chris asked flatly.

Lex groaned. "God, I hate this damn story. Way to ruin the mood, Drew." He exhaled. "I saw Renée at the mall about five months after she moved in with Corey..."

CHAPTER EIGHTEEN

About three years ago

Glass ceilings allowed the Arizona sun to illuminate the beautiful building. This must be how a colony of ants felt when some kid held a magnifying glass over them. Sweat trickled down Alex's nape and his back through his throwback Lakers jersey.

People milled about doing whatever possessed them to come to the mall. Had he not needed new kicks, he would've avoided this place. Alex hated being in this—he passed Victoria's Secret. He did a double take at the scantily clad model poster blown up in the window. *Okay, so maybe the mall has its benefits,* he thought, watching a couple of young girls inspect V-stings.

Nice.

Continuing his mall excursion, Alex watched some boys, who couldn't have been more than middle school age, spit game at a group of high school girls. To think that was him, Drew, Rand, and Chris once upon a time. He'd like to believe they had a tad bit more swag than that. The girls couldn't have been less interested, but the little dudes kept trying. Maybe one would get lucky and score the ditzy easy chick. Every group of girls had one friend who'd do anything and anybody.

Alex spotted somebody he hadn't seen in months through the crowd of people coming at him. Squeezing past a few couples seated outside of Cinnabon, he made his way to his prey. He was almost one hundred percent sure she'd try to avoid him if she knew he saw her. Alex headed her off just as she tried to pass.

Whoa! This close, she looked... haggard. Of course, she was still beautiful, but her brown skin had dulled. A bulky gray shirt hung off her as if it wore her instead of the other way around. Jeans that should have been skin-tight, bagged. Brown hair was in a sloppy bun. What shocked him more than her face bare of make-up and bronze eyes devoid of the light that shone in them was a black boot-like brace on her left foot.

"Hey, short stack," Alex greeted, holding back his astonishment. "Long time no see." He gripped her waist with both hands and would swear he felt bones. "How are you?"

She backed away from his hold. "Fine, how are you?"

"Livin' the dream," Alex responded, searching her face. Maybe she was sick, but that didn't explain the brace. His Spidey senses tingled. Something wasn't right. "What's up with the foot?"

Renée glanced at her foot as if she hadn't had a clue what he spoke of. "Oh! This?"

Yeah, now his entire internal alarm system blared. Renée Sutton wasn't a go-out-in-public-looking-like-roadkill type, and she didn't lie. And whatever she said next to explain her injury would be a lie. The way her voice raised an octave at her question screamed *I'm-stalling-to-get-my-lie-straight.*

"It's nothing," she replied. She gave a dismissive shake of her head. "I ran into a wall and tore a ligament. Crazy, right!"

Riight... His eyes cut at her in suspicion.

"I have to wear this little fashion, don't"—she twisted her leg like one of *The Price Is Right* models showing off a prize—"for a couple of weeks, but it'll be fine." She shrugged, an indifferent lift of frail shoulders.

At that precise moment, Renée adjusted her shirt. Alex's eyes bulged at the deep purple bruise near her previously hidden collar. He made quick work of smoothing his features. Inside, he felt like a tea kettle reaching its boiling point. Smoke should've come billowing out of his ears. He was so pissed.

Did Drew know about this? Her parents?

He kept his eye roll to himself as Renée hurried to reposition the neck of her shirt.

Too late, sweetie. Cat's out of the bag!

No one knew about this, and if left up to Renée, no one would. Call it stubborn, independent, or stupid, but she was the type of chick that would "ride or die." Her parents and brother were just as stubborn or stupid. This tough love, freeze-out bullshit to teach her a lesson was gonna teach all of them the ultimate lesson if somebody didn't swallow their pride.

He couldn't keep standing there. If he did, he'd throw her over his shoulders and fireman carry her ass out of this bitch.

Alex took a deep breath. "I gotta get going," he said, releasing his breath, "but take my cell number." He lifted her cell from an outside pocket on her purse. He programmed all his numbers and email into the device before replacing it. "Call me," he said, throwing some bass in his voice, "and I'll take you to lunch sometime—soon."

She balked at his domineering behavior but said nothing. Her lack of protest was more alarming than anything else. This shrinking violet routine didn't bode well for her mental health.

"Uh, okay, cool." Renée smiled, but it appeared forced, uncomfortable. She shifted her weight from foot to foot as best she could, with the boot hampering her movement. "Umm... You know my family's not talking to me, right?"

Alex nodded. Where was this going?

"Don't..." She paused, then started again. "Can you not tell them you saw me?" Joyless, honey-brown eyes pleaded for understanding.

"Yeah," he said with a sigh, "I can do that."

She gifted him with a genuine smile and wrapped her arms around his neck. Shopping bags clapped his back as she hugged him. He struggled with his protective instincts as he wound his arms around her tinier-than-usual waist. What was going on with her?

Three weeks later, Alex spun in his swivel chair. It was good being the assistant supervisor of the 24-hour call center where he worked. At the end of the month, when his boss left, he'd move into her position. He'd be the direct supervisor to over twenty phone bankers. The job wasn't as glamorous as, say, a private investigator, lawyer, or nutritionist. Still, he didn't come from a family of ballers like his friends. He wasn't jealous, though; it was a fact of life he'd made peace with long ago.

Besides, being twenty-three and pulling a little over thirty thousand a year—not bad. Plus, his GPA was a 3.0; he'd be graduating college soon with a finance degree. Things could be worse. He wouldn't complain. His life was on the right track.

On the last revolution of his chair, it slowed, stopped just shy of his computer. Left-facing the sidewall of his cubical, his chest tightened. In front of him were several pictures tacked to the fabric wall.

Hazel eyes gleamed. A sultry smile lifted the corners of full pink lips. Shoulder-length wavy strawberry blond hair framed one of the most angelic faces he'd ever seen. Ashley. She'd caught him staring and told him to take a picture to last him longer. So he had. That was eight months ago at a kickback at—somebody's—apartment.

There was nothing spectacular about the apartment. A stained futon. An entertainment center made of boxes and enough alcohol to own and operate a small liquor store. She and Renée had crashed the party. Ashley looked good enough to eat in a tight, red, halter dress and too-high heels. She'd called herself, giving him an eyeful of what he'd never get.

Yeah, he got quite a bit that night. Not the whole enchilada, but enough to last him until she realized they were perfect for each other. Who knew when that would be. Good thing he was a patient man. They'd agreed to keep their clandestine tryst on the low. Gazing at the picture next to it, he wondered if she'd ever spilled the beans to Renée.

God, *Renée...*

He ran a hand over his face, raked his fingers through his overgrown hair. In the following picture, she and Ashley were at the same house party. Milk chocolate skin glowed with health and vitality. Her smile stretched wide and ridiculously deep dimples adorned full cheeks. Renée's petite figure, although skinny, didn't look unhealthy for her five-two height. A black headband held brown spiral curls in check. Her black dress matched Ashley's in style but was shorter. The ever-present—until recently—light in her eyes dominated as usual. Showed her for the diamond in the rough she was. She and Ashley posed with one leg bent, and each propped a hand on their hip.

Alex sighed. That Renée was nowhere in the person he'd met a few weeks ago at the mall. Skittish uncertainty replaced confidence. He—

His desk phone rang.

Please don't let it be another customer pissed about their balance. He got the popularity of online banking, saw its merits. But no way should it replace a good old-fashioned checkbook. Too many people relied on banks to keep their records. While the bank system did a fair job, it wasn't infallible. Knowing when a purchase was made and how much it was for came in handy when claiming the bank stole your money.

He snatched the phone off the hook on the third ring.

"Thank you for calling Wells Fargo. Alejandro speaking, how may I—"

Speak of the devil.

CHAPTER NINETEEN

"I thought you wanted to go to lunch?"

Alex sat their tray on the table. Scooting into the seat across from Renée, he forced his long legs under the table. Once situated, he handed off her small brown bag of corn chips. That was all. He had three tacos and a steak burrito in front of him, and she had a piddly bag of chips without salsa.

Taco Haven wasn't the most upscale spot, but he hadn't chosen the place in his defense, which perplexed him more. She'd called, sounding almost frantic, and said she wanted to take him up on his lunch invite but couldn't be out long. Then she picked a place in Chandler. Thirty minutes from his job and where he thought she stayed. It had tempted him to put it off since it was past his lunch hour, but the desperation in her voice made him leave work early. She knew the place; why she ordered nothing when it was her idea to come here confounded him.

"We are at lunch," Renée replied, checking over her left then right shoulder every few seconds.

Alex shook his head while he chewed, taking a bite of a taco. When he finished, he amended her statement. "No. *I'm* at lunch." He took a sip of his drink, set the cup down. "I don't know what you're doing. Why'd you pick someplace so far out of the way? Damn."

Renée picked at a tortilla chip, broke it apart. Put it in the bag. She fidgeted with the shredded sleeves of her black sweater. "Hey, Corey loves this place, says their food's amazing."

Alex couldn't tell if she fidgeted due to discomfort or the fact that while he ate, he watched her. Stared at her. Studied her with open scrutiny. There was no help for it. Something was wrong with her, and she wouldn't look at him. Never once in the entire time since he'd walked up to her table outside had she glanced at him. At first, he'd assumed his height was the deterrent.

A large white and red umbrella planted through the center of the table provided shade, but the sun was brutal. Renée wore sunglasses, which wasn't abnormal. What was bizarre was her choice of outfit. Black slacks, a light-pink, collared shirt he figured was long-sleeved, but couldn't tell for the long sweater she wore.

She was bundled up like they were expecting snow, yet today had to be in the high eighties.

He unwrapped his burrito, and bit into it. Didn't take his eyes off her. Mmm... Not bad for unauthentic Mexican food. Alex dunked his burrito in the plastic container of salsa that came with his meal.

Leaning forward, Renée pushed her bony fingers through his hair. Moved his bangs out of his eyes. She gulped, as if clearing something significant from her throat. "You need a haircut, Alejandro," she said. He heard the smile her face lacked.

"Alex or Lex," he said around the food in his mouth, "you know that."

She dropped her hand, went back to playing with her chips. "Ashley calls you Alejandro."

Shit! That little hellcat could call him anything she wanted. There was something about her that called to him on not only a physical level, but on a primal level. He wanted to know her, just be lucky enough to say he knew a woman like that.

"Ashley has no home training." Alex laughed.

Renée jerked her head toward his food. "Is it good?"

"Mm-hm," he answered, mouth full.

"I knew you'd travel for good food."

He nodded in agreement but believed her as far as he could throw. That wasn't the saying, he knew. However, judging by her extreme weight loss, his version fit better. Saying he didn't understand the rouse would be ludicrous. Renée was what he referred to as too responsible. Too accountable. She'd decided, no matter if she regretted it now or not, to move out. Because of her independent, responsible, accountable ass, she'd suffer the consequences of her choice. Stupid girl. He loved her like a sister, and yet—

Renée removed her sweater. The heat had probably gotten to her. Sweat dripped down her hairline, raced along her chin. He saw that her collared shirt was open at the neck.

His mouth dropped open; his eyes distended so far he thought they'd fall out and roll across the table.

Bruises littered her collarbone—the unmistakable outline of a purple handprint wrapped around her neck like a gruesome choker.

Thank God she was busy folding her sweater and didn't see his face. Alex was sure it took him a hot minute before he found the ability to close his mouth. Appetite lost; he pushed his food away.

Done caring for her sweater, Renée made quick work of buttoning the top few buttons of her shirt. She thought she'd covered herself fast enough for him not to have seen the bruises. He wouldn't correct her assumption.

Eminem's "Love the Way You Lie" played. Alex jerked as if stunned by a stun gun, but the way Renée jumped was absurd.

One would think someone had poked her in the back with a hot-shot cattle prod.

Fumbling with her sweater, she found her cell phone in its pocket. Breathing hard, she answered almost as soon as her fingers made contact with it.

"No," she answered a question from the unknown caller. "I said no. I swear. Sorry. Yeah. Yeah. Yes. I'm so sorry."

Alex listened but couldn't hear what the other person said. Although, if the way Renée paled was anything to go on, he'd say she'd just been sentenced to the gas chamber.

"You cheatin' on me! Who the hell is Alex?" yelled a man's voice from behind the door.

Alex paced caged beast-style outside the closed apartment door. Gold numbers nailed into the middle read: 305. He huffed and puffed, scanned his surroundings. Damn, Renée. His previous conjecture had been correct. She lived thirty minutes from Taco Haven. In the most rundown one-story apartment complex Alex had ever seen. Once her call ended, she'd fled with flimsy excuses. With her abrupt departure, she'd unknowingly led him on a near car chase. Intuition made him follow her.

How could she live here? With a douchebag, who'd shouted at and degraded her for the last ten minutes.

He doubted anyone knew Renée lived in such squalor. Drew and Mr. and Mrs. Sutton wouldn't stand for her living this way—he hoped. A lesson was one thing, but he couldn't imagine them deciding she deserved this for defying them. Teenagers and early twenty-somethings defied their parents, tested boundaries, and shit. Asserted their independence. Did Renée deserve to live like this—? Alex continued to scan the area.

Trash covered the parking lot. Several vehicles parked in the lot had trash bag windows, or some were missing at least one window. Some didn't even have license plates. Making matters worse, some apartments had graffiti-decorated plywood windows. Others had graffiti-painted sheets hanging over the windows. At present, he stood in front of a door with a fist-size dent in it.

Did Renée deserve to live someplace one step up from being a trap community? He would've said house, but considering every unit's condition, community seemed to fit. Part of him wanted to call Drew. Another part didn't know if calling her parents would be more advantageous. A more significant part of him wanted to kick down the door, which could cause more harm than good. So, here he was, posted outside Renée's door, listening.

"When would I have time to cheat?" Renée shouted. "I'm always with you."

"Who's Alex?" Corey repeated.

Glass broke somewhere. Alex couldn't tell where the sound came from. He approached the door, trying in vain to see through the picture window to the left. The way the Venetian blinds were turned, he saw movement but no faces.

"He's my brother's friend and a friend of the family," she answered.

"Oh, so, how long has this been going on?"

"What?" Renée's voice rose an octave. "Nothing's going on. He's just a friend."

Alex glanced behind him. He hoped no one thought he was doing anything shady. Of course, if he were, he doubted anyone around here would bat an eye. He was sure this neighborhood lived by the famous credo, *Snitches get stitches.*

"I'm not stupid," Corey hollered, breaking into Alex's ruminations. "I know what that shit means—friend of the family. Please! How many times you fuck him?"

"I-What?" Renée stammered.

Bad choice. This guy was the type to take her stutter as an admission of guilt. Fuck! What should he do?

"We've never had sex," she finished. "I barely talk to him. I haven't talked to anyone. Not my family or friends since we moved in together. Today's the first time we ever went to lunch—"

The yelling stopped. There were a couple of thumps, thuds.

Then a blood-curdling scream... followed by faint gagging.

Adrenaline streaked through Alex's veins. His skin grew tight. Hot. He kicked the door. It did not crash in as he expected it would, like in the movies. The second time proved to be a charm. The frame cracked, and the door burst open.

He spied a backward, black hat covering hair Alex knew was a white blond strip usually spiked into a mohawk. Corey's khaki shorts-covered legs, straddling Renée's prone body which lay across a dingy, beige sofa. Sheesh, the apartment's interior was little better than the exterior.

Pale hands wrapped snugly around Renée's neck, choking her. The contrast of stark white skin against her brown skin shocked Alex. Ice-blue eyes pegged Alex with a caustic glare. Yet he didn't relinquish his hold on her slim neck. From the way Renée's eyes bulged and her mouth worked without sound, he'd guess the bastard had tightened his grip.

Alex charged over to the couch. Hands around Corey's puny bicep, he flung him off Renée. He punched him because he could. Blood dribbled from the corner of the jackass's mouth. Corey wiped the blood away with his dirty wife-beater.

Corey swung on Alex twice. Neither attempt connected. However, they threw Alex off balance. Corey scrambled to his feet, ran out of the apartment. Alex jumped to his feet and took off after him. This motherfucker was going to learn about picking on people weaker than him.

"Don't hurt him, Alex," Renée called to him. "He didn't know what he was doing."

Fo' real? She continued to protect—defend—a man who beat the shit out of her.

"Stay here," Alex bit out between clenched teeth. "Call the police!"

At that moment, Alex wasn't sure if he was angrier because he had to chase this asshole in his gray dress shirt, black slacks, and loafers, or at the pitter-patter of Renée's feet behind him, disobeying his orders.

Stopping for a breather at the end of the sidewalk outside the complex, he scanned the immediate area. Given the small community and even smaller parking lot, it didn't take long to ascertain that Corey had escaped or was hiding somewhere. Shit!

Breathing heavily, Alex turned to Renée, a short distance behind him. "Go call the police," he said, speaking in a tone reserved for children, the elderly, and idiots. Not that he thought her an idiot, but with Corey... intelligence wasn't in her.

Her eyes were bloodshot. Tears streamed down her face. She was more fragile than he'd ever seen anyone look before. Frazzled. Broken.

He didn't have time to comfort her. Alex ran to his Hyundai, got in. He would find Corey, call Drew, Rand, and drag Chris back from Flagstaff to whoop this motherfucker's ass. Once his keys were in the ignition and the car started, he flew into reverse. With mere seconds—maybe a minute—head start, Corey couldn't have gotten far.

Car hood facing forward, he found Corey. Perspiring, chest heaving from exertion, Corey stood in front of Alex's vehicle, a 9mm pointed right at him.

They stared at each other. Something had Corey turning his head to the right. The gun remained steady on Alex. Even in his precarious situation, Alex followed his gaze.

"No!" Renée shouted, running barefooted to where the sidewalk met asphalt. It couldn't have been more than a foot from where he idled and Corey stood. She must've screamed loud, considering Alex heard her through his closed window. "Corey! Stop!"

Her voice enraged Corey. His pallid face turned beet red, and his jaw locked into a firm line. A determined line. Almost as if in slow motion, Corey turned the gun on Renée. She skidded to a halt seconds before she would've stepped into the street. Froze. Deer-in-the-headlights stared.

Protective instincts Alex didn't recognize welled within him. These weren't of the hitting-a-woman-is-never-okay variety. His heart slammed against his ribs so hard he swore it would break free. This wasn't watching a buddy get a beat down and deciding whether to jump in. Someone else's fate, their life, rested in his hands at this moment.

The entire universe seemed to hold its breath, waiting for his decision. Was Corey bluffing? Yeah, he'd hit Renée, but weren't woman-beaters obsessed with the object of their affection? If he shot her, he couldn't have her anymore. Wasn't keeping her the point?

Renée's desolate brown gaze met his. Corey's finger tightened on the trigger.

Time for indecision ran out.

Alex threw his car into drive and stepped on the gas.

A shot rang out.

CHAPTER TWENTY

Two-day layover? Since when did road trips have layovers? The whole concept meant traveling the open road. Instead, they were still dicking around in Nowhere, Oklahoma. Okay, so maybe that wasn't the name of the city, but it might as well have been. Whether real or in movies, cities on road trip routes were always deserted, no matter the destination. No wonder these Podunk towns were staples in horror movies.

Staying in a seedy hotel no-tell hadn't been part of her plan. For fear of catching some hybrid gonasyphaherpalaids, STD, she, Ashley, and Chrissy cut open trash bags and wrapped the beds. It had been a noisy night with each tossing and turning on plastic, but it'd been a necessary evil. Had her stubborn brother not insisted on this impromptu group road trip, she would've been in Indiana by now.

Renée flung a glare at Drew across the convenience store eatery. Seated at the sole booth, deep in conversation with Alex and Chris, he missed it. Propping her elbow on the table, she rested her chin in her hand. She gazed out the dust-covered store window and groaned inwardly.

For logic-defying reasons, Andrew had deemed this two-day layover necessary. It conflicted Renée. Part of her wanted this over and done with. She'd have her closure and never look back or wonder what might have been. Another part suffered extreme guilt. Her parents didn't deserve this. They were wonderful, embraced her mood swings, her issues. Accepted her. If her race had ever given them pause, Renée never knew it. They treated her like she'd seen her friends' parents treat them; like their daughter. Without the apparent difference in pigment, few would guess they weren't related. Searching out people who hadn't done squat for her seemed a colossal betrayal. But she had to do this for her peace of mind. So... maybe the layover was what she needed to get her head straight.

Sighing, Renée stretched her legs under the table she, Ashley, and Christina sat at, far from the guys. Chris had been extra annoying since their argument. Whenever she caught him looking at her, there was always intensity in his blue gaze. Possessiveness. Thankfully, they hadn't had another moment alone. She'd damn near insisted one of her friends or Drew be with her at all times. Dealing with him couldn't be a priority, ever. Plus, he'd shown her a side of him that night that she hadn't expected.

Renée gazed at the guys' booth out of the corner of her eye. Suspicion narrowed her eyes. For once, it had nothing to do with Chris but her best friend sitting next to her. Christina. Her gaze was also on the guys.

"Are you checking out my brother?" she asked, bumping her friend's arm with her elbow.

Christina jumped as if startled. "No. I was zoning." She shook her head; black hair grazed the tops of her shoulders. "So, who are you looking for in Indiana? Did Drew find everyone you asked about?"

Renée studied her friend's flushed face and not-quite-direct gaze. Something was off there, but unable to put her finger on what it could be, she shelved her suspicion. "I guess a few of the people passed away, which makes sense, since some were pretty old when I was little. But he found a woman named Lynn Davis. She's my bio mom's cousin. Then there's my half-sister on my mom's side, Kathy. She's the one I wanted to talk to. Everyone else is sort of filler. He found a half-sister on my dad's side I didn't even know I had."

"Older or younger?" Ashley asked from across the table.

"Older. Her name's Shenae Williams. And finally, the person responsible for fifty percent of my genetic material"—she paused for dramatic effect—"Manuel Williams. My sperm donor."

"Ooh... Sperm and lunch!" Ashley pushed her half-eaten slice of pizza away. "I'm done." She grimaced at her discarded lunch.

"Wow! That's a lot of people," Christina commented. "It's a good start."

"Maybe." Renée shrugged with a nonchalance she didn't feel. "I figure I'll start with the least intimidating first, Lynn Davis."

Ashley made a very unladylike snort. "I see your bio mom's not on that list. Why's that? I mean, how intimidating could a crackhead be?"

They all laughed. Renée had long ago renounced any loyalty to her egg donor. If any bystanders heard some of their conversations, they'd assume they were prejudiced against addicts. Although she tried very hard to be open-minded—her mind could rationalize or sympathize with anything or anyone except drug addicts. She had no tolerance for them. Teens who experimented were another story; even though she never had, she could forgive that. But adults who shirked their responsibilities and chose drugs while knowing the risks...

Unacceptable.

Even if a person couldn't help being addicted, they weren't high all the time. In her mind, there were choices. Of course, she knew her outlook could be flawed; personal experience hadn't shown her any differently. So, yes, she made jokes about her crackhead egg donor. Besides, it wasn't like she went around assaulting random drug addicts or anything.

Sobering, Renée replied, "She's been MIA for years. She's popped out a few more kids along the way but disappears after they're born. Honestly, I don't want to see her. I know why she left, and while I disagree with her cracky ways... I know where her head's at."

Ashley winced. "I'm sorry. I didn't mean to touch on a sore spot."

Renée waved away her apology. "It's all good. I got over her a long time ago."

"Hey," Christina said, jerking her head toward the guys' booth. "What are they doing?"

She and Ashley looked over. Drew and Alex sat on one side, leaning over the table as far as possible without being on top of it. Chris sat on the other side, tilting his head toward theirs. Dressed in ballin' shorts and hoodies, they looked to either be a small basketball team planning their next play or an oddly outfitted army plotting world domination.

Whatever they were talking about, they were trying very hard to keep it on the downlow. Weird.

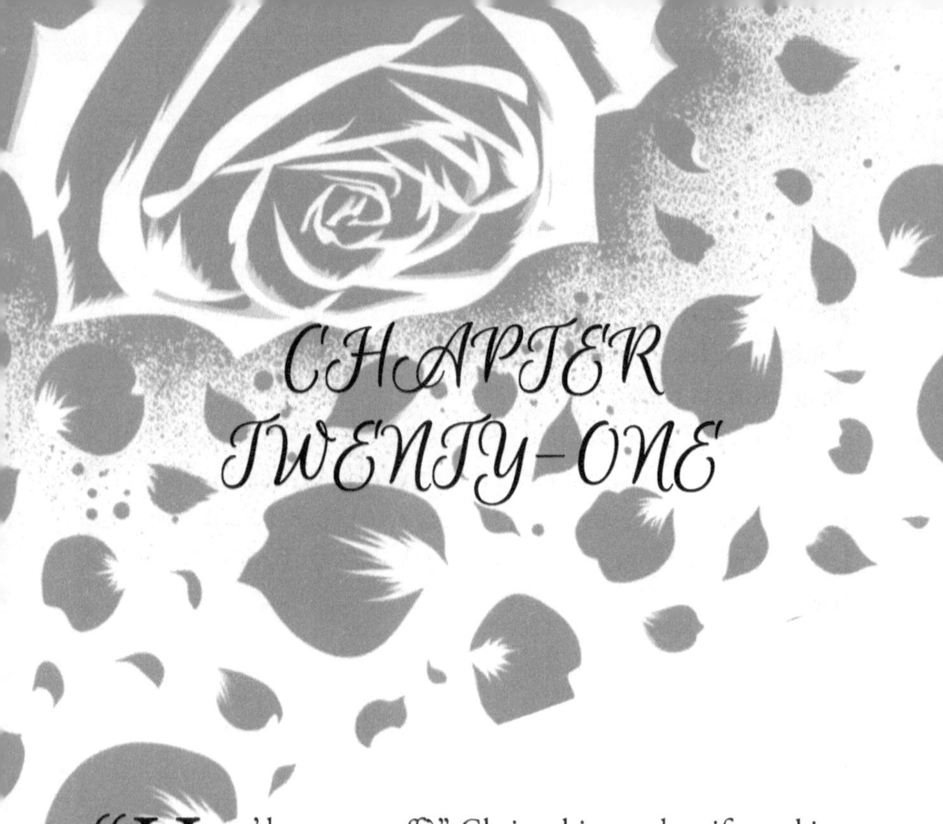

CHAPTER TWENTY-ONE

"How'd you get off?" Chris whispered as if speaking any louder would change reality. "You didn't go to prison—not that I know of, or is that another secret? Was leaving the state part of a deal or something?"

"No. I moved because it was easier on"—Lex looked right and left, then leaned in as if to ensure no one overheard their conversation—"Renée. And for me. I know what I did was good, but it fucked with me. I had nightmares. Went to counseling for a while—it helped. The nightmares stopped. Things got easier for me, but not for Née."

Drew assumed the same conspiratorial pose as Lex. "She stayed in that shithole apartment a couple months after that. Damn near barricaded herself in the place. She'd only see or talk to Alex, but every time she saw him, she freaked out. Tears, shakes, the whole deal." Shaking his head, Drew rolled his eyes. "Our parents thought they were giving her time to grieve, but when she stopped going to work and answering her phone and door, they went and got her. Forced her to move home—basically kidnapped her. She was bad. Panic attacks and nightmares. Bad."

Chris sat frozen. Unblinking. Mouth agape. Stupefied.

For two days, his mind reeled over what Lex and Drew had told him. At first, he thought they were yanking his chain. Lex killed a man...? Like, killed a man and nobody said shit about it for three years. They'd explained it more than once, yet nothing about this story made sense to him. The sullen, earnest expression on both their faces told him they weren't joking, but still...

He hadn't liked the guy Renée had been dating. With his platinum blond hair and trashy, wife-beater, skater look, Chris had known Corey wouldn't last. Of course, he'd never dreamed he'd be murdered, especially not at the hands of one of his best friends. He'd only been sure his and Renée's futures were destined to merge. However, his jealousy reached an all-time high as she got closer to legal age, and then she'd started dating. Yeah, not something he could stand by and watch. Faking disinterest got hard. No, fuck hard. It was impossible.

His original plan had been to give her time. He'd felt their chemistry, knew Renée was it for him. At least, he'd thought he knew his feelings, which was why he'd decided distance and perspective were needed. He'd wanted to make sure she wasn't a passing fancy. She deserved more than that, and his friendship with Drew meant that much to him. Wanting to give himself time to ensure he was capable of the total commitment being with Renée required, he went to stay with his grandparents in Flagstaff. If his feelings for her faded, then no harm, no foul. If they persevered, he planned to follow through on said feelings. He hadn't meant to be gone so long. Hours turned to days, days slid into weeks, and before he knew it, he'd been gone for over a year.

Upon his return, nothing had been as it was when he left. Lex headed to California the morning Chris got back from Flagstaff. They'd had no formal goodbye. Andrew had always been the most responsible of their crew, but he'd grown hard. Serious. And Renée. He had seen little of her. Drew talked about her. He'd catch a quick glimpse here and there, but she was pretty much a ghost. Their families celebrated anniversaries and some holidays together, so he saw her then, but she'd grown even less tolerant of him than before. He'd been thrown off his game. Rand, the cocky SOB, was the only one who hadn't changed at all.

God, he *was* as self-centered as everyone said. This life-altering event had happened to his best friends and, although he'd noticed a change, he hadn't thought to delve deeper. Oh, hell, who was he kidding? He had asked no questions. Not one. He'd been pissed about what he deemed rejection from Renée, then did what he did best: focused on himself.

He'd gotten lost in a sea of nameless, faceless pussy and the gym.

To this very second, even after learning so much about Renée, a woman he loved, he'd been self-centered. He claimed to want to give her the world while not considering what the world meant to her. Happiness to one person could be hell for another. His friends, who he would've sworn knew he'd be there for them, hadn't reached out to him. No, that wasn't right. They hadn't felt they could reach out to him.

It'd be one thing if he didn't care or didn't see a problem. But it bothered him that everyone saw him as this unreliable, one-dimensional person. When had he become this meat-headed asshole? This shallow man his friends didn't even trust? After hearing this story that impacted the most important people in his world, he vowed, to do better. He wanted to be someone people called upon in a crisis. Someone Renée called first.

No wonder she had such love for Lex. For all intents and purposes, he'd slain her dragon. Lex was the only person who'd proved he was worthy of unwavering trust. He still didn't like her reaction to Lex, and he couldn't promise to never get jealous again, but he understood. He'd just have to move heaven and earth to usurp Lex's position in her life.

Chris wanted to say something to Renée. What he would say, he didn't know. An apology wouldn't help. She'd probably be pissed he mentioned it, or maybe she didn't want him to know. He'd considered trying to get her to broach the topic, but that wouldn't work. In three years, she hadn't let it slip, and he doubted that'd change soon. Regardless, he promised not to repeat the story. Proving he was a better man started now. He couldn't break his word.

Scratching his head, Chris sighed. "So, were you charged with anything?" he asked Lex.

Lex shook his head. "It's called justifiable homicide. I ran Corey down to keep him from murdering Renée, which was a far more serious crime."

"You didn't serve any time?"

"No."

"Then why'd you leave?"

"For Renée," Lex repeated on a loaded sigh. "I saw how me being around affected her. I couldn't keep re-traumatizing her. My cousin offered me a place to crash in Cali. I put a transfer in at the bank. I lost my seniority, but"—he shrugged—"it was worth it. Renée started writing to me about a year ago, things got better. Now I'm back. The end. Drop it, Clark." Lex adjusted his fitted black hat as if to emphasize that the conversation was over.

Chris stared wide-eyed, open-mouthed, and dumbfounded at his two friends. The entire story just seemed surreal. How did so much happen in a year? How could everyone keep such a tremendous secret?

"Renée acts like she's over it, but I know she doesn't trust me like she used to," Drew confided. "I'll never get over failing her. You know, I felt it in my gut that something wasn't right—that freezing her out wasn't the best method, but I didn't say anything." Drew paused. Took a couple measured breaths. "Renée hasn't been in another relationship since then. I'm pretty sure she hasn't even dated. She never talks about it, and we never bring it up. So, you don't say anything either."

"I would never," Chris stated empathically, stretching his legs out on the seat. "Contrary to popular belief, I'm not completely heartless."

Tension passed, they all relaxed in their seats. They continued their lunch.

Taking a bite of his burger, Lex spoke with his mouth full. "You think you could've brought any more stuff?" he asked Chris, further dispersing the tension.

Oddly, Chris didn't mind the dig. After two days of obsessing over this thing that happened, he welcomed the light-hearted, good-natured ribbing. Their conversation had gotten mighty serious, too serious for a grungy eatery attached to a convenience store. Plus, the girls were probably wondering what they were up to. It surprised him they hadn't come over to investigate.

"I require a certain number of products to live day-to-day," he answered his friend.

"If you weren't one of my best friends, I'd swear you were a woman," Drew taunted, popping a chip in his mouth.

Chris glowered at him. "I care what I look like, bro. That's not gender specific, you chauvinist. Good grooming habits are essential."

Drew stared at him in disbelief. "Chauvinist?" He snickered. "That's a big word for Elmo," Drew said, feigning impressed. "You get that from your word of the day toilet paper? Chris...you need panties. Seriously, a bra and frickin' panties, man. I think Renée might have an extra purse if you need it."

Lex and Drew laughed.

"Fuck you both. I don't see women willing to stand in line for either of you."

Of course, because fate was just that cruel, Renée and the funky bunch sauntered up to the table no sooner than the arrogant remark slid past his lips.

"What are we whispering about, ladies?" Ashley asked, sarcasm drenching each word. She stood at the head of the table, wearing a fitted black T-shirt and worn jeans.

Lex vacated his seat; Chris assumed to allow Ashley to sit. Christina dropped into the spot so fast her long, goth-esque, ankle-length skirt got caught under her hand. She sort of fell into Drew. Neither she nor Drew looked to be in too much of a rush to adjust her position. Gazing at Drew as if he'd made the sun, a gentle smile spread across Christina's face. One corner of Drew's mouth curled into a secret grin.

What the hell?

Had Lex not chosen that moment to sit back down, who knew how long the girl would've stayed leaning on Drew with her peach, corset top disheveled. Blushing, she righted herself. No one seemed to notice the byplay between the pair; Chris did. He'd get to the bottom of it. Later.

Finally, he'd be close to Renée again. Not knowing what to say or afraid he'd slip and say something about what he found out, he'd been awkward around her. After their kiss and the few times he'd gotten to hold her, he missed being close to her. She was sexy in dark, skin-tight jeans and a black sweater with a sweetheart neckline. Knee-high stiletto boots added to her vixen appeal. Dark hair cascaded around her shoulders and down her back. The woman had no clue how attractive she was.

He sat up, moved his feet off the seat, and forced his long legs to fit under the table to make room for Renée to sit.

She took a seat...

On Lex's lap, much to Chris's consternation.

Heat suffused his body, his face. His fist and jaw clenched. Once again, his woman had relied on another man instead of him. Chris thought he could put aside his jealousy now that he knew the score, but...

"Dammit!" he gritted out between clenched teeth. "I gotta get out of here."

If he didn't, he'd punch Lex.

"What's up with you, dude?" Lex asked, genuinely confused.

He couldn't say. Now wasn't the time to profess his love for Renée. First, there were still some kinks to work out in that plan. Second, when he formally staked his claim, he wanted to do it privately, just the two of them. It needed to be unique, romantic, not in anger over a sticky floor toppling her on his friend's lap.

"Nothing," he finally grumbled.

"I leave for three years, come back, and now you're suffering from Tourette's?" Lex asked, amusement alight in his dark eyes.

Eyes steady on him, Renée quirked an eyebrow. "I think he might be PMSing."

Wrapping an arm around Lex's shoulders, she tossed him a saucy, crooked grin. Everyone, excluding him, laughed. No amount of understanding made him feel like being the constant butt of the jokes. Renée cozied up to Lex, sharing a laugh at his expense, grated on his last nerve. He needed to regroup.

Chris stood on the bench seat. Stepped on the partition separating the booth from the other half of the store. Hopping down on the other side of the booth, he headed to the front of the store. Yep, the objective for the day was to not punch his friend in the face. Walking away was the only way to prevent that at this point.

Their laughter seemed to increase as he shoved open the store doors. Chimes sounded as he stormed out.

CHAPTER TWENTY-TWO

Missouri

Miles and miles of empty mountainous highway stretched ahead of the Denali. Oppressive clouds spread across the violet sky as if someone had pulled cotton to its maximum. It was dusk. The sun had nearly disappeared below what looked to be some abrupt drop-off. As if the road and world ended in the far distance. Yet each time they covered that distance, the end got farther away.

Strange how the open road reminded Renée of life. Through all the crap that happened—some random events, some direct results of her poor decision-making—she'd survived. Each time something horrible happened, she'd felt that time would be the end, the end of her endurance. Yet life continued. Stretched on and on while she simply survived. Stopping to smell the roses wasn't a luxury she had. So, most times, she wished things would just...

Stop.

That she'd cease to exist.

But what she really wanted, she realized, staring at white line after broken white line of the road, was to live. Too many outside forces held far too much control of her world. Renée wanted—no, needed—to live.

She worried the corner of her bottom lip between her teeth at that revelation. Watching TV, reading books, and even people-watching gave her glimpses into people's lives. Women her age dated, went to clubs. Led productive lives. Dare she say, girls her age were contemplating marriage, even getting married and having babies. At the very least, they had hobbies. Her only goal each day was to make it through without a public panic attack. Each night, she strove not to have nightmares and peppered in between all that excitement she worked. Dealt with complaining ass, snooty residents at the luxury apartment community she managed. She didn't even like her job.

Honestly, she felt like a spectator in her own fucking life. If this trip relieved her of one-tenth of the loneliness and mental exhaustion that dwelled inside her, it was worth it no matter the outcome.

"Hey, Chris!" Alex called from the back seat, rousing Renée from her inner angst. "Guess who texted me the other day?"

Chris turned in his seat, which was directly in front of hers. She'd organized the seating arrangement that way on purpose. That way, she couldn't stare at him in a moment of weakness, and he couldn't work his magic on her.

"Who?" he asked, brows creasing.

"Your love slave, Samantha."

Renée's ears perked up at Alex's response.

Who did what now? She thought, glancing down to hide the frown bowing her lips. Unease swept through her. She wasn't jealous—she wasn't. "Who's Samantha?" Renée blurted with more bite than intended before she could stop herself.

Drew glanced her way briefly before returning his gaze to the road. "This girl Chris has had bench-warming since senior year of high school. Girl goes dumb"—his voice rose an octave—"for the D."

Something like a bowling ball sunk in her stomach. What was it he'd said the other night? Some shit she'd—as dumb as it may sound—believed about her being all he'd thought about for years. The only woman he wanted in his stupid arms. He'd said there had been no one else since he decided he wanted her. What a crock of shit!

God, I'm an idiot.

For one fleeting moment, she'd fallen for his bullshit. When would she ever learn? Leopards didn't change their spots. Tigers didn't change their stripes, and players played. She couldn't blame Chris. Players would be playas.

"They used to hook up. Chick's a freak. Down for whatever, whenever," Alex added.

Renée became very interested in her purse strap and the idea of hitting Alex with said purse. Guess there was a first for everything. She'd never wanted to harm Alex. Until today. Why'd he add to the whore's qualifications? She plucked at a loose thread. Her insides felt as if someone had wound them taut on a spool. Her skin was hot. Feverish. Breathing became damn near impossible.

Again, Drew turned, flashed a mischievous smile. His gaze returned to the road. "What do you mean, used to? That shit never stopped. She's the official president of the Christopher Clark fan club. Just a few weeks ago, they got thrown out of McDonald's for indecent exposure."

Oh, she didn't want to. She really didn't want to. Renée felt his stare burning a hole in the top of her lowered head, but she did it anyway. She glared up through her lashes at Mr. Popular. Seems he omitted his fuck buddy from his affirmation of love.

Asshole.

"Can we stop at the next rest area?" Christina's soft voice came from the back, drawing Renée's attention to her.

"Yeah," Chris assured, still staring at her.

Renée felt it and kept her attention on her friend to avoid looking at the prick. Although everything in her wanted to turn around and kick him in his ridiculous blond head. Why'd she even care? He wasn't her boyfriend. He could do whatever he wanted. What he couldn't do was play with her. That shit would stop immediately. No more holding her, kissing her. Definitely no more digital stimulation, even if he had terrific hands. After all, he-sluts had to be good at what they did. No wonder he ran so many smooth lines. They were part of the Playa Handbook.

"There should be a place to stop coming up in the next couple minutes," Chris continued, voice sounding as if he still faced the middle seat, which meant she wouldn't be turning around until they stopped.

Half an hour later, Chris stood under a starry night sky, leaning against a chipped metal railing. His nose was numb. It was so cold. On the other side of the barrier was a wooded area. However, he didn't see how the piddly freestanding metal discouraged people from jumping over it and going into the forbidden woods. He shook his head.

Whatever.

That wasn't his focus now. He glared at the nondescript brick building several yards away.

Lights lining the building provided a decent amount of illumination for the parking lot before it. The rest stop was deserted, other than the Denali parked crooked, taking up several spots, doors wide open. On one side of the building was a placard for the men's restroom. On the other, a placard for the women's restroom. Two silver water fountains were posted out front between both bathrooms.

Propping his foot on one of the middle rails, Chris folded his arms over his broad chest. His leather jacket squeaked with the action. He waited for his woman.

Chris ground his teeth. Damn, he could murder Lex and Drew's dumb asses. Of course, they didn't know why they needed to keep their fucking mouths shut, but who mentioned shit like that? Did bro code mean nothing anymore? If not for him, then surely for Lex; talking about another chick with Ashley around had to be a no-no.

Fuck! He shouldn't have lied to Renée. But he hadn't lied—not really.

Before Drew told him about his plan to house-sit for his parents, he'd fully intended to stay away from Renée. After three years of no reciprocation of any kind, he'd been willing to let go. Every man had a breaking point, and he'd thought he'd reached his. Until Drew mentioned staying at his parents' house. Something told Chris that if he didn't seize this opportunity with Renée... He'd lose the one woman who drove him crazy, challenged, and enthralled him, forever.

As corny as it sounded, she focused him. Gave him purpose. His clients at the gym and working out were the only things that had done that for him before. Now she did. So, of course, when he thought he'd made some progress, Alex's ass knocked him back to square fuckin' one.

Just then, Renée exited the restroom. Much to his dismay, she'd once again donned one of Lex's hoodies. For the first time in days, she was alone, but if he didn't hurry, she'd reach the Denali where Drew sat, legs hanging out the door in the front seat.

Chris pushed off the rail, rushed to intercept her. He caught her before she stepped off the sidewalk. Less than a foot away, he said, "Hey, can I talk to you for a minute?"

Without sparing him even a sideways glance, she continued as if he hadn't spoken.

He quickened his pace, as did she. Completely ignoring him, she hotfooted it to her brother.

"Andrew, can I pick the next song?" she asked saccharine-sweet, seemingly just to piss him off.

Drew hopped out of the driver's seat. "Yeah. Don't turn it up too loud. I don't want highway patrol coming out here. The last thing we need is to get arrested in St. Clair, Missouri."

"Who's gonna call?" Renée asked, leaning into the front seat. She grinned.

Because of her position, and his spot standing in front of the truck, Chris couldn't see what she played. Her naughty smirk spoke more than her silence. Whatever trick she had up her sleeve would torture him; of that, he was sure. She twisted a few nobs, then hopped out of the truck.

A heavy-hitting bass beat started, followed by a synthesized female voice. Most everyone under a certain age who'd heard a live beat by Lil Ju knew this rapper. *Oh, shit!* He recognized this song before the vocals started, Megan Thee Stallion's "Thot Shit."

"Oh, yeah!" Ashley shouted, coming from the restrooms, Christina and Lex close on her heels. Clapping her hands, Ashley swiveled jeans-clad hips. "This. Is. My. Song, right here!"

Christina had also changed. Instead of the long, flowing black skirt she'd been wearing earlier, she now wore light faded jeans like Ashley's. Her knee-high boots appeared to be a replica of Renée's. Both girls wore jackets not belonging to them.

Lex's cocky ass ground his crotch against Ashley's ass. She went with it all of two seconds before sidestepping him and joining

Renée beside the truck. Lex shrugged off the diss as if it meant nothing.

The girls danced together, laughed, and swayed their hips as the rapper rapped about being progressive, boning, and being a proud, independent woman. At least that was Chris's take on it. He liked the song. The beat was dope, but what he really enjoyed was Renée's hips rocking and waving. Moments like this, where she got to be happy and carefree, made him happy in ways he couldn't articulate. He'd only be more comfortable if he were behind her when she backed it up.

The rapper continued complimenting women's many attributes, including one of Chris's personal favorites, pussy.

In unison, the girls yelled, "Thot shit!"

A minute later, the song ended, and the beginning of an older song he was very familiar with started: Travis Porter's "Ayy Ladies."

Chris leaned on the truck's hood, watching. From their much closer vantage point, Drew and Lex watched. Their heads bobbed to the beat.

Renée grabbed Lex's hand, pulled him into the loose circle they'd created. When the song directed them to bend over and touch their toes... Renée bit her lip and bent over. Brown gaze steady on *him*, ass out; she rolled her hips. Swirled. Moving like a cyclone, she clutched Lex's thighs. Used them for leverage as she dropped low, then brought it back up, ass snug against what Chris would bet was an erection. All the while, she never took her purposely hooded bedroom eyes off him.

Lex had no clue this wasn't so much a show for him, but an intentional dig at Chris. His dark gaze was glued to *his* woman's ass, grinding on his dick. He grasped her hips, kept her pressed tight to his groin.

This had nothing to do with Lex and everything to do with Renée showing Chris what she thought of the Samantha revelation. Even knowing that pissed Chris off.

Instead of tunnel vision, he had tunnel hearing. Everyone's laughter sounded as if it were coming from a far-off cave. Fury dimmed the scene. With a lesser part of his brain, he knew Renée's blatant disrespect was her way of showing jealousy. He knew his friend was innocent, just enjoying himself the same way Drew was with Ashley and Christina dancing on him. Unfortunately, his rationale chose this moment to go on vacation.

Chris's mouth clamped shut. His jaw clenched. His breathing grew labored, and his nostrils flared on each exhale. Everything moved in slow motion. He felt as if he were in slow motion as he approached his so-called friend, his boy. Clearly, some sane part of him remained because instead of yanking Renée out of Lex's reach, he eased her to the side.

He'd deal with her later.

Something like curiosity passed over Lex's face, and that pissed him off more. Rico Suave should know precisely what the fuck he did wrong. Breezing into town, charming all the ladies with all that Latin sex appeal bullshit. Well, not his fuckin' lady, not anymore. Like a slingshot preparing to launch a rock, he pulled his balled fist back. Then released. Clocked one of his best friends in the jaw.

Somewhere behind him—or beside him—the girls screamed. It could've been one girl or all of them. He didn't care. Lex recovered quickly. Pushed Chris hard in the chest. The force made a loud *thud*.

"What the fuck, man?" Drew growled, prying them apart. Fists flew, and hands groped, seeking to inflict pain. "Stop!" he commanded with a hand on each of their chests. "Chill."

Lex calmed as fast as the fight began. Chris saw red. Was blind with fury. He bucked against Drew's restraining hands.

"What the hell is your problem?" Lex demanded.

One girl must have turned the music down or off because it was suddenly quiet. Quiet except for their breathing and Chris's pulse pounding in his ears. He jerked away from Drew. "Nothing, dude," he replied, wiping sweat from his brow with the back of his hand. "Guess my Tourette's is acting up again, huh?"

Rubbing his jaw, Lex glared. "You don't—you're a dipshit."

Fuck! He needed to get away from their judgment and open-mouthed stares. This shit with Renée had him losing his damn mind. "Screw you guys. Come get me when we're ready to leave," he said.

Without waiting for a response, he stomped off. Hopped the useless guard rail and walked away into the wooded area. Away from prying eyes.

CHAPTER TWENTY-THREE

The crunch of twigs and dry leaves minutes later alerted Chris to the fact someone was there. Shifting on the oversized boulder he sat on; he eyed the corner of the building.

"What's up, Hercules?" Renée teased, leaning back to the building. She crossed her arms over her ample chest, which was hidden behind the bulky beige hoodie.

Chris was so mad he couldn't even ogle her properly. He glared out of the corner of his eyes. "I'm surprised to see you," he snarked. "I thought you'd be attending to Lex. Did I break his pretty face?"

"Nope. Turns out he's not made of gingerbread. I can leave," she offered, jerking her head to the side.

He faced her head-on. "You know what I think is funny?" he asked, then angrily barreled on, answering his own question. "How you think you have the right to get pissed over something that happened long before"—he waved his finger between them—"but you expect me not to give a shit when you're basically having sex with one of my best friends, right in front of me."

For the first time in their acquaintance, Renée appeared guilty. Her gaze dropped to the ground. She kicked at a rock or something with the pointed toe of her boot. "It's not like that," she said so low he had to strain to hear. "I love Alex like a brother. He's my friend."

Chris inhaled deep through his nose, bought himself a few seconds before responding. Frigid air stung his nasal passage. He knew what she wasn't saying. The connection forged in those moments when Lex did the ultimate for her, saw her at her weakest: impenetrable. And he didn't want to penetrate it, he just wanted a place with her, and dammit, he was tired of hiding what they had. Holding her in public, dancing, being the recipient of one of her dimpled, award-winning smiles... he wanted that right.

Exhaling loudly, he said, "And Samantha's mine."

"Yeah," she said on a sulky pout, then glared up at him, "your homie, lover, friend. Or is the PC term FWB since that Justin Timberlake, Mila Kunis movie?"

"It's not like that, Renée," he grumbled, regarding her through narrow eyes.

To his total amazement, her eyes shone. Glistened. She sniffled, brought the back of her gloved hand to her nose for a moment. Her eyes stayed locked on something in the distance. Chris checked over his shoulder, following her gaze. Nope, nothing there. No bear to warrant tears. Was she crying—over him? Damn. His heart region warmed, melted.

She shook her head as if to clear it. Hard, amber eyes speared him. Determination, or stubbornness, mashed her gloss-coated lips. "Whatever," Renée said between clenched teeth. "I don't care." Agitated, she paced back and forth. "What complete and utter bullshit," she spat, before lowering her voice. "'It's only been you,'" she mimicked his deep drawl. "'Once I realized I wanted you, it's only been you.' Bullshit!" shouted in her voice. "So, what, do you use Samantha to fill the void of not having me? God, you're so full of shit!" She laughed humorlessly. She stopped pacing.

Thrown by her manic mood swing, he stood to find his bearings. Gulping, he ran his fingers through his hair. "Renée, I didn't have you at the time. Not even a hope of having you. I have no feelings for Samantha. I've never felt what I feel for you for any woman."

She threw up her hands. "Whatever, Christopher."

Now he knew he was in trouble. She never used his government name.

"I don't give a shit how many voids you,"—she looked him up and down, revulsion twisting her mouth—"fill. Do as many chicks as you want. Do so many that your penis falls off, which I hope is sooner rather than later for all of womankind's sakes. That way, you don't break any more hearts—whore!" she whisper-shouted.

He broke her heart. Chris was—wow! This was a night of revelations. First, she almost cried, and now he'd broken her heart? He gave himself a little shake to focus. Then he extended a hand to her.

She glared at the proffered appendage like scabs and puss covered it. "What?"

"Need a hand?"

"What?"

"Want a hand off your high horse, ice princess?" he asked with a frosty smile.

"Fuck you!" she snapped.

"I wish you would. Then maybe you'd stop treating me like I'm not allowed to make mistakes. I'm not perfect. You guys point that out to me on the daily."

"Not perfect, and a liar. Got it," she retorted.

He closed the distance between them. Standing almost on top of her, he looked down at her thoughtfully. "Did it ever occur to you I lied because she really doesn't matter? Did you ever think that maybe I sleep around because I'm very familiar with what it's like to be the kind-hearted, fat kid no one looks at twice? The perfect friend but never the boyfriend?"

Her eyes widened a smidge.

Chris continued, might as well get it all out there. "That was me. For years, I was the fat friend of Drew, Lex, and Rand, who—let's face it—have all been good-looking and popular since birth. Girls got close to me to get to them. I lost myself for a while." He shrugged, let his hands slap his thighs dramatically. "Got wrapped up in pussy. I'll admit it, I'm a man. But I have been trying."

"Oh, poor Chub-chub." Renée imperiously folded her arms. Her forearms nudged his chest. "Grow the hell up. You can't keep using your fat childhood to excuse your slutty ways. Get over it."

Chris quirked a brow. "You mean like you've gotten over your childhood issues? Or like you've gotten over your young adult issues and started dating again after Corey?"

Her entire face seemed to fall at the mention. Her mouth popped open. Even her arms limply fell to her sides, and he could've kicked his own ass. He hadn't meant to say that. Fuck!

"Who told you?" she murmured.

"Doesn't matter," he soldiered on, knowing he should shut up. "You can't hold everyone accountable for something one shitty person did. It's been three years, and you haven't dated. Haven't let anyone near you. Not family, barely your friends... and the one guy willing to give you everything, protect you, cherish you...? You turn away. Doesn't feel good to have someone throw your flaws in your face, does it?"

She stepped back. Hit the wall. "Go to Hell, Chris. Go to fucking Hell."

"I could." Why did he keep talking? His mouth just wouldn't stop moving. He felt her slipping away with each word he spoke, yet he couldn't stop.

"This feels like it. The last thing I wanted was to hurt you, so maybe I should go to Hell. But I won't. For once, you aren't going to get your way. You're so used to everyone tiptoeing around you and your crap attitude. Well, sorry, sweetheart. I won't cower. I'm a man, and as a man, I'm going to stand here and love you. I'm gonna be in your face. Piss you off. You're going to have to deal with it and your feelings for me because... I'm not going anywhere."

"Why did you do this?" she croaked as if she were fighting tears. "Have me even considering that you could be different, be an... option? If you would've just stayed the conceited man-whore, I wouldn't even care."

"Renée, I'm going to let you down. People will let you down. It's a fact of life. You hold people to these impossible standards, then the moment they show any sign of human imperfection... You're done. Don't you think you've ever let someone down before? You have. You let Drew down by cutting him out of your life. You didn't tell your parents about this trip"—he gentled his tone, looked around to encompass the space, then back at her—"because you know it'd let them down. Letting someone down doesn't mean you don't still love them. It means you have ass-kissing to do to get back in their good graces—if they really matter to you. I lied." Chris stepped forward, crowding her. "So, I'll kiss your ass, but I'll never leave you alone."

For extra emphasis, he kissed her freezing forehead.

She stared up at him, eyes big, round. Looking lost or hurt or confused. Renée slowly turned. Glanced back. Then walked away.

CHAPTER TWENTY-FOUR

Gary, Indiana

The following day, Chris stared at his reflection in the mirror of the hotel bathroom. He was wrecked. This felt worse than being hungover. Guilt, the ultimate bender.

Bedhead didn't begin to describe what was goin' on with his hair right now. Inclining his head, he inspected his bare chest. Pinched a wayward hair between his thumb and finger, yanked it out. Frowning, he rubbed one tanned pectoral, felt an upraised bump. A zit! No!

Shit with Lex and Renée had him pimple-stressed. He hadn't broken out since he was sixteen, or seventeen.

"What the hell is up with Chris?" Chris heard Lex ask from the other room.

"I don't know, dude. This trip's got everybody acting weird," Drew answered. "You guys gotta figure this shit out 'cuz you guys are my brothers."

Chris had no idea why they acted like a soundproof barrier instead of a paper-thin wall separated them. He fucking heard them talking about him. They'd all been tap dancing around the fight. He and Renée hadn't said word one to each other since their verbal smackdown.

As much as he hated to admit when he was wrong, he was wrong. His and Lex's fight, his subsequent argument with Renée—both were on him.

Renée had a right to be pissed about Samantha. He'd put the moves on her without nailing down the particulars. Of course, hearing about his sidepiece blindsided her. She pretended not to care, but he knew better. Her surly attitude was a defense mechanism. A man couldn't go into a relationship with a woman like her and not be aware of glitches, so to speak. They were long overdue for a relationship talk. What happened last night did not qualify.

Chris didn't think what he said was wrong, but how he'd said it needed work. Now with the girls in one double room and them in another, he'd have to go covert ops to hash things out.

"So, what's with this trip?" Lex inquired. "What are we supposed to do?"

Petty as he may seem, he was happy Lex didn't have all the answers for once. Maybe he'd have a chance to guide his woman through this experience. Even if Drew helped her through, it would be better than Lex playing Superman again.

"We gotta be here for Renée," Drew said as Chris turned on the faucet. "She's going through something. I don't honestly know how meeting these people will affect her."

After brushing his teeth and splashing some water on his face, Chris walked out of the bathroom. The conversation came to a halt as he came into view of his friends.

Sitting on the double bed closest to the bathroom, he grabbed socks from his bag and put them on. They could cut the tension in the room with a knife. As he put on his shoes and laced them, he felt the burn of Lex's and Drew's stares.

They weren't supposed to be like this. He pulled an undershirt on, then a blue T-shirt to go with his jeans. This relationship was the first relationship he needed to repair.

Chris stood, walked over to where Lex leaned against the dresser. Each gave the other a critical once-over. He shrugged, looked his buddy straight in the eye. Extending his fist, he asked, "We cool, man?"

Lex examined Chris, his fist. "Yeah, we're cool." He smirked and bumped fists with him. Both chuckled.

More than he saw, Chris felt Drew shake his head from where he sat on the other bed. An apology didn't need to be wordy among friends. This for damn sure wasn't the first time any of them had come to blows with each other, nor would it be the last. They were brothers.

He patted Lex on his shoulder, grabbed his leather jacket, and tagged Drew before leaving their room.

Renée sat on one of the double beds, swinging her bare feet. In front of her, on the ugly pastel comforter, was the composition book Drew had used to gather information. She'd forgone meeting the guys for a late breakfast. She wanted to jot down some questions.

Already, she was coming to these people out of the blue. The last thing she wanted to do was be unprepared. Of course, that'd been her original plan. But here she sat ten minutes later, after Ashley and Chrissy left to meet the guys, in her yoga pants and tank top. She hadn't written one word. What type of questions did an abandonee ask the abandoners? Now that they were in Indiana, Renée realized she might not have thought this plan through.

She sighed. And then there was the Great Chris Debacle. Her head reeled from the stuff he'd said. Why did someone who refused to leave her or give in to her do so much for her? For some reason, knowing he wouldn't go anywhere no matter how she behaved comforted her. It took the pressure off, eased the feeling that she had to live up to some standard.

God, she was crazy!

Renée threw herself backward on the bed. She needed to get her mind right and stop thinking about stupid Christopher Clark.

There was a knock at the door.

"Who is it?!" she called out without moving from the bed.

Ashley and Chrissy had keycards. If they wanted to get in bad enough, they could.

"Chris. Can I come in?"

She bolted upright. Talk about a twisted way of getting her prayers answered. "No!" she shouted.

Hefting herself from the bed, Renée trudged to the door.

"Why not?" he asked on the other side of the door.

Forehead on the door, she replied, "'Cause there's nothing in here that you *need*."

"That's not true," Chris said.

She smiled at the smile she heard in his voice.

"I don't see Samantha in here, so..."

"Just let me in," he demanded exasperatedly.

She opened the door. Sure, it wouldn't close; she went back to her spot on the bed farthest from the door and sat.

He sauntered in like he owned the joint. Really! Was there anything he didn't look sexy in? He looked like a model, wearing a simple T-shirt a few shades lighter than his blue eyes, jeans, and leather jacket. In a very un-Christopher-like manner, his blond hair was in disarray and damp. Chris went nowhere looking less than his best. What the hell? He sat at the end of the other bed, facing her.

"What do you want?" she asked, crossing her legs on the bed.

None too subtly, Chris stood. He sat at the end of her bed, scant inches from her. Turning to her, he answered, "I wanted to make sure we were okay."

"Don't worry about it. It's fine." She flicked the corner of the notebook's pages. Anything not to look him in the eye. Renée felt awkward with him now, since he'd scolded her. "I'm fine. I'm always fine, no matter what happens."

"No one is fine all the time. I can be there for you. I'll catch you… if you fall."

What? Renée laughed hard. She gazed at him in time to catch him scooting closer. Trying not to be obvious, she kept laughing yet scooted away. "That's the corniest line I've ever heard," Renée said, between fits of laughter.

Dropping all pretenses, Chris slid closer. Renée scooted to the wall.

"Stop it," he demanded.

Totally not expecting what he'd do, Renée gasped as Chris scooped her up. Cradled her in his arms. "What are you doing?" She squirmed, not really trying to get away.

Dammit! His big, muscular arms felt good around her. Safe.

"Shh… Let it happen," he crooned, smoothing her hair back. Getting comfortable on the bed, he flipped her, so she straddled his lap. He grinned. "Better? Wait." Lifting each of her arms, he situated one, then the other on each of his shoulders. He rolled his neck, purposely grazing her limp hands. "Lace your fingers, baby."

Head tilted, she cut her eyes at him in reproach.

Smirking, he arched his brows, challenging her disapproval of the endearment.

Who the hell was she kidding? Not him, and it was just the two of them right now. She wanted him and all the dreams he'd tried to sell her. This trip would emotionally bankrupt her. For once, she didn't resist.

Renée wrapped her arms tighter around his neck, bringing them nearly chest to chest. Chris quirked a brow in question. He shook his head as if to say he didn't want to know the reason for her change of heart. She smiled, rested her forehead on his shoulder.

He squeezed her ass playfully. "Hey, I don't want to ruin the mood, but I want you to look at something really quick. Then you can go back to smelling my neck."

Rolling her eyes, she sat up.

He held up his iPhone for her inspection. She leaned away to bring the screen into focus. A blurry thumbnail of some brunette in lacy, pink, boy shorts and a cropped white shirt, bending ass out, hands pressed on a door. Her smiling face flashed back at the camera, or rather a cameraman. The contact's name beside the picture read: First Round Alternate. Three numbers and four email addresses were listed below. Renée frowned in confusion.

"Touch the first phone number."

She stared at the phone for a long moment. Brushing his thumb across the screen to keep it from fading to black, he encouraged her with a nod. Curiosity made her do as instructed. She touched the number. He placed the phone to his ear.

"Sam?" he asked.

Oh, hell no! He did not just call this bitch with her sitting in his lap. Way to ruin a moment. She moved to get up. Wrapping his arm around her waist, he forced her to stay put.

"Yeah. Uh-huh. No."

He quieted, listening to whatever Samantha the slut said. Her jostling didn't faze him or his phone call at all. His one arm was stronger than her two arms and legs. Bastard!

Her fingers crawled up the nape of his neck, tunneled into his hair. Tresses soft enough to make any woman jealous slid between her fingers; she curled her fingers and yanked. Hard.

"Ow!" he bit out between gritted teeth.

Moving quicker than she thought possible, he took both her arms from around his shoulders, pulled both behind her back, and locked them together with his huge hand. He did all this without dislodging her from her place, straddling his lap, or the use of his other hand.

He mouthed, *"Be. Good."*

Shackled like a criminal, she could only wiggle her shoulders in retaliation. Shifting, her hips was out. The friction did interesting things to her when his obviously hard "Pole D" rubbed her embarrassingly aroused "Slot C." Her traitorous body had her pissed at him and herself. If he didn't watch himself, she'd bite his nose off. Renée scowled.

Humor twinkled in his bold blue eyes, which stayed fastened on her.

"Well, you're gonna keep missing it," he answered, continuing his conversation as if she weren't there. "We're done... We're done. You heard me... I can't kick it with you in any way anymore... Fine. I said what I said... Don't wait, I never asked you to... I won't get bored. I'm with who I'm supposed to be with." He grinned. Winked. "She's in love with me. It's gonna take my full attention to get her under thumb... No, it goes both ways... Whatever... Lose my number." He ended the call.

Turning the phone toward her, he made a show of deleting Samantha's contact info, their text messages, and his call log. He went into his address book, found her name. Shockingly, he had her cell and home numbers, three email addresses, including one she rarely checked. He changed her name to "My One and Only." Then he shoved his phone into his jacket pocket.

"Where's your phone?"

"What? Why?" she asked, confounded, and to be honest, pleased by his behavior. "It's under the pillow."

Releasing her hands, Chris searched under her pillow. He came back out with her phone. Totally without shame, he went through her address book.

Oh, no!

Glancing up at her, he gave her a *really?!* look. He turned her phone toward her. "*Town Bicycle*, huh? I guess I should be glad you have my number in here at all."

Renée shrugged, frowned repentantly. "You weren't supposed to see that."

"Doesn't matter," he said, and she believed him. He did fancy one-handed typing, then showed her the screen.

"My Man?" she read aloud, inflection making it a question.

Chris tossed the phone somewhere behind them on the bed, wrapped his muscular arms around her waist. He stared her in the eye.

She'd like to say insanity caused her to wrap her arms around his neck, forced her to play in his hair as if she were a lovesick schoolgirl. It wasn't. She wanted to be with him this way.

He ran his nails up and down her back. Chills skittered the length of her spine. They stayed that way, staring into each other's eyes, content being close for what seemed an eternity.

"Will you do something for me?" Chris asked, breaking the silence.

"What?"

"Tell me you have feelings for me." Sensing her discomfort, he swatted her on the ass to quiet her protest. "I'm cool with earning your love, but I need to hear it once."

Renée sighed. He had to ask the one question she didn't know how to answer. Whatever they had—and she'd admit they had something—defied definition or words. Sometimes she saw him and wanted to kick him square in the face. Other times, she wanted to crawl into his lap and let him pet her like a kitten. She loved and hated his high-handedness. The way he touched and picked her up without permission, yet treated her as if she were precious.

She took a deep breath. Let it out. Placing her forehead against his, she told him, "You infuriate me to the core of my being. You're unbelievably cocky. Most of what you say when you're not being hurtful makes no sense. Your sense of humor is corny and perverted—"

Slapping her ass hard and then pinching a handful of a cheek, he grumbled, "Tell me how you really feel." His brows crinkled.

"You take advantage of people and situations," Renée went on as if he hadn't spoken. "And when you look at me, it's like... the earth stops spinning. When you laugh, it does weird things to my insides. I hate to see you angry."

She smoothed his wrinkled brow with her thumb. As she lowered her hand, he captured her thumb, bit the pad.

Her breath hitched. "I feel completely safe to be any version of me with you. I hate that your eyes, your smile, your presence hypnotizes me. Your kiss literally makes me weak—it's embarrassing—don't laugh," she threatened as the corners of his delectable mouth curled. "You know exactly how to stop me from slapping you and instead make me want to kiss you. You're like a fungus. You just grow on a person. You're addicting." She smiled.

He rubbed his nose on hers, giving her Eskimo kisses.

"I just need you," she whispered, her eyes misting, "you know that, and I hate it. You're magnetic, dammit!"

His smile was indulgent. "Shh..." He peppered kisses from her cheek to her chin. "Okay. You can stop. I get it."

Renée raked her fingers through the back of his hair, held him to her. She shivered as his breath tickled her clavicle. "You ever bring this up in mixed company, I'll deny it."

"I won't," Chris agreed, nibbling her collar.

"So, no more Samantha?"

"Right," he said, then licked a trail up her neck that set her insides to trembling. He stared her in the eye. "I don't want any woman but you. I'm sorry I lied. Am I forgiven?"

Glaring at his puppy dog pout, she punched his shoulder. He grabbed her hand and kissed her palm. "No. I hate you," she said without steam.

He had the audacity to smile. "No more flirting with Lex, got it?" Chris sternly demanded, dropping the grin. When she would explain, he spoke first. "Gratitude's one thing. Rubbing *my* pussy on his dick—not okay. You wanna feel someone's dick, you feel this dick."

Chris took her hand roughly, stroked his denim-covered erection with it. Biting her lip, she held back a moan. He was hard as stone. His eyes drifted almost closed, half-mast. He groaned. Arched into her hand.

Liquid heat rushed to her center, between her thighs. Thoroughly soaked her panties. Ecstasy etched into his sharp, masculine, features. Unable to control herself, she leaned forward, mashing her lips to his. The moan she'd fought to hold in escaped.

Mm... He tasted good.

He let her hand go; she continued to stroke him. Renée undulated above his hardness. She allowed her knuckles to brush her swollen clitoris hidden behind her yoga pants. Chris put a hand on each side of her face. Stopped her before she would plunge her tongue into his mouth. He pulled away, barely.

Panting, his breath caressed her face. "I need to be inside you."

Renée couldn't agree more. She needed him inside her. She grasped his zipper.

Two quick beeps halted her.

The door creaked. Oh, crap!

Hopping up, Renée smoothed her hands down her hair and clothes. She straightened herself out. A loud *thud* sounded behind her, but the door opened before she could inspect.

Ashley, Christina, Drew, and Lex entered. Staring past her, they all laughed hysterically.

"Dude, what are you doing?" her brother asked between breaths.

Renée turned to see the top of Chris's head poking out from between the wall and where the bed met. What the hell?

"You pushed him off the bed," Ashley assumed, laughing so hard she clutched her stomach through her dark sweater.

To her surprise, Chris's booming laugh came from behind her. "She couldn't push me. She couldn't overpower this," he bragged. "She can't move the rock."

Eyes narrowing in suspicion, Lex asked, "What are you guys doing?"

"Talking," she and Chris answered in unison.

Drew stared at her, wide-eyed. "Talking? What would you two need to talk about?"

"Umm... he wanted some concealer. I think he has a zit or something," Renée said, playing the obvious opening she'd been given. She turned, flashed an apologetic smile at Chris.

"I can believe that," Ashley muttered.

CHAPTER TWENTY-FIVE

Bright, early afternoon sunlight shone spotlight-style on a small, dilapidated white house. The front yard was overgrown. In all honesty, the place looked as if it should be featured in one of those movies characters trespass on only to discover psychotic serial killers live there.

Trepidation coiled inside Renée's stomach to the point of pain. She stared out the Denali's window. They'd just arrived at Lynn Davis's house. Anxiety knotted her intestines so bad; she hadn't been able to eat breakfast. Laughing or trying to follow the breakfast conversation was impossible. She hadn't even attempted normalcy on the car ride here.

Inhaling deep through her mouth and out the same way, Renée gathered what little courage she could. On another breath, she opened her door and got out. She closed the door and went around to the driver's side.

Sea-green eyes gazed at her in curiosity. Drew lowered the window.

She leaned in. "I'm going in. I'll be back as soon as possible."

Drew's mouth opened as if to speak.

"Like hell you are!" Chris exclaimed, beating him to the punch.

Her brother's eyebrows shot up, nearly met his hairline in surprise. Drew's eyes narrowed suspiciously first on her, then Chris in the passenger's seat.

From the back seat, Lex stared wide-eyed at the back of Chris's head.

Renée shot him a wary, tight-lipped glance that hopefully screamed *shut up* as she intended.

"Weird," Drew said wryly, then he looked at her. "But right… I guess. I'm not letting you go in there alone. What if they're murderers or cannibals? You're like a bucket of KFC walking right to their door."

"Why's everything killers and cannibals with you? Statistically, I don't think there's as many people eaters as you think there are." Pointing to a large, dust-coated, unobstructed picture window near the front door, Renée asked, "How far away do you think you are from the door? You'd see if they pulled something."

Drew gave her a look that said *right*.

Sighing, she strove for compromise. "I won't go farther into the house than that front room." Off his skeptical expression, she vowed, "Promise."

"I don't feel comfortable with you going in alone," Drew reiterated, exasperated.

Oh, she'd had enough of this. Lynn Davis might not even talk to her. If she went to the door with the village people behind her, it guaranteed her failure.

"Well," she said, glaring at everyone in the truck before her gaze rested on the occupants in the front seat, "you have about one minute to get comfortable 'cuz it's happening."

"I don't think so, Née—" Alex said.

"It's gonna seem like an ambush if we all go in," she explained, interrupting him. "I'll text if"—she affected an ominous tone—"danger arises."

"Fine," Drew capitulated, like he really had a say in the matter. "But after an hour, make some excuse to leave. One hour, Renée."

She walked away without responding. It would take however long it took. Chris's invasion last night had kept her from writing questions, so she was flying by the seat of her pants.

As she headed to the battered front door, her phone vibrated. Without breaking stride, Renée pulled it from her purse's side pocket. Swiping the screen, she read the text:

> *If anything goes wrong or seems weird, text me first.*

The message was from Chris. Lifting her eyes heavenward with a shake of her head, she returned her phone to its place.

At the front door, she raised her fist to knock. The door opened before she followed through.

Standing before her was a surly-faced mocha-complexioned woman, who appeared to be in her sixties but was more than likely younger. Maybe mid-fifties, Renée guessed. Whatever her age, the years had not been kind. They'd hunched her back and marched all over the woman's leathery, yellowed skin. Grey streaked black—part kinky, part wild—curls jumped out of her scalp in every direction as if running from her withered face. Her loud floral housecoat almost detracted from the puff of sickeningly sweet smoke that rushed for freedom as she opened the door.

"Can I help you?" the woman rasped in a voice that spoke of decades of cigarette smoking.

"Umm... Yeah. I'm looking for Lynn Davis?" Renée stammered, unsure if she wanted this to be the person in question. Something about this woman screamed, "I'll cut a bitch for no reason," followed by a nasty smoker's laugh-cough.

Well, aren't you judgmental? You don't know this woman from Adam. Give her a shot.

Oh, God, she was doing precisely what Drew had done with his off-the-wall assumptions. She should kick her own ass for that sort of pre-judging.

"I'm"—wet smoker's cough (with her mouth barely covered)—"Lynn Davis. You Renée Williams, right?"

Whoa! Her eyes widened. That threw her for a loop. She recoiled a bit at the surname. It catapulted her to a time—a person—she'd rather forget. That last name hadn't been attached to her since before her adoption at ten years old.

"No. I mean, yes... kind of," she stuttered. "It's Sutton now. Renée Sutton. I was adopted. How did you know that—me?"

Again, Lynn did something between a laugh and a hacking cough. "Girl, please, I can tell one of Shelly's kids a mile away," she said, smiling one of the yellowest frightening smiles Renée had ever seen. "You look just like ya Mama. She was pretty 'fo dat booger suga'."

Her answering smile was slow in coming, uncomfortable. She wasn't positive crack hadn't made Lynn's acquaintance a time or two. "I wouldn't know. I don't remember her."

Nodding, Lynn turned on slippered feet and headed inside.

Unsure if she was supposed to follow, Renée hesitated at the threshold.

"C'mon in here. Don't want flies gettin' in or roaches. Those fly here, too."

Gross! Ducking, brushing off her arms, and searching around herself, Renée hopped over the threshold and hurried inside. She shut the door behind her.

Inside, a wispy haze, or a cloud of smoke, blanketed the house. It burned Renée's eyes and irritated her lungs as she attempted to follow Lynn into the living room. Along with the house, the room was cluttered. Like three or four stacks of paper away from an episode of *Hoarders* cluttered. Knickknacks and piles of old newspapers and bills filled every nook and cranny. The smell of clove cigarettes, mothballs, and formaldehyde permeated the house. What didn't have a stack of papers on it had a layer of dust.

Lynn sat on an outdated plastic-covered couch.

Renée looked around for a place to sit. In a corner, a rocking chair. Plastic covered the cloth cushion and fabric arms. How'd that happen? Other than an overstuffed shelf behind it, it was clear. She sat carefully to keep from knocking everything on her.

"Last I heard, you was in California," Lynn rasped.

"Nope. Arizona," Renée corrected.

Waving her answer away as if inconsequential, Lynn patted her housecoat pockets. Then she felt between the couch cushions. Plastic squeaked as her hands grazed it. "You missed Big Mama's funeral— 'bout a week too late. You was always her favorite."

To hide her eye roll at that blatant lie, Renée turned her head. She let her gaze wander around the room. Her eyes lit on the Victorian-style loveseat buried under mounds of paper and throw blankets. Cherry wood legs and beige, plastic-wrapped cushions triggered a memory.

Three-year-old Renée wore a teal jumper with substantial white flowers. She crawled into the lap of a heavyset, light-complexioned Caucasian or Native American woman. Ebony hair was pulled back into a tight bun. Large, warm amber eyes gazed lovingly at Renée.

Once young Renée settled into her afghan-covered lap, the woman, Big Mama, reached forward. Retrieving a tin container from the floor beside the seat, she opened it to reveal fortune cookies. A whole tin of fortune cookies. Returning her great grandmother's warm smile and adoring gaze, she reached her tiny hand inside and grabbed a cookie.

It had been their ritual. Of course, she didn't remember the day of the week, but they ate fortune cookies together whenever she came over. God, how could she have forgotten their ritual? Big Mama had loved her, and she'd adored her. To this day, Renée still loved fortune cookies because of her Big Mama. She was gone now, and Renée could never say goodbye—

"You remember Big Mama? This her house," Lynn said, breaking into Renée's reverie. "She was sad when y'all got tooken. She wanted to find y'all, but time got away from her."

Those words cleared the tears that her memory called forth. Snapping her head back around, Renée leered at Lynn as a myriad of emotions swirled inside her. Anger took center stage. "When we got taken?" she asked, incredulity raising her voice an octave. "We didn't get *taken*. Our mom left."

Unperturbed by her ire, Lynn continued her hunt. Finding her prize, a pack of cigarettes, she pulled one out. She placed it in her mouth and let the cigarette dangle from the corner. "Well, that's water under the bridge now," Lynn said, dismissing the most critical event in Renée's life. She studied Renée while once again feeling herself up in search of a lighter, Renée assumed. "Look at you, all grown up."

"I didn't know Big Mama passed away."

Lynn chuckled, then coughed a nasty wet sound. "Kathy didn't tell you?"

Renée shook her head in answer. Clearly, her older sister had been in touch with the family enough to know current events. How nice. She was the only one no one bothered to find. She didn't regret her parents or her brother, but the realization still stung.

"It don't matter. I didn't go to the funeral either," Lynn continued, shrugging her indifference to the death of a loved one.

She wasn't sure of the relation. If Lynn Davis was her egg donor's cousin, then Big Mama would've been her grandmother—maybe.

Just then, Lynn found her lighter. To Renée's horror, she lit her cigarette.

"So... what brings you here?" she asked, cutting narrow distrustful eyes at Renée.

"I was just trying to reconnect with my roots," she responded, trying not to glare as Lynn puffed away on her cigarette. "Wanted to see where I came from."

"Well, you came to the right place," Lynn said, cigarette drooping precariously from her mouth as she spoke. "Gary and Fort Wayne full of yo' people. You seen Kathy?"

"No, but I plan to. She doesn't live too far from here."

"Yeah, if you don't think Kalamazoo is far from here." Lynn hacked-laughed.

Her entire demeanor changed. She wilted in her seat; her shoulders slumped. Renée's heart felt as if it beat slower.

"Kalamazoo? Michigan?" she asked, voice hollow.

Before Lynn responded, Renée's phone vibrated. She grabbed it out of her purse and read Chris's text:

> *You have ten more minutes, then I'm coming*
> *in after you.*

About to put it away, not even finished rolling her eyes, it vibrated again. She checked the new text message, this text from Andrew:

> *I'm coming in if you don't reappear soon. I*
> *can't see you from here.*

"Sorry about that," she apologized.

"You popular," Lynn commented, ashing onto a nearby stack of newspaper.

That is a fire hazard waiting to turn into a house fire, Renée thought.

"I ain't got no cell phone," her misguided relative stated eloquently. "Nobody needs to be knowin' my every move—where I shit, what time I shit. That one of them iPhones? That yo' husband or baby daddy callin' you?"

Renée balked. "Neither. It was my brother. He's waiting for me. He's impatient. So, Kathy lives in Kalamazoo, Michigan?"

"Yeah. She been in Kalamazoo a few years. Want her address? I'll give it to you," Lynn offered.

"That would be awesome. I'd really appreciate it."

Hefting herself from her spot on the couch, Lynn laughed, which morphed into a cough. She trudged on stiff legs out of the room. "*Awesome,*" she said, mocking Renée's voice. "Still proper as hell. That'll tell everybody who you is. Whitest black girl I eva saw," she murmured, turning around a corner and out of sight.

Seems some things didn't change. A faint memory of being ridiculed for her speech as a toddler pirouetted through her mind. She stood slowly, so the chair didn't rock and tip the papers behind it.

Minutes later, she stood outside on the front porch. Lynn stayed just inside the door.

"Thank you for your help, Lynn. I really appreciate you talking to me," she said, grateful for the info regarding her great grandmother and her sister. As for the experience itself—the jury was still out on that.

A plethora of emotions wreaked havoc on her. She didn't know what to make of this visit.

Lynn waved away her gratitude. "I didn't do nuthin'. We family; that's what family do. This yo' last stop?"

"No. I'm gonna go see my sister and Manuel," Renée answered honestly, not seeing any reason to withhold the truth.

"Manuel?" Lynn flinched. "I don't know 'bout Manuel."

Eying the older woman with open curiosity, she started to ask if something was wrong, but Lynn halted her with a finger. She reached a hand back inside, brought out an envelope full of pictures.

"I got a million pictures of Big Mama. Ain't too many, but these is copies I got. I found a few baby pictures wit' yo' name on 'em and pictures of you and Big Mama," she said, handing her the envelope.

Tears welled in her eyes. For all her appearing not to give a shit, Lynn had a heart. Renée had never had baby pictures of herself. Her throat swelled. "Thank you," she croaked.

"C'mon now," Lynn said through a coughing fit, arms spread wide, "give me a hug."

Not wanting to be rude, especially not after Lynn gave her such a priceless gift, Renée leaned in. She held her breath the entire two seconds of the hug. It was worth it.

CHAPTER TWENTY-SIX

The following day, Drew lay on one of the double beds, deep in thought. Only with a small portion of his focus was he aware of Lex sitting on the other bed, fiddling with his cell phone. To his total annoyance, Chris's inhale-exhale pattern as he did bare-chested push-ups kept infiltrating his ruminations.

"No offense, but I wish they had three bedrooms here. This ain't sleep-away camp, and we aren't ten. Sharing a room with two dudes is weird," Lex complained.

Chris grunted as he—from what Drew assumed the sound meant—flipped to his back. "I can see how you'd be uncomfortable in the bed next to all this."

Drew lifted to his elbow, rested his head in his hand in time to catch Lex side-eye Chris.

"Yeah, that's what it is—jackass!" Lex muttered.

What the hell was up with these two? All the time with the arguing. These weren't meaningless jabs or the usual banter they indulged in but actual fightin' words. Hug it out, kumbaya, arm wrestle; he didn't give a fuck what they did. They just needed to get over this shit.

Bad enough, his sister had acted weird and quiet after she visited with her—cousin? She'd been contemplative, introverted, the rest of the day and into the night. Thinking to give her space to process, Drew hadn't pressed when she went to bed early.

In the harsh light of day, he worried for her. Renée was a contradiction of terms. Stronger than anyone he knew. But inside were these pockets of weakness. Landmines, that once triggered, wrought indeterminable consequences. Then there was the other complication he hadn't counted on.

Not true. He'd chosen to ignore the inherent difficulty in favor of proximity. To say that'd been stupid would be an understatement. Being here with Renée caused him emotional distress. Thanks to Rand fielding house and cell calls, their parents would remain ignorant of their children's disloyalty. Part of him understood his sister's reasoning. Part of him felt like a damn adolescent sneaking out of the house. For goodness sake, he was a twenty-seven-year-old man. Weren't the days of hiding from his parents supposed to be over? Shouldn't he be allowed to love whomever he wanted, even if it was his sister's best friend?

Shit! He needed to release some stress. However, to do that, he needed to be honest with his friends and sister. But he couldn't while this shit with Renée's biological family was going on. He'd intended to tell his boys, but not this way. Unfortunately, proximity was killing him, and he wanted alone time with his woman.

Drew took a deep breath through his nose, sat up on the bed. The sharp musk of Chris's sweat stung his nostrils. He exhaled through his mouth. He'd tell them and endure the ribbing that was sure to accompany the revelation, then plan some way to be alone with his lady.

"So... what do you guys think of Christina?" he exclaimed, employing the rip-the-Band-Aid method.

As he'd presumed, Chris had started a rep of sit-ups. Coming up on an exhalation, he rested his elbows on his knees. A neat, thick, blond brow rose over one deep blue eye. "I think if you want to date a chick with your best friend's name... that's on you. Just don't get us confused." Chris grinned.

Drew glanced at Lex, who looked about as shocked as if he'd been told he was Hispanic: it did not surprise him in the least.

Damn! He thought he'd been so careful. "Uh gross, dude, I don't call her Chris. And how did you know I was seeing her?"

It was Lex's turn to pin him with a droll stare. "We have eyes, bro. She slides past you, purposely brushing up against you with some body part. You stare at her like she's a melting popsicle you need to lick. Then with your whole, 'can you guys keep a secret,'"—said with more bass to mock Drew's voice—"bullshit at Big D's? Wasn't too hard to solve that puzzle," Lex finished in his own voice.

They laughed.

His chuckle was more relieved than from the stupid joke. Now that the secret was out of the bag, he could put in his request.

Before Drew said anything more, Chris stood and strolled into the vanity area. He returned, wiping the sweat from his chest with a hand towel. His sincere gaze landed on Drew. "Seriously, dude, if you're happy, I'm happy for you. You deserve a good woman. Christina's quiet, but if that's what you like, I'm not mad at you."

His and Lex's mouths dropped open with a pop. They exchanged astonished, crazy-eyed looks, then stared at their friend. Maybe this *was* one of those body-snatcher situations.

Drew found his voice first. "You feelin' okay, bro? Usually, if something isn't about you, you couldn't care less. Now you're happy for me?"

Chris draped the white towel over his shoulder. He leaned an elbow against the wall, feet crossed at the ankles. "Hey, I display human emotions from time to time. I told you I was trying to change."

"This new sensitive side of you is so... hawt," he kidded. "Can I get a hug, man?" Drew opened his arms toward his friend.

Chris glared.

"Are you almost done with your daily... routine? I need to shave and brush my teeth," Drew informed the narcissist, still thrown by the attitude adjustment.

Running a slow hand through sweat-dampened hair, Chris retorted, "Looking this good takes time." He kissed his bicep. "I have to make sure my adoring public gets the perfection they've grown accustomed to."

"Shut up!" Lex admonished Chris, then turned to Drew. "Wanna know something sad? He actually believes that shit."

Lex and Chris had made up after their fight, but it was tentative. He steered the conversation to a topic that wouldn't end in holes in the hotel room wall. "I got a favor to ask," Drew interjected before a verbal slap fight started. "Since Renée decided to forgo seeing her sister today, I want to make some time with Christina tonight."

"Like, adult time?" Chris interrupted. "You two serious or just fuckin'?"

"Serious. Real serious, I hope," he answered with an exasperated sigh. "Anyway, I'm gonna need help, so Renée doesn't get suspicious."

Chris returned to the vanity area. The faucet turned on.

"I'm down," Lex volunteered with a shrug. "You want me to take Née out so you guys can slip out?"

Running water cut off abruptly.

"No. I already talked to Renée. Since she decided to see her sister on her bio dad's side instead of the other one tomorrow, she wants to prepare notes or something. But Christina and I can't just leave, at least not alone. I need you to bring Ashley like it's a group thing, then you two can split off. Keep her occupied until I call you."

Lex sat ramrod straight. "Man, you know I'm in if it involves Ashley. I'll find a way to keep her out for a while."

A devious smile crossed his friend's face. Lex refused to give up on the fruitless Ashley venture. The chick wasn't interested, but if he wanted to torture himself, Drew would let him.

"I guess you're gonna get to spend some quality time with your favorite person—you," Drew said loud enough for Chris to hear.

Chris came around the corner. A private smile upturned the corners of his mouth. "Alone time. Just what the doctor ordered."

CHAPTER TWENTY-SEVEN

The restaurant was almost empty. Gary, Indiana, wasn't as big a place as Renée remembered. Due to the lack of suitable living quarters—Ashley and Lex's shared sentiments—their hotel was in Hammond, a twenty-minute drive from Gary. The dead IHOP they were currently seated at was in Merrillville, also twenty minutes from Gary. It seemed nothing worthwhile could be done in the city.

Or the state, her subconscious reminded her.

Kathy, her older sister, lived in Kalamazoo, Michigan. How hadn't Drew found the correct address? That never happened. She wasn't stunned. For years, she'd searched social networks for Kathy. Each attempt had been unsuccessful. Her sister appeared to live off the grid.

Out of everyone, Kathy was the most important. They'd both suffered at the hands of their neglectful, drug-addict mom. Their life experiences were unique, yet similar. She'd been all Renée had at one point. Adversity, sisterhood, and love forged a bond not even escapable by death. She needed to see Kathy. Not just to validate what they'd gone through, but to cement the knowledge that she'd overcome things most would never experience in their wildest, most frightening dreams. At least, that's what she believed would heal them. Maybe pave the way for a new relationship.

Sausage speared on fork tines waved in front of Renée's face. Like blown leaves, her thoughts scattered at the sight of the juicy brown meat.

"Bet you wish you weren't a vegetarian now, don't cha?" Lex taunted.

She grimaced. Using only her eyes, she followed the link a second before swiveling to meet Lex's laughing brown gaze. "That's disgusting. Do you know how—"

"Stop," Lex interrupted with his finger to her open lips. "Every time you start a sentence with, 'Do you know' after any reference to meat, it's followed by some nasty meat fact."

Reaching across her plate of hash browns and chocolate chip pancakes, Chris smacked Lex's hand away from her mouth. Lex's jaw tightened.

Why me?

Ever since their "almost sex", Chris had been acting territorial. He held her to the whole, not using Lex to make him jealous thing. The reminders weren't necessary; she got how wrong pinning Chris against Lex was. In all honesty, she hadn't known that was what she'd done until he pointed it out. Now that she'd seen what her over affection caused, she backed off.

She'd also stepped back from the subject of her and Chris. Wishy-washy wasn't usually her style, but he confused her. On the one hand, he'd done and said all the right things. But on the other, what he said he wanted was still a relationship. Gun-shy didn't explain how she felt about those. She wanted to believe his miraculous playboy-to-gentleman transformation, but she'd been wrong—very wrong—about a man before. Plus, this was Chris, not a random guy. Drew would have a cow, two ducks, and a chicken if they got together. More if Chris broke her heart. Renée didn't want to hurt her brother or split his loyalties.

"You know who we should've invited?" Ashley asked, not letting a mouthful of French toast keep her from talking. She answered her own question, "Rand. He could've funded this little excursion."

"Ashley, sweetie," Renée crooned condescendingly. "Remember, we talked about this? Independence good, using our friends bad."

Ashley's fork landed with a clatter on her plate. She snapped her finger. "Silly me, I keep getting those mixed up."

From his place beside Ashley on the other side of the table, Drew spoke for the first time. He'd inhaled his eggs, hash browns, bacon, and two pancakes like a prisoner afraid his food would be stolen. He pointed at her plate. "I can't believe you ate any of that. Regular pancake batter with chocolate chips added. Not too many, though, measure out twelve, and instead, three pancakes bring two," he said, voice high to mock hers and her order. "You remember that movie *Waiting*, right?" His brows rose. He tipped his head toward her plate.

"Oh, gross," Ashley grumbled, echoing her thoughts. "I'm gonna hurl. I'll be back." She excused herself and headed to the bathroom.

"Does anybody want the rest of my pancakes? I'm full—" The word hadn't fully formed on Christina's tongue before her brother scooted into Ashley's vacant seat and snatched the plate. Christina gasped at the sudden movement.

"I'll take that."

Blowing his overgrown bangs out of his face, Drew tossed her friend a sly wink. Christina blushed and pushed a strand of hair behind her ear.

What the hell was that about?

She'd been about to ask that burning question when Lex and Chris came down with a case of whooping cough. Renée gazed at one, then the other, suspiciously. Lex took up his napkin, held it to his mouth until his cough quieted.

"Anyway..." Lex said, regaining his composure, "I need to bring a book or something to the next place we go. Especially if we're gonna Thelma-and-Louise it all over the Midwest. Doom-scrolling social media holds only so much appeal. Sitting in the car is boring as hell. My entire ass was numb after your visit yesterday."

Damn. That was another reason not having everyone here would be better. Her original plan had been to visit Lynn and then Kathy since they both lived in Gary. Then they'd travel the two and a half hours to Fort Wayne, stay there two days, and finish the tour with Shenae and Manuel—in that order. Now, if she wanted to visit Kathy tomorrow, they'd have to drive over an hour and a half there, then backtrack.

Gas wasn't cheap. She'd started with minimal funds for this spur-of-the-moment trip. Meaning, Drew handled the entire cost of this adventure. Sure, everyone would pitch in where they could, but none of them were millionaires. Maybe they *should've* brought Rand.

No. Damn, Ashley's seed-planting ass.

This was her mission. Having anyone but her foot the bill was wrong.

Renée kept her guilty sigh to herself. "You guys should go do something," she suggested, hoping they'd listen. She'd feel less bad if she knew they were sightseeing instead of outside in the truck. Going in with her still wasn't an option in her book. "I can call you when I'm done at each place."

"Hell, no!" Ashley sounded off, announcing her reappearance. She took the chair in front of Drew's empty plate. "We aren't leaving you at a possible psycho's house, Née."

"Ash, I'm not some delicate flower. I've dealt with worse," she reminded everyone softly. "I'll be fine."

Drew polished off the last blueberry pancake, took a sip of his coffee, then spoke. "As much as I hate to say it… Ashley has a point. We aren't leaving you."

Chris stood abruptly. "Are we leaving soon?" he asked no one in particular.

"Yeah," her brother responded, one thick brown brow arched. "Probably in, like, ten minutes."

"Cool. I'll be right back. I'm gonna hit the shopping plaza across the street. Let me get your keys." Chris held up his hand, prepared to catch. When Drew hesitated, he added, "I'm not taking the truck. I just want to put my shit somewhere."

Waiting for a beat more, Drew finally reached into his pocket. He tossed Chris his keys.

Plucking them from the air, Chris spun around and strutted out of the restaurant.

What was his deal?

CHAPTER TWENTY-EIGHT

Plodding down the hotel hall to her room, Renée tossed her can of pop into the air. Catching it, cool aluminum slapped her palm; she cursed herself.

Dammit! Why would she play catch with a carbonated beverage?

This trip messed with her good sense. Or maybe her intuition was trying to tell her something. Her parents always said she was intuitive but accused her of ignoring it. Within her, something—and that was the best way to describe it—felt off.

Although meeting Lynn Davis had been incredible, especially getting the pictures, the experience lacked something. She didn't know what she'd expected to happen when she saw a member of her biological family, but it felt anticlimactic. That bothered her more than she cared to admit. With a loaded, shoulder-heaving sigh, Renée rounded the corner. And almost ran into one source of her confusion.

She plastered on a smile. "Hey, superstar, how's life in the OC?"

In blue-and red-plaid flannel pajama pants and a white V-neck tee, Chris arched a brow. "Do you ever get tired of making fun of me?"

With a dramatic tilt of her head, she lifted her eyes heavenward as if in thought. Shrugging, she sighed, a dreamy sort of sound. "No, it's like the gift that keeps on giving."

Chris gave her a heatless glare, then smirked. For the first time, his normal cocky air didn't cling to him. "Looks like we're all by ourselves tonight."

Renée's stomach somersaulted. They weren't technically alone in the hotel. Of course, there were other guests, but Drew, Chrissy, Lex, and Ashley were checking out the Indiana nightlife. So, yes, of their group, they were the only two here. But she was nowhere near as sure of him, or them, as she'd been a couple days ago. Tension swelled between them.

This couldn't be more awkward.

"Yep. Looks like it," she answered, rocking on her heels. Her eyes scanned the barren hallway of their own volition. They refused to look him in the eye, even though she felt his gaze on her like a heat-seeking missile. After a pregnant pause, she said, "Well, I better go. I have lots of questions to write and organize for tomorrow's visit. It's with that sister I never met before. Gotta be prepared," she rambled.

Finally, she looked into his eyes, expecting relief. She'd discontinued their awkward exchange. Instead, she found a storm brewing in his intense blue orbs.

"Fine," he growled. "Whatever. See you tomorrow then."

He went to pass her. She stepped in his path. Chris allowed her to impede his progress. Allowed because she knew for damn sure that if he wanted to get past her, he could. There was more than a foot in height difference between them.

"What's your deal?" she demanded.

He stared hard at her as if he could extract what he wanted to through osmosis. The only problem was she didn't know what he wanted. One thing was simple: he expected more than she'd given.

"Nothing. Nothing at all," he said, defeated.

Confused by his agitation and dejected attitude, Renée didn't stop him when he went to pass her this time. Continuing to her room, she glanced over her shoulder. He'd already disappeared.

Minutes later, Renée laid stomach-down on her bed. Black yoga pants bunched below her calf. She'd traded the composition book for index cards, thinking they'd be less intimidating. Shenae Williams was a great unknown. What did she ask a sister she only shared partial DNA with? What if Shenae didn't know she existed? Her sperm donor couldn't be the most upstanding person. Shit! What if Manuel had abandoned Shenae, too?

God! She could be broaching a complicated topic for Shenae. For the second time, she questioned the sanity of her surprise visits. No, it had to be done this way. Warning people gave them time to ditch her. Yes, they had the right not to talk to her, but this was important. This was her life. She wasn't spending the rest of it with this big question mark over her head or these unstable moods. If this was a sore subject for Shenae, they could commiserate over deadbeat dads.

Time marched on. She hadn't written one question.

Nope. Not entirely true. Written on one white card were the words: *What is wrong with Chris?*

Chances were good no one knew that answer, not even Chris.

One minute he held her, told her all those things a woman wanted to hear. The next, he was rolling his eyes and angry because she acted as screwed up as she'd told him she was. Why were people shocked when she proved she was damaged? Why did she care if Chris couldn't deal with her mental scars? She'd informed him she couldn't give him what he wanted. Yet he'd persisted. Then, when she didn't know how to do whatever he'd expected, he got mad.

Damn him!

Damn her!

She was supposed to be working through her anxiety attacks. Attacks that since he'd been—sheesh, she didn't know how to explain what he'd been. Present? Since he'd been attentive, her panic attacks had lessened. That thought made her heart flutter—stupid heart.

Her heart was broken. Not in a someone-broke-my-heart way, but in a cracked-in-pieces way. The never-been-quite-whole way. Could someone as ruined as she love? Did she know how? So many moments and people who'd come into her life were supposed to stay. Relationships between siblings, parents, and children lasted forever, yet hers hadn't.

Once denied those necessary skills acquired at birth—love and acceptance, from people genetically encoded to love you unconditionally—did a person get another chance to gain them? Were they nurture or nature skills? Her formative years were filled with deception, rejection, abuse of every classification, but no love. Love, a primary emotion, forever eluded her.

She shook her head to disperse her thoughts. That's why she couldn't do this relationship thing with Chris—if she believed that's what he wanted. He needed someone who knew what he needed when he got all upset for no reason. Whatever they'd started was at the flirtation stage. Ending it now would save him from being hurt and Drew from losing a friend. Yeah, it might hurt her a bit, but pain seemed to be the only guarantee in her life. She knew how to deal with it.

Renée hopped up from the bed. Wiggling each of her legs straightened her pants legs; she tugged her fitted maroon tank top into place. She grabbed her light hooded sweater that zipped in the front, then shoved her sock-covered feet into her black suede UGG boots.

While finger-combing her hair into a sloppy ponytail, her stomach twisted as if to protest her decision. "No, Renée," she scolded herself, snatching the keycard from the dresser and sticking it in her pocket. "Whatever this is… is over."

With that in mind, she left to end things with Chris. He deserved better, not some girl who missed his signals and left him in his room to… do whatever sad Chris did.

She marched down the deserted hall with long, determined strides. Soft music drifted from some room with a couple who probably thought music drowned out sex noise. At least she'd have something to listen to while crying over what never could've been. Renée rubbed her hands up and down her arms. The hallway was colder than her heated room. Her nose and cheeks were cold.

Must save money to have the hall cooler, she thought, outside the guys' room door. Inhaling deeply, she knocked, exhaled.

"Come in!" shouted Chris's accented bass.

Renée realized then that the door was ajar. A thick stack of takeout menus kept it from shutting entirely. She pushed open the door.

Her mouth dropped open.

CHAPTER TWENTY-NINE

Lights off. Pillar candles of varying sizes in maroon, rosy pink, and ivory were lit and strategically placed around the room atop clear glass pillar plates. Rose petals and caramel-filled Hershey's kisses littered the floor from door to vanity and on top of beds. An iPhone—Chris's—sat on a dock with speakers. A bluesy, soulful piano ballad—what she'd mistakenly assumed came from some over-sexed couple's room—played softly.

Slack-jawed, Renée stumbled backward. A portentous click of the door shutting fully under her weight sped up her pulse. The fresh, floral-fruity scent of passionflower enveloped her.

The room was... beautiful. Straight out of a Nicholas Sparks novel turned movie, but it wasn't the reason her heart raced.

Chris stood in the center of the room. Warm candlelight flickered. Illuminated his handsome face in a soft glow. His signature lop-sided grin tilted perfect lips. He looked like sex. No other description fit. The man was sex on two long, strong, black slacks-encased legs. A royal blue—one of her favorite colors on him—button-down didn't hide the rock-hard, chiseled chest it adorned. He held a single yellow rose with red tips, a fire-tipped rose—her favorite. Taped to the rose was a card with words written in pen that she couldn't read from this distance.

She took several unsteady, hesitant steps forward. Not wanting to get too close, but close enough to read the note. The penmanship wiggled as if he'd tried super hard to make it legible. Renée read to herself: *I kiss the ground you walk on.*

A boulder-sized lump lodged in her throat. She gulped in hopes of speaking. Opening her mouth, nothing came out. Her gaze swept across the room. Her mind worked to process the scene. Candles, music, roses... He'd even remembered not to gel his hair. She liked how light and golden blond tresses fell over his forehead. Tears pricked her eyes.

They'd seen each other what—an hour ago? Had he had time to do all this? What about being mad at her? His eyes spit blue flames earlier, now... this? That seductive smile? No one had ever done such a focused study of her. Used their knowledge specifically to woo her, make her happy. She wasn't the type of girl—at least, she'd never considered herself the kind—who inspired grand romantic gestures.

Blurry eyes gazed up, meeting eyes of the deepest blue.

"What is this?" she breathed.

Chris moved then, sat the rose on the dresser, then approached her. He extended his hand.

Neck craned to look him in the eyes; she gaped at him, then his hand. Her heart moshed with her sternum.

"Give me a chance, please," Chris's solemn request, hand reaching for hers. "Do you know how hard it was to do this without anyone noticing this stuff?" he asked with a put-upon sigh.

His flippant, oh-so-Chris response went a long way toward putting her at ease. This, their usual sarcastic/antagonistic banter, she could do. Something told her he'd used the tone specifically for her comfort. It worked.

Mock skepticism narrowed her eyes. "I could have been house-keeping or something. You told me to come in," she accused.

He nodded. "I was pretty sure it was you. My little show in the hall stacked the deck in my favor," he bragged.

Feeling a teensy bit on more level ground, though un-der-dressed, she crossed her arms indignantly over her chest. "So, now, not only are you conceited but psychic, too?" she charged, humor lacing her words.

"No." He grinned. "But I think there's something here. It's the reason we have all this... animosity between us."

"What're you talking about—animosity? It's hate, honey. Good old-fashioned hate," she teased for no reason but nervousness.

The ambiance didn't lend itself to this kind of conversation, or rather, debate. This was a let's-make-bad-decisions type of atmos-phere.

"Not to sound cliché, but there's a thin line between love and hate, Renée. And between us, that line is electrified, barbed wire fencing. We thrive on the sparks. Should make for an exciting 'how we met' tale for our children."

Her brow arched at that. Them with babies? *Puh-lease!* "What-ever, Christopher."

Jiggling his hand, Chris brought her attention to the fact that he hadn't lowered it during their entire exchange. "Please, come here? Let me try. If you feel nothing, then there's nothing, and I won't bother you again," he prodded.

Yeah, right! Nothing. Electricity sizzled between them, and they hadn't touched. What would happen if they kissed? She inwardly shook that thought away. No kissing.

Taking a giant leap of faith, she placed her hand in his. He yanked her to him. Their bodies made intimate contact. Her world shifted. Righted. She swallowed hard.

Chris wrapped one arm around her waist. In a natural move, as if they'd been dancing together all their lives, she rested her left hand on his buff upper arm. Grabbing her other hand, he inter-twined their fingers.

One piano ballad transitioned into another. Chris swayed them to the beat. Feeling a wild desire to lay her head on his solid pectoral, Renée straightened her posture. She dropped her gaze to keep from staring into his. Images of the stories they would tell trespassed in her mind's eye: them married, gorgeous little mocha-la-ta-cha-tatte babies with a mash of their features. Unbidden, a ridiculous, content sigh escaped her.

They weren't moving. She glanced up at his broad chest. His eyes locked on hers.

"Eyes on me," Chris commanded, "always."

Floored and aroused by his dominance, she complied.

As if on cue, the song playing changed. Another soulful ballad, but this wasn't an instrumental. This was a song, a singer she loved, a song that from now until forever would be her favorite: Gavin DeGraw's "More Than Anyone."

Shock of shocks, Chris knew the words. He mouthed them, ensuring she understood these weren't just the songwriter's words, but his to her.

He sang of a desire to be whatever she needed. Friend. Confidant. Lover. Pleaded with her to consider giving him a chance. He vowed to provide for all her needs. Her heart clenched as he pledged to love her more than anyone.

"What are you trying to do to me?" she croaked in a bewildered whisper.

Smirking, he reproached her, "Shh... We're dancing."

Renée couldn't watch him fall. And that's what was happening. He was falling, but not alone. As he lip-synced about being available for her anytime, she fell in love, too. But she needed to protect him. Loving him meant loving him enough to protect him... from her.

She steeled her tone, but unwilling to destroy the mood, didn't raise it. "Why are you doing this?"

"Listen to the song," he directed. "I want to show you that someone can care about you."

"What makes you think I need that?"

"'Cuz, no one ever has. At least, not in the exact way you need," he stated, self-assured.

Her eyes widened in surprise. "And you think you can?"

"I know I can. Do you remember what we talked about that summer before I lost my weight?"

Renée flipped through her memory Rolodex. Nothing jumped out at her. Oddly, she recalled every minute detail of negative experiences, but something as innocent as a conversation didn't register. What did that say about her mentality? Too much to contemplate now. She shook her head.

"Rand, Lex, and Drew were swimming," he prompted, attempting to jog her memory. Still, nothing came to her. He went on, "Some random girls followed me to your house. They teased me for not taking off my T-shirt. You were sitting on the deck reading. That Hanson song came on." He chuckled at the memory. "Even then it was old, but you loved it."

Oh, my word!

She remembered. Although it was a CD, not the radio. Hanson hadn't been a particular favorite, but their song "Weird" resonated with her. They'd sung of feeling invisible, alone, about not being impressive enough to stand out but being too weird to fit in.

Two years into living with the Suttons, she'd been struggling to find her place in the world and their family. Four ice cream sandwiches and as philosophical a conversation as a twelve and fifteen-year-old could have helped. The rest of the afternoon, she and chubby Chris shared secrets, laughed at dumb jokes, and made fun of the bimbos fawning over her handsome brother and friends.

"Yeah, I remember now," she said. "Do you remember the Isle of the Too Cute?"

He laughed a hearty belly laugh, which vibrated through him and shook her. "Hell, yeah! It's where we banished all *stereotypically* attractive people. I sent Mark Wahlberg, Jensen Ackles, and Jared Leto. Who'd you send?" His brows bunched as he struggled to remember. "Oh! Amanda Seyfried, Gabrielle Union, and Mila Kunis."

"You forgot Garrett Hedlund," she reminded him, enjoying the trip down memory lane.

"Oh, how could I forget?" he jested. "Do you remember what you said that day?"

Sheesh! Buzzkill. She didn't, but she knew whatever her adolescent self said was about to bite her in the ass. Renée shook her head.

"We'd finished our seventh ice cream sandwich, and you said, *No matter how invisible you feel, I'll always see you. We'll be weirdoes together.* You saw me that day. Not who I would become or my rolls. You saw me. Inspired me to embrace who I was. You helped me gain confidence when you felt like garbage. Endeared me to you without realizing it."

Blinking away tears, she stared, dumbfounded into his eyes. She had no clue she'd had such an impact on him. Funnier still, he'd had a profound effect on her, too. That day, her crush on him grew at an alarming rate.

"You stopped 'seeing' me because I didn't stay the odd man out while you have lived in a perpetual state of odd woman out syndrome. I never stopped seeing you," Chris asserted. "I may have gotten sidetracked, bought into my hype for a bit. But I see you. I always have. You belong to me. I belong to you. We weirdoes fit together."

How could he be so sure?

"Chris," she tried reasoning with him, "I'm not worth the effort."

His eyes darkened. "Who lied to you?"

"I'm not the girl people take chances on," she explained. "There's always something better than me. Even my biological parents knew that. My entire biological family knows that. I make no impression on anyone—good *or* bad. And no one cares how what they do, or don't do, affects me. Nobody loves me this way. I accepted that a long time ago, and all this"—she waved their joined hands to encompass the room—"gives me false hope."

Chris's lips turned down, his entire expression that of a woeful bleeding heart.

Realizing her error, Renée stiffened. "Oh, my God! I'm such a whiner."

"Why do you do that?" Chris scolded.

"What?"

"Make jokes when things get serious or when you're sad?"

"Because my feelings don't matter," she answered honestly. "And it's better to laugh than cry, right? I heard something about it taking more muscles to frown than smile." She smiled, then frowned, smiled, then frowned to lighten the mood.

"God, Renée, you're doing it again," he groused. "Just be real. Feel what you feel. You don't have to deal with it alone anymore. I'm with you," he said, rich, gravelly voice sinfully low.

"Chris, I—"

His mouth swooped down, crushing hers.

CHAPTER THIRTY

Chris couldn't help himself. He'd wanted to kiss her since she walked in. With a thin, gray fleece hoodie and black yoga pants on, she was dressed for running—something he wouldn't allow again.

Mashing his lips with hers, he took her mouth in a bruising kiss. He firmly pressed until the pressure caused her to gasp. Then he attacked with such fervor their teeth knocked. Not allowing that to detour him, he nibbled her plump bottom lip. Breath mingling, they both panted, needing more. And he obliged. His tongue delved inside her mouth, twirled around, and glided over hers. She massaged his, sucked it into her mouth. Desiring the same attention, his cock jerked in response. Without breaking their ardent kiss, he advanced. Forced her backward.

The backs of her knees hit the bed; Renée froze into a block of ice.

Nope, not tonight. Tonight, Chris would physically express his feelings for her. Claim her so thoroughly she never questioned who she belonged to again. He smacked her ass. She yelped and broke the kiss. Gripping her under the arms, he lifted her. Slowly. Let her body skate against his. The heat of her core sliding up the length of his erection almost undid him. Chills racked his body. Lust-glazed brown eyes looked upon him. Her lips parted in a silent gasp. Hoisting her up, her breasts came level with his mouth.

Dammit! Why didn't he strip her first?

"Wrap your legs around my waist," he growled.

She didn't move.

"Make me ask you twice, and I will rip through your flimsy pants and fuck you where we stand. I'd rather make love to you on the bed, but I'm flexible."

Yes, his manner was gruff, but they'd been doing this a while. Weeks of foreplay—a man could only take so much.

Renée trembled in his arms. After a tense second, shaky legs wound around his hips. Renée crossed her ankles behind his back. Thighs he'd underestimated the strength of, squeezed him hard. One arm around her back fastened her torso to his. Arms draped around his neck; her fingers slithered into the hair at his nape. Uncertainty lit her eyes.

Unwilling to allow her time to concoct another excuse for why this shouldn't happen, he took her lips fast—deepened the kiss immediately—forced his tongue past the seam of her closed lips.

He swallowed her moans. Reaching behind him, he pulled her boots off. Threw them. They thumped against a wall somewhere. He'd started the kiss, should've kept control of it, but when her slick tongue swirled around his, he felt drunk. An exhilarating surge of desire coursed through him. Overwhelmed him. Renée ground her hips, rubbing herself on the tip of his dick through his pants. Chris groaned.

He had to have her now. Lowering her to the bed, he unzipped her sweater in one swift motion. Shit, another shirt.

Crawling down her petite frame, he kissed her navel, then eased away. He stood at the edge of the bed.

Confusion marred her beautiful brown face. Her lower lip poked out in the most adorable pout he'd ever seen.

Legs spread. Chris grabbed her ankles. Dragged Renée toward the end of the bed. The tail of her ponytail trailed behind her. Crooking a finger, he beckoned her to him.

Ever defiant, she propped herself up on her elbows. A knowing smile flirted with her lips. When she arched a challenging brow, Chris threw his entire arm into the summons.

Renée grinned; twin dimples indented each cheek. She sat up.

"Arms up," he commanded in his best sergeant major bass.

With a saucy smirk and a brief squint of defiance, she obeyed.

Leaning down, eyes steady on hers, he snagged the hem of her tank top.

Her smile melted.

Yeah, baby, this is serious.

Grabbing hold of the offending material in both hands, he tore it down the middle. Unbound breasts the size of full, perfectly round grapefruit bobbed. Chris nearly swallowed his tongue. No bra. Hadn't expected that. Nipples, the exact shade of the Hershey's kisses sprinkled on the ground, pebbled under his intense gaze. His breath caught. Brushing one beaded peak with his knuckle, he dropped to his knees in front of Renée's parted thighs.

She gulped audibly. Her eyes tracked his every move.

He relieved himself of dress shoes and socks, tossed them aside. A quick tug at the bottom of Renée's yoga pants divested her of them. His eyes bulged at the unobstructed view of a neat, thin strip of hair stopping above glistening nether lips. Fuck! No panties either! She was killing him. He nearly shamed himself at the sight. His eyes flipped up to hers.

Tears filled their light cognac depths.

This wasn't his usual confident vixen, eager to show her shit that he'd found in some bar or club. Not a woman who viewed him as, as much of a conquest as he did her. This wasn't even the normal don't-give-a-shit Renée. Staring out at him was someone unsure, someone shy with vulnerabilities he understood.

He straightened to his full height.

Taking the comforter with her, dumping rose petals and chocolate on the floor, Renée scrambled to the head of the bed. She discarded each side of her ruined tank top. Back pressed to the wall, she burrito wrapped herself. Her eyes stayed glued to him. Fear creased her brows, pursed her lips.

Hands where she could always see them, he unbuttoned his shirt. Shrugging out of it, he allowed the garment to drift to the ground. He looked to make sure Renée was still with him. She was. Seeing his exposed chest, her gaze changed to something resembling wary, half-mast desire. Chris unzipped his slacks, released the button. Shoving pants with boxers down his legs, his erection, thick and heavy, sprang free. He stepped out of the bundle.

It required every ounce of self-control he possessed not to rip open that comforter and do what they both wanted. This situation demanded finesse. He climbed onto the bed, kneeled near the edge. Although he'd made no sudden moves, Renée curled her legs back so no part of her touched him. She stared at his dick. Licked her lips. Pre-cum beaded at the tip. Lurching forward, Chris nearly mauled her. Wide, scared eyes jumped to his face, holding him in place. Scaring her was the last thing he wanted to do right now.

"Come here."

Renée shook her head.

"You can keep the blanket. I promise not to touch you unless you ask," Chris assured her. "I just want to show you something."

She arched a skeptical brow.

"Not that—can't hide that."

That certainty got her to scoot closer. A decent gap separated them, but she was close enough to see something he'd shown to no one besides his doctors.

He pointed to deep, off-colored groves carved into both hips, down the outside of his thighs and buttocks. She slapped a hand over her mouth, but he heard the gasp, anyway. No matter how much he tanned, the stretch marks remained visible. Tanning made them less obvious but didn't get rid of them. It looked like a tiger, or some other wild animal had attacked him.

"Are those stretch marks? Guys don't get…" her sentence trailed off. Couldn't dispute the evidence.

"Yeah, we get 'em, too. And not for something worthwhile, like creating life. Growth spurts, drastic weight loss… I changed a lot that last summer," he explained. "These are constant, embarrassing reminders of the lonely, fat kid I used to be. You can't see them if I don't point them out, and I don't. Most women are too busy staring at"—he waved a hand at his muscular physique and above-average cock—"to notice them."

She nodded as if she understood.

Chris not only knew she did, but her scars were worse.

"I've never shown anyone, outside of my doctors, my insecurity. Not even my friends know," he confirmed, knowing she'd ask. "Just you. You're still the only person who gets to see me. I showed you mine. Please, trust me enough to show me yours," he implored. "*I* want to see *you*."

Watery eyes the size of saucers studied him. Wordlessly, Renée scooted back, repositioned herself at the head of the bed. She leaned against the wall.

He'd thought opening up to her, showing her that even the biggest asshole could be vulnerable, would help, but it hadn't. He'd content himself with—

She slid down the wall until she lay flat on her back. Sucking in a loud, measured breath, she held it and released the edges of the comforter. She bared herself completely to him.

Chris felt as if he'd been bestowed with some great honor. And he had. This was more important than love in Renée's mind. This was trust.

Lowering to his hands and knees, he crept up her body until they were nose-to-nose. A solitary tear escaped the corner of her eye, racing toward her ear. Swooping down, he licked the salty tear. Took it and her secrets into his safekeeping. With saintly patience, which caused his biceps to shake, he held himself over her. Waiting.

On her exhale, his face was awash in her sweet breath. Pointy nipples jabbed his chest. Breathing labored, she murmured the words he needed to hear. "Chris, touch me, please?"

"Won't stop until you scream, baby," he promised in a husky drawl, grinning.

His knee shoved her legs apart, providing his body with a nice cradle between her creamy thighs. Sweeping up both her arms, he lifted them above her head. Thumb and forefinger encircling her wrists, he pinned her arms to the bed. He nuzzled the left side of her neck. Found a three-inch-long scar too close to her carotid artery, traced it with the tip of his tongue.

As he sucked the skin there into his mouth, Renée whimpered. He released it with a pop. Moving on, he located the multitude of lash marks running the length of her ribcage. She knew he'd discovered them because the hand gripping her opposite hip tightened. He made a garbled noise in the back of his throat, a repressed growl. She wished he'd let go of her arms so she could cover the crisscrossed scars forming diamond shapes that appeared as if she'd tanned with a chain-link fence. Time healed the angry lines, but the discolored slashes were ever-present. He hadn't seen her back or the matching marks on the other side yet.

Sharp teeth and firm lips nipped her scarred skin. Under the pleasure-pain, Renée flinched. Shivers skittered up her spine.

Chris's face appeared in her line of vision. "Stay out of your head. You're beautiful."

Instead of resuming his ministrations on her sides, he rose over her. Went to her wrists; hard, smooth abdominals hovered above her face. Unable to help herself, she lifted her head as much as possible and licked the mountainous hills. His stomach muscles bunched, clenched. She swirled her tongue in his belly button. His heavy length twitched where it rested almost between her breasts. Moisture from the tip dribbled onto her skin. Chris kissed the crescent moon scar on the bone of her right wrist.

He let go of her wrists then, but she didn't lower her arms. He ran the tips of his fingers down her arms, tickling the sensitive skin. At her mouth, he dove right in. He kissed her with enthusiasm. She breathed his breath. He breathed hers. Their chests rose and fell in rapid succession as they devoured each other with startling hunger. She squirmed underneath him, bringing her core in contact with his lower abdomen. An erotic kiss. Tingles shot through her swollen clit.

Renée wanted nothing more than to have him inside her. Her own juices coated her inner thigh. She wrapped her legs around his waist. She brought her arms down, raked her fingers through his silky hair. Scratched his scalp. Chris moaned into her mouth, urging her on. Swiveling her hips, her mound collided with his abs. She groaned. Removing her hands from his hair, she dragged her nails up and down his sweat-slicked back. Reached, clutched the top of his firm glutes, then scraped from there to his back. Not a butt girl, but his ass was amazing.

Allowing their tongues one last tangle, she broke the heated kiss. "Please... please," she panted. "Inside... inside."

He looked down at her; his dilated pupils nearly eclipsed the mesmerizing blue. His ordinarily sharp features stood out even more starkly in the glow of candlelight. "I've never had unprotected sex—I promise. But I want you to trust me. I'll wear a condom if you want. Trust me to keep you safe."

She searched his face for any hint of deception, found none. Depo-Provera prevented pregnancy. She'd been on the shot for over two years, hadn't had a period the entire time. That was one worry down, but did she want to take this step? Her heart galloped, drowned out the music playing softly in the background and her ragged breaths. As she trembled beneath him, he shook above her.

Renée shut out everything screaming inside her that said no. Rocking her hips, she let her body say yes.

Chris kissed her forehead and mouthed, "Thank you." Then his golden chest rose in front of her face. She bit his nipple ever so lightly, twirled her tongue around the stiff peak. Tasted the salt of sweat and musk that was uniquely Chris.

Hissing, he snatched her left leg up and opened her to him. The tip of his erection played in her wetness. Renée's muscles clenched, anticipating his thick intrusion. He rolled his hips. The head of his penis disappeared. Renée quivered. On its descent, it kissed her wet hole. Retreated again momentarily. Expectation zinged through her veins. She inhaled through her nostrils. One fierce thrust seated him deep inside her.

Fire shot through her. She gasped. Stars flashed before her eyes. The sound Chris made was not that of a man, but a feral beast. He stilled, permitting her time to adjust to his girth. She had never felt so full before. He was breathing hard, holding back. He ground against her. Pubic bone met pubic bone. Renée's insides quaked as, pressed snug against her, he rolled his hips. Unimaginable pleasure tore through her as he hit a delicious spot within her, and her inner walls rippled around his length. Waving her hips, she strove to get him to move.

And move he did. He retreated, not all of him, but enough to make her clutch at him. Squeeze to keep him within her core. With torturous slowness, he sunk inch after smooth, steel inch into her. She felt each vein on his shaft as it slid into her. Before reaching the hilt, Chris rotated his hips, causing him to slip out, then glide in. He swiveled counterclockwise, dove deep. Withdrew.

Renée struggled to get air into her lungs. He felt so good. Her eyes rolled back in her head at the fire he stoked. Seeming to lose control, he thrust. His strokes were harsh. Powerful. In. Out. In. It felt as if he were touching her soul. Each thrust scalded her. If this was what burning was like, she wanted to burn forever with him. She strained against him; he pushed against her. They couldn't get close enough to each other. His balls slapped against her perineum, heightening her pleasure.

She was so close. Her stomach muscles tightened, coiled. Chris's grunts and her moans engulfed Usher's "Dive" playing in the background. He buried himself to the hilt, and her womb contracted. Her orgasm hit fast, drowning her in sensation. Her toes and fingertips went numb.

She hadn't realized she'd closed her eyes until she heard Chris chanting. "Open. Your. Eyes." He punctuated each word with a punishing thrust.

Doing as requested, she opened her eyes. He hunkered down, stared at her with a desire so hot it melted her. His kiss burned her before he pulled out. She reached out, pumped his shaft, slick with her juices. Balancing the bulk of his weight on his forearm, he leaned to the side, granting her better access. One pump. Two pumps. Three. He bucked into her hand, shuddered. Jet after jet of warm semen splashed her stomach.

Chris held himself steady for a moment before falling beside her. They lay, struggling to catch their breath. He scooted close, snuggling her side. Renée rested her head on his chest, ear pressed to his heart. The beat was erratic, yet for the first time, she was at peace.

CHAPTER THIRTY-ONE

Renée stared in wonder at the ceiling. Candlelight flickered, casting sinuous moving shadows that created a hypnotic rhythm. Her sigh pierced the quiet room.

I had sex with Christopher Clark; her mind chanted again and again. *Mind-blowing, life-altering sex with Christopher Clark.*

Now she understood what the fuss was about. The man was gorgeous and hung like a stallion. He'd chosen her to sleep with—hats off. Of course, in hindsight, she realized the stupidity of that decision, but she'd been lust-crazed when he'd asked. Anyway, if they were going to do it, then she'd wanted nothing between them. She believed him when he said he'd never had unprotected sex. Rumors about his sexual prowess never mentioned him being irresponsible. Somewhere in their afterglow, he assured her he got tested often and always carried the results on him.

With the postcoital bliss dissipating, Renée's nervousness and insecurity rushed back. She tucked the white top sheet around her nude body, shoved the ends under her. After they'd caught their breath, Chris strolled, unabashed by his nakedness, into the bathroom. She assumed he'd gone to freshen up. His return not even a minute later with a warm, soapy washcloth surprised her. He cleaned his seed off her stomach, placed a soft kiss on her belly, then took the washcloth to the bathroom, where he was now.

The bed dipped, signaling his return. Renée's eyes stayed locked on the ceiling. A firm yank stole the sheet she'd just adjusted from under her. Goosebumps sprang to life as the cool air hit her skin. Chris slid in next to her and covered them both. Spooning her side, his sleeping cock rested against the curve of her waist. He pushed a hand behind her head, so she lay on his massive bicep. His other arm draped over her middle. Grabbing her hand, he twined their fingers. The weave of her brown skin and his white skin was beautiful.

"You okay?" he asked near her ear.

A zing of electricity shot through her, reigniting her arousal.

"Did I hurt you, make you uncomfortable?"

Renée stared into the dimness, dazed. She couldn't be any less hurt. Somehow, the stress and sorrow, her constant companions, had disappeared. Chris did what Xanax hadn't been able to do in three years: relax her. Soothe her. Take her mind off everything except him.

Snuggling closer to him, she grazed his flaccid length. He hardened. "No," said with a sigh. "I'm fine. Are you okay?"

"Umm... Yes. Duh!" He chuckled. "I'm more than okay. The only way this moment could be more perfect is if you'd make me a sandwich."

"You're an ass." Renée laughed. If her hands weren't otherwise occupied, she would've smacked him for saying some dumb shit like that.

Chris nuzzled her cheek and ear. His whiskered chin tickled. Warm breath in her ear made her wet all over again.

"So, what do we tell Andrew?" he asked the dreaded question as her laugher died.

Shuddering in disgust, Renée shook her head. "I really don't want to think about my brother while I'm lying naked in bed with his best friend." She shot him a look from the corner of her eye, letting him know she was serious.

Thankfully, he didn't press the issue.

Renée didn't know how to proceed. They'd done the unthinkable. No turning back for either of them now. She felt the ties binding them together as if an actual lasso roped around her heart. Andrew would lose his shit when he found out. Somehow, she didn't think Chris would be too keen on keeping this low-key anymore. Although it was on the tip of her tongue to ask anyway, she wouldn't.

They hadn't defined what they were to each other, but he was the type of presumptive, possessive guy who wouldn't ask her to be his girlfriend. He'd declare it, and she'd find out when everyone else did. In an uncharacteristically submissive way, she got excited over the prospect of him telling her how things were going to be. Sometimes it was nice to have someone else take the lead. Hypervigilance and pretending to have all the answers all the time was tiring.

Comfortable silence encased them in a cocoon of bliss as they lay. No worries of tomorrow, of consequences for this union, penetrated their utopia built for two. Even their breathing was in sync. His hard chest rose. As she inhaled, her naked breasts lifted under the sheet. Did he feel the new connection?

Damn, when had she become so sappy!

"What *do* you want to talk about then?" Chris asked, breaking into her thoughts.

She shrugged; a lazy lift of shoulders that were, for once, relieved of the constant weight they carried. "I don't know. I haven't done this in years. What do you normally talk about after..." Renée paused, searching for the right word. Making loved seemed presumptuous and calling what they'd done sex or fucking didn't seem right either. "You know?" she finished.

Chris chuckled yet refrained from providing any clarification. His guffaw took on a peculiar, uneasy edge. Calming, he said, "You don't want to know, trust me."

"Why?" Now she had to know. "It's kinky, isn't it?" she guessed in a dry tone.

"No," his denial came out in a high-pitched voice. He shifted his body, laughing another uncomfortable laugh. "It's not kinky at all. I just don't usually have too many *talks* afterward."

She understood. "Ohhh... so it's normally wham-bam; thank you, what's-your-face?"

"Kind of," he admitted sheepishly. "Not that heartless, though."

"Well, if that's what you do, then..." Letting the sentence hang, Renée released his hand, moved to get out of bed.

Chris damn near tackled her, pressed his total weight into her to keep her still. "Whoa! Where are you going?"

"Don't want to mess with your routine," she replied.

"You know it's not like that with you."

"What makes me different?" she asked, then held her breath, waiting for his answer. She hated to admit it, but she *needed* to know.

Seeming to sense she'd stay; Chris resumed his position beside her. She readjusted the sheet that had almost slipped off in her pretend escape maneuver. He laced their fingers, stroked up and down her arm with the backs of his fingers.

His loaded exhale sent chills down her spine. When he still didn't speak, Renée looked at him out of the side of her eye. Chris's answering grin stole her breath.

With a tiny nudge, he stole her heart. "'Cause it's you, shortie," he stated in his uncanny southern drawl. "Since I was fifteen and those incredible amber eyes flecked with gold looked at me, you patted the lounge chair seat next to you and... I was yours."

Unbidden tears filled Renée's eyes. God, he could be sweet sometimes. Yet something within her had to play devil's advocate.

"This could be drunk talk. You know how people get all philosophical after smoking weed? You might feel different when you're sober."

Shaking his head, Chris pursed his lips. "Not possible. Neither of us smokes weed. How many ways can I say it, Renée? This wasn't a snap decision. I might seem shallow, but I wouldn't let things go this far," he said, tweaking her nipple under the sheet for good measure. "Not without putting serious thought into it. Shit! I left the city for over a year to think it through. That night I heard you sing, something happened to me. I want to be the type of man you deserve... someone good enough to be with you."

Renée chuckled, attempting to lighten the mood. "I had no idea your shallow waters ran so deep," she teased.

"Ha. Ha. Funny," Chris said. He untangled their hands and tickled her stomach.

She slapped his hand away. The way their bodies pressed intimately together tickled somewhere lower. Warmth blossomed low in her belly, crept up. Dang! One taste and she was ready for more.

"You mean something to me," Chris continued. "Once someone means what you mean to me, there's no going back."

Eying him with a hint of skepticism, she conceded, "Okay, let's say I believe you. What happens next? Where do we go from here?"

"Well, you lay with me a little longer." Chris peppered kisses down the side of her face. He lifted onto his elbow, stared down at her. Unfathomable emotion twinkled in lazurite eyes. Nudges to the shoulder closest to him forced Renée to roll to her side. The new position placed Chris behind her. "Before we get up and cover our tracks, I have a point to make," he stated, laughter coloring his playful statement.

"Oh?" Renée replied. Flirtatious mirth filled her tone.

A double tap on the outside of her thigh prompted her to raise her leg. Rough hands took a firm grip of her leg, held it high. A comprehensive, coarse-haired thigh wedged between her thighs. Tickled her smooth skin.

Chris's no longer sleeping, rigid member, nestled against her now sopping wet folds as if making itself at home. Sliding down the length of her slit, it stopped just shy of paradise. The tip pressed into her resistant entrance. Renée didn't think she'd ever get used to his size. Her hips wiggled of their own volition, desperate for the inevitable merging.

Simultaneous groans of frustration escaped their lips.

"Interesting point..." she panted, pushing her hips back into him.

"Isn't it, though?" Chris's harsh response. "I was just inside you. Now it's like I was never here. Let. Me. In," he demanded through clenched teeth, punctuating each word with a forceful thrust.

Renée ground her ass into him, creating delicious friction where he was lodged at her opening. She wanted—no, needed—him fully seated inside her. Now!

A large hand slid down her quivering stomach; going lower, he found her throbbing clit. Chris parted her labia. His finger, slick with her juices, circled the bundled flesh. Chills raced through her entire body.

"You like that?" Chris asked. Pure male satisfaction tinged his voice.

"Yes," Renée breathed.

"Then let me in." Rolling his hips, Chris tried to work himself in.

"I'm trying."

"You will not shut me out again, Renée," Chris growled in her ear. Shivers skittered down her spine. He gripped her side harshly, holding her still. "You. Are," he said each word on an almost brutal thrust. "Mine." With that, he slammed deep into Renée's walls.

"Yours!" Renée nearly screamed. Her shout wasn't from pain but from being filled completely. Heart. Mind. Body. And soul.

CHAPTER THIRTY-TWO

"What are you doing? I thought you finished that last night. Feeling a little OCD, are we?"

Renée glanced up at Ashley from the notebook she'd been writing in. Sunlight snaked in through the curtains. A strip of light streaked across the middle of her friend's face. Ashley's freckles were more pronounced under the sun's bold assault. Hazel eyes squinted, watching Renée with humor and a teensy bit of suspicion. One well-plucked eyebrow rose slightly.

Careful not to rouse more questions in her friend's mind, she discreetly placed her forearm like a bookmark over what she'd written. The notebook's cover flopped closed on top of her arm. Renée hoped the action appeared unintentional, although it was anything but. She prayed she successfully wiped the silly grin from her face that she'd worn since returning to her room last night. Every time she thought of what she and Chris had done—*four times*—a stupid grin materialized before she knew what was happening. Her cheeks ached from the number of times she'd caught herself.

Something in Ashley's gaze said she hadn't gone as unnoticed as she thought.

"You're stupid!" Renée said, going for nonchalance. "I'm just checking over some stuff. I woke up with... questions on my mind. More questions. Soooo... I was writing them down before they disappeared."

Why did that sound more like a question than an explanation?

Christina dressed in fishnet stockings, a dark, floral print, mid-thigh length skirt, and a red, cable knit, cozy sweater, which appeared a bit too big, given that the sleeves reached her knuckles, exited the vanity area. She eyed Renée curiously. "Née, you had something like—eight hours to think of questions? Unless you're planning to go all Spanish Inquisition-style, what more could you ask? And your phone has a notes app. Why are you writing anything?"

Humor drained from Ashley's face. She leaned her jeans-clad hip on the dresser across from where Renée sat at the desk. Full-blown suspicion lit her eyes. "What did you end up doing last night?" She crossed her arms over her long-sleeved, white, V-neck T-shirt-covered chest. "Eight hours? That's a lot of time to have on your hands."

Renée averted her gaze, lowered her head. God, was she smiling? No, not now! She couldn't smile while they were both paying far too much attention. Her cheeks burned. Oh, great! Thank the Lord for dark skin. They wouldn't be able to make out her—

"Are you blushing?" Christina asked.

Never mind. Of all the days for brown skin to fail Renée, of course, it would be today. Footsteps alerted Renée to her bestie moving closer.

Trying to play it off, she looked up. "Am I what now?" she responded seconds before one of the biggest smiles she'd ever felt stretched her lips.

Christina and Ashley traded wide-eyed, shocked gazes.

"What's that about?" Ashley asked, chuckling.

"Nothing?" Shit! Why was everything coming out like a question? Like she wasn't totally sure her answers were acceptable. Even her voice went up higher than usual. She tried again, "Nothing. I got caught up talking to Chris last night, so I didn't get to finish all my questions."

"You got caught up talking to Chris?" A healthy dose of skepticism layered Ashley's grumbled inquiry. "About what? Hair gel and push-ups?"

Was it so impossible to believe Chris thought about more than his looks? Months ago, she would've sworn he sat around kissing pictures of himself all day, but since he'd moved into her house, she'd seen another side of him. Yes, he was still more self-absorbed than most, but vulnerability, empathy, loyalty, and heart were also there. For the first time in a long time, Renée saw why her brother and Alex were friends with him.

How had she not recognized the kind-hearted, gentle-spirited, self-conscious chubby kid still in there? She'd labeled him. Decided who he was, stuck him in a box, then locked and threw away the key. Her entire life, she'd fought being labeled. She'd wanted to be seen as more than the abused, abandoned little girl, the adopted kid, the black girl. How ironic that she would be guilty of the exact thing she cut people to the quick for.

Renée rolled her eyes. "Ha. Ha." She glared at Ashley. "He's not that bad." She attempted to defend him without being too obvious. "Once you get past all that pretty boy crap."

This time, Christina's brown eyes narrowed on her. She stepped closer to Renée, as if invading her personal space would reveal untold truths. "What are you talking about—he's not *that* bad?"

Yanking her arm out of her notebook, Renée slammed her hand on the cover. "Is there an echo in here? He's not."

Ashley leered at Renée for hours, it seemed, but it was mere seconds. She squirmed under such intense scrutiny, fiddled with her discarded pen on the desktop.

Ashley gasped, mouth agape. Dismayed hazel eyes widened. "You slut!"

"What?" Renée jumped to her feet. "Slut! Why? How?"

At that precise moment, Renée saw understanding dawn on Christina. Her jaw fell slack, as if it'd come unhinged.

"What did you do?" Christina breathed aghast.

"We had a pact," Ashley reminded her, in a clipped tone. "Don't you remember the *We Hate Chris Clark and Will Never Sleep with Him* vow? You made us promise, and…" She paused, puffed out air through her nostrils, then continued, "You broke it!"

Someone give this girl an Oscar.

"Shh…" Renée cautioned, fanning both hands. Her brother could be anywhere. Drew was good at his job for a reason. If he even sort of sensed something more than the stress of finding her birth family was going on, he'd be tenacious. Dog after a bone style. And he'd find out, too. "Shut up, guys! Drew will kill Chris and have me committed if he hears you."

Hand to her heart, Ashley sighed. Slumped. She sagged against the dresser. "Of course, we won't say anything." Her words were calm. Rational. Very unlike her. "You're about to do something big." Ashley pushed off the dresser. She approached Renée like someone gauging a dog's temperament before petting it. She even proffered her hand with caution.

Renée latched onto the offered appendage to see where the Hell this was going. Ashley tugged her forward, toward the bed nearest them. She sat, patting the space beside her. Following her friend's silent plea, Renée sat. Chrissy got her other flank on the bed.

Christina rubbed her back. Ashley kept hold of her hand.

This felt like an intervention, or they were about to break some news to her—terminal illness type news.

"You had a moment of weakness," Ashley crooned. "We're all entitled to one every now and again."

Renée snatched her hand away. Shook Christina's hand off her back. She glared at them. "It was more than that," she protested. "I don't know what it's gonna turn into, or what I want it to become, but it was more than some temporary lapse in judgment."

Christina studied Renée. Her mouth dropped open, and her eyes bulged like she'd seen bigfoot superimposed over Renée's features. "Oh, my gosh!" Christina exclaimed. "Shallow stupidity is contagious."

"Shut up! It wasn't like that," Renée reiterated. "There were candles, music—we danced. Talked. This was so not the 'all the girls want me cuz I'm the bee's knees, Chris.' He thinks—a lot. More than any of us would imagine. He said I flipped a switch inside him."

Ashley's eyes leveled on Renée. "Yeah, his penis. It gets all big then goes down." Speaking once more in that damn soft voice meant to coax shy children away from mothers trying to leave them with unfamiliar sitters, she said, "Renée? After your relationship with He Who Shall Remain Nameless, you made me promise to slap sense into if you were ever stupid for some dude again. I'm trying hard not to slap you right now, but the struggle is real. Haven't you listened to any of my bad date stories? All dudes say sappy shit. It's bait."

Resuming the tender caress of her back, Christina picked up where Ashley left off. "Sweetie, he's that kind of guy. You know, hit 'em and quit 'em, beat 'em and street 'em? He wanted to get laid. Regular guys love the chase. For Chris, the chase might as well be an undiluted aphrodisiac. You're the ultimate catch. He caught you. But Chris is a catch and release type of guy. We've seen it hundreds of times."

Her eyebrows rose. A smirk flitted across her lips. Inside, Renée felt like an elephant kicked her in the chest. Fuck breaking. Her heart shattered. They were right. She'd give Chris credit. Maybe on some level he believed what he said—the mind is a tricky thing. He could've wanted to get her into bed so badly for so long that he'd convinced himself he had sincere feelings for her. But they were right. They were right.

Renée released a long breath and... deflated. Cloud nine couldn't last forever. She just never realized falling off would hurt so much.

Chris's attention span made a toddler on Christmas seem focused. He discarded presents midway through the first rip of wrapping paper if something prettier caught his eye.

Only years of practice feigning things were all right, and foolish pride kept her smirk in place. Inside, she was... hollow, desolate. She'd walked into his lair, eyes wide open. "Beat 'em and street 'em?" she asked, reaching deep for her familiar quick wit and sarcasm.

A grin eased Christina's troubled features. A plucked eyebrow rose. "You like that? I just made it up."

"Yeah, it's great," she said, trying for flippant, but her vocal cords were as raw as her emotions. She cleared her throat. "Anyway, it isn't a big deal."

Ashley snorted, gave her a tight-lipped smile. "Née, I love you like a two-dollar hooker, and I hate to break it to you, but... it's like that. And this is a big deal."

"Andrew and Alex love him to death, and even they say he's a player," Christina said.

"The only position you'll ever have on his team is MVFWB. That's only because you're his best friend's sister. He can't shake you without ruining a lifelong friendship. Stop this before you catch feelings for him," Ashley advised.

Shit! Didn't they know when enough was enough? Sleeping with Chris was a mistake of mass proportions. Got it!

A hard knot clogged her throat, making it hard to swallow. She needed a drink, several drinks. Hell, an acid bath would do right about now. She felt dirty and ashamed. Her stomach churned. Renée stared at her hands. When had she started ringing them?

"Let's drop this, okay?" Christina said, sounding uncomfortable.

Renée glanced up to find Ashley watching her. No, not watching, but looking through her. They'd been friends since childhood. Ashley *saw* her. Shit!

Ashley let out a long-suffering sigh. Her gaze turned sympathetic, pitiful. "You love him. Dammit!"

Christina and Ashley wrapped an arm around her.

Fucking embarrassing. Unbidden, tears pricked her eyes. "Shut up! Let me go," she gritted out between clenched teeth.

A knock at the door intruded on their unintended moment.

"What!" Christina called, gruffer than she'd ever heard before.

"Move it, ladies!" Andrew shouted.

Renée hopped up. She smoothed out her burgundy hi-low dress skirt and adjusted the braided belt. Then she pegged each of her friends with a murderous glare. "Not another word about this, understood? Especially not in front of my brother or other mixed company," she ordered. "I'm done with Chris. It was temporary insanity—I'm over it."

CHAPTER THIRTY-THREE

Using his hand as a makeshift visor, Chris shielded his eyes from the sun. Feminine laughter called his attention to the stairs leading from the hotel. Ashley, Christina, and Renée made their way toward the parking lot, where he and Lex waited next to the Denali. Like an ugly designer forced to walk the runway after the models wrapped in their creations, Drew brought up the rear.

The wind tousled the hem of Renée's burgundy skirt. The scoop neck dress provided a peek-a-boo view of her plump, chocolate breasts bouncing with each step.

Mm... Chris licked his lips. He'd tapped it four times last night. Yet he wanted more. What they'd shared meant more than sex. More than getting balls deep in something he'd been determined to get into for years. However, he'd be remiss if he didn't consider the idea, she floated about him feeling different once the sexual high wore off.

He'd done a lot of sticking and moving in his time. Faces blurred together, and names? Most of those disappeared from the slate immediately. What made this different? Renée. And the high wasn't sexual. Yes, the sex was fire. The type you lather, rinse, repeat. But this high went soul deep. His soul felt high on her soul. Her essence. It recognized it as its counterpoint. She inspired him to be more, strive for more. They were right together. Destined. Had him waxing poetic over her. One smile from her could right his world. One frown could destroy his entire life. Renée invented the slate. It couldn't be cleaned of her.

He woke up with a spring in his step today. Even forwent his prolonged grooming ritual in favor of getting out here to see her faster. Was there anything beyond obsession? If so, Renée was his. Watching the hypnotic sway of her hips made his dick hard. Instead of dampening as *she* assumed, his feelings this morning amplified. Chris stared into her eyes as she approached with her friends. He wanted there to be no mistaking his con-tinued interest and intentions.

Lex opened the door to the Denali. Bowed his head. "Your chariot awaits, m'ladies'," he said, using a horrible British ac-cent.

Dude tried too hard.

Speaking of trying too hard or trying at all. Renée seemed to avoid looking at him. Already, he'd tried to catch her eye several times. He could believe it was coincidental, her turning her head in the opposite direction one time. Even thinking she needed to dig into her purse like a champion spelunker another time. But she never avoided Lex, which for reasons no matter how rational, still pissed him off. Given his position, right beside the dude, she had no choice but to see him, at least in her peripheral. Yet, she persisted in shifting her medium brown gaze here, there, and everywhere, except at him.

What the fuck!

"Who's driving?" Drew asked, approaching the tail end of the truck. He flipped the keys over and over in his hand. Green eyes scanned Christina's petite frame imperceptibly.

Chris was above average at noticing certain forms of tension. A pheromone bloodhound. Those two were putting off copious amounts of the ectohormones. Had Renée not been icing him out or not so focused on her journey, she would have picked up on the vibe between her best friend and brother, too. Of course, that didn't explain why Ashley didn't appear aware of it. Maybe all the effort it took to spurn Lex's advances made her blind to other people. Although, her being self-centered could be part of it, too.

"It's your baby. You drive," Renée stated, gazing deadpan at her brother.

There were some people she didn't mind looking at. If she thought he'd let that shit fly, she had another thing coming.

"Nope. I'm good on that," Drew said, far too casual. This wasn't Drew-like behavior. He'd kill a man for daring to touch his beloved Denali. "This might be the only semblance of a vacation I ever get. Somebody else drive. I'll kick back in the back." Drew glanced sidelong at Christina so fast Chris wasn't sure he'd seen it.

"Do we know how to get to Fort Wayne, Indiana?" Christina asked. Her oversized red sweater slipped off her shoulder, exposing creamy beige skin.

Drew's eyes lit on the subtle action. A blush swept up Christina's neck, warming her cheeks. Drew's pupils dilated. Even, square, white teeth bit into Drew's bottom lip. The scam going on between these two was reaching a boiling point. How did this escape Renée and Ashley's awareness?

"No," Renée answered, "but who needs exact directions? We have a map." She rooted around in her purse a second, then held up a folded pamphlet-looking thing, illustrating her point. "And GPS. If Drew's not driving, I can—"

"Uh-uh," Lex interjected.

Thank you, Lord! For the first time since coming back, Chris found a use for his childhood friend's presence. Lex's outburst got Renée to glance in their—and by proximity in his—direction.

Sunlight caused her deep brown skin to glow and her red undertone to stand out. Golden cognac eyes refused to connect with his dark blue ones. Each time her gaze wandered in his direction, she'd snatch it away or focus on some spot above his head. Given their enormous height difference, her 5'2" to his 6'4," the insult was overt. And he took offense.

"Hold up. Rewind," Lex requested. "You wanna drive? You? The person who gets lost going from the bathroom to her own bedroom in *her* house? I've seen you hit the wall thousands of times as you round the corner going back to your room. The same wall. It's not new. It's always been there, but you hit it like it popped up out of nowhere every time. You even look surprised when you hit it. Now, you want to drive in a whole other state. Jesus, take the wheel. Or take me." He roared with laughter.

Renée pegged Lex with a droll stare. "Hilarious," she retorted. As they rolled, her eyes skated past him once more before skittering away.

Enough!

Chris's steps were deliberate, measured. He approached Renée. Invaded her personal space. She tried to hide it, but his effect on her was clear. His gaze never left her face. Her breathing quickened. She took an infinitesimal step back. Almost bumped into Christina. Burgundy straps crisscrossing the scoop neck of her dress fought to restrain ample brown cleavage. Each rapid breath tested the fabric's endurance.

Damn, they needed more alone time. But, no, they had another hurdle to jump in their relationship. What the Hell changed between last night and this morning? He thought they'd left things on a high note. Now, she couldn't stand the sight of him. If she kept playing hard to get, he'd out her in front of everyone. Cat and mouse got old fast.

Because of his too-close-for-polite-company stance, Renée had to lift her head to see into his eyes, which he narrowed in annoyance. Her eyes widened. This wasn't low-key, but he couldn't care less. Let everybody find out. She was his, dammit! The sooner everyone else knew, the better. Her heady, clean, floral, fruity citrus scent made it hard to stay angry, but not impossible.

Get a hold of yourself!

Stealing himself against her delectable scent, he grabbed for the map. Renée yanked it out of reach.

"Give it to me, short stack." He used her nickname, but his tone was anything but playful. "I'll drive."

"No," she balked. "You don't live here like we don't live here. We all read and hear just fine—well, I don't know about you, but we do. You don't know any better than I do where to go."

"Yes, I do," he affirmed, reaching for the map held behind her back. "I'm a guy. Guys have lead in their noses. It gives us a better sense of direction than women."

Inserting herself between him and Renée, Ashley burst into hysterical laughter. "Who lied to you?!" she exclaimed. "My sense of direction works fine, fuck you very much."

"Move," Chris commanded. "Nobody's talking to you. What are you—her bodyguard?"

Ashley scoffed. Then under her breath, she said, "If I was, I dropped the ball last night."

What did that mean? Renée was adamant about not telling anyone about them. So, what the Hell was that about? He would have asked, but Ashley barreled on in typical Ashley fashion.

"What makes you think you have lead in your nose?"

"I heard it on TV," he informed her.

"Aww..." Ashley crooned, patronizing. Head titled to one side; strawberry blond hair draped over one shoulder. "Sweetie, baby, honey, the people in the big box," she said, pantomiming the shape of a flat-screen television with her index fingers, "don't always tell the truth. FYI, neither do the people on your laptop. Kind of like that person you see in the mirror every day." She glared.

Got it! So, Renée told them. Their hive-mind mentality must've warped their experience into something sordid. Welcome back, sarcastic, ruthless Renée. If he were another man, her lack of faith in him would hurt. It stung a little. Fortunately, he specialized in Renée and her mercurial moods.

Cutting his eyes at Ashley, he demanded in a tone that brooked no argument, "Give me the fucking map."

Renée moved around Ashley. Glared at him. She slapped the map into the palm of his waiting hand. Avoided any form of physical contact. She sidestepped him to enter the open back door of the Denali. Brat!

Before she climbed in, Chris hooked a finger through the brown, braided belt around her waist and dragged her back several paces.

"Really!" Renée growled.

Sauntering up to the driver's side door, he turned and flashed a cocky grin. Served her right. She was lucky he didn't spank sense into her in front of everybody.

He got in the truck.

CHAPTER THIRTY-FOUR

Much like its owner, the house was sterile. Nondescript. Not too big, not too small. Unimpressive. Nothing stood out about it. Reminded Renée of the model apartments at the luxury apartment community where she worked. They sold dreams to prospective residents. Staged the models with furniture, knick-knacks, framed photos—placed towels in bathrooms. Bookshelves were brimming with fake books. The scent of fresh-baked choco-late chip cookies filled the air with an extra, artificial "this could be home" feel. All the trappings of home were present, but the models still missed the mark.

Home was more than just appearance. Some vital components transformed an apartment or house into a home. Renée didn't know what recipe created a home, but... She scrutinized the living room she currently occupied. Stark white walls were devoid of family pictures. A large, taupe throw rug covered pristine, hickory hardwood floors. A bland, overstuffed camel couch and loveseat were situated kitty-corner from each other. In the center of the room sat a brown, metal, glass-topped coffee table. Matching end tables on either side of the loveseat were adorned with transparent glass vases filled with white silk roses, and mounted on the opposite wall was a thirty-five-inch flat-screen television. Yeah, Shenae Williams's house was hollow, not a home, in Renée's opinion.

"What brought you out here?" the woman asked, reentering the living room as if conjured by Renée's thoughts. She handed Renée bottled water. Then returned to her seat on the couch.

"Thank you," Renée accepted politely. "Umm... I decided it was time to get to know my biological family. It's been a long time since I've seen anyone."

This was so awkward. She didn't know what she'd expected. Maybe some inherent familiarity. As stupid as it sounded, Renée thought there would be some unexplainable connection between them. Like blood recognizing blood or something equally corny and movie-like. But, as she gazed at the medium, brown-skinned woman who appeared to be somewhere in her mid-thirties, she felt nothing. No spark of recognition. No feeling of kinship. Nothing.

Yes, there were minor similarities. Almond-shaped eyes, a small frame, long dark hair, and a button nose. Those were gifts from their Hispanic father. Her darker skin was from her black mother. The red undertones were from her biological mother's Native American ancestry. With all that in common, Renée still felt nothing. Like an intruder.

"Sorry if I interrupted your day. Were you on your way to work?" Renée asked, nodding toward the form-fitting gray scrubs her half-sister wore.

"No," Shenae said, shaking her head. "Just got off about an hour ago. I'm just lazy and haven't changed yet."

Renée smiled. At least, she hoped she smiled. It felt wrong. Tight. Forced. This couldn't have been weirder. She hated small talk regularly. Sitting in some stranger's house trying to bring up painful memories politely was torture.

"Last time I saw you," Shenae said, then sighed, interrupting herself. Brown eyes shifted in thought. "You were two, maybe three."

"Yeah, I've changed a little since then," Renée commented stiffly.

"My mom didn't let me spend much time with Daddy back then. They had a lot of problems. One of those being your mom."

Awesome! Just what she wanted to hear. Why had she come here? She could've bypassed this one. It's not like they'd ever met before. At least, not within Renée's ability to remember. How much credible information could this woman have that a woman scorned did not taint? Now, here she sat, the daughter of the woman who'd come between her and a relationship with her father. This day kept getting better and better.

"Sorry," Renée said, even though she wasn't sure what she was apologizing for—being born? Causing a rift in the father-daughter dynamic? None of those were her fault. Their father might have chosen her mother, but he'd never done such a thing for her.

"Don't be." Shenae chuckled. "That's their business, not ours."

Renée nodded, because she didn't know what else to do. "So..." God, this was strange. "Do you see your—I mean our—dad a lot?" she asked, highly aware of the way her voice cracked when referring to a man she had no recollection of as dad. The acid of betrayal churned her gut. Randall Sutton was her dad.

"I didn't," Shenae confirmed Renée's suspicion of her and her biological mother being the catalyst behind destroying Shenae's childhood. "But after I had kids, things changed. They needed a grandpa. So, I started having him around more."

The repeated tapping of Shenae's foot signaled her discomfit with their topic, too. Good. Renée wasn't the only one feeling like the subject of an old-school R&B song.

"He's good with kids?" Renée asked, stunned. She figured a man who'd cheat on his woman and then pick the side chick didn't have a great moral compass. Plus, from the sounds of it, he'd abandoned

Shenae, too. Who'd of thunk he'd want anything to do with kids since he couldn't be bothered with his own?

Shenae gave another derisive laugh. "Girl, don't get it twisted. He's only good with kids he didn't father. Just ask Manuel Jr. He can tell you all about that."

That sparked her curiosity for several reasons. One was that neither she nor Andrew had dug up any contact information on her half-brother. He didn't exist in the cyber world, which was weird. Everyone has some information online nowadays.

"What happened?" she asked, genuinely interested in some part of this conversation that wasn't super uncomfortable.

"*Our father*," Shenae said disdainfully, "stole little Manuel's identity a few years back. He screwed up his credit badly. Got arrested and then skipped out. There was a warrant out for Manuel and everything. Manuel's still fighting to clear his name. He won't come around any of us anymore."

Damn! Now it made sense why they couldn't find information on Manuel Jr. Andrew was the best P.I., and if he couldn't find anything, it meant there was nothing to be found. Manuel Jr. probably got help in hiding his information, so he didn't have this problem anymore. Her biological parents were real winners. Sheesh! Neither of them seemed to have a paternal or maternal bone in their body. To think Manuel Sr. was on her list of people to see. Wonderful.

"Should I not trust Manuel senior?" she asked.

"That's up to you," Shenae said sympathetically. She shook her head. "If there is something you specifically want to know, he's your best bet. But use your best judgment. Take him and anything he says with a grain of salt. Keep your eyes open."

"Okay," she said, nodding and taking her half-sister's words under advisement.

"So," Shenae said more upbeat, "are you still a Williams, or did you get married?"

Renée almost spit out the sip of water she'd taken during the lull in the conversation. Screwing the water bottle cap on, she carefully swallowed, then laughed. And laughed. Her eyes watered. Married? Her? Right!

"Me?!" she screeched. "To whom?"

Unbidden images of Chris came to mind. Dammit! That man wouldn't leave her alone. He didn't know he occupied so many of her thoughts, but he penetrated her defenses and struck her square in the feels, leaving her to put her wayward feelings into perspective. Part of her wanted to believe he felt something for her. Who went through the trouble of decorating a hotel room, buying candles, an outfit, etcetera, etcetera, to get ass? That made little sense. It wasn't just the hotel either. He'd been doing little things for weeks. She didn't want that to be part of some perverse need to have her. But it made more sense than thinking that he'd morphed into a hopeless romantic overnight. What Ashley and Christina said was true. But she hoped it wasn't, and even if it were—which it was—she'd never out him to Drew. It was embarrassing enough that her friends knew she'd fallen for his act. She couldn't take it if Alex or Drew knew, too. Her laughter subsided with thoughts of her embarrassment and shame.

"Me, married?" she asked soberly. "Umm… No. My last name is Sutton. When I was ten, I was adopted."

"You have time. You're still young," Shenae advised as if that were at all what Renée wanted. "You could find Mr. Right Now 'till Mr. Right finds you."

Renée fought her eye roll. She laughed instead of correcting her sister's assumption. The only man her idiot heart wanted was an asshole. If he weren't, they still wouldn't work. Reasons abounded for why their two brands of crazy could never make a relationship work. Her brother was one of the biggest. They didn't date each other's friends. No matter how distant their relationship got, that fact remained. Some ill-fated relationship wouldn't come between her and Drew.

"I always wondered about you," Shenae continued, bringing their conversation full circle. "I didn't know where you ended up. Though I heard from different people that your grandmother ordered everyone in her family to stay away from you."

Anger torched her burgeoning ease. "My grandmother told people to stay away from me?" she asked, hoping she'd misheard. "And people listened? Why? I was a little kid."

Shenae shrugged. "The Johnston family is old-school. Right or wrong, the matriarch is the last word on everything. Her word is law."

Not only did she descend from drug addicts and child abusers but also manipulative sociopaths. With such a stellar family tree, it's a wonder she wasn't more fucked up.

"They took in my older sister, Kathy, though?" Confusion colored her tone. "And all the other bastard children? What was so wrong with me?" The question was rhetorical. She knew all that was wrong with her, but she'd been a little kid. Surely, her crazy hadn't manifested so young. Even if it had, what about family loyalty? Blood was supposedly thicker than water, right? She was a kid who'd been abandoned by her mom, abused by her uncle. Why leave her alone?

Sympathy-filled brown eyes stared at her. Shenae shook her head. "All I know is they're old-school, like voodoo and curses, old-school. You were more articulate, proper like me. My mom said they thought you were possessed or evil."

Evil? She'd been called evil before. Renée shook. Her heart raced. Sweat beaded on her upper lip and forehead. The temperature seemed to drop and rise all at the same time. She couldn't get it together. Her vision blurred. One word, reverberated in her ears *evil*.

Seven-year-old Renée stood in the center of a modest, large kitchen. Her clothes weren't threadbare but didn't fit how they should. Ugly, yellow-stained linoleum chilled her feet. She wiggled her toes against the cold. Several cabinets hung above ugly off-white tiled counters. Each cabinet had a small keyhole lock. All were closed except for one cracked open. A blue box of strawberry Pop-Tarts sat empty on the counter.

Light brown doe eyes stared into angry denim blues. Sweat seeped from huge pores. Pale skin tinted gray from too many years of smoking. The overweight woman standing over her was not happy.

"These are for everyone. Not just you," Genny yelled, spittle barely missing Renée's face. A very long, stringy, dirty blond ponytail swung, punctuating each angry word.

She didn't want to be bad; the group home didn't feed them enough. She was starving. Renée would've gotten something else, but the locks were different on the refrigerator. Her long, thick nails only worked to unlock the snack cabinet. Cabinets staff ate from all the time. Kids never got snacks, though. Had she known the overnight staff didn't sleep, Renée would've been quieter. Except for moonlight trickling in through the windows, it had been dark. Genny was nowhere to be found when she'd crept up the stairs.

"You're a selfish, evil little girl," Genny scolded.

Tears welled in her eyes. She was just hungry.

CHAPTER THIRTY-FIVE

*S*eated around a large wooden oval table, were people Renée swished she didn't know. These people had power over her future. She got no say in the end, and no matter what put her in this position, they were going to judge her. Literally.

An authoritative-looking brunette man with an intimidating, thick mustache and tired, discerning green eyes sat at the head of the table. In front of him, a folded, white cardboard nameplate read: Judge White. Everyone seated at the table in the conference room had a nameplate, which, to her, meant they didn't know each other. Shouldn't people deciding the fate of a ten-year-old girl at least be familiar with each other? None of them gave a crap about her, but shouldn't they know the case? She guessed not.

Glancing to her side, Renée watched her CPS caseworker, Gary Olsen, thumb through a file folder. She supposed the overweight, middle-aged Caucasian man with black frame glasses that kept sliding down his nose needed to get his notes together. He probably didn't even know who she was since she only got graced with his *presence when he came to rip her from one placement and throw her into another.*

"Returning to my home isn't an option. She's not welcome back." Bobby Greensburg, seated across the table, stated in her hoity-toity way of speech, matter of fact.

This further proved her theory about them not caring about her. Why would they ever subject her to being in a room with a woman who did the things Bobby did? Her stomach was in so many knots it felt like someone was crocheting a blanket inside her tummy. It took everything in her not to vomit at the prospect that they considered sending her back to Mrs. Greensburg's house after what she'd told them happened there.

"It's your assertion, then, that this child lied?" Judge White asked, steepling his fingers and watching Mrs. Greensburg closely.

"Yes," Mrs. Greensburg lied confidently. "She exaggerates. If she didn't want to stay, that is all she had to say. Running away, making up stories...? She needs help. Renée has issues that are above my ability to deal with."

She might as well not be here. Why was she? They weren't talking to her. Most of the time, they weren't even looking at her. No one asked her what had happened. Everyone had read some report, written by somebody that told somebody that reported it again to somebody. But she was right here, and no one would ask her what happened. As scared as she was, she'd tell. She wouldn't lie. Bobby Greensburg and her family shouldn't breathe on kids. They were the sick ones. They had issues.

"She crafted the entire story?" Judge White asked. "Two of your son's friends never lived at your residence? You didn't permit her to drink alcohol? Starve her when she threatened to expose the level of abuse in your home?" Lifting some papers, he read. "There was no inappropriate conduct on behalf of anyone living in your home?"

Renée's heart leaped a little. Although he seemed hostile and unaffected, the judge sounded like he believed her, or at least didn't believe Bobby, which was better. He could think of her as a liar, or exaggerator all he wanted, just as long as he didn't believe Bobby either.

After telling what her uncle did, Renée had learned some fundamental truths. People believed what they wanted to. They thought about what was fathomable in their own minds. If they couldn't imagine it, then it was impossible. She might tell white lies from time to time. She was still a kid, but she never lied about what mattered. However, it was easier to label her a liar or exaggerator than to admit the truth. Because if people believed her, they had to admit they'd failed, which Renée learned. No one liked to admit failure. So, they pacified themselves by making her the damaged one, her the villain. She didn't try to get people to believe her anymore. It was an exercise in futility. She would cast enough doubt on the other person, so no one believed them either.

"I'm not lying, Judge," Renée interrupted. She knew it was pointless, but no one else was standing up for her. "I told her I would tell. She didn't let me eat for a week."

"You understand this is your last foster placement, don't you?" Judge White asked her. "Black children, and children your age, are harder to place. You're unadoptable."

Whatever hope filled her heart died a quick death.

"Your Honor," Bobby interjected.

Oh, no! Renée held her breath. Bobby was going to retaliate. She would die if she had to go back to her house. They would kill her.

"She needs a lot of help," Bobby went on. "She's an evil little girl, suffering from a personality disorder. I'm not surprised she would lie about my family. Just saddened. I tried hard to provide her with a loving home."

There goes that word again.

"Renée didn't seem like herself after her last visit," Alex commented, lying across the double beds of their hotel room. "Did she tell you what happened?"

Andrew glanced at Alex and shook his head. No, she hadn't, and it pissed him off. Once upon a time, she wouldn't have hesitated to let him know if something bothered her. Now he had to pry it out of her.

"I tried to get her to talk. Even got her three shots of Patrón at dinner," he replied, remembering his attempt to ply her with alcohol to get her to open up. He'd taken her to a nice dinner. She loved sushi. Yet, the more buzzed she got, the less she spoke. "She kept avoiding the topic the moment I brought up her half-sister. After an hour, I gave up."

What he wanted to do was go back to Shenae Williams's house and demand to know what happened. Why his sister had to take medicine as soon as she got in the car. He didn't know if she should go into these people's houses alone anymore. Anything could happen to her, and he wouldn't know until it was too late.

"Think we should be worried?" Alex wondered.

Alex always looked out for Renée. He trusted him with his sister's life, unlike Chris, who in grand Chris fashion hadn't said word one in concern for Renée. Laying on the floor, hands behind his head, he stared at the ceiling as if everything were right in the world.

"Not yet, I don't think," he answered Alex, but glared at the side of Chris's head.

"You should go in with her next time."

Yeah, right! Andrew's head whipped around. Wide eyes stared at his friend. He liked his testicles right where they were. If he even acted like he might go in with her, Renée would relocate his testicles for him.

"Man, did you just meet Renée?" he quipped. "She will have two goats, five chickens, and a cow if I try that."

Alex laughed. "Just a suggestion, my bad. Maybe you should call your mom?"

Even worse idea than going in with her. Their mom would have an entire farm if she found out what they were doing. What he'd helped Renée do.

"Not in this lifetime. What would I say?" Andrew asked rhetorically. "Renée's being quiet? My parents don't even know we're here. It would kill them."

"What if she goes into shock? This isn't Arizona. There's no psychiatrist to bring her out of it this time. We're fucked if she goes catatonic or something," Alex warned.

Sometimes Alex's concern seemed overboard. Andrew eyed his friend through skeptical eyes. He worried about Renée, too. But Alex's interest sparked questions he'd never considered before. He needed to monitor him.

Renée's hand, which held her cell phone shook. Tears welled. She felt stupid. Of course, this would happen. She'd come all this way. So, this outcome made total sense. If it weren't for bad luck, she'd have no luck.

Sun illuminated the hotel room as Christina entered. Something was different about her friend. The ruffled skirt of her pink floral dress swayed with an extra bounce in her step. Disquiet compressed thin lips, yet in the depths of her dark eyes, happiness shone. Confusion momentarily eclipsed her distress.

"Hey, girlie. What're you doing?" Christina asked, eyebrows creasing in bemusement. "Aren't we going to meet your sister, Kathy?"

Pain lanced Renée's heart. That'd been the plan. Renée cleared her throat before speaking. "We were, but I talked to her. She can't do it today."

Christina examined Renée's face. "What do you mean, she can't do it? You can't do it any other day. It's not like we live here."

This was the Christina people rarely got to see. Yes, most times she was mousy, but she wasn't a coward. Just shy. She possessed quiet strength. When roused, she was just as fierce as Renée.

If anything could make her smile, her meek friend's outrage at her expense was it.

"Apparently—and I'm quoting her—she can't stay stuck in the past anymore. Seeing me would take her back to a time she'd rather forget. She said maybe sometime in the future." The disappointment was hard to hide. It was a living, breathing entity. Right now, it lived like a lump in her throat and a queasy feeling in her stomach.

Her sister might have said she wanted to forget her past, but Renée heard: "I want to forget you." The person who could validate her and her experiences, her life, wanted to forget her. Possibly had already forgotten her.

Watery, sympathetic eyes bored into hers. It was almost too much for her to bear. "I'm so sorry, Née. I know she's the one person you wanted to see."

Renée leaned on Christina's shoulder for a second. Squeezed her hand. She loved her even more for knowing that without her saying the words. Her broken heart sealed a bit.

"It's fine." She raised her head. "I just thought seeing her would've made it all real, you know. Sometimes my memories are surreal. When I look back, it's like I'm watching someone else's life."

"I'm sorry," Christina said, frowning. "Is there anything I can do for you?"

Unfortunately, the person who could do something for her didn't want her. Who would help her find herself now? She wanted to disappear.

Not true. She felt invisible already.

Only one thing to do. Renée sighed. "Could you get my pills for me and not tell anyone what happened? I feel like enough of a loser already. I don't want the 'aww... it's gonna be okay' frowns."

Christina patted her shoulder, hopped up, and went in search of her pills. "Why would you feel like a loser? She's the loser for not wanting to see you."

Damn! She was going to make her cry. Renée shook her head. "No, she's not. She wants to do what I should have done a long time ago. Get over it. I'm stupid for thinking she'd want to skate down memory lane with me after all this time. I mean, if I hadn't reached out to her, she probably never would've reached out either. Guess I didn't mean as much to her as she did to me."

"It's her loss, sweetie," Christina commiserated, handing her the pill bottle. "She's missing out on knowing an amazing human."

"Not that amazing. I'm evil." Renée regurgitated the long-standing consensus about her.

"Who says?" She scoffed, sat next to her. "I've known you for a couple years now. You literally found me in tears in the mall. You could've walked by, dragged Ashley away. But you stopped and listened to me cry about being broken up with. You bought me coffee and ice cream. Took me shopping. What evil person does that? You go to bat for everyone but you. And you're funny as hell."

When said with such conviction, she didn't sound so bad. She smiled weakly. "Thanks, Chrissy. You're sweet like a chocolate-covered strawberry."

"It's sexy!" Christina laughed. "Sexy like a chocolate strawberry, weirdo."

"What? Not as good as beat 'em and street 'em?" She laughed, reminding her of their discussion a few days ago.

"No! It's plagiarism. Mine was an original." Wrapping an arm around Renée's waist, she gave her a quick squeeze. "Let's ditch the boys, go get Ashley, get some Cinnamon Toast Crunch, and explore Indiana now that we don't have to pit-stop in Kalamazoo, Michigan."

CHAPTER THIRTY-SIX

"**M**y baby. My baby girl," Manuel Williams gushed to his wife. His white smile contained the wattage they warned you about exposing your retinas to. "Look at you all grown up," he said to Renée. "I haven't seen her since she was four years old. Her mother brought her to say goodbye before taking her away to Arizona."

Renée's eyes bulged. She gazed around the ostentatious living room to keep from outright glaring at the contributor of half her genetic code.

This house differed from Shenae's. Cherry wood-trimmed faux antique couches with gaudy, floral fabric backing and matching cushions. Unlike Christina's delicate floral-patterned outfits, these colors were loud and didn't match on any level. Tried too hard to be elegant, but the velvet fabric was timeworn. Deflated cushions indicated they'd seen much ass in their day. All the furniture appeared expensive but was imitation luxurious. Which wasn't as shocking as it should be, considering Cheryl, her sperm donor's buxom, Caucasian wife, carried herself similarly. Big, over teased, brunette hair streaked with gray. She was a lot of woman. She wore knockoff designer clothes, costume jewelry, including giant Wilma Flintstone pearls, and overpowering perfume.

What shocked Renée was the multitude of pictures on the walls. Baby pictures of Shenae, and who she assumed was Manuel Jr. Professional and candid photos of Shenae and her two daughters. A family picture of him, Shenae, and Manuel Jr. hurt more than it should have. But it did. Because while she'd pined for the family that threw her away, they'd moved on as if she'd never existed. She wasn't even a blip on their radar.

And he dared to say her biological mother took her away. From all the stories and what she knew firsthand, he chose to leave. When she and Kathy were taken into the foster care system, Arizona state contacted their fathers. He could have stepped forward and raised her, but instead, mysteriously fell off the face of the Earth. Manuel had never looked for her and signed his parental rights away. Now, he had the nerve to act like the slighted one. Wow!

Anger bubbled inside her. "Wait a minute. What do you mean, took me away?" she asked, not disguising her agitation. "You weren't around a lot before we left."

"Is that what you think, sweetheart?" Cheryl responded, all condescending, like anyone asked for her opinion.

"That's not what I think," she confirmed. "That's what I know," she corrected.

Sympathy spread red painted lips. "Sweetheart, that's not true. I'm sure from a child's perspective it seems that way. And with no one to confirm or deny, it became your truth. For the five years I've been married to your father, he's talked nonstop about you."

If she called her sweetheart one more time, Renée would scream. Narrow eyes observed the happy pair in disbelief. Her gut tightened.

"Cheryl's telling the truth," Manuel backed up his wife, hugging her shoulder. "I failed a lot as a father, but when I found out about your mom leaving, I wanted to find you. I didn't know where to start. I promise I wanted to find you. They didn't notify me about my rights being severed. Before I knew it, time passed, you were grown. But you're my little girl. I've always loved you."

She glared. Yet, her heart softened. Anger, betrayal, and sorrow warred within her. This wasn't the story her caseworker had told her. If what he said was true, he'd had no clue about her adoption until it was too late. To help her through childhood depression and abandonment issues, her caseworker told her that her biological mother had died. After she reached adulthood, she learned that wasn't the truth. CPS wasn't above lying when it suited them. It was possible Manuel's story was true, which meant she'd spent years being resentful and angry for no reason. Renée was so confused.

A man who didn't want his kids wouldn't hang pictures of them around his house, would he? She didn't know.

"I don't know what to say," she said, voicing her confusion. "It's hard to believe you looked for me for twenty years."

"Believe it, *mi hija*," Manuel exclaimed, upbeat. "It's one hundred percent true."

"Your dad was so sure he'd see you again one day that he's kept you under his insurance at the steel mill all these years. I'll give you the card before you leave. We have it around here somewhere," Cheryl said, then gave a strained laugh.

Manuel joined with an uncomfortable laugh of his own.

They were so weird. Maybe it bothered Cheryl that he had children outside of their relationship. A child who materialized on their doorstep demanding answers. Some women thought of children as baggage. Yes, he had Shenae and Manuel Jr., but Shenae was in her mid-thirties, and Manuel Jr. wasn't much younger from what she gathered from the pictures. Her being in her twenties meant she might need him more than his other two children. Who knew? Honestly, she wasn't sure what type of relationship she intended to have with him after today. Her emotions were jumbled.

"You know what?" Manuel said, standing suddenly. "You should stay for dinner. Maybe a couple days so we can catch up, get to know each other. I've got a lot to show you."

"Umm…" Whoa! Quite the offer. One that would make Andrew's head explode. It already made her head hurt a little. "My brother's waiting for me. He wouldn't appreciate sitting outside in the car for a few days."

Manuel and Cheryl chuckled.

"See, Cherie told you she was mine. She's got her daddy's sense of humor," Manuel complimented, continuing to laugh.

"Yeah, she does," Cheryl agreed. "She looks like you, too. Only more feminine. She could be a model if she didn't get your height."

Renée gave a small laugh, but that was all the commitment she would make. Manuel was short, maybe five-foot-five or five-six. She could admit she might have gotten her height from him. However, comparisons stopped there. Skin a few shades lighter brown, he had inky, close cropped, black hair. His face was square and too small for his body. All his features were compacted into the middle like they were afraid to branch out. No, she wasn't the hottest thing walking, but she didn't think she favored him, either. Nor did she find Cheryl's statement particularly funny.

"Hey! Short is sexy," Manuel joked.

Her eyes widened; her throat clogged.

"Sorry, did I offend you?" Manuel asked, catching her shock.

"No." Renée shook her head. "You surprised me. I say that all the time," she confessed.

They shared a comfortable, conspiratorial smile.

Manuel approached, cautiously placed a hand on her shoulder. "Oh, my sweet Renée. I'm so sorry we lost so much time. We can make up for that now, though."

Why was she so emotional today? Sheer willpower fought down the lump in her throat. She didn't feel the instant connection she thought she'd feel, but she felt something. It was a start. Every relationship started somewhere.

She patted the hand on her shoulder before deftly shrugging out from under it. Touching was too intimate for this new acquaintance.

"Is there somewhere I can make a quick call?" Renée asked, standing.

"Sure, sweetheart. We're going to get dinner ready," Cheryl informed her. "You can make your call here."

"Thank you." Renée pulled her cell phone from her purse.

Manuel and Cheryl went toward what must be the kitchen.

Andrew glanced at his phone display. Sighing in relief, he swiped his finger across it and put the phone to his ear.

"About fuckin' time. You're still in there?" Andrew asked in place of a greeting.

"No, I'm right next to you. I'm wearing my invisibility cloak," Renée joked. "God, you're such an ass. Of course, I'm still inside. Where else would I be? They want me to stay for dinner and a couple of days, too."

Andrew's head shook before she finished her sentence. She must be crazy. "Hell no, Née!"

"Chill," she directed. "I already said no. But I am staying late, though. And I need you to be cool with it," she said quickly, probably sensing his objection.

What to do? What to do? Alex watched him expectantly. He ignored Ashley's continual taps on his shoulder. Andrew exhaled loudly.

"Fine," he relented. "Your judgment has been good so far, I guess. Stay for dinner. We'll all go back to the hotel. Call when you're done."

"Really?" Renée squealed, sounding surprised. "Thank you, Drew. I love you. You're the bestest big brother ever."

Then why did he feel so stupid? A sharp pang of sadness struck his heart. Seemed the only way to get her to admit she loved him was to indulge her.

Ashley flopped back against her seat in a huff and intentionally kicked to his seat. She was a brat, too. He lifted his eyes heavenward.

"Shut up! You're going to make me blush or throw up," he teased.

Renée giggled. "Okay, I've got to go. Lucy and Ricky Ricardo are cooking dinner."

"Okay, Little Bit. I... you," Andrew said, using their cheeky endearment.

"Aww..." Renée crooned, touched. "And I... you, big brother. Bye."

Andrew's insides warmed at the rare moment of affection between him and his sister. Until...

"What the fuck! Ashley!" He shouted when a powerful blow hit his back through the seat. Andrew turned an evil eye on his sister's friend.

Her eyes bulged. Usually, pale skin appeared even paler, making her freckles stand out. "Wasn't me, fucker!" She huffed indignantly, crossing her arms over her small chest.

His glare shifted to his friend seated beside her. "May I help you, dick? Break my seat; you buy it and me a whole new ride, man."

"Where is she?" Chris asked through tight lips.

"Who?"

"Who else? Shit!"

"None of your business. Renée's my sister, and she's fine," he stated matter-of-factly, pushing the button to start his truck.

Wind sweeping his neck warned him to move. Andrew jerked forward and dodged left before Chris's hand connected with the back of his head.

"What is your deal, Clark?" Alex interjected before Andrew could.

"We're not leaving her," he demanded.

"She wants to stay to eat. What am I supposed to do?" Andrew asked, still shocked at this uncharacteristic protective edge he heard and saw in his friend's demeanor.

First Alex, and now, Chris. What the hell was going on with his friends? Yes, they all cared for Renée, even Chris, in his own way, but none more than him. Treating him like he couldn't handle things pissed him off.

"Tell them to set five more places or saddle up, and we can all head to the corral or something," Chris's insolent offer.

"This is her thing, man," Andrew said calmly, trying to defuse the situation. Things were getting intense. They were all on edge and cramped in the Denali. Cooler heads needed to prevail. "We can't interfere."

"Why does everyone just do whatever she wants?" Chris grumbled. "Someone needs to stand up to her."

"You're one to talk," Christina grumbled from the far back.

"Chrissy," Ashley hissed, turning to stare at her friend.

Okay, he didn't know what was going on, but he didn't like it. Something felt off. The air was charged with more than their usual sarcasm and irritation. It was another vibe he didn't particularly care for or know how to name. Plus, in the pit of his stomach, deep, where he didn't want to acknowledge, sat a brick. Gut-churning intuition. Maybe he shouldn't have given in so easily. Andrew put his foot on the gas and eased his vehicle away from the curb. Thin fingers flicked his ear.

Ashley.

CHAPTER THIRTY-SEVEN

Renée nearly jumped out of her skin. She spun around.

"I'm sorry," Cheryl apologized, looking abashed. "I wasn't listening—I swear. I was coming to tell you dinner will be ready soon."

"It's okay," she assured her. It wasn't her house.

"Sounds like you're pretty close to your brother," Cheryl commented, proving her earlier statement false.

"Thought you weren't listening?" Renée quipped.

Cheryl laughed. The loud sound seemed exaggerated and made her feel uncomfortable for reasons she couldn't define. Even being in the living room alone with the woman caused unease. She didn't want to retake her spot on the loveseat, afraid to put herself at a disadvantage with her. Cheryl was nice enough, but Renée felt ill at ease in her presence.

"You caught me, sorry," Cheryl apologized insincerely. "So, are you two close?"

Damn! Pry much.

"I guess," Renée answered. Things between her and Andrew were complicated. She didn't want to talk to this strange woman about it. "We were when we were younger."

"That's good." Cheryl smiled. "I bet you and little Manuel would be close, too. I've gotten very close to him and Shenae. He's around every other weekend."

Renée's brows furrowed at that news. Shenae had said the exact opposite the other day. Manuel Jr. wouldn't want to be near Manuel Sr. if what Shenae told her was true. Or was Cheryl lying?

Why would she lie? This made little sense. She wasn't looking for a replacement for Andrew. They had unresolved issues of their own already. But this trip healed some of those issues for her. He'd taken her to dinner after her meeting with Shenae went south and she'd ended up having an anxiety attack and rushing out. Of course, she hadn't told him what happened. However, his being there with her made things better for her somehow. Anyway, she didn't want to trade brothers. And why would there be a difference in Cheryl and Shenae's stories? Who was lying?

"Look what I found," Manuel announced, breaking into her thoughts and re-entering the room. He held several large brown leather binders. "Photo albums!" He held up one for her inspection. "They're pictures of the whole family in these, some of you as a baby, too."

Her heart stopped momentarily. She'd never seen baby pictures of herself. There were pictures galore of her and Andrew at home on The Wall of Shame/The Wall of Fame. Ashley and Christina both had pictures of themselves at their homes and could trace their lineage decades and decades back. She couldn't trace her own image farther than first grade. Renée only had one picture from that time, and the rest didn't start until her tenth birthday. Dumb as it might sound, she envied all of them for having those ties to their pasts when she didn't.

Her heartbeat was erratic. "That's crazy," she breathed. "I've never *really* seen pictures of myself as a baby. I think I have a vague memory of seeing one when I was little—velvet red dress, white ruffles. That's it. My parents don't have any."

The word slipped out before Renée considered her word choice. She didn't normally censure herself when referring to her parents. Seeing Manuel flinch at the word *parents* made her wish she'd thought before she spoke. Here he was giving her this giant gift, and then she trampled all over his feelings.

"I mean my adoptive parents," she rushed to correct herself.

Cheryl was at her side at once. "It's okay. We know what you mean." She smoothed her hair, and Renée cringed inwardly. "Your dad's just over-sensitive. He even cries at commercials."

Renée sank onto the couch to keep the woman from continuing to touch her. Something about Cheryl rang all her alarm bells. The visit was throwing her off more than she realized.

"You do? I do, too," she confided, hoping to bridge the divide her careless words created. "I used to cry at McDonald's commercials. I won't bore you with the details, but the baby doesn't get the McDonald's, and I bawl like a little girl."

Everyone laughed. The tension eased.

Manuel set the photo albums on the coffee table. "Hope you're hungry. Cheryl made a full breakfast for dinner thing. You like pancakes?"

Renée's stomach growled on cue. "I love pancakes. They're one of my favorite foods."

Cheryl grinned. "Let's eat then."

"This is you." Manuel pointed to a picture in the open photo album. "Hard to believe you're so skinny now. You were such a *gordita*. God! Such a fat baby. We used to pinch your cheeks and rolls all the time."

Not wholly immune to criticism, Renée felt a bit triggered by that description, even though she didn't resemble the tubby baby in the pictures at all anymore. She tried to laugh it off, but her stomach cramped at the thought, making her sound strangled.

She settled on speech instead. "It doesn't even look like me. I was adorable."

"Yes, it does," Manuel said, bumping her arm with his elbow like they were old chums with a secret. "You're just a little taller and thinner now."

Renée smiled awkwardly.

Dinner was delicious. She had three chocolate chip pancakes smothered in maple syrup, golden hash browns with Tabasco sauce, and pulp-free orange juice to drink. Cheryl cooked well. Afterward, they retired to the living room, where they were looking through more photo albums. Manuel hadn't lied—he had tons of pictures and, yes, pictures of her as a baby. She would have enjoyed browsing the albums more if she wasn't sandwiched between Manuel and Cheryl on the couch. The happy-family portrait they painted didn't work for her. And them flipping pages in her lap made her anxious. Too much too soon had her stomach doing flips. Plus, Cheryl's perfume was choking her.

"Are you okay?" Cheryl asked, concerned. "You don't look so hot."

Compliments just kept on coming. No, they hadn't technically called her fat. Well, technically, they called her fat, but that was past her. Not current. Though current Renée experienced the self-esteem jabs as if they were delivered on her now.

Renée pressed her hand to her stomach. "I think I might have overeaten."

Pearls from Cheryl's silver charm bracelet smacked Renée in the face as Cheryl laid the back of her hand on her forehead. Renée didn't know which was worse, the clammy hand against her skin or the overwhelming rosewood, patchouli, and—acid—fragrance that assaulted her nostrils. The scent never dissipated, just recharged each time Cheryl moved.

"Hmm..." Cheryl hummed thoughtfully. "I know you planned on leaving, but maybe you should stay here tonight."

Renée shook her head, dislodging the hand affixed to her forehead. Thank God! "My brother won't like that."

"I'm sure if he knew you were sick, he wouldn't mind," Cheryl tried to soothe her. "Give me his number, and I'll call him."

Thick bangs and long lashes hid the suspicious glare Renée tossed Cheryl out of the corner of her eye. Whether or not intentional, condescending tones tap-danced on every one of her nerves. Cheryl seemed married to the tone of voice. Renée's stomach somersaulted.

"I don't know." Renée hesitated. Something didn't feel right, or maybe she didn't feel right. Either way, her knotted guts told her not to give her Andrew's number.

Sitting stiflingly close, Manuel turned to her. Hot breath bathed her face. "If you don't want Cherie to, I can call. At least he'll know what's going on."

She didn't—her stomach gurgled. Her eyes darted back and forth. "May I use your restroom?" she asked, leaning forward and placing the photo album she'd been holding on the coffee table.

"Sure," Cheryl agreed, standing to allow her to pass. "It's right down that hall, first door on the right. You can't miss it. It's the only room with a toilet."

Renée tried to smile, but she was positive it came off like more of a mangled grimace. Clutching her stomach, she ran to the bathroom.

Moments later, still holding her middle and moving slower, she returned. Her eyes bulged at the sight before her.

"What are you doing?" Renée snapped.

Cheryl scrambled to her feet. "I'm sorry. You sounded bad in there. I called your brother for you." She held Renée's phone out to her.

Renée snatched her property, retrieved her purse from the coffee table, and sat across the room on the loveseat. She would have stormed out, but her intestines were trying to escape her body at present.

"Sorry," she infused as much contrition in her voice as possible, given the circumstances. "I didn't mean to snap. I'm not feeling well."

"It's fine," Manuel assured her. "Being sick in a strange place is uncomfortable."

"What did my brother say? How did you bypass the lock on my phone?"

"He was fine with you staying tonight. There wasn't a lock," Manuel explained.

Made sense. Renée often turned the lock function off. Usually, she didn't leave her phone or any belongings around people she didn't trust. She hated having to unlock her phone whenever she wanted to glance at something. She would have used the lock here, but she hadn't planned to leave her phone out of her sight.

"Really?" The news about Andrew was shocking. Earlier, he'd been adamant about her not staying. "Wow!"

"Told you he'd understand," Cheryl gloated. "He sounded really nice."

Renée smiled tightly.

"We're going to get the spare room set up. You look at the rest of the photo albums," Manuel suggested, standing and ushering Cheryl out of the living room before Renée responded.

Forces beyond her control compelled her to check her phone. She appreciated the gesture. But why would modern-day Ozzie and Harriet use her phone? You don't go into someone's phone without permission. Not only her phone, but her purse, too. Where her phone had been.

Scrolling through, nothing seemed changed. Of course, they were in their fifties, maybe even late fifties, early sixties. If anything like her parents, they wouldn't know how to do more than make calls, and barely that. She stuffed her phone into her purse and reached for a photo album.

White-hot fire tore through her abdomen. Pain of the blinding variety stabbed her. She lurched to her feet and staggered to the bathroom.

Gripping the toilet, she prayed for mercy. None came. Every couple seconds, she dry-heaved, but not a pancake or hash brown revisited. If she could throw up, it might relieve her stomach pain some. It had to. Dizzy. Sweaty. Hot one minute, cold the next. She felt like garbage.

"Think her brother believed she took an Uber back and left her phone?" Cheryl's muffled question filtered through the wall.

A loud crinkling and snapping followed. Sounded like the summer she and Andrew got an inflatable pool, unpacked it from the box, and then shook it out to blow it up.

Renée searched her small confines with her eyes. They weren't in the bathroom with her, but from the sounds of it, they were in the next room. Their walls were paper thin, apparently. She fell back on her haunches. What were they talking about?

"Seems like it," Manuel's garbled reply. "If he didn't, he'd be here."

"... Won't get through if he tries to call. Buy her... going to Arizona?" Cheryl's unintelligible question.

Renée tried to stand, couldn't. Her body was laden. Breathing labored, heart beating too fast for her liking. And she didn't understand what they were saying. Her head was cloudy. Shaking her head, she attempted to focus. Strained to hear their conversation clearer.

"She's an emotionally unbalanced black girl," Manuel stated. "White people took her in. They know anything's possible."

"Hey! I'm white," Cheryl said, offended.

"I'm saying Post Traumatic Stress Syndrome comes in handy. She's going door to door in this day and age. Anything can happen. Nothing's a stretch."

"Shockingly, she's not less trusting," Cheryl mused. "Looking at those pictures, she was like a lost puppy who found its way home."

Tears welled in Renée's eyes. What was happening? She knew she didn't like that woman. And her conniving "father." How could she be so stupid?

"We'll move her later," Manuel suggested. "Two or three in the morning. How long until she's out?"

"Ten—twenty minutes," Cheryl replied. "She's small. The amount I slipped her should have taken her out immediately. She was feeling it when we left her, though. Twenty minutes tops."

"Glad I never stopped that life insurance." Manuel yawned.

Renée's heart seized. What had she done? She'd walked herself into some weird insurance scam she now couldn't walk out of. And her phone was in the living room. Damn it!

Crawling it is, then. Renée's world tilted as she lowered her hands to the ground. Good thing she'd never gotten up, or this would be ten times harder. She could barely see.

Reaching up, Renée twisted the doorknob. Slow to avoid making noise. It clicked. She eased the door open. Thank God the hinges weren't old in this fake house. She glanced left then right, and her blurry vision cleared enough to reveal a closed door beside the bathroom. It must be where Manuel and Cheryl were. Renée crawled through the open doorway toward the living room. Her abandoned purse rested on the loveseat.

Grabbing her purse's shoulder strap, she pulled the bag to the floor. The edges of her vision wobbled, shrank. She blindly unzipped it, reached in, and rooted around until her hand connected with the desired object. This would be tricky. Squinting, she fought the encroaching darkness. The display light leeched away the limited sight she regained. She swiped, poked, and prayed. Then lay on the ground, phone next to her head.

"Uh… hello?" a male voice answered.

Whose voice she didn't know. The lights dimmed—her ears filled with water or cotton.

"Please, help me," she whispered, then the lights went out.

CHAPTER THIRTY-EIGHT

"Who is it?" a female shouted through the door.

"My name is Christopher Clark, ma'am," Chris yelled. He surveyed the surrounding area.

Lower middle-class neighborhood. Nothing too spectacular about the area. Neighbors were spread quite a distance from each other. He tapped his foot impatiently. What was taking this bitch so long? Although the ambient temperature was chilly internally, he was on fire—fuming mad.

"What do you want, Christopher Clark? It's two in the morning," the woman bellowed.

Chris nearly broke down the door. Drew barreled past him, foot at the ready to enact his thoughts. He put a rough hand to the center of his best friend's chest. Tight-lipped, he shook his head.

"We're trying to sleep. Come back tomorrow," the woman requested.

Right. Tomorrow. Chris's woman had called him after not talking to him for three days. When he started to lay into her, dead air met him. Worried didn't describe his emotions. He heard a man and a woman talk about moving her, and he flipped.

"Move your hand, man," Drew whispered.

"No!" he mouthed, shaking his head. "Wait."

If they didn't play this right, they'd never find out what was going on. A feeling in the pit of Chris's stomach told him something was wrong.

"I can't come back tomorrow, ma'am," Chris said, using the politest nerdy voice. He glanced at Drew, shrugged. "My friend Steven and I were wondering if we could use your phone. It's an emergency."

"We're living in the twenty-first century, Christopher. I find it hard to believe you don't have a cellular phone."

"That's her," Drew whispered. "The woman who called me. She said Renée left in an Uber heading back to Arizona. It was ridiculous. I thought Renée was messing with me. It was this stupid bitch!"

Chris took several calming breaths. None worked. "Shut up!" he mouthed. "If she hears you, we're screwed."

Dark brows knitted in confusion.

"I have a phone, but it's dead," he answered, ignoring his friend. "Please, miss, we'll be out here all night if we can't get a ride."

A crack signaled the opening of the door.

"Come in, Christopher. I'll get the phone. Wait here," the woman instructed. She turned and retreated down a dimly lit hall.

Over the threshold, Chris scanned the room immediately. The black and gold bag he saw Renée exit the car with earlier sat on a short hall table. Drew nudged his shoulder.

The woman reminded him of Roseanne Barr from back in the day, except she had large, helmet-shaped brunette hair with gray streaking both temples. Hideous makeup adorned a chunky face. Fake jewelry decorated her like a human chandelier, and she wore a peach dress that hung like a tent on her plump frame. She returned with the phone. Her eyes lit on Drew.

"This is my friend, Steven," he introduced Drew. "He got scared and didn't want to wait in the car."

Understanding shone in the woman's muddy brown eyes. Nodding, she said, "I'm Cheryl. Nice to meet you." She handed him the portable phone.

Drew pushed him aside. "OMG!" he exclaimed, outrageously flamboyant. He bent to get a better look at Cheryl's necklace. "Are those real pearls?"

Chris arched a brow so high it almost hit his hairline. If the situation weren't dire, he would have fallen on the floor, dying in laughter.

"Yes, they are," Cheryl bragged, cheeks coloring. "Have you ever seen anything more beautiful?"

"A pearl necklace," Drew said in an ignorantly, stereotypical, exaggerated feminine voice. He giggled. "Scandalous."

"Oh, honey, eat your heart out," Cheryl offered, leaning forward, elongating her neck to allow Drew a closer look.

Drew struck. Wrapped his hand around her neck. Her mouth popped open.

"If you scream or kick me, I will slit your throat," Drew warned, spinning her around until her back pressed into his chest.

Cheryl whimpered.

"Find Renée."

He didn't have to tell Chris twice, or at all, for that matter. Chris marched toward the back of the house. The house was too quiet. Eerily quiet. Two adults lived here, so he didn't expect a ton of noise. But Cheryl appeared wide awake. There should be noise from a television or something.

"What are you doing?" Cheryl asked, strained from her airway being restricted. "This is called breaking and entering. It's illegal. I *will* call the police."

At her indignation, Chris spun around. "I dare you to. 'Cuz I'm pretty sure kidnapping's illegal, too."

"I'll make you a deal," Drew offered low, threatening. "If my sister's okay, *I* won't call the police. But, if you hurt her... You and your husband will end up strange smells in a vacant house."

"Our house isn't vacant."

Chris heard Cheryl's clueless statement as he stormed through the cramped house.

The place was a life-size dollhouse. Complete with tacky furniture. His grandparents had one in their attic, looked just like this. Instead of smelling of formaldehyde and mothballs, it reminded him of the candle store he couldn't go into in the mall because of the putrid mix of fragrances. Off the living room was another corridor. He turned left down it. Two doors were on the right and two on the left.

As he approached, the second door on the right opened. Dark eyes widened when they landed on him—his narrowed. A short, very unattractive man with a square face and bushy mustache raised his fist. Chris smirked. He couldn't help himself. This troll thought he could take him. In what world would they be equally matched? The idea was laughable.

Squeezing his hand, he realized he was still holding the portable phone. Who still had a home phone? He didn't have time for this.

The man charged. Chris lifted the hand holding the phone and advanced. Before he thought better of it, he bashed the man over the head. Hard. He fell unconscious.

Grunts and shouts echoed from the back of the house. Loud cracks and booms shook the walls. Cheryl struggled. Andrew slapped a hand over her mouth, muffling her screams.

A minute later, Chris appeared. Limp, unconscious Renée draped over his arms. Andrew's stomach dropped. His grip on Cheryl's neck tightened unwittingly. Muscles tensed. His heart battered his ribcage. Shit! He'd failed again. *How could you allow this again?*

"Is she dead?" he breathed, chest heaving. His gaze zeroed on his sister, and his vision swam. Wiggling caused him to loosen his grip and drop his hand from his captive's mouth.

"Did you kill my husband?" Cheryl sobbed.

He tightened his grip. Andrew hoped Chris killed the mother-fucker. She gagged, and he relaxed his hold.

"No," she cried, trembling. "She needs her stomach pumped."

"You better hope that's all she needs," Andrew said through a thick throat. He pushed the woman away so hard she tripped and fell on the floor. "If it's not, I promise you—I'll find you."

Chris snatched the purse off the hall table. "She's barely breathing. We need to go—now!" he growled.

They started for the front door.

"Did you kill my husband?" the chunky woman repeated, fretting from the floor.

He opened the door, and Chris exited. Andrew stepped to the threshold and grabbed the doorknob.

"Now, it's your turn to worry," he said darkly. Then slammed the door.

CHAPTER THIRTY-NINE

Everyone sat frozen in varied forms of stress. Lex sat, legs spread, hands clasped, and head down. Ashley leaned against Lex's shoulder, staring into space. Sitting legs drawn, knees together and to the side, Christina fidgeted with the hem of her skirt and chewed ice she got from a plastic cup that Drew refilled dozens of times, then sat it by the foot of her chair.

Chris focused on what he could control, his breathing. It was four PM. Around five AM, they admitted Renée to the hospital and moved from the ER to a private room. Ashley, Lex, and Christina had taken an Uber from the hotel and met them there. It took a lot of convincing for anyone to believe Drew was family. So much so, that they called his and Renée's parents. Saying Randall and Susan Sutton were livid would be an understatement.

While they pumped Renée's stomach, none of them were allowed in, nor were they during the myriad of other medical tests and procedures. HIPPA regulations meant none of them would know any more than the bare minimum about her condition. The important thing was she was alive. Although she wouldn't be if they hadn't reached her when they did. He'd never been more scared for anyone in his life.

Another essential point, Drew wouldn't speak to him. Not even when the police questioned them about the incident. He checked on everyone's welfare except Chris's. Drew paced the waiting room, sat next to Christina, and soothed her every fifteen minutes. Tragedy had demolished the need for secrecy. The only person who didn't know about Christina and Drew now was Renée. With everything going on, Ashley hadn't blinked an eye at their revelation. The same, however, could not be said about the revelation of his relationship status with Renée. A situation that was still very much complicated. No one spoke to him. He was *persona non grata*. Forced to sit alone in the farthest corner of the small family waiting room.

Chris didn't handle being ignored well. Typically, it irritated him. Today, working on no sleep and fear for his woman, deep breaths were the only thing keeping him from exploding. Of course, he understood the gravity of the situation. Consideration of his friends' grief stopped him from confronting any of them hours ago. But, dammit, he was grieving, too!

Did they consider him?

No. A voice whispered in his mind.

Well, that would stop now. His patience snapped.

He jumped to his feet—time to tackle the lesser of two beasts. Chris approached Ashley. Watery eyes, more green than hazel with grief, met his. Annoyance entered, nudged sadness aside.

Lex lifted his head. "Not the time, Clark."

"It never is, is it?" he replied. "Can I talk to you?" he asked, gaze shifting to Ashley.

"I'd rather not."

He could always rely on Ashley for brutal honesty. "Please?" Chris implored.

Raising her head from Lex's shoulder, she stood with all the speed of a snail. One side of her strawberry blond hair was mussed from where she'd leaned on Lex's shoulder. Without a word, she shuffled to his timeout corner. She sat. He remained standing. Chris stayed an arm's length away just in case she and Renée shared the same views on nuts and anger.

"Why hasn't Renée spoken to me in days?" he asked, too stressed for niceties.

"That doesn't even kind of matter right now," she said, voice devoid of its usual fire. "Renée is lying in there fighting for her life. I'm not gonna stroke your fragile ego."

He sat then. Left one chair open between them. Chris turned hard eyes on her. "See, that's the problem right there," he pointed out, tone calm, but far from gentle. "You all think I'm this emotionless drone. Walking around caring for nobody but myself. Why would I go get Renée? Lex was there. He could've gone with Drew. It didn't have to be me."

Looking taken aback, Ashely stayed quiet. Thoughtful.

"I'm human," he reminded her. "I have feelings, vulnerabilities, and shockingly insecurities. Do you think I could hit and quit my best friend's sister? You think that little of me?"

"I don't know what to think of you," Ashley said, shaking her head.

"Why did Renée stop talking to me?" he rephrased the question.

Ashley exhaled loudly. A look of resolve passed over her features. She licked her teeth. "She told us what happened," she said, confirming what he suspected. "Chris, you're a douchebag. Like, a grade A, pussy hound, asshole."

Let it never be said Ashley ever pulled a punch. Damn!

He blinked to absorb each of her blows. She might as well have kicked him in the nuts.

"Thanks," he stated sardonically.

"Let me finish," she requested.

Chris nodded, tight-lipped.

"You're not a good guy. You use women for—whatever you use them for—you have money, a place, a car... I don't know what else you could want that you don't already get easily. But you use them. Take advantage of them."

"This is not better," he said under his breath.

She wiped a hand over her pale face. "I've never seen you be different. And Renée's not stupid. She may have had that thing with Corey, but that was something different. She doesn't play stupid girl. So, there must be something in you she sees."

"Agreed on all fronts," he concurred.

An upraised hand palm out requested his silence. He waited.

"*I've* never seen *you* be different," she reiterated with emphasis. "But since whatever started between you two, Renée's been different. Even with all this shit going on, she's been flirty, giddy, and just... different. She smiles more. Makes more actual jokes. Her panic attacks don't seem to happen as often. And I've seen you care for her, which is weird."

"I love her," he proclaimed. Chris gazed into her eyes.

Ashley searched his eyes. Minutes passed, or what seemed like minutes. Thin lips curved into a warm smile. She hauled herself to her feet, attentive gaze fixed on him.

"If she wakes up, tell her that." Her smile faded, and her eyes teared.

Chris stood and pulled her into his arms. Ashley allowed the comfort for a moment, then yanked away. She eyed him warily.

"One step at a time, Clark. You're freaking me out," she quipped.

"When she wakes up, I'll tell her," he corrected.

"In the meantime, you have someone else to talk to," she reminded him.

"Yeah, I'm good on that. One beast at a time."

She rolled her eyes and strolled away. Right. Over. To. Drew. His eyes narrowed. Drew leaned down. Ashley whispered something in his ear, pointed at him. Drew glared, nodded, and started walking. In Chris's direction.

Sweat pooled under his arms. He couldn't stand Ashley! No boundaries. Limits were mere suggestions to her.

Despite the apparent tension between them, Drew sat next to him.

"What do you want?" he asked, but it sounded more like an accusation.

He hated being on these terms with Drew. They'd been friends since before they knew how to speak. Part of him wanted to back away from Renée if it meant things between them would return to status quo. However, a more significant part of him, the region containing his heart, couldn't walk away from the woman who made life worth living. She made him human. Made him a better man. Losing Drew's friendship would destroy him. But there wasn't a choice; losing Renée would kill him.

Chris blew out a long breath. "Thanks to Ashley, it appears we need to talk."

Across the way, Ashley flashed him an ironic smile and waved. He flipped her off.

"Something funny?" Drew asked, recalling his attention.

"No," Chris answered immediately. "None of this is a joke. My woman is laid up in the hospital after being fucking poisoned. I'm sitting here, possibly losing my best friend. No, nothing is funny here."

"That's exactly what's confusing," Drew said, pounding the armrest with his fist. "You're talking about my sister. *My* sister. I don't judge you for any of your exploits, but you go behind my back and choose the one woman who should be off-limits to you. How long have you been sticking it to *my* sister?"

Chris took several deep breaths to regain his composure. Drew was angry and frustrated. No question about it. He could throw himself all the pity parties, but speaking of Renée like she was just some booty? Not while he had life in him.

"Do you think I would risk our friendship just for a chance to hunch on your sister?" Chris asked, intentionally crass.

Drew's flared nostrils confirmed he received the message Chris intended. "You understand if we weren't in a hospital, I'd beat you, right?"

"I'm right here, dude," Chris taunted. If that's what they needed to do, then they'd do it. Consequences be damned. He didn't want to lose his friend or his woman. Drew required him to be the villain right now, and he'd be that if their friendship survived.

"How long, man?" Drew inquired. "Help me understand this. Otherwise, you will be my first homicide. Which says a lot because last night I could've broken that lady's neck—no problem."

"Yeah, I could've ended both their lives," Chris commiserated. "The police better—"

"Chris!" Drew snapped at the end of his rope.

Why was he stalling? "I'm in love with her, Andrew," he exploded. His eyes watered instinctually with his seriousness. "I'm in love with your sister. I've been in love with her for years. I don't know the exact second the love started, but it's grown consistently. I tried to get over it, dude. I did. I left for an entire year. Remember?"

Drew nodded.

"I only started pursuing Renée a month and a half ago. When we got there to house-sit," he admitted. "No sooner. I would never use her for just something to get into. If you believe nothing else, believe that. I haven't been seeing anyone else. Haven't dealt with another female in any way, shape, or form."

"I know," Drew interrupted. "Samantha's been blowing up mine and Rand's phones. This explains that, at least. Though I wouldn't rule out your tires being slashed by the time we get back."

Progress. Drew wasn't as mad.

"Why didn't you talk to me before?" Drew asked. "If you've felt this epic love for years, why not tell me before now? You've been puttin' chicks on the catch-and-release plan for a minute. So, I'm confused about where all this love and devotion came in."

He expected that. Reforming one's lifestyle, or owning up, meant owning one's past. Chris had a lot to answer for, but every dog had his day, right? Renée was his salvation.

"You've never been the fat kid, Drew," he explained. "Invisible. Oinked at when noticed. Bullied. I'm human. When I dropped that weight... I went crazy. Women throwing themselves at me was new. Dudes were hitting me up on social media wanting fitness tips. Shit blew my mind. I wish I'd been strong enough to know better or not to be affected by the attention, but I wasn't. I took advantage of unfamiliar circumstances, but that gets old. When the high wore off, I took stock of who was there, no matter what. Renée fits that bill and so much more. I love her."

Drew studied him for a long minute.

Chris hoped his friend saw his sincerity.

"Does she love you?" Drew asked.

That was the million-dollar question, wasn't it? He wanted to know that answer too.

"I think so," he replied. "But I don't know. If she doesn't know, she will, because I'm not going anywhere. She will feel my love."

Drew shifted in his seat. He chuckled. "You know how weird this is, right?"

"Very," he agreed.

"I still want to punch you," Drew admitted. Whether serious or joking, Chris wasn't sure. "Maybe run your head into the corner of the wall or something." Drew shrugged. "I'll get over it, though, man. It kills me she wanted you over me—not in that way."

"I get it. You did right by Renée," Chris assured his friend. "She doesn't blame you for not being there when Lex was, and she didn't call me over you. Personally, I think Renée's more upset with herself for disappointing you. But I know she adores you. More than even she realizes."

"Damn," Drew breathed. "When'd you become so wise, Obi-Wan?"

They laughed.

"My mind is spinning," Drew confided. "So much is going through my head. Life is so short. We have to live in every moment. Seize the day. I'll feel better when Renée wakes up. Of course, she might not feel better when our parents get here."

"Yeah, that's a whole other set of issues," Chris agreed.

"Among many," Drew said, smacking his jeans-clad knees. He hefted himself to his feet. "If my sister ever experiences one iota of heartbreak because of you, I'll kill you. I'm a P.I.—a good one—I know how to hide a body."

CHAPTER FORTY

Something stabbed her eye. Wouldn't let her continue sleeping no matter how hard she squeezed her eyes shut to ignore it. Her brain nagged her to wake up.

Renée rolled to the side. At least she tried to, but a sharp pain pierced her left arm. Her eyelids drifted open; she blinked several times trying to get her bearings. Open blinds. The sun had been the culprit interrupting her sleep.

Her first thought: *Where the Hell...?*

She tried again, slower, to lift her left arm. Experienced the same painful tug. Glancing over, she inspected herself. An IV was taped in the crook of her arm. Her heart rate accelerated. If she hadn't felt it, the monitor sounded it. Breathing grew shallow. Why was she in the hospital?

The door across the room creaked open. Rationally, the worst it could be was a doctor. But irrationally, Renée tensed as every instinct went on high alert.

Honey blond hair eased through the crack. Then came a tan, chiseled face and glacial blue eyes. Chris. Her pulse slowed.

"Look who's awake," Chris said, his tone bright but strained.

"How did I get here?" she croaked. She coughed to clear her raw and itchy throat.

Chris entered, closing the door behind him. He approached the side of the bed and sat. Renée watched every ripple and bunch of muscles through his T-shirt. The guy was a frickin' work of art. Donatello, Michelangelo, eat your heart out! She just wanted to rub her hands and body all over his—Wait! Wasn't she supposed to be mad at him? Her thoughts were jumbled. Brain fog was the term that came to mind.

"I brought you," Chris's sinful deep drawl broke her train of thought. With the back of his large hand, he stroked her cheek. "How you feelin'?"

The way his eyes scanned her, examined her, rattled her nerves. Whenever he looked at her, her system went into overdrive. Was she supposed to feel bad? Obviously, she was in the hospital.

"My head's foggy. Like I took too much Benadryl or something," she voiced her honest assessment. Her stomach also felt hollow, like she hadn't eaten in years. "I guess I'm okay. What happened?"

He took her hand in his. He intertwined their fingers. "You were poisoned by your freak of a biological father and his crazy wife," Chris growled. "I'm guessing you called me cuz you were scared, which surprised the hell out of me."

Poison? She searched her memory. Hazy images of looking through photo albums. Odd pancake dinner. Her stomach started hurting. And... there was nothing. Black void.

They'd poisoned her. Didn't that only happen in Lifetime movies and soap operas? People poisoned other people. *That happens?!* And why would Chris be surprised she called him?

"Why are you surprised I called you?" Confusion laced her words.

His thumb caressed her hand. "Whatever they gave you must cause amnesia," he joked, giving her his signature lopsided grin. "You've been ignoring me for three days. Calling me for help..."

Right! That's why she was supposed to be mad. She shook her head.

"All that happened," she breathed. "It seems like a dream. Told you nobody can love me," Renée kidded—sort of.

Chris released her hand. He bumped her hip, a silent request for her to scoot over. She complied at once. It didn't escape her notice how easily she agreed to his direction. Weeks ago, she would have balked at his heavy-handedness; now, she scooted. Perspective must come in near-death experiences.

He got in bed. The heat of his gigantic body and his dark, masculine scent caused her hormones to riot. He wrapped an arm around her shoulder and rested it behind her head and neck. Hard bicep and pectorals were more comfortable than she expected.

Once settled, he spoke. "How does what those people did make you unlovable?"

She snorted. Didn't Chris get it? "I'm part of him, which means his evil craziness is part of me, too," she explained. "That's why no one ever looked for me."

"No, you're not."

Renée sighed. No one understood. "You don't—"

"Stop," Chris interrupted her rebuttal. "I already have evidence to the contrary." He paused dramatically.

She kept her peace. Curious to hear this proof.

"First, no one is born evil, just like nobody is born racist. Both behaviors are learned. So, you can be part of him every day, all day. It doesn't make you evil. Second, I love you. I'm in love with you. So, you're not unlovable."

Why weren't the monitors beeping? Alerting nurses and doctors of her distress. Her breath caught in her chest. He'd come for her when he was mad at her. Stubborn, maybe. Dumb, absolutely not. Could he love her, as he claimed? Did she love him?

Chris carefully lifted her hand attached to the IV arm. He kissed her knuckles, then put them down. His tender handling of her would be her undoing.

"See?" He grinned. "Something this beautiful couldn't be unlovable."

Her dry lips twitched. "Are you talking about you or me?"

"You're doing it again," he chastised.

"What?"

"Making jokes when things get real," he reminded her. "This is serious. They could've killed you, Renée. And for what? Insurance money? Like a random dead chick turning up in their house wasn't gonna raise some red flags?"

Tears filled her eyes. Chris lifted her as if she weighed nothing. He scooted into the center of the bed, spread his legs, and placed her between them.

"Stop manhandling me," Renée chided. "My brother's gonna assassinate you. And this is against hospital policy."

"No, he won't," Chris said casually. "He knows already."

"*What?!*" Renée jerked, yanking off the pulse oximeter attached to her finger. Bells chimed. Chris clipped the monitor back to her finger. The bells quieted. She settled into his embrace. "How are you still alive?"

"Once you called, I had to tell him," Chris enlightened her. "He came with me to get you—and let me just say, nobody plays a gay man like Andrew. He really commits."

They laughed.

"He can't be your sole protector forever," he continued. "But you need to open up to him again. He loves you more than anything," Chris advised. "Well, I guess, not more than his girlfriend. Oh, my bad, fiancée."

He was right. Renée had punished Andrew for so long for a situation that was of her own making. Pride had kept her from admitting what was happening with Corey. Andrew was her brother in every way that mattered, and—

Renée swiveled around to face Chris.

"His what now?" she asked. "How the hell long was I asleep? Who's his fiancée? Don't you have to be dating someone to get affianced?"

"Hey, you miss a lot in thirty-six hours." Chris laughed. "Once Drew knew you were out of the woods, he got all philosophical. He decided—and I quote—tomorrow's not promised to anyone. So, he *carpe diem'ed* and proposed to Christina."

Her jaw fell slack. "My Christina!" she shouted. "My brother proposed to my best Christina?" Renée gritted her teeth. "I knew it! I had a feeling. I should strangle both of them. They're lucky I love them, or they'd be dead. No wonder Andrew's so cool with us. Ooh!"

Chris forced her face forward and head down to rest against his chest. His deep laugh vibrated his chest and, by extension, her body. It did interesting things to her lady bits, considering she only wore a fifteen-sizes-too-big hospital gown.

"Wanna hear a funny story?" he asked once he sobered.

She shrugged. "Sure."

"So, I was talking to Ashley, right?" he said mockingly, chipper. "She told me about a little talk she and Christina had with you."

Renée rolled her eyes. "Ooh! I can't stand her! And?"

"And next time you decide to write your man off, talk to me first," he appealed. "Bitch me out so I can at least explain myself."

"My man?" She scoffed. He presumed too much. But if Andrew already knew then... "Fine. Is there anything else I should know? Did World War III start in Nebraska? Gas prices go down?"

"Actually, yes," he answered casually.

Renée turned slack jawed. "Gas prices went down?!"

Chris shot her a droll stare.

"Fine. Sorry. Fine. I was just trying to lighten the mood. Sorry," Renée apologized. Old habits die hard. She preferred humor when things were too serious. Renée required a certain amount of levity with her drama.

His deep sigh said more than she cared to hear. But he said it anyway. "Your parents are on their way. They know everything."

Renée relinquished all her body weight to Chris. She rested her head on his chest. The euphoric feeling of being able to trust someone with her entire being momentarily eclipsed dread. Yes, her friends provided support. She could be herself with them, but this intimacy coupled with support was different.

"Super!" she retorted sarcastically. "This day keeps getting better and better."

Steely arms gripped her in a bear hug. Chris placed his lips to her ear. "You have no idea how scared I was for you," he whispered. Goosebumps broke out all over her arms. Tingles raced up and down her spine. "I'll be right here when your parents get here," he assured her. "But first, you need to answer a question. Can you do that—without making a joke?"

She gulped. Couldn't help it. Things were upside down. If he did something like propose, she'd die. Die!

"Umm... I think so. Ask and find out." She chuckled nervously.

"Please," he pleaded.

Fidgeting with her gown, she nodded.

"In case you didn't catch the two other times, I said it," Chris said, then paused for a beat. "I'm in love with you. Do you at least have feelings for me, too?"

Ugh! She wasn't good at emotional talks. Verbal expressions of love and all that came across as corny when she saw them on television. Her mind and heart might say one thing, but her mouth saying it would ruin it. She was more of a horror girl.

"Chris, don't be weird."

He frowned. She knew it without having to see his face because his shoulders sagged behind her. However, she wasn't done. He needed to understand.

"Thank you for coming to get me," she powered through. "It means more than I can ever express."

"Renée," he reprimanded.

Damn! "Okay, okay." She inhaled to her toes. Then let it out. "I love you. I'm in love with you. I've been in love with you since I was in eighth grade. And puppy love before that. Happy?"

Chris pressed a chaste kiss to her cheek. Renée needed more. Before he backed away, she turned. She wrapped her unencumbered arm around his head and pulled him close. His lips descended. Fire spread through her, and she forgot all about being in the hospital. Her lips trembled under the force of his. Chris's tongue barged into her mouth; permission be damned. Entrance was demanded, and she relented. A moan escaped her lips. He swallowed it whole. For passionate minutes, their tongues dueled. She could get used to this.

Breaking the kiss, Chris smiled. "Thanks, brat. Love you, too."

CHAPTER FORTY-ONE

Renée picked at tape clinging to a microscopic arm hair. Hospital tape always seemed to find the tiniest hair and yank the crap out of it. All afternoon she'd felt this pinch in her left arm, aside from the irritating IV, yet couldn't find the source of the pain until now. Funny how minute nuisances emerged as distractions when waiting for your world to crumble. Or was she the only person who fidgeted and fixated on anything to keep from focusing on what one perceived as impending doom?

Somewhere in the hospital were a livid Randall and Susan Sutton. Chris had gone to get an ETA ten minutes ago. The fact he hadn't returned yet was a bad sign. Her stomach did a move impressive enough to make a gymnast proud.

She should never have done this road trip. Her brother, bless his heart, wanting to regain her trust, put his, and the lives of their friends, in danger for her. For a stupid quest to find something, she realized after her first stop. The sum of a person's experiences, morals, values, the content of character, and loved ones form a person's identity. Self-identification was personal. Not some formula mixed in a lab. Blood determined the potential for hereditary health risks. It didn't make a person who they were. Didn't make her, more, or less, valid. Needing to understand her past and heal from it wasn't wrong. Her past, no matter how volatile, was part of what made her, her. A part Renée needed to reconcile with her present. Where she went wrong? Dismissing the love and care her parents, brother, and friends showed her in favor of obsessing over people she didn't know.

Her room door creaked. Renée jumped. Almost ripped all the tape off her arm and pulled out the IV. Patting the offending adhesive in place, she held her breath. Cast her gaze to her lap. She was prepared for her parents' ire.

Quiet greeted her. She looked up into wide, round, frightened dark eyes.

"You whore!" she blasted. "How could you?"

Christina flinched as if struck. Her skin paled. She gasped. Tears made her dark eyes glisten. The corners of Renée's mouth inched into a smile.

"So, we're gonna be sisters!" she said. "Come here, girlie."

Fear not yet receded; Christina shuffled toward the bed. She sat in the chair Chris bypassed earlier. Renée pegged her friend with a flat stare. Color slowly returned to Christina's face. She approached the bed. Grabbing her hand, Renée jerked Christina to her. Finally, her friend cracked a smile. They shared a quick hug.

"I'm sorry," Christina apologized. "I was scared how you'd react. Andrew said he'd tell you. And I didn't want to lose you as a friend. I love—"

"Calm down," Renée coaxed. "First off, I'm not your mom; you should never fear me. Second, there isn't anybody in this world better for my brother than you. And third, you could never lose me."

Christina flashed a smile and retook her seat. "You know they're mad, right?"

Renée resettled herself on the bed. Smoothed the now destroyed IV tape. "Unfortunately." She exhaled loudly.

"You're a brave girl," Christina complimented. "Chris? And now your parents? You haven't even talked to Andrew yet. Ash and I are here if you need us."

"Thanks."

The door cracked open again. Their heads swiveled in that direction.

Her father's tall, broad frame entered the doorway first.

"Time to face the music," Chrissy whispered conspiratorially. She pushed her chair back and rose.

"Wish me luck," she mouthed.

Her father patted Christina's shoulder as she passed him. "See ya in a bit, darlin'."

Christina granted him and her mother one of her token bashful smiles and sped out of sight down the hall. Randall, complete with brown Stetson, flannel, and worn jeans, sauntered in. Close behind him, Susan decked out in black slacks and a fuchsia blouse. Her nails were freshly done, and her polish matched her top. Gone was the fun-loving, vacation-bound Mom and Dad, and in their place were Mr. and Mrs. Sutton. And they meant business. Not even laugh lines hinting at past mirth were evident on their faces.

Booted and heeled feet click-clopped against the hospital floor. Sky blue and emerald gazes tunneled into her. Renée's stomach tightened. Shame and guilt were oppressive weights. They rounded the bed. Her mother sat in the chair. Her father sat on the end of her bed. Their expressions were stern. Neither spoke. If the lump in her throat was indicative of her expression, then moisture-coated, wide apologetic eyes and a downturned mouth greeted them.

The intermittent beeping of her monitors provided an ominous soundtrack to their silent standoff. She didn't know what to say. Her mouth dried. They stared. Why weren't they yelling or accosting her? She'd nearly killed Andrew? Why—

The whir of her blood pressure cuff inflating broke their stalemate.

Tsking, her father, shook his head back and forth slowly. "Renée Marie Sutton," his gruff drawl laced her name with so much anger he was calm. Almost bored sounding.

"Hey, guys," she said, relying on the levity Chris despised. "How was Hawaii?"

Her mother blinked several times, astonished. An unimpressed flat stare replaced confoundment.

"Fantastic," Randall answered deceptively light-hearted, "until the phone call that our daughter nearly died from being poisoned and was rushed to an Indiana hospital."

"Is life not exciting enough for you?" her mother queried; brows knit. "Were you looking for an adrenaline rush? Going into strangers' houses—blood or not—alone, unprotected? I don't understand what possessed you to do something so crazy. You and your bonehead brother could've been killed."

Leave it to Mom to dive in. Dad shared her ironic sarcasm. He entertained it even in the gravest circumstances. Mom didn't do evasive maneuvers; she steamrolled her victims. No BS.

Renée shifted. Picked at the tape. Looked everywhere but at them. Sorry, wouldn't suffice. She'd hurt them. Hurt Andrew. Band-aids and A&D ointment didn't heal metaphorical gunshot wounds to the heart.

"I'm sorry." Lame! But it was all she had. "I didn't mean to hurt you. Andrew wasn't ever in any unnecessary danger, I promise. It wasn't my intention to hurt anyone. I thought this would help," she rambled. Tears obstructed her vision. Renée wrung her hands to keep from ripping out her IV.

"Did you find what you were looking for?" her father asked in exasperation.

She winced. Sorrow descended. Clouded her mind, tightening her jaw. Renée gazed at her parents through thick, tear-laden lashes.

"Yes," she whispered. "I've always felt like nobody loves me. Even when people said it, I didn't trust it. I couldn't. All my experiences with love hurt. My biological parents were supposed to love me and look at what they did. My sisters, family, all people genetically hard-wired to love me left me," Renée explained. "Since birth, there's been something about me that just pushed people away. I thought if I met these people—people I was supposed to feel something for—everything in my world would right itself. But when we met—it didn't. I felt nothing. The only time I feel whole is with you guys—and my friends—and I'm sorry."

Susan Sutton jumped out of her chair like it bit her. Warm, soft arms embraced Renée. Enveloped her in the love, support, and all the belonging each of her spontaneous visits lacked.

"Oh, you silly, foolish, silly girl," her mother cooed, pushing her head into her bosom. Her mother's familiar perfume surrounded her. "We aren't worried Andrew would have been hurt. Have you seen that big, corn-fed boy? Of course, we care, but we know he'll be fine. You are our baby girl. We didn't adopt you because of some God complex. Because we weren't spending enough a year on Andrew. Or because we enjoy high-stress situations and sarcasm. We didn't save you. You were intelligent, strong, and resilient long before us. And would have succeeded all on your own. You didn't need us, but we needed you. We adopted you because, from the moment we saw you, we knew you were ours. Not our adopted daughter. Our daughter. Our family.

"Do you know how beautiful you are here"—she pointed to her heart—"and here?" Gently lifting her head, she caressed Renée's cheek. "We couldn't imagine our lives without you. And you nearly took *you* from us with this half-cocked stunt. You complete our family. You couldn't be our daughter any more than if we conceived you ourselves. And look what your brother and friends did for you... You are now, always have been, and always will be... Dearly beloved."

Beautiful large crosses were carved into Honduras mahogany arches. Tingles started in Renée's toes. Raced up her legs. It could've been the silver open-toed heels. They pinched. She wiggled her toes. Cool air caressed her exposed, overheated skin. Rolling her shoulders, she sought to loosen the knots. Wool warmed the perspiration-slicked crook of her arm; she held a death grip on the proffered appendage. Knees locked, she didn't think she could walk. Like a domino, she'd topple over if he let go.

"Don't let me fall," she whispered, clinging on vise-grip style.

"Never," he vowed. "Never."

Nothing frightened her more than when she'd realized her biological mother wasn't coming back twenty-three years ago. No matter how neglectful she'd been, she was all Renée knew then. Then she and Kathy were separated. And she'd been abandoned all over again. Loss, betrayal, and violence became staples in her life after that. Trust was a luxury she couldn't afford for her entire childhood and part of her adolescence.

Through her adoption, she gradually found trust. Three and a half years ago, while looking for something she already had in spades but wasn't capable of fully appreciating, she'd been poisoned. Trust crumbled like a sledgehammer to stained glass. Not trust in her friends and family. Her faith in them grew to bulletproof proportions. However, she lost complete trust in herself. Working with Dr. Mendoza and support from her nearest and dearest rebuilt her self-esteem in ways she'd never believed possible.

Violins and ground bass in D Major reached their crescendo through the double doors. Renée's stomach dropped. Nerves made her comfortable lace sweetheart neckline itch. She refrained from acting on impulse. A delicate cough did little to clear her clogged throat. Maybe she'd overstated how much trust she had in herself. She glanced down. Blood red toenail polish matched the red velvet carpet under her feet. Clammy hands fought to hold on to the silk-wrapped handle clasped between them. Her breathing increased.

The music coming through the doors moved into a diminuendo. Wood creaked as the old doors opened. Petals shook under the minor earthquake taking place inside her nervous system. Tulle grazed her arms.

"Relax, kiddo," came the gruff direction from beside her. His smile made laugh lines and crow's feet prominent on his tanned face. Her father delivered two reassuring squeezes to her upper arm. "Stop watching your feet."

She raised her head. Flower petals littered the red carpet. Candelabra were on either side of the aisle.

Randall led their slow procession. Ninety inches of ivory illusion tulle trimmed with scalloped lace cascaded around her petite frame and trailed each of her steps. Lace and tulle swished, rustled, as she moved. Glancing to the left and right, she saw her loved ones. And one she never expected...

Big black springy curls adorned the java-skinned woman's head to the left. Onyx eyes glistened. A purple dress complimented ample curves. Full lips parted into an attractive smile showcasing pearl white teeth. Two years after her road trip, Kathy finally came around. They weren't super close, but Renée was okay with that for the first time.

Her best friends stood to the left of the aisle. Gorgeous, vintage, maroon, A-line dresses flattered Ashley and a heavily pregnant Christina. They beamed brightly. Strawberry blond and coal black hair clashed prettily. On the right, Andrew, Rand, and Alex were quite dapper in their wool, Tom Ford tuxedos, which matched her father's. Her brother grinned and winked.

Her gaze drifted, and her world righted—tailor-made, virgin wool fit wide shoulders to perfection. Satin lapels begged her to pet his hard, muscled chest. Chris's single-breasted Prada tux caused her heart to palpitate for a whole other reason. When his mouth tilted into that same lopsided grin, her nerves and everyone else in the room melted away. Midnight-blue eyes sparkled with unconditional love and acceptance.

Of course, Renée trusted herself. More importantly, she trusted him.

The white-haired minister stepped into place behind Chris. The music faded. Once at the altar, her father presented her.

"Who gives this woman to be married to this man?" the gravel-voiced minister asked.

"Her mother and I do," Randall proclaimed loud and proud, drawing laughter from their guests. Randall shrugged, lifted the blusher to her veil, and kissed her cheek. He replaced the veil and placed her hands in Chris's. Her future. Her man saw her imperfections perfectly and loved her despite them. And she loved his cocky ass, too.

"Dearly beloved..."

Dearly Beloved Soundtrack

1. Mario – Let Me Love You (Chris's song to Renée)

2. Bruno Mars – Count on Me (Story Anthem)

3. Pink – You Make Me Sick (Renée's song for Chris)

4. Gavin Degraw – More Than Anyone (Chapter Twenty-Nine)

5. En Vogue – Giving Him Something He Can Feel (Chapter Nine)

6. Christina Aguilera – Voice Within (Chapter Ten)

7. Black Eyed Peas – My Humps (Chapter Nine)

8. Charlie Daniels Band – The Devil Went Down To Georgia (Chapter Ten)

9. The Village People – Macho Man (Chapter Ten)

10. Garth Brooks – Friends In Low Places (Chapter Ten)

11. Pink – Fuckin Perfect (Ashley To Her Friends)

12. Maroon 5 – One More Night (Chris & Renée's Relationship Anthem)

13. Travis Porter – Ayy Ladies ft. Tyga (St. Clair, MO Rest Stop Boogie)

14. Lil' Wayne – How To Love (Renée's Issues with Relationships)

15. Pink – Trouble (Chapter Ten)

16. Robin Thicke – Sweetest Love (Chris & Renée Together)

17. Yelawolf – Good Girl (Chris's Issues)

18. Robin Thicke – Blurred Lines (Chapter Eleven)

19. Quindon Tarver – Everybody's Free (Epilogue Dearly Beloved)

20. Usher – Dive (Chapter Twenty-Nine)

21. Train – Drops of Jupiter (Renée's Journey)

22. Nate Dogg – Never Leave Me Alone (Chapter 20)

23. Megan Thee Stallion – Body (St. Clair, MO Rest Stop Boogie alternate)

Acknowledgements

There is a certain stigma surrounding children who grow up as wards of the court. I'm not even sure the world knows that they've pigeon-holed these kids. Used circumstances outside of their control to paint them with an unfair broad brush. Labeled them damaged. Broken. Unlovable. Oftentimes, children are removed from bad homes with their biological families and placed in homes worse than most can ever imagine. It's not all the states' fault. Social workers are burnt out by overwhelming caseloads. What started with good intentions, often ends with another form of neglect for innocent children who've already seen too much. Experienced too much. Suffered more.

Foster care is the worst, best-kept dirty secret. The amount of trauma inflicted on foster children is outrageous. Appalling. There's not enough light shone on the situation. For some reason, society would like to believe only good comes from placing children in the state system and foster homes. I wrote this novel to share some of the horrors that befall children in the state system. To destigmatize the idea that these children are somehow unworthy and deserving of mistreatment. Bring awareness to the damage that follows some through adolescence and well into adulthood.

These people who survive the system aren't any more predisposed to being bad people than anyone else. It's the world that causes them to feel less than. Statistically, most of the people placed in the state system and foster care don't make it to adulthood. When they do, they often struggle in many ways because they're ill-prepared to deal with life. The foster care system is less about care and more about money. With all that being said, there are good people that I've been lucky to meet. Who saw me as more than a neglected and abused black little girl. Genuinely took an interest in my well-being. Money didn't entice them. Accolades for "saving" a poor child weren't their motivations. They saw something in me worth nurturing. I'll forever be grateful to them. Through them, I survived and learned to become more than my circumstances. I learned that I was Dearly Beloved.

Thanks to:

Sandy Nicest

Cheri Estrada

Nick & Sue Mavrolas

Katy Buehler

Bailey

Kathy Bass

Special thanks to:

Becky Horwitz

Melanie Zuverink

Pam Sadler

Amber Holbrook

Elena Johnson

Honorable Mentions:

Thank you for editing my work thoroughly Claire Ashgrove. Also, thank you, Romana Mihai for your assistance editing.

Roseanna Bruton for being an awesome friend and beta reader.

All of my guy friends who I used as inspiration for the friendship between Andrew, Chris, Lex, and Rand. And a big thank you to the men of RT TV, the YouTube channel that helped me get the men's banter just right. The amount of hours I spent watching their channel is insane, but totally worth it.

If you like dark urban fantasy or dark paranormal romance

Turn the page for a sample of

Dead Inside

by Wilt Rhys

writing as

Piper Anderson

The Inauguration of Chaos

Delphi, Greece, 1,020 years ago

THE SUPERNATURAL WOULD cease to exist. Danae Rossi couldn't breathe. Her lungs burned. Erratic thumps of her heart sounded loud to her ears. Each footfall against the cold, stone floor of the grandiose Radulescu crypt rivaled the fiercest thunderstorm.

Crypt—hmph? Danae would have laughed at the ease with which she thought the word, if anything could be humorous in this moment.

Decades ago, such musings would've wrought light-headedness and palpitations. Supernatural: beings capable of shifting shape. Beings that possessed magical abilities and outlived mortals. Beings, like her. She'd been young, ignorant then. Neither description suited her any longer. These people were her friends, family. This place, her home. Her heart palpitated for a different reason now. For this news, she bore.

...to everything, there is a season, a time for every purpose. So it is written, now is the time, a time to fall. The time for more hate than love, more sow than reap, time of chaos for all ye supernatural. A

time of great sorrow, time of much woe. Now is time for Vampire Royals, to Raj they must go...

The prophecy filled the limited space unoccupied by terror in her mind. This mystical passage catapulted her from her quarters, sent her running through the massive underground dwelling.

She passed *Chief Vampire Royal Guardsman*, Sebastian Cantemir, his second-in-command, Gawain, and the newest addition to the guard, Sebastian's son, Emilio. Her heart ached for the oblivious males.

Would they survive? Would any of them?

These morbid ponderings hastened her steps. She needed to reach the queen.

"Your Majesty," Danae blurted seconds later from the entryway of the nursery. She paused, swallowing hard. "It has been written. Your cousin and his army shall attack. The Vampire Royals will not survive."

Soft, ethereal laughter came from the petite, gold-cloaked, hooded figure standing beside an intricately carved wooden cradle. "Ah... dear, White-witch. I could destroy the barriers guarding your thoughts with much ease."

Danae wiped a sweaty palm down the front of her red servants' cloak. She knew the queen would sense her shields. However, she'd hoped to ease into the discussion her abrupt delivery belied.

"My queen, this is prophecy from the Book of Being, not a vision. We must take it seriously."

A pale white hand extended from the gold cloak. Glided back and forth across the top rail of the cradle.

With her back facing her, Danae could not gage the queen's reaction. Her own heart constricted. The hair on her nape and arms stood on end. Intuition bellowed time was of the essence. The queen needed to understand the magnitude of the situation.

"What can Balkan do which has not been done?" Queen Ana-Marie drawled in a bored tone. "His Daywalkers have failed time and again. And they walk in sunlight. If that advantage has not aided him thus far, what could?"

Danae sighed. If only that reasoning staved off the inevitable. If she were a mere servant this knowledge might be easier to bear. On second thought, it would not. Queen Ana-Marie brought order, peace, to the supernatural. Things her cousin, the ex-King Balkan, never did in his six-century reign. Not one sound-minded supernatural could relay such news and not recognize it for the catastrophe it was.

In the decades since the queen's ascension to the throne, she and Queen Ana-Marie had forged a friendship. Dare she be so bold as to say, they had become sisters? That knowledge doubled her burden. How did one inform their sister of her and her family's imminent demise?

"Fifty years have passed, Madame," Danae pointed out, voice cracking. "His army has grown in strength and number, along with his hybrid young. We do not possess similar advantages."

"How does he continue to find reasons to be unhappy?" the queen mused. She turned, pinned Danae with narrowed, beguiling eyes. "The Fates should have destroyed him. Simple deposing for creating those hybrid abominations was too good for him."

Danae pushed back the hood of her cloak, ran a hand through her chin-length, ebony hair. Legs aching from her sprint through the crypt, the weight of Queen Ana-Marie's gaze nearly felled her.

The queen's flawless white skin glowed with eternal youth. High cheekbones and a small, pert nose were perfect complements. But her eyes were the *pièce de résistance.*

Hypnotic and almond-shaped, one iris was deep green with a jagged pool of golden-brown citrine reaching out from the pupil. The other iris was yellow with the same pool of golden-brown citrine reaching from its pupil. When Queen Ana-Marie set eyes upon someone, she could be denied nothing.

With untraceable speed unique to her breed, Queen Ana-Marie crossed the room. She sat in a large, floral-engraved, throne-style chair and lowered the hood of her cloak. Lustrous, deep red waves cascaded to her waist. "Come. Sit with me, dear Danae. I worry for your health. You look unwell."

"Your Majesty, please," Danae pled, voice cracking. She cleared her throat. "I would never come to you with such distressing words with any uncertainty. Ana-Marie, I implore you, prepare the guard."

She never addressed the queen informally, even when requested. The queen's knitted brows confirmed Danae's words had the intended effect. A wave of the queen's hand pulled out a smaller chair, scooted it near hers. She patted the seat.

On shaky legs, Danae entered the nursery and sat.

Queen Ana-Marie was silent, eyes fixed on nothing in particular across the room. "I see," whispered moments later. "When is the battle to take place?"

Danae's heart became lead in her chest. Her stomach dropped. This was what she wanted, the queen to grasp the seriousness. Now that she had, her friend's forlorn look was unbearable. A hot tear rolled down her cheek. She shook her head. "The time is undisclosed. However, intuition says the time is near. Less than one rising."

She once envied the immortal inhabitants of the royal crypt. Although long-lived, witches grew old and passed on to Raj. Secretly, Danae wanted to be as the half-human, half-demon vampires were, forever young and beautiful. Here, watching the queen's expressionless face, empty eyes and stiff posture, she didn't wish to be witch or vampire. All would meet their end...soon.

Reaching over the cloth-covered arm of her chair, Danae placed her warm hand on one of the queen's much cooler ones.

For long moments they were still, absorbing the quiet comfort the other offered.

The queen's gaze shifted.

Danae followed her line of vision to the cradle. No, not the cradle. Through it, to what was held within. Princess Valora. A crimson tear slithered down the queen's cheek. She roughly brushed it away.

It occurred to Danae then, she would never know the obvious pain the queen experienced. The loss of young. The joy of bringing life into the world. Prophecy stated they would all perish, servants and Vampire Royals alike, her. Her heartache soared. Shifting fabric called her attention to the present. Danae focused on the queen.

Upper lip curled away from lengthening fangs. Unique eyes glowed. Queen Ana-Marie yanked her hand from underneath Danae's.

Danae started.

"What of my young?" the queen snarled, facing her.

"The book did not say. It stated a time of chaos would befall the supernatural. Races will fight each other to near extinction. The warring will lead to exposure to mortals, which will incite the Most High's wrath. Eventually, he'll destroy The Fates and all supernatural."

"What. Of. My young, Danae?" she demanded.

Danae gulped. "Prince Isaac and Prince Nico have long since reached the Immortal Age. They must battle with the king consort, the guardsmen, all of us to protect you."

"And what of my Valora?" Queen Ana-Marie turned slightly, as if to glance toward the cradle. She jerked to face Danae. "I refuse to stand idly by, helpless, cradling my young while we are destroyed. You and the Royal Guardsmen are sworn to protect me. I am bound by a force beyond even The Fates comprehension to protect my young. Must I choose between my..." her voice broke, she cut off abruptly.

Half-crazed, desperate eyes bored into Danae's.

"If there be nothing I can do for my sons... please"—she swallowed, seconds passed before she finished—"help me spare my daughter our fate."

Tears welled in Danae's eyes. She fought them, for once started, they'd never cease. The panic and despair she observed in the queen's frantic gaze was a punch to her abdomen. What could she do? The Fates' will would be done. Perhaps—an idea came to mind. Danae chanced a brief glance toward the cradle then back to the queen. "There may be a way, Your Majesty."

Queen Ana-Marie's fangs retracted. Red eyebrows furrowed. "A way?"

"To save Princess Valora."

Hope sprang to life in the queen's eyes. "Why such suspense, dear friend?" She took both Danae's hands in hers. "Our time is short. Speak now."

Her mouth went dry. She hadn't meant to give the queen false hope. There was no guarantee she could still preform such magic. If The Fates became aware... the consequence would be death. "I have not attempted this in years. And I have never performed such magic on a person—vampire or mortal. But, I may be able to cloak the princess. If successful, she will be incapable of being sensed by supernatural or The Fates."

Before the last word fell from her lips, Danae was alone. One second she sat hand-in-hand with the queen. The next, her hands were folded in her lap, and the queen's chair vacated. Not even wind denoted the speed at which the queen traveled.

"Do it," Queen Ana-Marie commanded from beside the cradle, hood covering her bowed head once more. In another, faster-than-discernible movement, the queen had the infant vampiress swaddled in a gold velvet blanket and in her arms.

They needed to hurry, but the abruptness with which the queen made the decision concerned Danae. If Ana-Marie did not understand the ramifications of such a request, all could be lost.

"Your Majesty," Danae hurried to elaborate, "if The Fates trace my magic they will destroy the babe with me. If successful and the royal family is destroyed, Valora can never rule. Her Seal will be dormant. It will be as if she no longer exists."

"Is this your lone objection?"

Nodding, Danae stood.

In the span of a heartbeat, Queen Ana-Marie approached. Wide, crimson tear-filled eyes leveled on Danae. She placed a feather light kiss on her forehead and one cheek. Then she handed Danae the baby.

Danae cradled the infant in wooden arms.

"Go now," the queen ordered. "Cloak her. I care not for the throne. Raise her among the mortals. Protect her with your life—as if she were your own. If I, Victor, or either of the princes survives the impending battle, we will call to your mind. Remain open to us." She gazed lovingly at her daughter, brushed back a blood red curl from her daughter's forehead. Crimson tears streaked Queen Ana-Marie's pale face. Somber eyes fixed on Danae. "Promise you will love her, care for her as your own."

Unable to speak past the lump in her throat, Danae nodded.

How could this be the end?

Queen Ana-Marie pulled Danae into cool, strong arms. Squeezed. She pressed a kiss to the baby's forehead. "Leave this place. Now!"

The command came not from a queen, but wrenched from the soul of a grieving mother.

Danae spun around. Ran as if the *Dark Majesty* was on her heels. Wind tousled her hair, ruffled the ends of her cloak. She sprinted towards the secret tunnel that led out of the crypt.

Dense fog and mist whooshed past her. Seconds later, the thud of several pairs of booted feet on stone sounded behind her as fog and mist morphed into males. Guardsmen. The queen must have summoned them through her telepathic link to all royal servants.

A short time later, Danae emerged from the underground passageway. Gazing around the lush, green mountainside and up the stone benches of the Delphi theatre, she wrapped Princess Valora tighter to protect her skin from the deadly sun's rays. A muttered incantation cast a transportation spell.

The first battle cry sounded as they teleported through space and distance.

Light, reassuring touches of each member of the royal family fluttered against her mind. She and the baby rematerialized in an unknown village where night had fallen.

Danae quickly located a vacant domicile, entered, and cast a protection spell over it. Her heart pounded. For hours she cowered in a corner awaiting news of the battle. She clutched the resting young to her bosom. Then...

One by one, the Vampire Royals' presence vanished from her mind. Prince Isaac. Victor. Prince Nico. And last, with a strained, whispered *"Thank you,"* Queen Ana-Marie. The vampire royals were destroyed.

Tuesday, June 27th, 1000 years later, St. Joseph's Hospital Phoenix, Arizona

HANGING ABOVE CLOSED double doors, a standard circular clock's long, black minute hand struck twelve, midnight. Cries of a newborn baby pierced the doors of the delivery room.

ELSEWHERE IN THE world, and for the first time in a millennium, a new entry appeared in the Book of Being. It read: For unto the supernatural an heir of pure noble blood is born, a daughter is given: *The government shall be upon her shoulder: and her name shall be called Zenith Royal, Portent of Peace, Most Powerful, Princess of Compassion, The Everlasting Queen.*

Chapter One

Present day Rome, Italy

TALON CANTEMIR'S GAZE traveled the length of his muscled forearm. His large hand rested atop the black marble counter. Long, pallid fingers obscure an object fisted in a vise grip.

Squeezing tighter, a lion-sized roar tore through his lips, piercing the silence. Reverberated through the room followed by a loud...

Pop!

Dense red nectar of life seeped between his closed fingers, ran over his knuckles, pooled on the marble.

"Dammit!" a thunderous male voice shouted from beside him. "That was the last one! You know what this means. And not only did you get it all over yourself, but, your mother's new counters. Does this make you proud?"

Oh yes, very. The one vampire warrior in existence disgusted by blood. No, not blood. Bagged, donated blood. Yeah, he was real proud. Was it his fault he had taste buds?

"Four rogue vampires attacked me night before last," his father rehashed in a low, gruff tone. "I'd just left one of the courtier's palazzo. How do you suppose they knew of my whereabouts? Or breached the compound's shield?"

Talon bowed his head. Strands of golden-blonde hair slipped over his forehead, tickled his eyelashes. He studied the bloody mess he made of his hand, glanced at his white silk shirt. Lots of blood stains there too, it'd be a bitch to scrub off.

He kept his head down, but not out of shame. Nor did he fear his father. Talon feared what he might say. Anyway, it wasn't as if Sebastian Cantemir expected an answer. His father adored talking at him. Not to him. Fates forbid his son might say something intelligent.

"Your mamma narrowly escaped decapitation leaving the Liakos palazzo last night. Luckily she sublimated to fog before the silver-plated machete pierced her flesh."

"I get it, *Comandante*," Talon bit out between clenched teeth. This wasn't new news, just one of many training tactics his father employed. Guilt. The *compound* was magically shielded, invisible to mortals, rogues, and non-privileged supernatural. The walled-in city housed the largest concentration of supernatural. *Vampire Royal Guardsmen* and their counterparts of other breeds protected it. Somehow, the *courtiers* had become the unofficial law. If rogues were getting in…? "I will not allow the courtiers to continue their plotting. I'll make you and Mamma safe."

"How? By bending over? Handing them the blade to sever your head from your shoulders? This will help you blend with the mortals. Yet this simple task is too hard for you."

Thanks for the sunlight to that wound.

"That's what I'm trying to do now," Talon continued, ignoring his father's gibe. "This solution—finding the Vampire Royals mortal descendant," he said in an ominous tone, "seems facile, and farfetched."

"It is not for us to question The Fates' will," Sebastian snapped, hitting the countertop. The sound of cracking marble rent the air. "We've been over a millennium without their guidance, punished for things, not of our doing. No sealed queen or king.

We're not converting mortals. White-witches haven't spelled our females' bodies, giving us no vampire young. If the incessant warring doesn't bring about our race's extinction the lack of young will. The supernatural won't survive another thousand years. The prophecy must be fulfilled."

Talon couldn't concentrate. The sulfuric and burnt rubber stench of old blood made him sick. He felt it drying on his face and hand. No matter, he knew how this song and dance went. His father's blind faith in the mystical trio of angels who created the supernatural astounded him. Sebastian refused to see reason.

"Your inability to do this jeopardizes us all, *Talon*." Contempt turned his name into a curse.

He was the prophesied savior of the supernatural and his family. Why couldn't he do this?

Hand-to-hand combat?

Check.

Weapons?

Master of all, there wasn't one he didn't know how to use, dismantle, and rebuild.

Feeding from a donor bag...?

Couldn't do it to save his existence.

Talon turned. His eyes traveled up, up, up the mountain that was his father looming beside him. Their resemblance was striking. Both were broad-shouldered and lean. Sebastian appeared larger from Talon's sitting-on-a-barstool vantage point. In truth, they were the same height, six-six. They shared dark blue eyes. However, the similarities ended there.

His haircut was shorter, modern. Sebastian's golden-blond locks were shoulder length. Their most important difference could only be seen when one examined the non-beating heart of the individual male. He didn't possess his father's blind faith. Talon preferred solid, indisputable proof. Perhaps there were other differences, too. He knew he had dried blood on his face, but his father...

Jaw tight, his pale face harsh, livid. Arms crossed over his chest. Blood spatter peppered his cheek and forehead.

Non bene.

"Father."

Sebastian growled.

Damn! He never slipped and called him that. Sebby didn't allow it. But, need to appeal to whatever got his father dubbed chief by the *Vampire Royals*, whatever once made him an esteemed leader, made Talon forget himself.

He began again, "*Comandante*, there is no proof Princess Valora existed, or that she ever bore young to produce this descendant. This journey to America to find the alleged descendant could be a hoax. A trick to leave you and Mamma unprotected."

"I am far from weak!" Sebastian smacked the countertop again almost breaking it in half. "You forget, I trained you and your brother."

Talon stared at his father, deadpan. "If this is a false prophecy and you and mamma are destroyed, how could I restore our name? How would the supernatural be saved? They would be in the same chaos they've lived in for over a millennium. The only difference, no royal guard to protect them."

"I can't speak for the other breeds of guardsmen, but if I were to perish my second would succeed me. If we both should perish, you would lead the Vampire Royal Guard."

He wouldn't touch the remark about his father's second-in-command. Talon considered Gawain family. The male was loyal to Sebastian, even trustworthy, but dedicated to the supernatural? Not in a way that mattered. However, he would set his father straight on one thing.

"No. I will not." Implacable resolve steeled his tone. "If this turns out to be a fool's errand and you and my mamma are destroyed. I will not lead the VRG." No matter how misguided, these were his parents.

"Will you be joining your brother then?" Sebastian asked evenly.

Talon wasn't fooled. This was no innocent question. It was the calm before the storm. And the storm would be off the charts. Beyond a tsunami if he didn't defuse it. The topic of his brother, older by over a thousand years, inspired many long rants.

"Disgrace your family further," his father barreled on, preventing Talon from interjecting. "Force your *cara mamma* into hiding, shame her for delivering two *defective* young." His eyes lit up, glowing orbs of blue fire. "You would sentence her to destruction by my hands or that of the rays of the sun? All because you believe you know better than The Fates?"

Sebastian stepped close enough that Talon's elbow bumped his torso. His top lip pulled back from his teeth, incisors, and canines lengthened.

About the author

Advice writers receive: Write what you know.

I know darkness. I grew up in Scottsdale, Paradise Valley, and Glendale, Arizona. Knowing the uglier sides of life there weren't a lot of options available to me. At least, that's what the world would have me believe. I could've succumbed to the hopelessness and despair that come with having the kind of childhood and adolescence better suited for a Lifetime Channel movie or a cautionary tale. Become a statistic. Or I could allow my past to fuel my creativity.

I devoured anything I could read as an escape. Writing became my calm in the storm. My constant. I published my first book at ten years old. Through college where I studied Social Work, trying to effect change from within the system—I wrote. Modeled a bit. Sang. Became an on-air radio personality. Acted. And still, I wrote. Poetry. Screenplays. Novels. Even placed in the 2010 Beverly Hills Film Festival. All roads lead back to writing. Now, I write dark. Dark paranormal romance. Dark urban fantasy. Psychological and supernatural thrillers. And dark contemporary romance under the pseudonym Wilt Rhys. Because the one thing life's taught me, what's done in the dark comes to the light.

Find me Online

Website: www.piperanderson.com
TikTok: @thepiedwriter
⌾ @that_chick_piper_tv
Want to be part of my ARC Team?
email: Piper@piperanderson.org

www.ingramcontent.com/pod-product-compliance
Lightning Source LLC
Chambersburg PA
CBHW021209310726
48971CB00006B/1498